LEGACY OF SHADOWS

The Unraveling

S.J. Winter

Winter Publishing

ISBN-13: 979-8-218-91865-1

Cover design by: Oliviaprodesign
Printed in the United States of America

For anyone who has ever faced a system built to break them—and chose to resist anyway.

CONTENTS

W
N
S
E
Valoria
Umbrahold
Aeloria
The House of Fas
Rynoriah
Las a' Chual
Aluinn
Brilane
Thalyora
Pyragarde

CHAPTER ONE

Blythe

Northeastern Auroraheim

Blythe's hands trembled while the funeral pyre burned down to its final ember. She folded her arms tighter across her body, the cold biting deeper than it should have. The wind teased her ebony hair across her face. Let the strands hide her. Better that no one see her unraveling.

Her rebel friends—those who'd fought beside her in the Dark Realm—stood in silence around the fire. Quentin lingered on the far side of the pyre, his figure darkening as the flames waned.

She wasn't sure she could count him among them. Not after he'd dragged her into the Dark Realm and a fate she never chose. Not after Miles had died trying to protect her there.

She stepped back from the pyre, her boots rustling over brittle leaves.

Hera, her closest ally in the rebellion, stood next to him, motionless, chin held high. Blythe couldn't see her face, but she saw in her mind the tight, disciplined calm she always wore. Hera had fought beside them in the Dark Realm, losing Miles just as brutally as she had. She held herself like a blade sheathed in control. Blythe wished she had even half that steel.

The pyre wasn't enough, but it was the only closure she'd been allowed: a small mercy her uncle, Demetrius, had granted. He led the rebellion against the corrupt Council, yet his failure to guard the portals had unleashed demons across the realms.

Miles had loved her—and died for it.

They'd barely escaped the Dark Realm themselves, fleeing demons with no time to carry his body out.

"Miles was a good lad," Griffin muttered, his voice ragged, like it had scraped against something before surfacing.

"You're not crying, are you, Grif?" Octo's mouth twitched in something that might have been a grin—but didn't quite land.

Blythe blinked.

Octo was a warrior and probably stood at more funeral fires than normal fires she'd lit in her life. Maybe he'd stood at enough pyres that this one didn't shake him the way it shook her. Still, the words scraped across her raw nerves.

"'Ere's nothin' wrong wi' feelin' yer feelings and expressin' 'em," Griffin bristled, emotion easing the hardness of his voice. "Least, that's what Aenwyn's always tellin' me."

"Don't listen to Octo," Hera said from Blythe's other side, startling her. When did she move there? "Women like sensitive men."

Her words were meant to tease, but Blythe heard the pain underneath. Hera had meant Miles. He'd been sensitive.

Her chest tightened, a pressure blooming where Miles's absence lived.

She turned from the pyre before anyone could see the tears in her eyes and started toward camp. The Council awaited —the same people who had sentenced her for using magic she never wielded.

A branch cracked behind her. The cold pricked sharper, as if her body recognized him before her mind did. She turned. Quentin stood at a pace away. His presence clung to her like a wet leaf stuck to her shoe.

He'd been her lawyer, her betrayer, the man who hid his rebellion ties and drugged her "for her own good."

"May I walk with you?" Quentin asked. His voice was missing its usual cocky lilt—quieter, almost... careful.

Her thumb moved over a fraying seam on her cloak; she needed something tangible to keep herself anchored.

A shrug was all she could manage.

Two strides and he was next to her. They walked in silence toward the camp. A branch gave way under Blythe's boot; she didn't flinch. A gust of wind lifted the edge of her cloak.

She picked up her pace, chasing thoughts of tea and a blanket—anything warm enough to disappear into.

He paused briefly, then held out his coat. She shook her head, and he put it back on.

"Could we talk, please?"

A dry leaf drifted past on the wind, skimming the way before her. She watched it swirl and dance before it drifted into the trees, wishing she could follow—weightless, unburdened.

Deeper within the forest, an owl called—sharp, abrupt.

Blythe clenched her jaw. "You're welcome to."

Miles would've said something ridiculous—Keep walking, Blythe. One foot, then the other. The ground evens out eventually.

But maybe he was wrong.

"How long are you going to ignore me?" Quentin's tone bore an edge, the strain of held-back annoyance.

Her shoulders stiffened, heat prickling up her neck.

"As long as it takes me to forget your lies."

"Yeah. Unfortunately, there've been... a few," he said, looking at the ground. "I already explained why I couldn't tell you about being in the rebellion—and why I put you under. If I'd known then what I know now, I wouldn't have done any of it."

His voice caught.

Had she let him believe she blamed him?

Maybe she had.

The forest thinned, and the camp's orange glow flickered through—warm against the cold.

"It wasn't your fault," she whispered. The words hardly made it past her lips; she half expected them to crumble midair. "If you hadn't taken me... the evil would still be loose. Miles and I—we wouldn't have seen it coming. We'd be dead. Or worse—caught by the Council."

That would've made Benjamin happy—he'd watched her sentencing with barely concealed satisfaction.

Her steps faltered, a breath escaping before she could swallow it back. She turned toward him, shoulders tight, head held high just enough to say she wasn't running anymore. The wariness stayed—but she didn't shut him out.

She lifted her chin. "We have bigger problems."

The rebellion was marching toward the corrupt Council, and demons were slipping unchecked into both realms. One way or another, this war would end with someone paying for what had been done to their world.

She turned and walked a few steps in silence, then inhaled—words gathering, reluctant to surface. "And the mate bond—you owe me the truth about that."

The question slipped out rougher than she meant, clumsy and too honest.

"Hera shouldn't have told you," he said, his gaze fixated on the ground. "I would have preferred to ignore it, but she had to say something..."

Her brows knit. "How did she even know? That doesn't seem like something that would come up in casual conversation—or at least, I don't think it would."

"She figured it out. Hera sees more than most." He stopped walking, and Blythe matched his pause, glancing over. "Fae imprinting exists, but it's rare—and it's never crossed races."

He looked up, and even with no color in the night, she imagined his hazel gaze seeking hers.

"In full honesty, I knew the moment I saw you. Getting to know you... deepened it." He shuffled his feet, "Imagine how weird it would've been if I'd said something before the trial, or while we were running. It never felt like the right time."

Looking down, he whispered, "I didn't want to scare you off."

His gaze caught hers, a pull that made her feel unsteady,

like the moment before a wave breaks.

She looked away, watching the darkness behind him.

"I understand if you never feel the same," he continued. "As far as I know, no Fae has ever imprinted on a human. I didn't know what to do with it, so I tried to ignore it. I hoped we'd never have to talk about it."

His gaze lingered, slow and heavy enough that her breath stumbled.

He turned and walked on, boots stepping softly. She held back, then followed.

She let his words take hold before catching up, her footsteps loud within the hush. She reached for his arm, fingertips grazing his sleeve—then he turned.

Her fingers remained in the air a moment too long. She curled them into a fist and let her hand drop, wishing she'd reached for him sooner, back when it might have meant something.

"I would've said we had a chance. Before the drugging." She bit her lip before continuing. "There's trust to rebuild. I don't want you hurt. But I don't even know what a mate is. Is it like... werewolf imprinting? If that's even real. I mean, I've just read about it in fantasy books..."

"It's real, and something like that," he said. "But Fae mate for life."

His hands disappeared into his pockets, shoulders pulled inward as if preparing for something. "The feelings are mutual —usually. But with you being human... I don't know what happens now."

She couldn't accept that they were bonded forever. She hadn't asked for this. Neither had he. If he could prove it wasn't just who he was, maybe they could be something. But to imagine being anything felt like a trap, not a choice.

She searched the sky for something steady. One star vanished behind a drifting cloud. Maybe that was her answer.

Hope dimmed as easily as starlight.

CHAPTER TWO

Blythe

Northeastern Auroraheim

The fire muttered low, its flames lipping at half-charred wood. Smoke drifted upward, carrying embers with it. Blythe cocooned herself deeper into the blanket, the coarse wool grazing the underside of her jaw. The tin cup in her hands radiated faint heat, just enough to take the edge off the night air.

From across the clearing, she watched Demetrius speaking with Quentin. Their posture was relaxed. Quentin was playing along, masking whatever he really felt. It set her teeth on edge. Easy smiles. Controlled gestures. Too controlled.

Avoiding her uncle wasn't wise, but it was easier than admitting the suspicion rotting in her chest. It had been manageable during patrols and the endless tasks she kept volunteering for.

She should have been training with him, learning to steady the magic that still flared when she was overwhelmed, sparks licking at her fingertips. But duty and worry kept stealing her hours. And the longer she waited, the more she felt herself thinning at the edges, her magic fraying with her focus.

If he didn't suspect she was up to something by now, he'd have to be clueless. And if he was anything like her father —sharp, watchful—he wasn't clueless.

She took a sip, eyes focused on the clearing. Most of the rebels had turned in for the night. Werewolves and vampires kept watch in the shadows, while during the day the others took turns patrolling the perimeter. The rebellion was a patchwork of races the Council insisted could never coexist—and yet here they were, guarding each other's backs.

Originally, the guards watched for the Council's forces. Now they watched for demons too. The tension never eased.

Blythe watched as Demetrius disappeared into his tent.

The quiet left too much room for memory. Her thoughts drifted to those who were not there.

Bertolf had stayed behind to hold the line while they escaped, and she still didn't know if he'd survived. The not-knowing gnawed at her.

The fire cracked louder. She looked up. Quentin moved into the light, slower than usual, shadows dragging behind him. Her grip tightened on her cup as he took a seat next to her with a heavy sigh.

"Have you heard anything about Bertolf?"

Quentin's expression tightened. "No. I asked Demetrius about him, and he said he would see what he could find out."

They sat in silence for several minutes before Quentin spoke again. The pinch in his brow betrayed his stress. "There's a meeting at dawn. Demetrius sounded... excited. That doesn't feel right."

Demetrius hadn't told anyone what he was planning. Unease twisted low in her stomach. She didn't know her uncle well enough to know whether that should alarm her.

"I've got a sinking feeling we should be worried." She took another sip of her tea, relishing the way it coated her throat, briefly warding off the cold.

"I asked him about the wyvern spotted yesterday in the village to the south of here. He didn't seem concerned." Quentin picked up a stick and poked a log back into the fire.

She listened—owls, shifting leaves, and creaking branches were the only noises aside from the snapping and popping of the fire. Quentin spoke again, interrupting her thoughts. "He's leading us all north. Apparently, whatever he's excited about is related to that." Quentin drew slow circles in the dirt with his stick.

The words slipped out before she could stop them. "I

know which way we're going." The sharpness in her voice surprised even her. "Sorry. I'm—was—an archaeologist."

A pang of nostalgia hit her, spreading fast. She pushed it down, turning her sight skyward.

"Polaris is the same here as it is in the human realm. Like the continents, all of the stars are the same. But it doesn't feel the same."

She pressed her thumb against the cup's rim. "I've come to terms with my magic, but that doesn't mean I'm ready to give up what I had… everything I worked for. My routine. My clarity. My old life."

His question fell lightly, but its weight struck her core as solid as stone. "So, you're still going to leave us when you get the chance?" Quentin glanced up at her.

She looked away toward the distant tents where her friends slept. She saw in her mind Hera's steady breath, Griffin's snoring, and Octo's twitching fingers, and the thought of leaving them made her heart ache.

She didn't want to assume his tone, but guilt worried her. She wasn't responsible for his feelings or the imprinting. She hadn't chosen any of it.

No answer felt honest. Every version sounded like an excuse. "I couldn't if I wanted to. I'm wanted, remember?" She looked deep into the flames. "I do care. I'll stay until both realms are safe." She locked eyes with him and lowered her voice. "If the rifts here are crawling with things from the Dark Realm, then the human one is too. Humans aren't equipped to handle that. I'll stay and help until I know everyone in both the human and magic realms is safe." She paused, then added, "And, maybe someday, I won't be a wanted criminal."

Quentin's jaw tightened, but he said nothing—just reached for her cup and set it down before standing.

Something in his movement felt deliberate. She stood too, instinctively, and they faced each other in the light of the dying fire. "Good. That's my plan, too," He offered a wan smile. "Now's just the question of how. I'm not sure about you, but I feel a bit ill-equipped to take down the Council, your uncle, and whatever his plans actually are."

"You're not alone in that... I'm sure he really does want to take the Council down. I don't trust what he plans to replace them with." Blythe scanned the shadows, conscious of how quickly whispers became dangerous rumors in camp. "We need to find a way to meet without my uncle knowing, so we can figure out what to do about him." If Demetrius suspected them, he'd shut her out. Or worse. "We need to help the humans. But someone has to stay and watch him."

The words tasted sour, even though they were true. Blythe didn't like how easily duplicity came to him. "I watched the two of you speaking... It looked... easy. He trusts you."

"He didn't trust me enough to tell me whatever his grand scheme about the portals was. He said we would leave people to protect them, and claimed we did, but obviously, we didn't, or they failed. If he trusted me, he'd have warned me. If they failed, he'd have said something. But he didn't. And that says everything."

Quentin rubbed his arms and set down the sticks. "If he knew they would be unguarded, then he knew I would disapprove. Perhaps that's why..."

A chill crawled up her spine.

Blythe watched Quentin staring into the waning embers of the fire.

"He did give a status report about the Council," he said, glancing at her as if gauging whether she could stomach it.

She shifted, tension prickling along her back.

"And it is...?" she prompted.

"Do you remember when Demetrius and I spoke about the new regulations the Council was going to announce?"

She shut her eyes, just long enough to remember life before everything unraveled. A lifetime ago—before the House, the dark realm, the unraveling. "Yes?"

"Well, we finally got word of what they are, and you're not going to like it." He shifted his feet.

"I'd have been shocked if I did," she said with a wry smile.

"They're building checkpoints now," Quentin said, his voice subdued. "Along trade paths and border zones. Officially, it's for 'protected commerce,' but you know what that really means."

Blythe's throat tightened, tension spreading down her neck.

"They pushed race-based separation before. They claimed it prevented conflict. Now they've wrapped it in economics." He shifted. "Commerce as camouflage. Just another mask for control."

The last of her smile vanished. Cold settled low in her belly, familiar as the dread she'd carried since receiving the Council's letter. The same dread that had never really left. She'd seen this before. Different world, same cruelty.

Her voice dropped. "Segregation dressed up as safety. Again."

Quentin nodded, eyes on the embers. He didn't speak. He didn't need to. "I suspect this will hinder news travel and cripple our double agents' mobility," he said in a hushed voice. "They'll know who's moving and when."

She rubbed her trembling hands together. "And people will thank them for it. For the 'safety.' For the checkpoints. For the walls."

He took up the stick again to stir the coals, then tossed it onto the fire to help feed it. "There's also a curfew. No one is to be out before sunup or after sundown."

"They're not just fencing us in," she said. "They're dividing us. And once we're divided, silence will follow."

"I heard something about Ben, too." Quentin's voice lowered slightly as he studied her face.

Blythe pressed her lips together, grounding herself. She didn't want to hear it—but she needed to.

"And...?" she prompted, her tone steadier than she felt.

"He's been given a job by the Council," Quentin said,

shifting his weight on the log. The fire snapped between them, a veil of smoke dancing across his face. “Since the House won't let him in—and they can't force it to name him Keeper—they found another use for him.”

She froze. “Let me guess, something that perfectly fits his righteousness and attitude problem.”

Quentin huffed out a laugh, the sound muffled by the wind rustling overhead. “Not exactly ideal for his attitude problem, but perfect for soothing one of his deepest resentments.”

Blythe exhaled, already preparing herself. “Me.” The word tasted like iron.

“You and I.” His grin was crooked but didn't reach his eyes. “We've officially made the Council's most wanted list. And Ben's been put in charge of hunting us down.”

A sudden pressure wound around her throat. She knew Ben, her half-brother, would relish the chance to remove her and claim the Keepership by default. She stared into the fire, watching a coal collapse to soot.

“Of course,” she said. “I never played cops and robbers with him as a kid. Now we get the grown-up version—higher stakes, fewer rules.”

Quentin chuckled, the sound thin and sharp in the cold night air. “At least you were never accused of cheating while playing that game.”

“Not yet.” Blythe's smile trembled, bitter and brief. “But I have a feeling Ben will find a way to rewrite the story.”

Quentin blew into his hands, breath fogging in the cold.

Blythe removed the blanket and offered it to him. “The tea warmed me. You take it.”

The change in his expression was slight, playful, something half-familiar but long missed. “We could share it.”

Her guard snapped up before she could stop it.

Shadows hid whatever glimmer she was sure twinkled in his eyes.

"Why, Quentin Hendrix, I do *declare*—are you propositioning me?" she drawled. Quentin blinked, confused, and she laughed. "Sorry, I forgot you wouldn't know references from the human realm. I'm guessing, historically speaking, no one spoke like that here?"

"Not as far as I know." Quentin smiled. "I can't take the blanket when I know you'd be cold." He wrapped it around her again. The rough wool caressed her neck, but his closeness eclipsed everything else. He smelled of woods and earth. She wasn't sure she'd ever noticed that before.

She dragged herself back to the moment.

"So, this issue with the portals and my uncle," she said. "I think if anyone has a chance of getting into his circle, it's you." Her voice faltered on the word you.

"Octo—"

"Wasn't asked to lead the first big move of the rebellion," Blythe cut in, sharper than she intended.

"Of course he wasn't. The prince of the mer-people is kind of important," Quentin countered. "The mer-people have always been the closest allies of the mages. Our group could've been killed in the dark realm. We're expendable."

"Or we could have just disappeared into the human realm and avoided all the danger, leaving them high and dry."

"But we never would have, because we have loved ones here we couldn't abandon, and he knows it," Quentin said with a sigh.

"Not everyone does," Blythe whispered, the words cooling the moment between them like a draft.

He smirked at her. "Yeah, but you're a hardened wanted criminal. He knew you weren't going anywhere." The comment drew a soft laugh from her.

They stood eye to eye as the waning ember died, and the clearing dimmed around them. After a few minutes, Quentin spoke.

"I'll talk with Octo and see if he feels like you do, that I'm the one best able to get that information, or at least worm my way into the inner circle." He seemed more resolved than uncertain now, like he'd already decided, but wanted her approval first.

"It won't be Griffin. Demetrius thinks he's too much of a lush to trust with anything. Eyra's still living her double life. Hera's too high on the wanted list. If she were caught... well, they wouldn't want her knowing anything."

She shifted, willing herself not to picture what might come next.

"So, you or Octo." A tightness coiled in her chest at the thought of Quentin being pulled into her uncle's confidence. Maybe she was afraid of what would happen to him if her uncle discovered he was spying.

"Me or Octo," he said, watching her. She didn't answer; she just searched his face, looking for hesitation or hope. She wasn't sure which frightened her more.

CHAPTER THREE

Blythe

Traveling North in Northeastern Auroraheim

"Could you walk a little louder?" Hera's voice cleaved through the hush, dry as dust, just shy of a laugh.

To anyone else, it might've sounded like irritation. But Blythe knew better. Hera's sarcasm was a familiar blade—sharp enough to remind her that stealth wasn't optional.

"I'm pretty sure I could." Blythe tossed the words over her shoulder with a grin. Hera was already catching up, her boots whispering over the frost-bitten ground.

They moved north again. Always north. To Blythe, progress felt like fits and starts, slowed by their numbers and the need to stay invisible. The Council despised most of the rebellion, and they no doubt knew her Uncle's faction was moving against them. The Council's hunters didn't miss much. The Valkyrie missed even less.

They were fugitives now—not just to the Council, but to anyone loyal to the Council's laws. And in the Magic Realm, most people were there.

"Any word on more goblins?" Blythe asked, her voice low as Hera fell into step next to her.

"No," Hera replied, eyes sweeping the forest. "But we've spotted gargoyles. And a wyvern."

The memory of their first scouting mission: gargoyles shrieking overhead, the air saturated with a stench that clung like rot.

"Yeah," she said. "Not a fan."

"Same," Hera said. Then, casually, "I saw you and Quentin talking last night."

"We did." Blythe tried to push the memory aside. The shared blanket, the quiet warmth. A glance at Hera confirmed what she already knew. Hera had seen. Hera always saw.

"It's okay to still have feelings for him," Hera whispered kindly, holding a branch aside so Blythe could pass. "He did what he thought was right. When you're on a mission, you follow it through. And I know he was afraid that if you left before the Dark Realm mission, the Council would find you. You were safer with us."

Blythe's jaw locked, tension coiling at the base of her skull. Hera hadn't been part of that conversation. That burden had belonged to Quentin. Not her.

"I get it," Blythe said after a beat. "But he could've run it by me."

"He could have," Hera agreed. "But from what I understand, Fae men don't always think through the consequences, especially when it comes to the ones they've imprinted on. Though now that I think about it, that could apply to many men in all races."

Blythe shook her head. "I'd rather not generalize. Maybe some are like that, but I'm not writing off an entire gender or race based on a few."

"Point taken. I'll save my sweeping generalizations for the Council. Still, Quentin's not the first to make a mess trying to do the right thing. Doesn't make it easier, though." She smiled as she cast a quick look at Blythe. "And he is a good guy, deep down."

Blythe exhaled hard, the sound sharper than she meant. "So I keep hearing." Her hands clasped the worn leather strap on her satchel, clutching it firmly as the breeze kicked up. "I agreed to give him another chance, I just—"

Her words wavered as the world fractured into chaos—branches snapping, feet stomping, voices swelling in alarm.

A strong arm cinched her waist. Instinct flared. She twisted, elbow ready, until Quentin's voice cleaved through the noise, quiet but insistent at her ear. "Gargoyles and wyverns incoming!"

He released her and broke into a run. Blythe followed without hesitation, boots skimming the leaf-strewn ground.

"There's a clearing ahead!" Quentin called over his shoulder. "If we can reach the far side, we'll have a clean line of sight and better angles to take them down."

Blythe nodded, running close behind. The din of steel and wings overwhelmed the forest. She knew they had little time to take up their positions.

A shout rang out behind her: "Blue squad, break left! Red, break right!"

She and Quentin veered left with the rest of the rebels assigned to that squad. To her right, the clearing opened up—sparks and arrows already arcing skyward from the far side. She didn't dare look to see what they were shooting at. She'd find out soon enough.

Quentin caught her hand and pulled her into the brush, ducking low as they edged forward for a better line of sight. She pushed down a branch and chanced a look at the sky.

Cold rushed through her veins.

Slate-gray gargoyles zigzagged through the sky, their wings slicing the air as they dodged incoming fire. Behind them came the wyverns, dragon-like at first glance, yet clearly different. Blythe remembered Hera's lessons: two legs, no forearms, and venom in place of flame.

One wyvern banked hard, throat pulsing as it aimed. A jet of poison struck an elf who had broken cover to fire. His cry burst through the bedlam, his skin bubbling as the din of shouts, roars, and wings swallowed it.

Quentin raised the crossbow, steady next to her, and fired.

The bolt struck its flank, and for a breathless moment, nothing. Then came a loud crack in the air as the gargoyle exploded, stone shards raining down in a jagged hail.

She scarcely registered the shockwave before figures dismounted from the backs of the remaining gargoyles and wyverns. Not riders. Not soldiers.

Creatures. Twisted figures in dark armor, appendages too long, eyes radiating with something ageless and wrong. One dropped from a wyvern's saddle and hit the ground running, its mouth spreading into a grin far too wide for its face.

Blythe's mind stuttered. Offensive spells—gone. She cursed herself for not practicing more.

“Any time now, Blythe!” Hera barked from her right. “We know you've got something in that magic arsenal of yours!”

Blythe inhaled sharply, forcing down the panic. She grasped at the first spell that surfaced. “Tharn kai'ven!” she shouted.

Her feet rooted, energy surging downward. A heartbeat later, tendrils sprang up from the earth, snatching one of the dark-armored creatures and dragging it down. More followed —writhing vines and earthen limbs reaching upward, pulling enemy after enemy into the ground.

Her gaze locked on the battlefield, the spell holding fast. With each creature dragged under, her strength ebbed as though the soil fed on her willpower. Her vision tunneled, the edges softening and going black.

“Blythe!” Quentin's voice sounded impossibly far away. Her knees buckled, and darkness swallowed everything.

Blythe opened her eyes to the sky. The moon hovered heavy above the trees, spilling a cold, uneven wash of light. Blythe stirred, the blanket's coarse fibers scratching her skin. Turning her head, she saw a fire burning nearby and a few figures at its edge.

Quentin sat close, his gaze fixed on the fire.

Flying on Ellira, pressed against him.

That night in the House, he carried her to bed and brushed a kiss along her jaw.

The memories pulsed through her, reckless and alive.

Don't go there, Blythe.

She hoped the darkness hid the blush spreading over her cheeks.

Sleep. That's what she needed.

Not dreams like that. Not now.

"You're awake."

She hadn't noticed Quentin move. Still drifting in the blur between sleep and waking. "You had us worried," he said, kneeling next to her. His hand lifted, hesitated, as if to brush her face, then fell.

She forced herself upright.

"Easy, Kit," he said with a tender smile. "You burned through a lot out there. I was a little worried you were going to take us all down."

"What happened?" Her head spun. She let herself sink back down. Sitting up had been a mistake.

"You dug too deep into your magic."

A voice jolted her. She turned to see her uncle's shifting silhouette come into view, crouching next to her with that same quiet, unsettling ease.

"It appears you forgot the first lesson I taught you."

Blythe frowned, "The truth behind the Council?"

Demetrius's lips curved slightly. "Okay, wit warper—maybe not the first lesson. What did I say about magic?"

"Know your limits," she said, closing her eyes for a moment.

"That one," he agreed. "You're getting more powerful, Blythe. If you're not careful, you'll burn yourself out." His smile thinned. "That was a good move—vines dragging them down. Your earth magic is strong."

A compliment. Did that mean he wasn't upset with her for keeping her distance? She couldn't decide if it was worth unpacking—or if she should just let it go for now.

"It's late; she should rest." Quentin's voice bore a thread of annoyance. Quentin could fake civility with Demetrius—just not when it involved her. Was he being protective?

She blinked. When her eyes opened, Quentin leaned over, drawing the blanket higher around her.

"We should move you into a tent," he whispered. "We set you up here while we finished setting camp and… other matters." His words faltered, eyes sliding away.

What was he hiding?

Her throat felt raw as she spoke. "How long was I out? Is everyone okay?"

"Hours," Demetrius replied. Then, turning to Quentin, he added, "Could you give us a moment?"

Demetrius's unreadable stare unsettled her almost as much as the thought of being left alone with him. And why hadn't he answered her second question?

"Quentin?" she whispered, her eyes pleading.

"Everyone's okay," he murmured kindly, though his mouth tightened as he glanced at Demetrius. "Hera, Griffin, and the others are fine. Not a scratch. We did lose some… she really should sleep," he added, hesitating.

Under the low light, his eyes caught hers, shadowed and uncertain. Something flickered there—fear?

"It's okay," she said, forcing herself to sit. Her body was leaden, akin to the flu-like feeling after that half-marathon in college—heavy, burning, impossible to shake. "After we talk… maybe you could help me to my tent?"

She gave a slight smile. Quentin sighed, shoulders sagging under a hidden load.

"Of course." He rose, glancing between Demetrius and Blythe, before turning to walk away.

Demetrius's inflection held a mocking lilt. "Do I need to warn you about the dangers of romance during a rebellion, again?"

"No." She held his gaze. Had he said the same to Quentin? Probably not. The possible hypocrisy stung, but she forced herself not to react.

She pulled her knees up, shivering as the breeze cut through.

"We need to resume your lessons," he said, standing up. "Your power runs deep, and we need you at full strength before facing the Council."

"I understand," Blythe responded quietly, her stare settled on his face, hunting for cracks in his composure. She drew a breath, then chose courage. "Do you know how those creatures made it into this world?"

His eyes narrowed. "Why do you ask?"

Did he think she was naïve?

"I was under the impression we'd left people behind to guard the portals—to keep them contained."

He slid his hands into his pockets. "Camp is safe. The Warlocks reinforced the wards. It's when we travel that we're vulnerable. Overall, I think we handled the attack well."

He still wasn't answering her question. In the wavering firelight, the look on his face was hard to read: focused and something else. He was studying her.

"It's important, Uncle," she said quietly. "If we let those things out—"

"Why assume we did?" His voice steeled. "The Council —"

"Didn't breach the portals to release the Warlocks. We did." Her fists clenched beneath the blanket, heat rising up her neck. "They couldn't be expected to put guards back in immediately, we were—"

"We did," he snapped. The words struck home, sharp and sure. She wasn't ready for them. A trace of something crossed his face and vanished.

"You don't need to worry about these things," he said, his tone eerily steady.

She remembered the battle they'd had to escape the Dark Realm after going in. How had he escaped on his own?

"How many did we lose?" She wasn't sure she wanted to

know. "Quentin said everyone was fine, but then said we lost some... I'm assuming he meant the people I knew were fine..."

He shrugged. "I haven't heard the tally yet. Those you traveled with before are all fine." He turned and started to walk away, tossing over his shoulder, "Tomorrow afternoon, we resume your training. Get some sleep."

A different ache, sharp and instinctive, pressed beneath her torso. Something was wrong. More wrong than the attack, more wrong than Demetrius's evasions.

He hadn't answered her question.

"Uncle," she called.

Demetrius paused mid-stride. Slowly, he turned back toward her, the campfire's light carving his features into something sharp and unfamiliar.

"What is it, Blythe?"

"You didn't tell me how the creatures got through." Her voice fluttered despite her effort to steady it. "You didn't tell me why they're here."

A beat.

A trace of something crossed his face. Annoyance? Amusement?

Then he advanced toward her.

"You're asking the wrong question," he said.

Her breath faltered. "What does that mean?"

"It means," he said, dropping his volume, "that you're assuming the creatures are a problem."

Her stomach dropped. "They killed our people."

"They killed some," he corrected, tone cool as steel. "But they killed far more of the Council's scouts. And they will kill more still."

Demetrius's smile was thin, reptilian. It didn't reach his eyes. "The Council has armies. We do not. But the Dark Realm? It has... resources."

Her heartbeat pounded. "You're talking about demons like they're weapons."

"They are," he said. "Unpredictable, yes. Dangerous, yes.

But pointed in the right direction? They can do what we cannot."

Her mouth went dry. "You're planning to use them."

"I'm planning to win." His eyes gleamed with something fever-bright. "The Council will never expect it. They'll be too busy fighting the monsters to notice us slipping in behind them."

Blythe's voice cracked. "You're unleashing them on innocent people."

"Innocent people die in every war," he said, shrugging. "Better theirs than ours."

Her breath snagged. "This isn't strategy. This is slaughter."

Demetrius leaned in, his darkness engulfing the fire's glow. "You're thinking like a child. I'm thinking like someone who intends to survive."

Her skin crawled. "Miles died fighting those things."

"And now they can help us avenge him."

Her heart jumped. "He would never—"

"He's dead," Demetrius snapped. "And we are not. We use what we have."

Blythe withdrew as if struck.

Demetrius straightened, brushing imaginary dust from his coat. "You'll understand in time. Power calls for sacrifice. And you, Blythe—" His gaze swept over her, assessing, calculating. "You were born to wield it."

He turned away, his speech drifting back like smoke.

"Sleep well. Tomorrow, we begin shaping you into what this war needs."

He disappeared into the dark.

Blythe sat frozen, the cold sinking down to her bones, deeper than exhaustion, deeper than fear.

He wasn't just hiding something—he was becoming something. Something dreadful.

And now she knew the truth: Demetrius wasn't fighting the Council.

He was becoming worse than they were.

CHAPTER FOUR

Blythe

Traveling North in Northeastern Auroraheim

"Did it go well?" Quentin squatted next to her, holding out a tin cup of tea. Her stomach tightened. Nothing about tonight had gone well. Not the creatures. Not the casualties. But none of it compared to the truth she couldn't unhear. And now that she knew, she couldn't pretend she was on his side.

Blythe accepted it and encircled her hands around the mug before taking a careful sip of the hot drink. She gazed down at the murky tea, missing the House, its steaming hot beverages, warm baths, and rooms that never chilled in the winter. She closed her eyes, letting the warmth seep into her bones.

"Well?" he pressed.

"As well as it could. He wouldn't tell me why the creatures are out." He had told her, just not in a way she could repeat without unraveling.

She let the heat settle in her chest.

"I'm sure he'll tell us all when it suits him." Quentin settled next to her, leaning back on his palms to look up at the sky through the branches of the trees. Something in the sound of his voice told her he didn't believe Demetrius would. He wouldn't. Not now. Not ever.

"Maybe," she agreed. They sat in silence, both lost in their own thoughts.

"We should get you to bed," Quentin said after a while.

"I can't." Blythe frowned, staring into the now cold tea. The heat and comfort she'd hoped for had vanished. She set down her mug and stood.

He reached toward her shoulder, hesitated, then pulled back, fingers dragging awkwardly to the back of his neck. "You should at least try."

She worried the inside of her cheek.

Smoky city streets rose in her mind, panic devouring everything.

"We need to figure out how to help the humans." She looked up into his face. "We're more equipped to handle those things... but if that's happening in the human realm..." She suppressed a shudder. "Their military might fight them off. But civilians?"

"One night isn't going to be enough for that. But if you're looking for my thoughts..." He moved closer, slipping an arm around her. Heat flared under his touch on her back. Leaning in, he whispered into her ear. "Better we look like we're being intimate than discussing what could be considered treason."

She hated how easily he could pull her off balance.

"It's not treason to talk about helping the humans," she sighed. "Or are you just looking for an excuse?"

She didn't pull away, even as he drew her near, his hand cupping her cheek, warm and steady, more tender than she'd expected.

She sucked in a breath as his touch set her skin ablaze. Her pulse hammered, electricity sparking through every point of contact. Before she could stop herself, her fingers clenched around his arms, tense and unsure. Her thoughts burst in every direction; a rush of heat tangled with longing and uncertainty.

His gaze held hers, open but braced, as though he expected rejection and needed permission all at once. Her eyes glanced to his lips, then back to his eyes. He was so close. His look didn't waver. Then, quietly, he said, "If you don't want this, please tell me."

Did she want this? She honestly wasn't sure how she felt. What would she have done in his place? The more she thought about it, the less certain she became.

The moment paused in time, tender and fragile, a heartbeat away from becoming something else, to becoming something more than words.

She broke into a subtle smile. "I thought we were only discussing plans."

Life was hard enough. Flirting could be harmless fun. It wasn't her fault that it meant more to him than it did to her. Yet guilt held onto her like smoke. His smile, when it came, filled something in her she hadn't realized was empty.

"We can do both, Kits." His breath was warm on her cheek, his mouth drawing closer to hers.

Even as heat spread across her skin, her mind clawed back toward the problem they'd tried to hide under closeness.

"What is that? Kits?"

"It's short for *kitsune*. Beautiful. Clever. A little dangerous," he said. "You've outgrown the kitten nickname." His smile sent a warmth deep in her belly. She needed to change topics, fast.

"So, what should we do?" she asked, raising her chin upward, their gazes meeting. His thumb brushed across her cheek before sliding down to rest behind her neck.

"Octo and I will speak tomorrow when we're on watch. I'd hoped to do it today while we travelled, but things didn't go as planned. Still..." His eyes searched hers. "I think it may be best for you and Hera to go to the House."

The mention of the House twisted a flicker in her chest. She didn't know if she wanted to see it empty again.

"You'll be able to get the two of you in," he continued, "and find out what's really happening in the human realm. We can't make a plan to save them if we don't know what's going on."

Blythe swallowed hard.

If Demetrius was willing to sacrifice innocents, then she couldn't stay under his command.

Going to the House wasn't just reconnaissance; it was

the first step away from him.

"Okay, but what do we do then? If we find out the human realm is being overrun..."

His nearness sent her thoughts scattering. Every time she tried to focus, awareness of him tugged her back into the pull of desire.

"I have a friend you can contact. He's someone who can notify the Council, if he hasn't already."

She moved backward. His hands fell away, and the blanket fell from her shoulders.

She clenched her fists, the words ripping out too quickly. "You have got to be kidding me."

"They're the only ones with the armies to take care of it —"

"Quentin, they want me dead!" She lowered her voice, a flicker of movement at the clearing's edge catching her attention.

"They want all of us dead at this point, I'm sure. But my friend can help, I didn't really mean—"

"You mean like how you helped with my case?" Blythe cut in. Quentin froze, then pushed the words out again, stiffness edging his voice.

"No. He's a sleeper agent in the human realm. He can help guide what comes next. How to help the people—"

She held up her hand, stopping him abruptly as a frigid spike drove along her back. That term didn't belong here. It belonged to shadows from her past wearing familiar faces. "Sleeper agent?"

She'd heard that term before.

From her father.

The memory hit hard, sharp as a stone through stained glass.

She had been young then—barely twelve—padding barefoot down the manor stairs at night, wrapped in a blanket and curiosity. The study door had been left slightly open, lanterns burn-

ing low. Inside, her father stood near the hearth, speaking in that clipped tone reserved for Benjamin, her half-brother.

"Sleeper agents aren't trained to act," Dorian said, standing by the hearth. "Not unless the Council calls them."

Blythe moved nearer to the doorframe. Benjamin was stretched out in one of the chairs, playing with the rug's fringe as if he weren't listening, but the stillness in his shoulders told her otherwise. He was always paying attention.

"They gather," Dorian continued. "They watch. They send back what matters." He rubbed his jaw. "They rely on the Houses—and us—to relay less immediate information. For critical information, they'll risk magical communication. They are not to be interfered with. The Council gives them freedom to act as they see fit if they believe something requires emergency intervention."

She hadn't understood it then, but the clipped edge in his voice had tightened her stomach more than the words.

She blinked hard, the present slamming back into place.

"He's a sleeper agent, so wouldn't the Council know already?" Her words spilled out faster than she'd intended. "Isn't this his job? Shouldn't the Council have done something by now?" Her voice dropped. "Is he going to give me up if I contact him?"

Quentin said nothing. The air thickened, damp and clinging, as if she were breathing through cloth. Her pulse thudded in her ears, too loud in the quiet.

She looked around, but the clearing was empty except for them. Clouds slid over the moon, shadows pooling deeper around them.

The fire lay dead; embers reduced to ash.

Quentin shifted his weight, scanning the dark. "Maybe we should talk in one of the tents." He paused. His lips curved, half daring and partly amused, but tension wavered at the corner of his mouth. "We could kiss on the way in, make them think we're having a private rendezvous."

Blythe cursed her blush, and she clumsily reached for

the blanket, pulling it tighter around herself. "No... our tent mates are probably asleep. I don't want people assuming things." She twisted a frayed thread on the blanket until it snapped. "Especially not in a tent with others."

"They already think we did," he said with a low chuckle.

Her cheeks reddened. She remembered the night he had carried her upstairs. What had everyone thought happened then?

Blythe sighed. "I guess I can see why they would..."

"Everyone needs an outlet," he said, his tone lazy, humor tucked into the words.

He reached up, slow but sure. His fingertips touched her temple, sweeping an unruly strand aside.

Then his thumb traced along her cheek, gentle, as if re-acquainting himself with every line.

She looked up just as the moon broke free, throwing its shadows long and thin across the ground. In that sudden clarity, their eyes met, his face finally visible in the low glow.

"Can we please stay focused?" she said. The sound of her voice caught—thinner than she'd meant. Her skin still felt electrified by his touch. He lowered his hand, a small, knowing smile pulling at his lips.

For the first time since the pyre, she saw the difference clearly.

Yes, Quentin had hurt her. He'd lied, drugged her, dragged her into a war she never chose.

But he had never wanted innocents to die. He had never looked her in the eye and asked her to ignore suffering.

Demetrius had.

And that made Quentin... not safe, exactly, but safer than the man she'd once trusted most.

She took a breath, tried not to give in to the part of her that wanted to touch him. If she did, what would she land in, a real connection or something dressed up to look like it?

"Of course." He smiled that impish grin again, moving closer to her and lowering his tone, "It's not likely he'll arrest you." He paused briefly, reaching out for her again, and she let him pull her close. His voice firmed, the softness slipping beneath something more calculated. "He's a double agent. Miles spoke with him before you were charged. That's how he knew to send for me." Her look held steady. "If the Council has a plan, he'll know." She watched his jaw tighten. "And if they don't... then it's on us to find a way to save both worlds."

"No big deal," she said.

She caught the shift as Quentin looked to the sky. Blythe also looked up, watching the slow, drifting clouds pass over the scattered stars.

"We'll figure it out... we have to." He still sounded convinced.

She looked back at Quentin, his nearness warmed the cold edge of the night. For a moment, she let herself lean into the warmth radiating from him.

Did she care about him? Maybe. But Blythe knew better than to fall headlong into whatever this was. Love? Lust? Both had teeth. Both could masquerade as comfort until they consumed you whole.

"I think it's time for bed," she said. Quentin nodded, releasing her and wrapping the blanket securely around her.

"Goodnight, Blythe." He bowed dramatically, drawing a chuckle from her.

"Goodnight, Quentin." She walked past him and paused outside her tent, turning back briefly, but the campsite too dark to see anything. She turned again and quickly went inside, letting the flap snap shut behind her.

As she settled into bed that night, her mind tugged backward toward the life she'd left behind. Alone in the tent, the quiet pressed close, thick as wool. And beneath it all, the question she couldn't shake: could she ever go back?

CHAPTER FIVE

Blythe

Northeastern Auroraheim

The sun had barely cleared the horizon, and heat was already shimmering off the sand around her. She pushed her sweat-damp hair off her forehead. Blythe knelt down in the sand, brushing grit from a piece of carved obsidian, too smooth and precise for any known civilization. A chill bled through her glove as she turned it over. A faint glow pulsed beneath the surface, subtle but impossible for her to ignore.

Not for the first time, she wondered if magic had followed her here, halfway around the world from the House she had fled. Her lungs tightened, breath snagging in her chest. She pushed the anxious thought away.

Behind her, a junior researcher called out, asking if she'd found anything interesting.

"No," she said quickly, tucking the shard into a soft leather pouch already half-full of things she couldn't explain.

Later, in the tent, she logged it as weathered volcanic glass. Filed. Shelved. Buried with the others that she pretended not to see.

Dig sites were predictable. Magic and love never were. That summer had felt clean, sterile, and controlled. A thousand miles from her father's world of soft-spoken spells and hidden doors.

And yet each artifact she found pressed against the part of her she tried to forget.

She wasn't outrunning it, only layering sand over her past. Her questions. Her heart.

The tent flap rustled.

She turned.

But the canvas behind her rippled, shadows sliding across it like liquid. Shelves warped. Faces spread across them, familiar but wrong in every detail.

The sand throbbed beneath her knees, pulsing like a second heartbeat.

The dark stone on the shelf hissed.

Voices surged from the artifacts, not names but sharp, accusing tones. A trial with no courtroom. A verdict with no defense.

Hands reached from the sand, white, fractured like porcelain, clawing upward.

Her father stood in the doorway.

"You should have stayed away."

His voice held no anger, only the cool certainty of someone who'd kept too many secrets.

Blythe recoiled. The sand swallowed her boots.

"I didn't want to come back to the House," she choked. "I want to live my life!"

Dorian stepped aside.

Benjamin appeared, quiet and calm, stones gripped in both hands. They buzzed in tandem with the sand. She sensed their power crackle in the air. Blythe tried to speak, but she couldn't. She couldn't move. Couldn't scream. The space between them felt merciless, heavy with something she couldn't outrun. Benjamin lifted the stones. His gaze was cold and hard as the obsidian she'd uncovered.

"It's time for you to die now, dear sister."

Blythe woke with a start, lungs heaving as if she'd sprinted through her sleep. The canvas walls of the tent filtered in birdsong, gentle and patterned.

She clenched the sheet, grounding herself in the waking world. Her heart hammered, frantic as if trying to bolt from her chest.

Across the tent, Hera's cot was empty. Of course it was. She trained before dawn; she always had.

Blythe used to be invited, but she'd refused enough

times that Hera had stopped asking. She should train; the tightness in her muscles reminded her of that.

Footsteps outside snapped her awake.

"If I don't get up now, someone else will make me," she said under her breath.

With a groan, she extended her hand toward her clothes tucked under the covers, a trick she'd picked up in Alaska to avoid the morning cold. The fabric was warm, but the warmth did nothing to ease the cold knot forming beneath her ribs.

She had just pulled on her boots when the flap burst open.

"Blythe!" Aenwyn barreled into the tent and threw herself into Blythe's arms, her hug fierce and grounding.

Blythe laughed despite herself. "Hello, Aenwyn."

Pink and purple flower embroidery on the fabric brushed Aenwyn's forearm, and spiked violet hair skimmed her cheek. Her new ear piercings glittered within the low light.

"Do you like it? Nreman says it's too much, but I don't care." Her grin was irrepressible.

"I do. It suits you."

Nreman followed her in, quieter. His tunic bore vines embroidered in green thread, and his boots were dusted from the trail.

"It is too much," he muttered. "Please don't encourage her."

Blythe gave a slight wave. "Not getting involved."

She bent to finish tying her boot.

"I'm glad to see you both," she said. "I worried about what happened after we split to go to the human realm."

"Oh, we're fine!" Aenwyn chirped. "Demetrius sent us home to check on family and gather information before rejoining the group."

Blythe stretched, muscles aching from yesterday's travel. "And what did you find?"

Nreman lowered himself onto the floor.

"The Council knows about the demons flowing into the

Magic Realm—"

Aenwyn added, "And they've twisted it."

"They've blamed you and Hera," Nreman blurted. "Said you conspired to overthrow them."

Aenwyn hissed, punching his shoulder. "We weren't going to say it like that."

"I don't agree with it," he grumbled, rubbing his arm. "I just didn't want to wait."

Blythe's breath hitched, the words landing sharp and heavy. She'd known that was what would happen. Better to blame the two escaped convicts the world already knew about than to admit there was another who had broken free from what was supposed to be an inescapable world of torture.

Again, she'd been left unaware while enemies crafted her story in ink.

She sank back onto the cot.

"Why didn't anyone tell me sooner?" Her voice stayed calm, though the calm felt like a lie.

Aenwyn didn't flinch. "Because it's false. The others didn't want you to panic over their lies. I hate repeating them." She frowned. "But I thought you should know. I would want to know."

Aenwyn's tone snapped sharper than Blythe had ever heard, enough to make her blink.

"I need to know what they're saying," Blythe said. "Last time... last time I was blindsided. Quentin sold me a song and dance about how we'd win because they had no case. Clearly, the truth doesn't matter. So I need to know what nonsense they're making up."

Her fists tightened around the cot's edge until her knuckles blanched.

Aenwyn settled next to her, running her hands through her hair.

"You're right. I'm sorry. I didn't want to be a messenger. But that wasn't fair." She swung her legs as she sat there. Her careless and unguarded demeanor almost made Blythe forget how old Aenwyn was.

"I'll accept the apology, even if it comes once every hundred years." Nreman looked up from where he was seated with his legs folded on the floor.

She ruffled his hair. "Once every decade if you're lucky."

Nreman's next words came in a lower voice, the confidence draining from them. "They shouldn't be able to twist everything. But they do."

"We should go," Aenwyn said, standing. "Demetrius asked us to check in before the gathering."

"But we came to see you first," Nreman added, lowering the timbre of his voice. "We trust you. And... you're right. Something's wrong. The portals, the smear campaign—none of it adds up."

"I don't trust the Warlocks," Aenwyn whispered, her gaze flicking toward the tent flap.

Nreman gave a dramatic salute. "We're with you. Red aura and all."

"Aura?" The word slipped out before she could stop it. She'd heard the term before, people in the human realm claiming to be able to see them. It shouldn't have surprised her that Aenwyn—or anyone in this realm—might be able to see them too.

"Your uncle's is... muddy. Yours is bright red," Nreman said. "Red's good. Strong."

"Red like blood?" She glanced down at her hands, half expecting to see it there.

"Red like passion," Aenwyn corrected. "Courage. Awareness."

"Demetrius has black and gray," Nreman added. Aenwyn shot him a look.

"Stop interrupting me."

He smiled sheepishly. "Sorry. We've traveled together forever."

"A hundred and fifty years is long enough," Aenwyn agreed.

"A hundred and fifty?" The words slipped out before she could catch them. "I thought you were training him."

"I am," she responded with a grin.

"He's basically a baby," she added.

"Teenager," Nreman said, shoulders hunching.

"How old are you?" Blythe asked, eyeing them both.

"Two hundred," Aenwyn said proudly.

"Child," Nreman muttered.

A laugh threatened, loosening something tight in her chest.

"Does training really take that long?"

"There's a lot to learn," Nreman said. "And the world changes. We commune every decade to feel the shift."

The tent flap snapped open. Hera filled the entrance, hands planted on her hips.

"I wondered what was taking you so long. But I see now."

"I was just coming," Blythe said, rising quickly. The tent suddenly felt smaller, the air too tight around her ribs.

"No need. The general called for a full meeting. We'll train later."

She turned and left.

"Aenwyn?"

Aenwyn had just hopped off the bed but paused, turning to face Blythe.

"Yes?"

"Have you ever seen the Council?" Blythe's teeth pressed into her lip. "Do you know what their auras look like?"

Nreman shook his head.

"We're not granted audiences with them."

"Sorry," Aenwyn said, giving a tender smile. "If I had to guess… their auras would be black."

Nreman nodded in quiet agreement. Aenwyn bounced out with her usual cheer. Nreman followed, more reluctant. Blythe hesitated, gripping the sword resting on her hip. The words black and gray snagged in her thoughts, refusing to let go. She'd mocked aura readings once. Not anymore.

If he was corrupt… she'd have to be the one to stop him.

CHAPTER SIX

Blythe

Northeastern Auroraheim

Blythe trailed Aenwyn and Nreman into the clearing at the heart of camp, where the morning hush still hung over the damp ground. She scanned the modest gathering—no vampires or werewolves, though after their overnight watch, their absence made sense. Elves chatted with the bark-skinned creatures gathered at the forest's edge. Octo, Griffin, Hera, and Quentin stood quietly to the right of Zelos Dredmore.

Her stomach tightened the instant her glance fixed on Zelos. Demetrius's second-in-command was cruel, ambitious, and loyal only to power. His pale face angled toward another of his kind—equally washed-out and still. He adjusted the tie holding his long white hair; his movements were precise, almost ritualistic. He nodded to one of the warlocks and glanced toward Blythe. His gaze was sharp enough to make her wonder if he'd caught her staring.

She looked away and tripped on a root. Heat rushed up her neck, but she forced her shoulders loose, pretending the stumble hadn't rattled her. She kept her gaze low when she drew closer to the group. Across the clearing, Aenwyn and Nreman joined her uncle as he appeared from his tent. The sight of his dark hair now cropped short loosened a tightness she hadn't realized she'd been holding. He looked less like her father. Strange timing for a change like that. He smiled as Aenwyn said something to him, her face animated as always.

"Hey, Kits," Quentin said, the sound of his voice pulling her back from her thoughts. In the time she'd known him, his hair had grown longer—unkempt at the edges—and the stubble on his jaw looked like it had settled there for good. He smiled, small and uneven, studying her, his expression caught somewhere between hopeful and cautious. A slow, traitorous warmth curled through her at that smile.

"Hi," she said, stepping beside him. She hadn't meant to lean in—but closeness drew her anyway. His presence steadied her.

He leaned in, sliding an arm around her waist, turning his face to speak into her ear as he pulled her closer. "I went to speak with Demetrius this morning and overheard him talking to Zelos." He glanced over to where Zelos and Demetrius were conversing. "We'll have to relay plans by word of mouth to complete our next steps. If we gather together, it'll raise suspicions." He paused. "I think they're suspicious of *us*."

She turned her head until their faces were only inches apart.

"What did you say to him?"

She smiled, the kind of smile meant for secrets — even as her hands trembled.

"I asked him about the unguarded portals."

Quentin must have sensed her nervousness; his free hand took hers, steadying her.

"Yeah, he probably wasn't happy about that," he said. "We'll need to be more careful."

"Makes sense." She turned as Demetrius and Zelos moved toward the center of the circle.

"Before that, I spoke with Octo," he murmured. "He got word from Bertolf. He made it out—he's been warning the werewolf clans that Demetrius hasn't been protecting the portals. That the demons are escaping because no one was guarding them."

A cold ripple slid down her spine. Bertolf alive. Bertolf fighting. And Demetrius seemed to be letting the world burn.

Quentin's jaw tightened. "Demetrius doesn't know Octo told me. I'm not sure he even knows that Bertolf is alive."

Blythe scanned the gathered crowd. The fiery leaves stood out sharply against the somber gathering. Overhead, the blue sky expanded wide, and a flock of geese-like birds passed in a V-formation. She might have called them geese, if not for their shimmering green plumage and their wings brushing the air with a soft, whispering sound. Her attention returned to the ground when she sensed someone approaching on her free side. Looking down, she saw Griffin standing there, his hands folded over the head of his axe.

"I s'pect," he said in a voice so low she had to strain to hear him, "we're 'bout to find out if we've been paranoid for nothin'—or if we oughta drink a bit more to prepare for the wors'."

Blythe nodded, though the thought of drinking twisted her stomach when she remembered the night with Quentin and Miles. If it hadn't been for Aenwyn and Nreman, that would have been a rough day after. Maybe not here. Not now.

"Greetings, friends," Demetrius's voice rolled out—smooth and practiced—interrupting her thoughts. Blythe looked up, inwardly cringing at the smile Demetrius shared with the group. It was the kind of smile that made her skin crawl. It was too polished, too self-satisfied for her liking. She hoped he wouldn't call on her or even look her way. Something about him made her skin prickle.

"I am sure many of you are curious about what is going on in the lands beyond our parameters. We are traveling north to a stronghold that will serve as our home base for the upcoming invasion of the capital."

Blythe glanced at Aenwyn and Nreman behind them. Aenwyn twisted her fingers; Nreman gnawed a fingernail, his brows drawn tight. She suppressed a shiver.

"Our dear fairy friends, Aenwyn and Nreman, bring us good news." Lately, he looked more and more like the warlocks he worked beside. Maybe he just needed more sunlight. Less time in tents. "They tell us the Council has not indicated to the public that they know there is a full-fledged rebellion against them. It has come to their—and my—attention that the defenses we put in place to guard the portal to the dark realm are not holding as well as we had hoped."

A stir ran through the group, tight murmurs and uneasy stares.

"What protections?" Quentin whispered. Blythe glanced over at him.

"The attack yesterday was proof of it. We can expect more while we're on the move." He looked around the group. "We will travel during the day; they are weakest in the sunlight. At night, we stop. The Warlocks have been able to provide us with protection, and the Vampires and Werewolves have done a good job keeping an eye on the few that test our barriers."

He smiled again. "These attacks are not just happening to us—they're spreading." Folding his hands in front of him, he continued, "This is just as well. It will keep the Council's troops busy cleaning up that mess and leave us the opportunity to strike." He paced as he spoke, his eyes settling on each face in his audience. "Don't worry about the demons," he said. "The Warlocks have placed protective wards. Our way ahead is secure."

"Yeh? And what about the others out thar?" Griffin grumbled. "We've passed small towns. They're not prepared for such evil."

Quentin's jaw flexed, tension tightening the line of it. She squeezed his hand, he offered a reluctant smile, and she returned it, understanding his anguish. How could Demetrius think it was a good thing that evil was escaping? Even if it occupied the Council's armies, innocents were dying. The only tense faces were her friends'. Most looked unfazed—a few even pleased. Were she and her friends the only ones who felt the wrongness? A shiver slid beneath her clothes.

"Those who agree with us have joined our cause as we have moved through their lands." He nodded to a few of the newcomers. "Those who have chosen to remain behind and live under the tyranny of the Council... well, this is what happens when you follow dictators and refuse to stand up for what is right."

Was he saying that if people didn't follow him... they should die? Blythe felt sick. Quentin's grip on her hand tightened.

"So, basically, fuck anyone who doesn't stand with us," Hera said from behind Blythe.

Blythe's free hand curled into a fist, tucked under the flap of her cloak where Demetrius couldn't see. That wasn't rebellion. It felt like cruelty dressed up as purpose.

"We continue north," he announced, his voice controlled. "I've learned of a weapon—one that could finally allow us to defeat the Council. I'll be assembling a small team to join me on a quest to retrieve it."

His gaze swept over the gathered crowd, skipped Blythe, and lingered on Octo and Eyra, who had just arrived.

"We should reach the northern shore in three days. From there, we'll cross the sea in teams. Once my team reaches the landing point, we'll set out to recover the weapon's fragment. The rest of you will remain behind to establish a base and await our return."

Demetrius presented plans to send people for volunteers, supplies, and recruits. Blythe's focus slipped, Demetrius's voice fading as she turned the words over in her mind. What weapon could he be talking about? Whatever it was, could they trust it wouldn't cause needless deaths? He didn't seem to care that the escaped demons were on a killing rampage. If people disagreed with him, they wouldn't receive protection. How did that make him any better than the Council? What kind of leader saw innocent deaths as a strategy? If this were a rebellion, maybe the world needed a third choice.

"We must all work together," Zelos said, stepping forward. "Do not worry about the losses, for there are always casualties in war. They're a necessity on the path to peace."

Blythe glanced at Quentin. How odd that he would say

that. He knew they were all disturbed by the prospect of demons and other creatures flooding their world, killing indiscriminately.

"Excuse me." Blythe stepped forward, the words leaving her before she realized she'd spoken. Her pulse thundered, breath thinning until the world narrowed to the space between them. Her uncle looked at her with an expression she couldn't decipher. His brows drew together, and his mouth tightened into a thin line. He and Zelos were staring at her—along with everyone else in the clearing.

"What are you doing?" Quentin whispered.

She ignored him.

"What about the humans?" she called out.

Demetrius's voice projected an edge. "What about them?"

"Are the demons escaping into their world, too? If so, they're not capable of protecting themselves..."

"We have no way of knowing what's going on in the human realm," Zelos said. He spoke with a flatness that made the topic sound barely interesting.

"Shouldn't someone check?" she asked, her voice thinning as the last of her resolve slipped.

"That could be something else the Council is handling. After all, they're the ones who insisted on separation between the realms. Our focus cannot be on the casualties that may occur. We get the weapon, and we take out the Council. That's all." Zelos spoke in a low voice, his dark eyes flashing red —briefly yet clearly. Her throat locked, and Quentin's hand touched her arm, guiding her a step back.

"You said the council insisted on the separation between realms?"

"Blythe," Hera hissed.

"Yes?" Demetrius's eyes tightened just a bit.

"Are you indicating that you do not want separation between realms? Does this include the dark realm?"

What was wrong with her? Why couldn't she just stop?

Zelos leaned toward Demetrius and whispered something. The only word she caught was unbound. It sounded like a title. Or a threat.

Demetrius nodded.

"Blythe, we can speak about this later." His tone was too smooth and controlled. A warning wrapped in civility.

The words she swallowed burned all the way down.

Demetrius and Zelos turned and left without ceremony. Blythe stood rooted. Shock swept through her. Others quietly packed, their faces unreadable in the rising light. In two days, Demetrius would have his prize—whatever it was, wherever it dragged them.

"We can't let him get the weapon." Hera stepped close, her whisper cutting through the noise. "Don't move," Hera murmured, just as Blythe began to turn. "Eyra overheard them. It's old magic—strong, volatile." Hera drew a slow breath. "You need to stop asking questions."

"We need to get to them first," Blythe whispered. Hera made a low drone of agreement.

"We'll talk later," Quentin whispered from her left. He gave her a look—heavy enough to settle in her chest—then turned toward his tent. Hera followed, her shadow long and silent. Blythe waited a beat, her throat constricting, each moment weighted.

CHAPTER SEVEN

Blythe

Northeastern Auroraheim

The day blurred past in a haze of stinging noses and quiet, coiled nerves. Blythe spent the journey quietly absorbing the subtle buzz around her, listening for any hint of how the others had taken the morning's meeting. By the time they paused for lunch, her face stung from the cold.

Most of the conversation centered on the demons breaching the magic realm. Few spoke of the human one, and those who did seemed unconcerned. And a cold question pressed in: what did they truly think of humans?

From her childhood lessons, she remembered that long ago, there had been no barriers between realms. That was how humans came to know tales of deities and demons—not as myth, but as fragmented history. Yet she couldn't recall whether anyone had ever explained how the people of the magic realm viewed humanity now. Had they left that part out? Or had she blocked it out herself?

She couldn't tell if they trusted the Warlocks. Their quietness carried an edge — tight, watchful. And she was starting to feel it too.

Blythe, Hera, Quentin, and Griffin were on perimeter duty during lunch, so they paired off and moved through the trees, watching and listening for any sign of trouble. She and Hera walked together, giving them a chance to discuss their plans.

"I think we need to leave as soon as possible," Hera said softly, surveying the surroundings.

Blythe glanced at her, surprised by the strain tightening Hera's jaw. Hera didn't rattle easily.

Hera met her eyes for a beat—steady, unflinching—and something unspoken passed between them.

Not fear. Resolve.

"Leave for where?" Blythe cupped her hands around her mouth, trying to warm her frozen fingers.

"The House." Hera held a branch aside and let Blythe pass first. "If we can find any information about an ancient weapon capable of taking out the Council, the House would have it."

The word "House" alone made her stomach tighten.

"Are you sure? I'd think the Council would've made sure such information was destroyed if it even existed." Blythe stepped carefully over a large root. The last thing she needed was to eat dirt in front of Hera.

"You forget, or maybe you don't know, that the Council once answered to the Keepers and the leaders of each race," Hera said, offering Blythe her hand as they crossed a narrow stream. Blythe declined and managed to do so without making a fool of herself. For once, her boots found solid footing on the slick rocks. "The Keepers guarded not just the portals, but also knowledge. That was their power over the Council. The Council couldn't stop the House from choosing you. The Houses hold a great deal of power. There's a reason your father got away with what he did."

Blythe's breath hitched. Hera's voice eased something tight in her chest.

"I know that's not easy to hear," Hera murmured.

Blythe nodded, swallowing hard. Hera didn't reach for her, but the space between them felt steadier all the same.

"Have you talked to Quentin and the others about this idea of yours?" Blythe asked, pausing to peer through some brush before continuing.

"Yes. It was Quentin's idea, actually." Hera stopped and turned to face her. "He and Griffin are going to see if they can get help from the Fae and the Dwarves against Demetrius and the Warlocks."

"But Demetrius has people out recruiting more troops..."

"They're going to tell them what's really happening." They resumed walking. Blythe tugged her wool cap lower over her head, wishing she were sitting by the fire, eating with the others. That would come soon enough, once those already eating could trade places with them.

Hera had told her the Valkyrie were adapted to frigid temperatures. They often trained at high altitudes, where the air was thinner and the cold sharper, so they would be more potent in those environments. Hera had mentioned that some Valkyrie trained for heat, but most didn't bother.

"Why would anyone trust them over Demetrius's people?" Blythe winced as her foot snapped a twig with a loud crack.

Hera moved without a sound. Blythe wasn't sure how she did it, but she was jealous.

"I forget that you don't know much about them..." Hera lifted a hand, motioning for her to be silent. She drew her sword, and Blythe followed suit. They waited; the only sounds were the birds overhead and the swish of air through the foliage.

A pair of warlocks rounded a tree and approached, carefully stepping over the underbrush.

"You two ready to eat?" one asked.

"Always," Blythe said brightly, hoping their hearing wasn't sharper than Hera's.

"You need to work on your stealth," one of them commented dryly as he passed.

"Yes, I do." Heat rushed up Blythe's neck.

Hera shot her a sidelong glance once the warlocks were out of earshot.

"You're rattled," she said quietly.

"Maybe," Blythe muttered.

Hera's shoulder brushed hers—barely there, but intentional. “Stay close. We’ll get through this.”

Hera sheathed her sword. The two of them followed the path the warlocks had come from. They walked in silence back toward camp and were soon joined by Griffin and Quentin, who looked as though they, too, had been wrapped up in talk before being relieved of duty.

Hera's nod earned two in return—simple gestures, but the quick exchange told Blythe there was more beneath it.

Watching Hera move among them—calm, sure, already strategizing. She hadn’t realized how much she relied on Hera until now.

If she had to run, if she had to fight, Hera was the one person she trusted to stand beside her.

She studied Quentin and Griffin as they walked. Why would they be listened to more than someone else? She'd have to ask Hera when they could speak privately.

Once back in camp, the four grabbed food and sat around the small fire, eating quickly. Others were already packing up the makeshift lunch site and working to erase any sign they had ever been there. She watched as a pair of tree creatures dragged branches across the ground, smoothing out footprints. A werewolf was repacking some bags, and an elf buried the refuse they had created. A flick of magic would finish the job.

“A piece of bread for your thoughts?” Blythe offered Quentin a torn crust, her voice light.

Quentin looked at her, brows drawn in puzzlement.

“Sorry… It's a play on—never mind. You wouldn't know the saying.” She popped the bread into her mouth and chewed. Once she'd swallowed, she asked, “I was wondering what you're thinking.”

“Honestly?” Quentin stirred his stew, then lowered his voice. “I've been trying to figure out when you should go. I think tonight, during the shift change, is your best chance.”

He frowned and took a bite before continuing. “We won't be able to gather much, unfortunately. You'll have to leave with what you've got." He peeked about casually, then added under his breath, "We need you gone before Demetrius resumes your training."

"Why?" Blythe asked, taking another bite.

"We can't risk him learning more about your power. I'm worried that whatever he's after, he may need you to get it." He stared into the stew, jaw tight, as though searching for words.

Blythe waited until someone passed by and was out of earshot before leaning in. "How do you know that?"

"Octo overheard Demetrius talking. He said this thing—whatever it is—was created by the most powerful witches and wizards, and that it might be dangerous to the wielder." Quentin's tone lowered further. "I suspect they see you as expendable."

Blythe swallowed hard. "Okay. Hera and I will go to the House. You and Griffin will find help?"

Quentin nodded. They focused on their food for the next few minutes as people bustled around them, cleaning up. Once the coast was clear again, Blythe leaned toward him to speak.

"When and where will we meet up again?" she asked, setting down her spoon. "It's unlikely we'll be allowed to rejoin the rebels..."

"Once Demetrius notices you're gone, Octo is going to tell him that you and Hera went to retrieve some tomes you remembered seeing at the House and decided not to bother him with worrying about your safety. Octo has already suggested to your uncle that we go and gather recruits from the Fae and Dwarves—and he actually agreed."

A gust of wind swept through camp, lifting the edge of Blythe's cloak. She pulled it tighter, trying to steady her thoughts.

"So Griffin and I won't be sneaking off. We'll be collecting our supplies and leaving at the same time—hopefully distracting enough that you and Hera can slip out unnoticed." He picked up the dry bread beside him and took a bite, chewing with the grim determination of someone forcing down bark.

Dry, tough, nearly inedible—but it was food.

"He's going to be angry we left." She dipped a piece of her bread into the stew to soften it.

"Probably. But he'll never let on to others that he is. It would ruin his reputation as a 'nice guy'." He finished his food and stretched out his legs. "As for your question about when we'll meet up again—the rebels have ways of communicating. Octo's going to let us know where their home base is, so we can then let you know. He said they'd be crossing the sea. That's bound to be a cold and miserable trek." He grinned gently at her. "Here's to hoping this works out for the best."

Blythe helped gather the leftovers of lunch, her mind churning as she cleaned plates and sorted gear. They refilled their canteens at a nearby brook, then slipped back into the march north.

The plan settled uneasily in her mind. When they resumed marching, she drifted beside Hera, looking at her uncle and Zelos as they moved toward the front.

Hera glanced at her as they walked. "You're quiet."

"Just thinking," Blythe said, though the tightness in her chest thinned the words.

Hera didn't push. She simply walked closer, their arms brushing now and then—a silent reminder that Blythe wasn't facing any of this alone.

She still wanted to believe her uncle was a good person. The dark realm had left its influence on everyone. She hadn't come out unaffected. It felt like that place had taken something from her—something she hadn't gotten back, leaving behind distrust and anger. Maybe it wasn't the dark realm that had changed her at all, but the loss of Miles.

How could someone not be affected? There was no way the Warlocks could have been there for so long and come out unchanged. Maybe they'd changed. Or maybe this was who they'd always been.

She scanned her small circle—Quentin, Hera, Octo, Griffin. Could she trust them? She didn't know. But she'd have to. Without them, she'd be adrift in a world she barely understood.

Overhead, a flock of birds veered south. For a moment, she wished she had wings of her own to go anywhere but north. Whatever Demetrius sought, it wouldn't end well. A heavy dread lodged low in her gut, solid and unmovable.

CHAPTER EIGHT

Blythe

Northeastern Auroraheim

The sun slid under the horizon, bathing the camp in warm orange light as rebels began their evening routines. The sky softened to rich violets, and shadows extended across the ground.

Blythe helped start the dinner fire—the first trace of routine in a night full of unknowns. Around her, rebels clustered in small groups, counting rations, sharpening blades, talking quietly about hunt routes and foraging plans.

Octo and Griffin assembled with Demetrius, Zelos, and the other leaders in her uncle's tent, their voices quiet and intense. Meanwhile, Hera approached Blythe, her expression unreadable in the firelight.

"Could you assist me with getting some water?" Blythe nodded, and the two slipped away, canteens in hand. Blythe caught Quentin's eye as he headed towards the tent to attend the meeting. He stilled—a glimpse of emotion crossed his face before he masked it. She caught his gaze and gave a slight smile.

It was possible she wouldn't see him again. If the Council caught her and Hera, they would be dead.

Something unspoken tugged between them, heavy enough to tighten her shoulders. The thought snuck in that maybe this was a sign she was developing deeper feelings for Quentin.

"You know," Hera whispered, "I think I'd have to work to be as loud walking as you are."

"It's a gift," Blythe joked.

Hera smiled, a rare moment of levity.

As they walked, the forest moved into shadow, making it harder for Blythe to see Hera ahead. She grasped the hem of Hera's tunic to stay close, trusting Hera's night vision to guide them through the trees and jagged roots. Hera saw effortlessly in the dark. Blythe didn't. Simple as that.

The quiet thickened around them, settling against her skin. Neither of them spoke as they moved.

They'd no choice but to leave without supplies—only their canteens, whatever they could fit into their pockets, and their weapons. Hera had managed to stuff her pockets with jerky—enough to hold them until they could raid somewhere or forage for more food. Anything more would have raised suspicion about their excuse for fetching "water."

After what felt like hours of cold and stumbling, Hera finally murmured, "We should rest."

They found shelter between a pair of boulders at the base of a mountain, huddling together for warmth as the temperature dropped. She pulled up her hood as a wintry drizzle began to fall, shivering as it soaked through.

"This sucks," she mumbled, her teeth chattering.

"Sucks?" Hera cocked her head.

"It's a catch-all human term for a miserable situation," Blythe explained, trying to coax heat back into her limbs.

"Yes. That would be an appropriate term for this, then, I suppose," Hera replied, her voice carrying a rare trace of amusement. Blythe tightened her cloak and hunched into it.

Eventually, the rain tapered off, exposing a sky dotted with stars, beneath an almost full moon. Blythe lifted her head. Clouds drifted aside, stars scattered across the black like flecks of glitter. She drifted into an uneasy sleep, the cold and hard ground making comfort impossible.

◆ ◆ ◆

Cawing birds jerked her awake, loud and abrupt as a slap. She looked around, and alarm rose when it dawned on her that she was alone. Hera wasn't there. She rose and scanned the area frantically, her breath drawing in quick, visible puffs in the cold dawn air.

Hera couldn't have been taken—because they would have taken Blythe, too, wouldn't they? Blythe stretched out her sore muscles.

"Hera?" she whispered, moving to the edge of the boulder. She crouched down and peered around it.

Beyond the rock, frost glazed the earth, and half-bare trees grabbed at a bleak sky. There was no sign of anyone.

She imagined this was how contestants on Alone and Afraid felt—cold, exposed, and stupidly alone.

"Blythe, where are you going?" Hera's voice came from above. Blythe looked up to see her perched on a rocky outcropping.

"I was going to look for you. Where'd you go?" Blythe returned to the shelter of the rocks, relief surging through her.

"I went up for a better look at where we need to go. The good news is I know exactly where we are and where we need to go."

"And the bad news?" Blythe asked, bracing her arms against the cold.

"We're going to have to go past a town. It isn't a big one, but it's a mage town..."

"Meaning they'll string us up before they listen?" Being mistaken for common criminals was one thing, but being blamed for unleashing evil upon the world was far worse. Mage towns were loyal to the Council; a glimpse of her face would be enough to condemn her.

"Let's go," Hera said, carefully climbing down. They set off again, Hera moving silently through the brush while Blythe stumbled along behind her.

"I thought you were a hunter or something in the

human realm?"

"I was an archaeologist," Blythe grumbled, pressing a hand to her sore shin.

"Archaeologists don't trek through forests?" Hera asked, barely slowing enough for Blythe to catch up. "Must be nice—relics waiting politely in open fields."

"We do, but we don't usually have to worry about how loud we are. I went to Peru for a dig and needed to get through the jungle, but we bushwhacked our way through the worst parts. There wasn't all this scrambling above roots and rocks," Blythe said, ducking under a drooping branch.

"Peru—one of your human cities?" Hera held a branch back for Blythe.

"A country," Blythe corrected.

They continued in near silence, Blythe focusing on where she moved and on not getting whipped by branches. By the time they stopped to eat the meager rations Hera had pilfered from the camp, Blythe felt certain there was no way they'd be able to pass the town quietly.

They didn't rest long before resuming their grueling pace. The sun made its slow ascent and descent as they traveled the harsh, unrelenting landscape. It took most of the day for them to reach the town's outskirts.

"We'll have to wait here," Hera whispered, crouching behind a thick bunch of brambles. "There's no way we'll be able to pass in daylight."

Blythe looked up toward the shadowed sky. "It shouldn't be too long a wait."

She settled in, leaning back against the trunk of a tree and stretching her legs out in front of her. She kneaded her aching calf. She kept hoping the pain would stop eventually. But miles don't get easier; they just wear you slower.

She became aware that she wished Quentin were next to her—someone warm to lean against, someone who made the dark feel less vast.

Blythe broke the silence first. "I thought you'd left," she

said quietly. “Or been taken.”

Hera shifted, drawing her knees up. “I went to scout. “I should’ve woken you,” A rare note of regret threaded through the sound of her voice. “You looked… worn.”

Blythe huffed a breath. “Still. Waking up alone out here isn’t exactly comforting.”

“I know.” Hera glanced over, her features unreadable in the dim light. “When we first met, I didn’t think you’d last a day in all of this. But you’ve kept going. Through things some wouldn’t survive.” She paused, then added, softer, “You’re no Valkyrie. But you carry yourself like one.”

Warmth and ache knotted in Blythe’s chest. “Coming from you, that means something.”

Hera gave a single, clipped nod—her version of affection—and the hush settled around them again, less sharp than before.

Night finally bled across the sky. Hera rose first, silent as ever, and Blythe followed. They tried to slip past the town, avoiding detection as best they could.

Blythe and Hera hunkered down behind a thick cluster of bushes on the outskirts of the mage town. The town itself was a modest collection of stone and wooden buildings, their windows dimly lit by lamplight. Soft coils of smoke rose from chimneys into the glittering dark. Voices seeped through open windows—some joyous, some weary. Somewhere, a dog barked once, then again, then stopped. Cutlery scraped upon pottery behind a warped doorframe.

“Quick and quiet,” Hera whispered, her gaze darting toward the dimly lit route. “No one sees us.”

Blythe gave a sharp nod, and Hera gave the signal. They moved. Each step ahead felt loud, her very heartbeat threatening to echo through the quiet.

They kept off the main path—shadow to shadow, building to building. Hera's pace changed with every sound—a breath, a shift, a creak—and each time, they paused, brittle and alert, before slipping forward again.

As they rounded a corner, Blythe heard a low murmur of voices. Hera raised a hand, and they pressed against the side of a building, peeking around the corner to see two mages deep in conversation near a well. Their cloaks bore stitched symbols—some faded, some still bright against the dusk—as though they hadn't changed clothes in weeks. Their faces looked hollow, skin pulled tight over sharp cheekbones. Whatever the Council had done here, it showed in every face she saw.

The men's voices floated down the path in broken pieces as they left the well, their pace slow but sharp-eyed.

"Another town hit," one murmured. "Dark Realm creatures again. Same pattern." His head turned toward the shadows. He didn't seem to see them—yet.

A branch cracked in the forest, followed by a man's laughter.

Hera pressed back, her hand inching toward the sword at her hip. "Patrol," she whispered. Blythe quickly placed a hand on Hera's arm to stop her. "They'll cut us down if they spot us," Hera whispered, sharp and low.

Before Blythe could respond, the men resumed their conversation.

"I can take them before they see us," Hera breathed. A tightness climbed her throat. Killing them would stain her hands in a way she wasn't ready to face.

"Why now?" the first man asked, pulling jerky from his pocket. "Why do you think they got out?" One of the patrolmen tore into his jerky, chewing with slow purpose.

"Council blames it on that Valkyrie again—and the half-witch," the other grunted, ripping a strip free and cramming it into his mouth.

Blythe's stomach gave a faint growl. She clenched her fists, willing it to be silent. Hera didn't glance her way, but Blythe felt the shared tension between them.

"Council'll blame anyone," the first said, jaw working through a thick bite. "Hell, they'd finger the stars if they thought it'd stick."

The second let out a short laugh. “Capital's got a stink all its own. Smells like pride—and cheap perfume. You can catch it a mile out.” He elbowed the other, and they both snickered.

Hera didn’t move. Her eyes stayed razor-focused, her expression locked and unreadable. Blythe imitated her posture—every muscle locked.

The men passed without a glance, still wrapped in their tired banter and strips of dried meat.

A few paces ahead, one of them pulled a pulsing communication stone from his pocket. “Looks like the boss wants a word,” he muttered.

“Yeah?” the other replied, just as an image appeared within view, hovering in the distance between them.

Blythe stifled a gasp. She'd know those keen jade eyes, that dark hair, and that glare anywhere.

Benjamin.

“Have you found them yet?” he snarled, venom dripping from every word.

“Not yet, Captain,” said the man holding the stone. “Someone claimed they saw a couple of figures pass through here, but we haven't spotted anything.”

“Then you're not looking hard enough,” Benjamin snapped. “They're halflings. They shouldn't be that difficult to track.”

The man glanced at his partner, who shifted uneasily.

“We'll keep searching and report when we find them,” he said at last.

“See that you do. Alive or dead. Dead would be preferable—but I'd enjoy delivering their sentence myself.” His grin was wicked, and cold shot through her, sharp enough to steal her breath.

The men ended the call and shared looks—then broke out laughing.

“It's pathetic, really,” one chortled. “He loses the Keepership to a halfling runt, and the Council tosses him a bone—'lead the charge,' like it's some grand honor. All he's doing is their dirty work. So when he fails, they can be done with him."

Their voices trailed off as they walked away, still mocking her half-brother, their voices fading into the dark.

When the boots were finally distant, Hera gestured. They crept out, moving quickly and sneaking through the last stretch of town toward the edge where branches thickened into cover.

They were two steps from the trees when the shout broke the night. Blythe's breath caught—almost there.

"Hey! You there!"

Blythe's body reacted before her thoughts caught up. She twisted toward the voice, her pulse thundering through her as her eyes found a mage standing down the path—young, sharp-lined, his posture too composed for someone just stumbling into strangers.

His arm lifted slowly, fingers arranged in a practiced gesture.

"Explain yourselves," he said. The sound broke the quiet. Blythe flinched. Hera didn't wait. Her hand secured around Blythe's wrist.

"Go," she spat.

They moved fast, ducking low as they ran. Leaves and detritus crackled beneath their feet, branches catching at their sleeves. The chase behind them intensified, spreading out like spilled ink.

They didn't stop until the shouting cracked apart behind them and was swallowed by the woods. Hera followed Blythe, one hand still clenched on her sword hilt, ready at a moment's notice.

"We can't stop," Blythe whispered, lungs aflame.

Hera nodded, looking back in the direction they had come. Blythe pushed aside her fatigue and pressed on through the thick gathering of trees. Hera took the lead, as if she knew which way to go.

"We need to cut west, then head south," Hera said, adjusting their course.

Blythe scanned the sky for Polaris, using its steady glow to orient herself where Hera was leading.

Time blurred into aching legs and burning lungs before the trees finally thinned into a clearing.

"We should rest here," Hera said. She sat down, and Blythe collapsed next to her, her muscles throbbing from the breakneck pace Hera had maintained to put distance between them and the town.

"We can't rest for long," Blythe whispered, though she wished it weren't true. "I'm sure they'll raise the alarm, and troops will come after us."

"...If we're lucky. If not..." Hera's tone lowered. "It'll be the Valkyrie who responds." Blythe couldn't see her face, but she knew the look—hard, set, unyielding.

"Unfortunately, they know roughly where we are. It's just a matter of time." Hera presented a piece of jerky to Blythe, who accepted it, studied it, and then responded.

"Sometimes..." Blythe hesitated. "I wonder if it would have been better if they hadn't rescued me after my sentencing." She curled her hands tight in her lap, willing the sound to stay small, swallowed by the dark. "I wouldn't have to keep running, the portals would be closed, and..."

Her voice felt too loud in the quiet, the admission scraping raw on the way out.

"Don't say that," Hera murmured. "Without you, they still would have found a way into the Dark Realm. This all would have still happened. Plus, on the upside, I'd say the conversation between those two mages is clearly a sign that not everyone is blindly following them." She took another bite of jerky, chewing before speaking again. "Demetrius will face the same problem. Some people follow without question, but I'm sure some won't. Quentin is more optimistic—he'd probably say most won't." She chuckled. "I'm not that naïve."

Blythe nodded and took a bite of jerky. "Maybe you're right."

"I usually am," Hera said, the cheer in her voice more

grounded than mocking. She popped the rest of her jerky into her mouth before taking a swig of water from her flask.

If nothing else, Blythe was glad she wasn't alone in being on the Council's Most Wanted list. Hera's sharp eyes—and sharper sword—were something to cling to.

CHAPTER NINE

Quentin

Northeastern Auroraheim

Quentin flung open the tent flap and flinched—cold air knifed across his face, unsoftened by the night. Frost snapped beneath each step as he crossed toward the supply tent, the air fogging with each exhale. He tried not to picture Blythe and Hera somewhere out in the cold, huddled against whatever shelter they'd managed to find.

The thought hit a tender place he'd been trying hard not to touch. They needed to move fast.

"Ready?" someone asked. Griffin's voice cut through his thoughts, and he looked up to see the dwarf emerging from the tent, two bulging packs in his arms.

Quentin nodded, taking one of the packs from him and slinging it onto his back.

"As ready as I'll ever be," Quentin said.

Griffin flashed a quick grin. "By stone and flame, ye look like sleep wouldn't go near ye."

"Maybe not," Quentin muttered, adjusting the straps. His mind was still on the gloom they were about to walk into—how far the rebellion had pushed them, and how much further it might. The pack felt heavier than usual.

"Where's Eyra?" Quentin shielded his eyes, peering toward the distance as if he expected Eyra's silhouette to appear.

"She's back with the council," Octo said, the sound of his voice rolling in slow behind him. Quentin turned; he hadn't heard the large man's approach. He and Hera could sneak up on a kitsune. Octo was walking up the slope, bare shoulders resisting the wind, grass catching on his pants as if it wanted to hold him there.

"Demetrius wants intel before anyone makes a move," Octo added.

Quentin readjusted the pack on his back. "If she makes it back."

His eyes wandered, unfocused. The plan—or what served for one—was splintered at best. Eyra had grit, but trust felt tenuous—fragile enough to snap over a misplaced step.

"And you?" Quentin asked. Octo's face tightened, like the words were dragging something heavy behind them.

"Demetrius needs me here," Octo said, voice flatter now. "Diplomacy." His hand went up, gesturing without precision. "Talk to the royals. Get them aligned. Build something new. A new council, maybe."

Quentin let out a short, dry sound, something between a laugh and a scoff. "A new council—with Demetrius pulling the strings? Sounds like a takeover dressed up for a party."

Octo shrugged. "I know my parents are not going to be keen to go against the Council, and they are even less keen to help Demetrius." He looked around. "Most leaders I've spoken with question how he escaped. They think he must have made some dark deal to get out. I'll be stalling leaving the group as long as I can."

"And do you agree? If he did, should we really be going along with him?"

Octo didn't argue. His jaw set firm. "It's what I've been asked to do. I figure we may be trading one evil for another, but at least the new rulers won't grip as tightly."

Quentin couldn't argue with that.

Griffin had been quiet until then.

"Sounds less like buildin' peace and more like splittin' stone with a rusty axe," he said, in a hushed tone.

Quentin nodded without meaning to. "We'll see." But the doubt hadn't left him. It sat heavily, pressing against every step they took forward. Demetrius had plans—and Quentin was no longer sure where they aimed.

Octo scanned the tree line, then turned back to Quentin and Griffin. “Before you head out—I wanted you to know. Hera and Blythe were spotted, but they escaped quietly. I'm guessing they already know the Council's goons will be waiting for them wherever they're headed. Still, figured you'd want the heads-up.”

Quentin gave a curt nod. “Thanks for the intel.”

Cold air closed around them as they left the last glow of camp behind.

They walked through the lush thicket for some time until the clearing opened wide, moonlight pooling across the frost. Quentin advanced. He whistled, gaze lifted—tense, expectant.

Griffin shielded his eyes. “How long until Ellira's here?”

“Soon,” Quentin said. “She's been shadowing us. Careful, but close.” He stretched to shake off his nerves. It didn't help. It didn't work. He knew they'd be riding for a while and wanted to move while he still could. He heard the sound of large wings flapping against the wind. A giant brown-and-gold dragon with gleaming scales emerged from above the tree line, circling slowly before landing in front of them.

Ellira let out a low groan, pushing her nose into Quentin's body. "Hey, girl," he murmured, stroking her shiny scales. "You ready, Griffin?"

Griffin eyed Ellira warily. If Quentin didn't know better, he'd swear Griffin's skin was two shades paler than it had been when they reached the clearing.

“As ready as I'll ever be,” he said, slowly approaching the giant beast.

Quentin helped Griffin up and then climbed on in front of him. He gently kicked Ellira in the side, and she rose into the sky. Griffin held tightly to Quentin, squeezing his eyes shut. “I guess you Dwarves weren't made for flying,” Quentin chuckled.

“Aye,” Griffin groaned. “We're for the earth—below it or

atop it. Ne'er above." He let out another groan and pressed his face into Ellira's neck. "Is there such a thing as air sickness? I feel like me innards' been tossed in a barrel o' grog and rolled down a mountain."

"Just please don't throw up on Ellira or me. Aim over the side."

"If I do that, I'll fall. Better on you," Griffin groaned.

Quentin grimaced.

Quentin effortlessly steered Ellira by pressing his heels —left for left, right for right. They flew south, leaving the frozen north behind. His stomach clenched—home hadn't been home for a long time. He wasn't sure what to expect. Wind tore past his ears, making it too loud for them to converse. If Griffin hadn't been nauseous, Quentin knew he'd be firing questions nonstop.

He turned away from Griffin's groans and the thought of home, concentrating instead on Blythe. It felt like something essential had gone with her. He could see her in his mind, how she had looked last night before she and Hera slipped off into the darkness. She was dressed warmly, and the green of her cloak made her eyes practically shine.

He forced them away, irritated at himself for letting them creep in—disgusted by how easily they took hold. He couldn't let himself wander there, not when she could so easily reject him and leave him heartbroken. This wasn't how it was supposed to go. He was meant to meet a Fae who would imprint on him, or not imprint at all, and have a normal relationship. Fall in love, marry someone… if he even chose to marry.

That had never been his plan.

But Blythe... Blythe was different. When he met her, his dreams of being the Fae lawyer hero, bringing back peace and unity to the Magic Realm, looked like they were fading to gray, and a new dream emerged. He saw himself and her together until the end. The thought of life without her seemed like an abyss he could never escape.

He needed to figure out how to get her to forgive him,

to see past his lies and the truth about who he was and what he felt about her. He should never have followed Demetrius's plan. He had thought for sure she'd want to help them.

He had felt angry at her—for being so selfish and naïve enough to think she could hide in the House forever.

How long could that really last? Was the House a match against the evil flooding the worlds?

Her forgiveness was all he needed. Without it, he wasn't sure what he would do. If things somehow broke their way, the council would be dismantled, the evil from the dark realm sealed away, and he could disappear into academia—just another professor with too many books and regrets.

Lately, she had seemed less cold. But he couldn't tell if she was softening toward him or pretending because the mission demanded it?

CHAPTER TEN

Quentin

Flying west over the continent of Auroraheim

From the back of a dragon, time felt distorted—too fast and too slow at once. Ellira flew high enough that, from below, no one would see a Fae and a Dwarf traveling together. Griffin wore his cloak with the hood raised over his head, staying close behind Quentin in the hopes that, if they were seen, people would assume he was a stocky child flying with his father. They both hunched low to help Ellira cut through the wind. Quentin kept his eyes on the horizon as the landscape below gradually shifted from frost-covered ground and trees losing their leaves to patches of green.

The warmth was a welcome change, but it scarcely alleviated the tight worry lodged in his chest. Ellira let out a low, rumbling growl. Quentin scanned the sky and saw a winged silhouette moving rapidly toward them. He tried to rationalize what it could be. *Friend? Foe? Another traveler?* But no—their path cut straight at them.

"Griffin, hold tight!" Quentin shouted over the wind. "We've got company!"

Griffin lifted his head to see what was coming. "What in the beard is that?"

Quentin narrowed his eyes, trying to make out the figure. It was another dragon, larger than Ellira. The rider on its back was only a shape against the clear blue sky. There was no way of knowing what they wanted, but Quentin wasn't about to wait to find out.

Quentin gripped Ellira's sides with his knees and prepared for evasive maneuvers.

Ellira roared and veered sharply to the left just as the other dragon swooped down toward them. The sudden movement jolted Quentin and Griffin, but they held on.

Quentin's brain spun. Their intent was obvious—this wasn't a friendly approach. He and Griffin weren't exactly wanted—but the fact that they were together would raise uncomfortable questions. If he were questioned again, he could truthfully say he didn't know where Blythe was. But no one would believe him—not after the last time she escaped custody.

They couldn't afford a confrontation now, not when they were so close to their destination. Quentin urged Ellira to fly faster, hoping to lose their pursuer.

The enemy dragon let out a resounding bellow, closing the distance. Quentin squinted against the sun and finally saw the rider's face. He didn't recognize them. They raised a hand, and a flash of light—magic—shot toward them.

Quentin steered Ellira into a steep dive. The spell whizzed past, narrowly missing Griffin's head.

"We can't keep dodging!" Griffin shouted.

Ellira's chest heaved beneath them.

"I know!" Quentin shouted. They couldn't lose a dragon in the sky, not without magic or combat training. Hera would have decimated their pursuer.

For once, he was grateful Blythe wasn't here. Hopefully, she was safer than they were at the moment.

How could they lose their pursuer?

Then a single, desperate idea cut through the panic. He remembered a narrow canyon not far from their current location. It was a treacherous place to fly—there was no guarantee it would work—but it was their only chance.

Quentin guided Ellira toward the canyon, the air rushing in their ears as it whipped past them on their breakneck descent.

Griffin gasped behind him, breath ragged with fear. His

grip on Quentin was painful, but there was no time to reassure him—even if he needed it. He hadn't flown a canyon run in years.

As they neared the canyon, Quentin cast a quick glance back. He saw the enemy dragon trailing them, attempting to follow into the canyon, its rider shouting orders and trying to force it into the tight space. The dragon's bulk made quick maneuvering in the canyon difficult, and flying above would make attacking them harder. Quentin knew this was their chance to buy some time.

He focused on the way forward, navigating the tight spaces with precise skill.

Quentin steered Ellira into a sharp turn.

Ellira plunged further into the canyon. As she flew, Quentin scanned their surroundings, searching for a hiding place.

"There!" Griffin pointed ahead. "I see a cave."

Quentin squinted. The entrance was slightly concealed by rocks and shadow. He looked back but couldn't see the enemy dragon. If it didn't see them go in, this might just work.

Quentin steered Ellira toward the cave, urging her to slow down. The cave was small, though it gave brief sanctuary. As they entered, Quentin could hear the enemy dragon's frustrated shrieks ringing out across the canyon.

Ellira settled inside the cave, her wings folding neatly as she crouched. Quentin and Griffin dismounted quickly, ducking inside the shadows.

The cave air pressed damp and frigid to their skin. They pressed into the stone, bodies stilling instinctively, listening for the sounds of the enemy dragon.

The canyon had shielded them—for now.

Quentin watched the entrance, his mind racing as he tried to decide their next steps. He knew they needed to move quickly once the enemy dragon gave up looking for them.

"We'll stay here until it's safe to move," Quentin whispered. "Once it clears out, we'll find another route. We can't risk staying too long."

Griffin nodded, his eyes studying the cave's interior. "Aye, and hope they don't dismount and come down here to find us." Griffin reclined on the cave wall. "Who do ya think that was?"

"No idea, but they weren't friendly… my guess would be from the Council."

Griffin grunted his displeasure.

The minutes crept by, each one stretching taut. They could hear the dragon's roars and the thump of its wings above the canyon.

Griffin sat with his eyes closed, listening.

"When I shut me eyes, me ears pick up more," he grunted. "Us dwarves, we're bred for the dark. We've long learned to trust what we hear, not just what we see."

"Makes sense," Quentin conceded.

While they stood, the last ringing of the dragon's thunderous cries thinned into silence. The pursuit had stopped—for now. It might have flown off or simply gained altitude, but he couldn't check without risking being seen.

"They can't fly forever," Quentin said. Griffin grunted his agreement.

As the last traces of the dragon's presence slipped away, Quentin moved towards the cave entrance and peered out. He signaled to Griffin. "It's time. Let's move."

They slipped out of the cave, and Ellira launched back into the air, staying low within the canyon walls. Quentin relied on his knowledge of the area to find their path so they wouldn't have to emerge until they were closer to his hometown. He watched the terrain while Griffin kept an eye on the sky. Their nerves taut as they threaded through the tight, twisting passages. Quentin sagged as they cleared the canyon, muscles unclenching. Ahead, craggy summits rose silhouetted by a stunning sunset of pinks and purples. He exhaled slowly, eyes fixed on the mountains—solid, distant, and untouched by the upheaval they'd left behind.

CHAPTER ELEVEN

Blythe

Somewhere in the continent of Auroraheim

Days flowed into one another as they walked. They stayed in the woods, picking what berries and fruits they could find. This area was much more wooded than it would be in the Human realm; Hera explained that measures had been taken to preserve nature as much as possible—that was one thing everyone in this realm appeared to agree on.

At one point, Blythe had grabbed something that looked like an elderberry but turned out to be a poisonous shadevine berry. They couldn't risk making a fire to cook meat, so they were careful with their meager portions of jerky.

By the fourth day, desperation won out—they stole a magic carpet that had been carelessly parked and left unsecured. The sky was crowded with clouds, so they flew high, covered with mist. By nightfall on the fifth day, the House came into view. They descended slowly, landing at the edge of the clearing, holding their breath while they surveyed the silhouette rising from the trees. Blythe could see the barn and the tree she had crashed into when she tried to take the cursed bicycle to get to the Council meeting. She looked up at the sky, half expecting to see Ellira's golden wings, Quentin perched atop her, grinning. But no—just clouds and silence.

They would not be coming.

"The coast appears to be clear," Hera's voice brought Blythe back to the present.

"That seems odd to me," Blythe whispered. "If the Council is trying to find me, wouldn't they think I'd come back here?"

"I agree," Hera's shoulders dipped. "It could be a trap... but what else can we do?"

Blythe thought for a moment. "Maybe we could trigger something to draw out whoever might be waiting for us?" She cast a quick look down at her hands. Was she ready to try?

"Like what?"

A small smile crossed her face as she looked up at Hera. "Magic."

Hera cocked an eyebrow and gestured for Blythe to proceed. Then she drew back and crouched down on her heels, hand on the hilt of her sword.

Blythe drew a steady inhale. She remembered something she had seen in her magic book that had seemed interesting. She hoped the trick would work.

She sat down on the ground, crossing her legs, and let her eyes fall shut. She trusted Hera to keep watch while she tried. She forced the image of herself and Hera emerging from the woods by the barn into her mind, picturing it as clearly as possible. She was going to make it look like they were walking out of the trees, hoping to trick any guards into revealing themselves so they could strike.

She visualized every detail—the stride, the tilt of Hera's sword, the confidence in her eyes. Anxiety prickled as she held the image steady. The image fed into her magic. A prickle of energy gathered in the tips of her fingers. She formed an image of everything: the rustling leaves, the way they moved, even the sound of their footfalls. She said the memorized incantation as quietly as she could. She couldn't risk giving away their position just to cast this spell.

Blythe opened her eyes. A faint stirring appeared across the clearing at the far side of the barn. Two figures—perfect replicas of Blythe and Hera—stepped out of the woods. They moved naturally, indistinguishable from the real thing. They looked around, poised for an attack. The illusion Hera even held her sword, ready to strike.

Blythe glanced over at the real Hera, who looked on in wonder, tense and ready for any sudden movement. She turned her attention back to the clearing and the House. Moments passed—then a rustling came from the trees, closer to where they were. Blythe saw a bush move, followed by the crunch of footsteps.

"It's working." Hera tightened her hold on her weapon.

Blythe stayed focused, holding the illusion as the figures drew the enemy toward their trap. Two men burst from the woods, weapons drawn, charging straight at the illusory Blythe and Hera. The guards looked around, realizing too late that they'd been deceived.

"Now!" Blythe hissed.

Hera sprang into action, launching herself at the nearest guard. Blythe rose, shifting her concentration from keeping the illusion to aiding Hera. She chanted another spell, sending a gust of wind to disarm the second guard.

It only made him stumble.

Blythe lunged, her blade flashing too slowly. He turned, sword already swinging. She raised her blade at the last possible second, meeting his with a jarring clang.

The guard quickly regained his balance and pressed forward, his blade slashing toward her neck. Blythe blocked, but his strength nearly knocked her off balance.

Instinct snapped into place. She twisted away, ducking and sliding out of reach before he could strike again. She slashed for his side. He moved aside and cut across her arm. Pain ripped through the wound, driving her backward in a burst of white-hot shock.

The guard advanced.

Blythe's mind scrambled for a spell, a tactic—anything.

"Mixed-blood trash," the man sneered. "Orders say dead or alive." His grin widened. "I prefer dead!"

He closed the distance between them, his eyes lit with a wild thrill.

She swung broadly, panic driving her more than technique. But the guard was dogged. He raised his blade for the killing blow—then something yanked his strike off course. The shift was so sudden that she stopped abruptly, stunned as the guard was pushed back, stumbling away from her.

Blythe watched as the guard's weapon flew from his hand, clinking to the ground. Her heart pounded in her chest as she tried to steady herself.

She pushed herself upright, palm braced against scorched stone. Her vision swam, but she still made out the guard sprawled on the ground, unmoving.

Her gaze met Hera's, who looked as though she was having the time of her life. "How about he's dead instead, hm?" Hera grinned at Blythe.

"Thank you," she breathed, her voice trembling with relief and residual fear.

Hera's head turned sharply, and she grabbed Blythe by the wrist. "We have to move."

Blythe heard a shout, but before she could look, Hera began to run, pulling her along.

Adrenaline drove her forward as she tore up the back porch stairs. The door swung open just as she reached it—thank the stars—and they staggered inside.

Blythe spun around.

A swarm of men burst from the tree line, thundering across the clearing like a wave of fury. At the front was Benjamin, his face contorted with rage, eyes lit with a hatred that didn't belong in any living man. His mouth curled into a snarl as he raised his hand.

A bolt of lightning sizzled to life in the palm of his hand.

Blythe froze.

The air snapped.

The bolt hurled toward her, a jagged spear of white-hot energy.

Then: SLAM.

The door shut with an ear-splitting bang, the wood shuddering under the force of the impact. The sound of the bolt against the door reverberated through her body.

Inside, stillness descended—thick, electric, trembling.

It settled heavily in the pit of her chest.

Hera sheathed her sword. "You did well, all things considered. But you need to stay focused."

Blythe turned toward Hera, who was already assessing the room.

"What things are considered?" Her stomach clenched. If Hera hadn't stepped in, she'd be gone. She let her sword fall to the floor and leaned back against the door, exhaustion rushing through her as the endorphins faded. "I'm not cut out for this."

"We don't have time for self-pity," Hera's tone sharpened. "You won't get better without practice—and you skipped too many sessions when you were with the camp." She fixed Blythe with a solemn look. "Unfortunately, life didn't give you time to truly train for all of this. We just have to make do."

Just then, a heavy crash from the other side of the door sent both of them flinching back. Blythe leapt away from the door she had been leaning on.

"The House won't let them in, right?" Hera scanned the dark, windowless room.

The air hung dense with the musty fragrance of ancient wood and wax. The sole source of light was from the dancing flame of an old candelabra hanging overhead, casting restless dark shapes on the walls.

Blythe looked down at her arm, pressing her hand over the wound. It was bleeding but not gushing—so that was a good sign.

"Not unless I tell it to," Blythe replied, her voice trembling softly. "At least, I think so?" She looked briefly up at the ceiling, her heart beating rapidly as she sought reassurance. "You're not going to open for them, right?"

The House knew her. It recognized her as its Keeper; it wouldn't obey anyone else.

As if in response, the door rattled under another violent blow. The sound resounded through the room, a heavy thudding that rattled the walls. Then, the House responded by erasing the door entirely. The sudden quiet that ensued was palpable, interrupted only by the soft snap of the House shifting.

Blythe smiled and leaned against the wall, letting her head fall back on the cool stone.

"Thank you," she said.

Maybe it was in her head, but she thought she felt the House sigh as relief rolled through the stone like a friend welcoming her home. She closed her eyes and slid down to sit on the floor. The room had started to spin. She wasn't sure if it was exhaustion or blood loss.

The House shivered behind her, a soft tremor grazing her in something close to comfort. Then light unfurled from the wall, flowing through her limbs in a slow, even throb. A soft red shimmer rose from her skin, brightening until it beat with power.

Was she seeing her aura?

It flared once more, then lowered to nothing.

Hera moved forward and pulled a cloth from her pouch, wiping away the blood, exposing a wound already sealed—weeks of healing done in seconds. Hera and Blythe exchanged a look before Blythe turned back to the wall.

She rose and placed her hands against it. "Thank you."

It was strange how a place could change in her heart. She once hated this House with every fiber of her being, avoiding it at all costs. But now it felt like a sanctuary—a place where she belonged. Home.

Relief slipped away too fast. Her mind rehashed the fight, the hesitation, the slip, the cold blade against her arm.

Hera rested a hand on Blythe's shoulder. "You'll do better."

"And I'm sure you'll have to save me... again." A humorless sigh escaped her, and she stooped to retrieve her sword. There would never be enough time to become who she thought she had to be.

She might not be able to fight, but she could research.

Looking up at the ceiling, she whispered, "Let's see what you've got for us. We've got some worlds to fix."

With a final pat, Blythe moved away from the wall. She looked at Hera, who had been standing back during her exchange with the House. Curiosity and concern mingled in Hera's expression.

"Let's go find out what my uncle is after," Blythe said with a smile. She took the stairs two at a time, a small fire sparking back to life in her chest.

CHAPTER TWELVE

Quentin

Fae Mountains

The sun rose above the horizon as Ellira descended toward the little town at the top of the mountain. Quentin had forgotten how breathtaking a sunrise over the Lumarthiel Mountains could be. Their other name was the Glimmercrest Mountains—given for the way sunrise and sunset lit their peaks with a glistening glow.

And yet, despite the beauty, with each flap of Ellira's wings bringing them closer to the landing zone just outside the main gates, anxiety curled low in his gut. He wasn't returning home for comfort. He was returning because he needed the Fae to help against Demetrius and the Council. Ellira glided down toward a green opening in the mountains, and Quentin spotted the ring of stones marking their landing spot.

Ellira descended smoothly until her four feet touched down upon the moist earth. Quentin hopped off and was quickly followed by Griffin, who slid off after him, landing with a heavy thud. Quentin straightened his jacket, then came forward to pat Ellira's nose.

"Thanks, girl," he whispered into her glossy scales, pressing his brow to her neck. She made a soft burring sound and nudged him gently with her nose. "Alright, Ellira. I'll see you soon."

She groaned once before lifting off. Quentin braced himself against the gust from her powerful wings, his coat fluttering wildly as she rose into the sky.

He watched her fly off, feeling momentarily abandoned,

as if she'd left him to face judgment alone. He wished Blythe could see this place—his home, his sky. He wondered if she was safe.

"So these are the Fae Mountains, then?" Griffin said from Quentin's left. Quentin looked down at his friend and nodded.

"Well, look what the Griffin dragged in," came a low drawl from behind them, setting Quentin's nerves on edge.

"I din't drag anyone anywhere," Griffin grunted, turning to face the man approaching them.

"Don't listen to him." Quentin stiffened as he turned to meet the approach.

The figure's long legs carried him with lazy confidence over the terrain. He tossed his long blond hair over one shoulder.

"Aw, come now, big brother; you wouldn't be turning your dwarf friend against me again, would you?" The figure's white teeth flashed in the waning sunlight as he grinned. Where Quentin was dark-skinned and dark-haired, his brother was his opposite: skin so pale it was almost translucent, hair so blond it was nearly white. He was tall and slim; Quentin matched his height but not his build.

"No, Iain. I wasn't turning him against you. I was merely suggesting that he ignore your snide remarks," Quentin said, beginning to walk in the direction Iain had come from. "I was hoping to avoid your usual sparring matches."

Griffin jogged to catch up as Quentin quickly passed Iain and headed towards a gap in the circle of stones. "I've no problem with a healthy debate."

"It's never a healthy debate," Quentin said.

"Now, now, don't be like that, Quentin." Iain fell into step alongside Quentin with ease. "No need to be so serious. Besides, is that any way to greet your dearest sibling?"

Quentin snorted.

"Well, that's a charming sound," Iain said, brushing his hair behind a pointed ear.

"I don't need to be charming with you," Quentin muttered, speeding up.

"Aye! Ya wouldn' wanna leave yer pal behind in a strange place, would ya?" Griffin had to jog to keep up with the long-legged pace of the two Fae.

"Sorry, Griffin," Quentin mumbled, slowing down.

"Mother will be thrilled you're back. She's been grumbling for months about having to do your work..."

"What work?" Quentin rolled his eyes. "Presiding over competitions and celebrations hardly seems like work."

"That's not all you're supposed to be doing, Que, and you know it." Iain's tone turned steelier.

"Oh, you mean kissing the Council's boots? Is that the other job you're referring to?" Quentin stopped and turned to face him.

"We don't kiss anyone's..."

"Since when?" Quentin folded his arms over his chest, trying to still the tremors in his fingers.

"Since they started overstepping their bounds," Iain's voice lowered. He looked around, leaning in toward Quentin before continuing, "Something is going on... something unnatural..."

"You don't say?" Quentin rolled his eyes. "It almost sounds like what I said before I left..."

"And perhaps Mother should have listened..."

"And you." Quentin poked Iain in the chest.

"Úra?" Iain placed his hand dramatically against his chest.

"Yes. Níra —you." Quentin inhaled before continuing. "I seem to recall you disagreeing with me when I went to speak with mother."

"Oh, look, it's almost like you never left," a light voice said from behind Quentin.

"Isolde..." Iain began. Quentin didn't need to turn to see the look that he was sure she was giving her twin brother.

Slowly, he turned to see his younger sister, Isolde—Izzy—standing a few paces away. Her long hair was pulled back, the fading light making it hard to tell which color she'd dyed it this time. She loved changing her hair to match her mood, much to their mother's chagrin. She wore a long dress that blew gently in the mountain breeze.

"Izzy," Quentin whispered. He couldn't quite read the look on her face, but when she ran to him and threw her arms around him, he couldn't help but smile. He wrapped his arms around her and held her tightly.

"Eryn'la ura'nal e'llis sa'nir," she breathed, a small sob escaping at the end.

"Eryn'la ura'nal e''lis, al'sa, pa'ra'ne," Quentin answered quietly. Izzy sniffled and slowly pulled back, gliding a hand over her face.

"Don't ever leave like that again, okay?" She said, sniffling once more.

"I won't. R'yal," Quentin let his arms drop to his sides.

"Who is this bonnie angel fallen from the heavens?" Griffin said from behind him.

A glow flared to Quentin's left as Iain lit a torch. The wavering light revealed their faces in a blur of shadows and light. Griffin stepped forward and offered his hand. Izzy giggled as he lifted it and brushed a kiss across her knuckles.

"Griffin," Quentin warned.

"Oh, stop, Aithar!" Izzy smacked Quentin's arm once Griffin released her hand. Smiling at Griffin, she said. "Since my brother isn't polite enough to introduce us,"—she shot him a withering look— "My name is Isolde, but I go by Izzy. I believe you already know my twin brother, Iain. Quentin is our older brother."

"Ah, thank ya, luv." Griffin smiled. "It's an honor tah meet ya. I did meet yer twin, but 'twas years ago."

"Come," Izzy said, taking Griffin by the hand and leading him along the path. "Welcome to Aeloria, the Fae capital city." She guided them through the opening in the stones, and they all looked up the winding path toward the glowing city at the top.

Quentin heard Griffin gasp behind him, a sharp intake of breath that told him he'd never seen anything like this. Dwarves were rarely welcomed in Fae cities, and the view ahead of them was breathtaking. Quentin exhaled slowly. The Fae, for all their elegance, could be just as exclusionary as the Council. That was a truth he'd long hoped to change.

"Aeloria, or the Crystal City, is noted for the magical light that seems to emanate from each pearly stone throughout its walls and all the buildings within," Izzy explained to Griffin as they began the ascent to the city. "Our people live scattered throughout this mountain range, but this is where our government resides."

"It's the home of our royal palace," Iain called out from behind them.

"Our?" Griffin looked back at Quentin, who sighed.

"My mother is the Regent Queen," Quentin confessed hesitantly. "Queen Lyriana Sylvannis-Hendrix."

"So that makes you…" Griffin began.

"He's the heir apparent," Iain's voice gave nothing away about what he thought of that. "And no, I have no interest in the throne. That comes with work—I'd rather avoid that." Quentin started to laugh, but stopped when Izzy shot him a look.

"We've been mates fer years, an' ya only just noo tell me?" Griffin shot Quentin a pointed look.

Quentin shrugged. "It never came up."

"Quentin here has been off trying to save the world," Izzy said, lifting her chin and smiling affectionately at her older brother.

"Aye, he's done a good job o' it, too," Griffin said with a smile. "He's a natural-born leader."

"That he is!" Iain agreed. "Much better than me."

"Okay, we can change topics any time now," Quentin mumbled.

"He's a bit humble, too," Izzy said, smiling down at Griffin. "He puts off a lot of bravado, but once you start complimenting him, he gets all sheepish. It's adorable."

"Stop, really," Quentin groaned.

"Ah, if only we could, big brother!" Iain sang dramatically.

"Imagine growing up with these two." Quentin moved quickly to take the lead up the path. "They're insufferable."

"But you love us!" Izzy sang. Quentin heard feet rapidly approaching behind him, and before he could turn and look, Izzy jumped onto his back, causing him to let out an "Oof!"

"You're too big for this!" Quentin continued walking as she hung onto him, as if she'd never grown up at all. She rested her chin on her arm, peering over his shoulder.

"I'm just helping you train," she giggled into his ear. "You could always be stronger!"

"I don't need your help with that," he grumbled.

Their lively banter continued when they came close to the castle gates.

Quentin's earlier dread had dissipated before the boisterous personalities of his younger siblings. He almost forgot that he was about to face his mother—almost.

CHAPTER THIRTEEN

Blythe

Fasbridge Manor, Upstate, NY (Human realm) / Auroraheim (Magic realm)

Blythe led the way up the stairs to the second floor. The rugs on the steps muffled their footsteps, but once they reached the wooden floors of the upstairs hallway, the sound resounded within the walls, a hollow echo that made the silence feel louder. She remembered when this House buzzed with life—her father, stepmother, brother, travelers moving through different realms; there was always someone around.

The air resonated with unspent energy, alive despite the emptiness. Prickles of anticipation ran along her arms, raising goosebumps. As she passed each open doorway, she peered inside, her senses finely attuned to any hint of movement or sound.

"What are you looking for?" Hera asked. Blythe heard her stifling a yawn.

"Making sure Benjamin isn't lurking about," Blythe replied, stopping before the door to the study. "Or anyone else. When Dorian—er, my father—was the Keeper, it wouldn't let anyone in or out without his explicit permission. Only the welcome family was an exception. I'm not quite sure how that worked. Did he instruct the House on who could come and go? Or did the House decide on its own?" She looked back at Hera. "I don't know if I was supposed to give it instructions or something. Like, 'By the way, House, my brother wants me dead, could you not let him in?" The door creaked open before she laid a hand on it.

Hera's hand went to her sword, still sheathed on her belt, but Blythe raised a calming hand.

"It's just the House," she whispered. "It won't permit anyone but me—or anyone I bring with me—to enter this room. It's the Keeper's Study."

She tried not to think about the many times she'd been in this library, both the good and the bad. The room was filled with the musty scent of books and cigar smoke, threatening to stir the past she wanted to forget.

Blythe hurried toward the metal spiral staircase, her boots clanging on the wrought iron steps. The staircase twisted up to a second-floor balcony with matching railings. From the ground floor, rows of books lined the walls, with a table and other pieces of furniture scattered about. Her footsteps echoed faintly as she climbed. She slowed once she got to the top, stopping to stare at the old typewriter that had altered her life so profoundly, which seemed like a lifetime ago.

She slowly approached the large wooden desk, its surface polished smooth by years of use. Her fingers glided over the detailed grain of the wood, feeling where her father previously had rested his hands—where she had learned the truth about her past.

She rounded the desk to the oversized leather chair and perched on its edge, ready to jump up at a moment's notice. The leather creaked lightly under her weight.

"Okay, old friend," Blythe murmured to the room. "Is there anything you can share with us about what's happening in the Human Realm?"

She sat in deep quiet, waiting for the familiar clickety-clack of the typewriter's keys. Instead, something cold and solid bumped against her foot. Blythe glanced down and saw that a newspaper had appeared. She bent to retrieve the rolled paper, opening it with care. The faint scent of ink and aged pages rose from it, carrying her back to mornings when her father read the news at this very desk.

The headline leapt out at her: "Mysterious Creatures

Swarm Out of Adirondack Mountains Cave, Spreading Havoc."

"Well?" Blythe started at Hera's voice; she'd almost forgotten she was there. Hera stood across the desk from her, silent as ever. One of these days, she was going to give Blythe a heart attack. Blythe needed to attach a bell to her— at least when silence wasn't required. "What does it say?" Hera rested her hands on its surface.

Blythe steadied herself before reading the article about a town called Wells, New York. After a few moments, she summarized aloud for Hera. "Unprecedented emergence of monstrous creatures from the caves of Chimney Mountain... zoologists baffled... casualties mounting... the entire town of Wells evacuated. Monsters tearing through homes." She reread the word monsters more times than she could count.

"Law enforcement and emergency services are struggling to contain the situation... but they have yet to identify these creatures," Hera read over her shoulder.

Hera's eyes widened as Blythe set the paper down on the desk, her face reflecting disbelief and concern.

"Kind of a miracle anyone has survived, huh?" Hera said, moving to perch on the edge of the desk.

"Quentin mentioned a friend who might help us clean up the demons in the Human Realm," Blythe said, exhaling deeply. She wished Quentin were here to see this, to steady her when the world felt like it was unraveling.

"Are you talking about Tavian Locke?" Hera asked, crossing her legs and leaning back, her attention riveted on Blythe.

"Yeah. Do you know him?"

"Yes... Unfortunately." Hera looked away from Blythe.

"Hera?" She lifted an eyebrow, and Hera let out an exasperated sigh.

"Okay, yes, I know him far more than I'd like to know him." She cleared her throat. "I knew him from my time with the Valkyrie. He was around the capital building a lot, and, well, he and I may have gone out for a bit."

Blythe leaned forward. "Go on."

Hera rolled her eyes. "It was a brief period of questionable judgment that absolutely won't interfere with our possibly working with him."

"But do you trust him?"

Hera sighed before answering. "Yes. He and Quentin have been close for years. Tavian's a mage. His family has had ties to the Fae Royal Family for centuries—something about a key event that linked their families long ago. They're also connected with the Council." She picked up the paper, her attention absorbed as she perused the article for herself. "Though I know the Fae Royal Family tends to work with the Council, much to Quentin's chagrin."

Hera's tone made Blythe pause. "What does Quentin have to do with the Fae Royal Family?" she asked, reclining in her chair, puzzled.

"What?" Hera looked over the edge of the paper.

"Never mind. How do we contact Tavian Locke?"

Before Hera could respond, the typewriter clattered into action. Blythe's heart thudded as she watched, her gaze riveted to the page until the typing ceased. She looked down at the fresh sheet and read aloud.

"I can call him."

"...Call him?" Blythe echoed. "Like, magically summon him, or ring his cell?"

The typewriter resumed its clattering.

"What did it say?" Hera asked, leaning in to catch a glimpse of the text.

"It's been done."

"Does the House always sound vaguely homicidal?" Hera muttered.

"Pretty much, yes." Blythe chuckled. "Let's go get some food, and then we can try to find out some information about whatever my uncle is after." She paused, thinking for a moment. "Let's hope that the guy's arrival won't blow up what little peace we've scraped together."

Peace was fragile enough with Benjamin still out there,

waiting for his chance.

"Why do you say that?" Hera hopped off the desk.

"Because I'm finding it very hard to trust new people these days," Blythe muttered, rising from her seat and following Hera down the spiral staircase, her steps clattering as they descended.

"From what I know, Tavian is a decent guy. He didn't hit on every Valkyrie he encountered, so that's saying something." She grinned. "Most of those sleeper agents acted like they were starved for female attention when they came to make reports or meet with their higher-ups." She shrugged. "I guess human females just didn't do it for them."

"So... are you saying this Tavian was cool with human females, or that he just had more respect for women in general?" They walked out of the library and started down the hallway.

"No idea." Hera smiled back at Blythe. "But, I guess we'll find out. Right? You're half-human, so if he respects you, that's a good sign?"

Blythe sighed. "I just hope he's a trustworthy double agent... as trustworthy as someone who betrays one side to earn the other's trust can be."

"Try to say that ten times fast," Hera said with a laugh, then immediately gave it a shot. She stumbled halfway through, sending them both into giggles as they made their way down to the kitchen. The smell drifting down the hallway made Blythe's mouth water and her stomach growl. "Your turn," Hera poked Blythe.

"I'll pass on that... let's eat instead."

CHAPTER FOURTEEN

Blythe

Fasbridge Manor, Upstate, NY (Human realm) / Auroraheim (Magic realm)

Her dreams since the dark realm always began the same way: her mind turning cruel, forcing her to relive Miles's death over and over again. Each time, the scene grew more grotesque, his lifeless body twisting in ways no living being should bend. The air crackled with the sound of his bones snapping.

His blood flowed thicker and darker. She could hear his final gasp and feel the slick heat of his blood on her hands. Every night she slept, the dream changed, the details mutating, but the end was always the same. Miles, broken and gone.

The truth struck her like a blade, refusing to soften.

The dreams had ebbed away when she and Hera left the camp, but now, back in the House, they were back. And they had shifted again.

Now, it wasn't just Miles. In the twisted landscape of her nightmares, her uncle appeared—but he looked different. His face was a mask of fury, his eyes depthless and black, like something had ripped its way inside him and now wore his body as a costume.

Demons twined around him in thick, writhing chains, their faint whispers filling the air with words she couldn't understand—yet somehow felt in her very core. When he spoke, it wasn't his voice. It was the same inhuman voice she had heard during her possession in the dark realm.

Hearing that voice again hurled her back to that awful

time—and the dream shifted again.

"Hello?!" Blythe's voice rang out, but disintegrated into the smothering silence surrounding her.

A laugh answered, floating through the stillness.

"Hello, dearie," the voice spat. "May I borrow your body for a while?"

"That'll be a no from me!" Blythe's sword swung, meeting only empty space.

The cackle vibrated within her mind, a twisted symphony within the darkness.

"Sorry, we don't adhere to consent in my world. Now, be a good girl and hush!" Stars danced before her eyes as a blow struck from behind. She lurched, struggling to regain her balance, fighting the disorienting onslaught of her invisible foe.

Cold, unseen hands pushed her to the ground. She flailed, dropping the sword and clawing at the invisible restraints. She fought, grasping but failing to connect with anything. How could she win against something she couldn't see or touch?

"Help!" she screamed. "Help me! Please!" Tears rolled down her face as she struggled. "Quentin!" His name escaped from her throat before she could stop it, with instinct, longing, and fear taking over. "Hera! Griffin! Miles!" Her voice faltered and quivered on Miles's name, realizing he couldn't save her. He was already gone.

"Miles…" She breathed. His name was a fragile prayer, a whisper of love she couldn't let go. Her pleas dissolved, sinking into the blackness with her.

Her strength withered as her unseen assailant's laughter swelled, the phantom hands pushing her down into the abyss.

She lay huddled on the ground, knees drawn close, her body quivering from quiet sobs. The air still beat with the echo of her struggle, marked only by the tears slipping down her face.

Blythe drifted in and out of consciousness within the void. There was nothing but stillness. Space and time were lost in the black expanse. She was trapped within her own mind, cut off from the outside world. She wasn't sure how long she'd been there before the thought crept in that dying might be easier than this.

She strained to listen for any sound. Still, the hush devoured everything, slowly, mercilessly eroding her sanity.

There were no battle cries. Not even the eerie cackle.

Primal fear took control. This couldn't be it forever.

Every attempt to move met resistance. The more she struggled, the stronger she felt herself sinking into quicksand.

Laughter washed through her mind. "You squirm so beautifully," the voice breathed venomously. "Miles is gone… perhaps Quentin should be next."

Blythe's thoughts tumbled, desperate to reclaim control—to shatter this sinister hold. Was this really happening? She was in the House, right? She couldn't be attacked there. Or had the demons got in while she slept?

She struggled to speak, finding the strength to yell elusive. Every time she tried, her cry vanished into the void—a mocking quiet, reveling in her weakness. Her vulnerability.

"Please," she said. "I don't know what you want."

Silence.

As the seconds lengthened into eternity, her spirit faltered, despair ready to engulf her. Tears cascaded down her cheeks.

Miles's death was in vain.

The thought hollowed her chest, guilt gnawing at her as if she had failed him.

He had died in the dark realm, and all they'd done was unleash eviler.

How could she have failed? She and Hera had made it to the House.

A light appeared in the distance.

"No," the voice sounded weaker.

She moved and found that her bindings were loosening.

"This isn't real," she whispered, her voice croaky from

screaming.

"No," the voice rose—her chains tightening.

She summoned her willpower, focusing on the memories of her loved ones—what she knew was real; their faces, what they were fighting for. A flame kindled in her, burning brilliantly. The voice recoiled with a yell.

"So stubborn," Miles said. Was that his voice—or just the memory of it?

"Yes, I'm stubborn," she thought. "I won't lie down and die."

Defiant to the core, Blythe rallied the pieces of her shattered self. She drew from her deepest well of courage and determined love for her companions, channeling them into a single, unyielding thought: "You don't get to take me."

She closed her eyes against the piercing light that blazed up from within her, destroying the void and breaking what bound her. The shadows vanished like mist beneath the morning sun.

Blythe's consciousness returned to her body as her mind reclaimed its dominion. She opened her eyes and saw her uncle standing before her—his face distorted once again into the disturbing mask of malice from her dreams. His empty, soulless eyes bored into her. When he spoke, it was that identical voice again.

"Blythe..." he rasped, his tone layered with a thousand twisted whispers, each more venomous than the last. "You can't run. You can't hide."

She gasped as dark figures surfaced around him, each one shadowy and faceless. The Council. They were all shrouded in the same darkness, emerging from the ground as living smoke, towering above her as she lay on the floor. She could feel the power spreading from them, bearing upon her.

"Uncle?" she asked, her voice cracking.

"Not your uncle," he responded. "We are one, and we will get rid of everything and everyone you love."

Demonic chains wound around his body, pulling him toward the shadow figures of the Council.

One by one, her friends stood next to him—Nreman first, his face distorted in fear as the shadowy tendrils entwined around him. Then Aenwyn, her mouth open in a mute shriek. Octo, Bertolf, Griffin, and Hera followed, each yanked into the void. Hera's eyes found hers for an instant—steady, unafraid—before the shadows tore her away.

Finally, Quentin was positioned before her, his face calm, though his eyes brimmed with sorrow. The shadows squeezed around him, tugging him into their grasp. His voice was soft—a hushed tone that barely reached her through the choking dark.

"It's okay, Kitsune. You'll be okay."

And then he was gone.

Blythe jolted upright, lungs dragging in uneven air, the traces of her nightmare lingering within her mind as an intrusive thought. She pressed her palms against her eyes, trying to force the horrifying images out of her mind's eye.

She wished Quentin's voice had been real, not just a phantom in her dream.

She grasped her blanket as she tried to ground herself in reality. Her room was faintly lit by moonlight shining through the curtains, the night's silence a vivid contrast to the madness that had plagued her sleep. She ran her fingers through her sweat-dampened hair, her hand trembling as the image of her uncle's possessed face faded, but not nearly fast enough.

She swung her legs, hanging off the side of the bed, the warm floor centering her for a moment. Blythe placed her feet on the wooden boards, focusing on the feel of them underneath her soles, trying to push the nightmare away, but her mind kept floating back. What did the dreams mean? Could they be more than just nightmares? What if they were a warning? If so, how? She'd never had prophetic dreams before. Had she?

If the Council was moving, Benjamin would be at their side. She couldn't forget that.

Doubt settled within her chest. She wanted to believe it was just a dream.

"Blythe?"

Hera's voice was sharp, edged with haste. She stood in the doorway, framed by the soft radiance of the hall. A single-strap top clung to her, paired with tight-fitting leggings and a leather belt slung low on her hips. Her sword was gripped in her hand, fingers pale around the hilt, as if she'd been ready to hack through the door.

"I heard you screaming," she said, stepping forward. "The House wouldn't let me in until just now... Are you okay?"

Blythe's skin was clammy, but beneath it a chill lingered, the same cold that always came when danger pressed close.

Blythe shoved damp strands of hair away from her face. Her heart rate pounded, but she forced herself to nod. "I... I think it was just a dream. I don't know."

The floor was firm beneath her feet, yet she still felt as if she were perched on the brink of an abyss. She turned, moving on autopilot to the bathroom. She turned on the cold water in the sink and cupped her hands beneath the stream, splashing it onto her face. Droplets ran down her cheeks, icy against her overheated skin.

Hera didn't move from the doorway. She stood with her sword still in hand, glance held on Blythe's reflection in the mirror. "Then why did the House keep me out until now?"

The words crept down Blythe's spine like ice water.

She met Hera's eyes in the glass, her grip tightening on the sink.

"I don't know," she said. And that terrified her most of all.

CHAPTER FIFTEEN

Quentin

Aeloria, Fae Mountains

The gates parted, allowing them to enter the shining city. Though the sun had set, the walls and buildings glowed with an unearthly light, emitting a gentle luminescence over the streets and their inhabitants. Quentin followed Izzy and Iain, who were cheerfully pointing out restaurants and shops to Griffin, their voices bright with excitement.

"You have to try the pastries at Auraline's Bakery," Izzy exclaimed, her eyes sparkling as she held Griffin's arm.

"And there's a blacksmith down the road who makes the best weapons. They supply all the weapons and armor for our armies. Another shop makes the fancier ones for ceremonies, but they're not nearly as effective," Iain added.

"I doubt he's here for weapons, Iain," Izzy frowned at him.

"Oh, and he's come for pastries, I suppose?" Iain rolled his eyes.

"I'm happy to git both while I'm 'ere!" Griffin laughed, scanning the area as he took it all in. As they walked, he joked with Quentin's siblings, his eyes wide with wonder at the vibrant city.

Their joyous laughter surrounded him, warm and bright, but he felt none of it. All he saw was waste, wealth, and power that could have gone toward resisting the Council. The city, with its lavish displays and excess, mocked the dire circumstances of their reality. He'd seen towns without even running water. The Council and the Fae elders did far too little to care for others. His father used to say a nation's worth should be judged by its poorest citizens. Though his mother called it a pie-in-the-sky idea.

They passed the bustling town square, where people came and went from markets and restaurants, some heading home, and others preparing for a night out on the town.

The glow from the buildings reflected off the paved stones, creating a surreal atmosphere. The air was thick with the blending aromas of rich food from nearby taverns and the subtle scent of night-blooming flowers from the gardens. The townsfolk's joyful conversation as they enjoyed the evening stood in sharp contrast to Quentin's stern resolve.

They reached the grand staircase leading up to the castle built into the hillside. Quentin watched as Griffin paused to look up. The castle dominated the skyline, its architecture equally grand and majestic. The stone steps were worn by centuries of travelers, and the towers seemed to reach for the stars themselves.

Quentin inhaled.

“How long's it been since ye were 'ere?” Griffin asked as Quentin stopped beside him.

“Five years,” he said, letting out the breath. The city hadn’t changed—but he had, and he no longer fit the shape this place expected of him.

He glanced at his siblings, who were bickering as they went up the steps, leaving Griffin and Quentin behind. He envied their juvenile debates. He wished his worries were so simple. They were sheltered from them—from the weight he carried. His mind was consumed with the task ahead and the state of the world.

“Que, are you okay?” Izzy had stopped at the top of the steps, looking back at him.

Her concern warmed something in him he hadn’t realized had turned cold.

He put on a smile. “Just thinking about what we need to do next.”

She twisted her lips to the side, clearly unconvinced, then skipped back down the steps to rejoin him.

"Come on," Iain grumbled. "Why are you taking so long?"

Izzy patted Quentin on the arm before grabbing Griffin by his. Together they ascended the steps—each one feeling a step closer to the confrontation Quentin dreaded but knew was necessary. He looked up at the tall, ornately carved doors, remembering the portrait engraved on the aged wood: a fae upon a dragon gliding above the castle in the mountain.

The doors opened, exposing a grand hall lit by chandeliers that appeared to float in midair.

As he entered, the sounds of murmured voices and the quiet shuffle of luxurious fabrics reached his ears. Courtiers and nobles mingled, their laughter resonating off the marble walls.

He looked past them, knowing what he would see: a beautiful woman seated upon a dais in an ornately carved chair trimmed in gold. Three smaller chairs stood on the platform just below her. Her long red hair was pulled into a braided updo, threaded with pearls and gold cords around her crown. Her gown radiated in the ambient light as if covered in millions of golden stars.

Quentin took another deep breath before stepping forward, his siblings and Griffin following behind. This was his moment, his chance to speak, to sway his mother toward the urgency of their plight. He could only hope that the city, with all its wealth and power, might be persuaded to act before it was too late for their world.

If not, by the time they realized the danger was truly coming to their protected city, it would already be too late. They were safe now, but that wouldn't last forever.

Quentin approached his mother, bearing the burden of every eye upon him. Nobles and courtiers became silent as he walked, their murmurs replaced by an anxious suspense. His mother turned to face him.

"Mother," Quentin began, bowing out of respect, "I need

to speak with you about something urgent."

The Queen's face softened, and she motioned for him to approach. "Of course, my dear." She smiled broadly and rose from her seat, moving quickly down to the floor where he stood. "Oh, my child! I have been so worried about you. When I heard you had chosen to represent that halfling—"

A trace of anger flared in his chest, quick and hot and instinctive. No one got to belittle Blythe. Not even his mother.

"Mother," Quentin began in a low voice.

"I'm so glad you are safe, and that the evil escaping from the Dark Realm did not consume you." Though she said the right words, her eyes didn't match them. "Come, let us speak in private, and you can tell me about what you have been doing during these many years you've been gone."

She escorted him through a side door into a smaller, more intimate chamber embellished with luxurious wall hangings and furnished with rich chairs. The city's lights shed a gentle radiance through the ornate glass panels, creating motifs on the floor. As the door began to close behind them, he heard the noise from the other room rise again, then fade as the doors shut—leaving them in a deep hush.

"Oh, my dear boy, it has been far too long." She slowly sat down, motioning for him to do the same. "What's troubling you?" Her slender brows drew together as she studied his face.

Quentin sank into the seat opposite her, resting his hands on his knees while leaning forward. His eyes remained locked on the woman he had to convince to believe him. This felt more stressful than most court cases he had faced—even worse than leading Blythe's case against the Council. "Mother, you mentioned the evil that is escaping, and no doubt you've heard the rumors that Blythe and Hera are the cause of it."

He paused, noticing the slight narrowing of his mother's eyes before she nodded. "All is not as it seems. The Council has lost its way. They no longer adhere to the laws of solidarity that have kept our world in peace for centuries. The Dark Realm's influence is spreading, and I fear it will soon reach our borders and consume the Fae. The human realm—and much of our world—is already feeling its effects. We need to act now, to use our resources to stop this, and the Council, before it's too late."

His mother sighed, her eyes wandering to the window. "I am aware of the growing danger, Quentin. But our people rely on us for their safety and prosperity, not to take care of the rest of the world." Quentin clenched his jaw but remained quiet. "If we do too much for others, we will put our own people at risk. It's destabilizing. I will not risk that—and you shouldn't want to, either."

"Destabilizing?" Quentin's voice sharpened. "People are dying. Evil is pouring into both realms, and it won't stop until it consumes everything. We can't just sit here in comfort while the world burns."

The Queen's posture hardened, and she met his eyes as if seeing straight through to his soul. "Do not presume to lecture me on the responsibilities of a ruler. I am doing everything I am able to ensure the safety of our people. They are my primary concern."

Quentin stood, his anger rising. "That's not enough! Use the wealth and power we have here to make a difference. If we ensure stability beyond our borders, it will prevent unrest from infiltrating here. If we don't act now, there won't be a nation left to protect. That evil isn't going to stop at our borders!"

His mother's eyes flashed momentarily. For a moment, neither spoke. The Queen searched Quentin's face. His father used to joke that Quentin was just as stubborn as his mother, and heaven forbid they ever stood at odds over something important, because no resolution would come.

"Very well," she said quietly. "I will call a council meeting, and you may make your case to discuss redistributing assets and dealing with the threat. But understand, this is a delicate balance. We must proceed with caution. We have always been on good terms with the Council, and we cannot risk damaging that." She scrutinized him for a moment. "We cannot afford to cross the Council as many have. You've seen what they're doing."

Quentin forced himself to relax his clenched jaw before speaking. "I do see that. But I also know that caving to tyranny will not provide the peace and security you hope it will." Her eyes narrowed, and he quickly pivoted. "Thank you for giving thought to my side. That's all I ask."

Quentin spoke patiently with his mother, recounting his travels and the life he'd led over the past several years. When their conversation had run its course, she raised a quiet signal that it was time to go.

Quentin exhaled, a delicate strand of hope twisting at him, thin and uncertain but there.

As he stood to leave, the doors opened, and the Queen's advisor—tall, severe, with eyes which missed nothing—entered the room. "Your Majesty, there are urgent matters that require your attention," he said, shedding a wary, assessing glance at Quentin. The Queen nodded. "Of course, Aldric. I will attend to them shortly." She turned to Quentin, her gaze softening.

"Go, rest for now. We will speak more later."

Quentin bowed and turned to leave.

“Quentin." His mother’s voice stopped him. He froze, his jaw tensing as he turned back to face her. "I am hoping that your being back here means you are ready to step up and face your responsibilities." Heat prickled behind his ribs, the same old pressure, the same expectations. She raised her hand to stop his reply. "We will talk about that later as well. Go, rest." She turned back to Aldric.

"Always the last word," he muttered, shoving his hands into his pockets as he exited.

Quentin made his way back across the grand hall, where Izzy, Iain, and Griffin were waiting. Their faces lit with attention and anxiety as he approached. Quentin’s shoulders stayed tight, the sound of his mother’s words still coiled inside him.

“So, what happened?” Izzy asked, her eyes growing large as she scanned his face.

"Will she send steel an' soldiers, or leave us swingin' axes alone against them cursed hordes and that snake pit o' a Council?" Griffin slurred, vowels sliding together like melted butter. He held a stein of something—clearly, Iain had started him on the Fae Ale. Griffin was in for a rude awakening if he drank the way he usually did. Quentin noticed that there were half as many courtiers in the room now, with still more drifting out. Some even looked relieved as they slipped out. Of course, they scattered; without an audience to impress, they had nothing left to perform. Well, at least someone was getting out while things were still pretty.

Soon, only the four of them remained. They moved to a table to eat. Griffin sat beside Izzy, while Iain rested upon the table a few seats down.

Quentin sighed and dropped into a chair next to him. "Mother agreed to call an adviser's meeting to discuss our situation... though I doubt they'd do anything but talk."

Iain clapped him on the back. "That's great news!"

"It's at least a start," Izzy offered with a small smile. "You've always been good at making your case. I'm sure you'll be able to convince the advisers."

Guilt prodded him; she believed in him far more than he believed in himself right now.

"Aye! I'm sure ya 'ave nothin' ta worry 'bout. Now let's eat. I'm starving—and these wee foods won't do!" Griffin slammed down his tankard, causing the plates of tiny canapés to jump like surprised insects. He wiped his mouth with the back of his hand and grinned at them.

Quentin smiled. "Yes, let's go eat."

Quentin breathed in the city as they wended through the busy streets toward Iain's favorite tavern. The soft illumination of lanterns bathed the cobblestones in gold, and the fragrance of roasting meat and spiced ale thickened the air. Griffin cracked a joke, and Iain and Izzy broke into laughter. Quentin couldn't help grinning too. Griffin was mangling the punchline so spectacularly that even Iain nearly spluttered on his laughter.

Blythe's presence dwelt just beyond reach, a darkness stretched across the edges of his thoughts. Was she safe? He hated being this far from her, hated the not knowing. The trace of concern never quite faded, even while he entered the tavern doors, the raucous cheer swallowing him whole.

CHAPTER SIXTEEN

Quentin

Aeloria, Fae mountain region

The sun appeared over the jagged mountains, shedding golden light across the rocky landscape. Houses dotted the mountainside, where fae citizens had built small farms and homesteads for centuries. Quentin wasn't sure how much longer that peace would last now that the Dark Realm was oozing into their own. He shivered, imagining shadows crawling over the peaceful farms.

The castle's sun-washed white walls caught the dawn's glow, casting a harsh brightness that threw long shadows over the courtyard below, where Quentin stood.

The breeze bore the smell of dew on stone and foliage, mingling with faint traces of wood smoke from the city. Quentin's breath lingered in small puffs in the chill morning air. He couldn't shake thoughts of Blythe. Her absence gnawed at him. No news is good news, he told himself. If the council had captured or killed them, it would have made headlines by now.

Quentin sighed, the sound dampened by the vast landscape. The anxiety was acidic on his tongue, though he knew he should join Griffin for breakfast. The memory of Izzy's laugh—light and unrestrained—filled his mind, bringing a small, reluctant smile to his lips. Both she and Griffin were hopeless flirts, their merry banter filling the tavern last night with the light of a hearth. He couldn't tell whether they truly liked each other or were simply glad to have someone clever enough to match their wit.

The sun's heat started to chase away the cold as he stood

there, torn between the pull of family and the weight of his thoughts.

The clock tower in the square began to chime, its deep notes reverberating between the mountains surrounding the mountaintop city. He listened as the sounds of the city slowly came to life with the hearkening of dawn from the clock's bells.

"I wondered if I might find you here," Izzy's voice came from behind him, accompanied by the rustle of skirts.

He turned to see his sister ascending the stairs, her flowing white gown billowing in the breeze that fluttered past him. Her long blond hair streamed behind her as she reached the top and took a few short steps to join him at the edge of the parapet.

"Just taking in the sunrise," Quentin said with a forced ease, turning back to lean against the wall.

"It's always a magical sight," she said, leaning forward against the parapet. Quentin watched as she closed her eyes. He turned his gaze back to the city.

"Though," she continued, "I've wondered how it must look from somewhere else."

He often forgot that their mother kept his sister more confined than either he or Iain was. He had once tried to argue that she should be allowed out more, but her childhood health problems had left their mother fearful of letting her stray too far.

They stood in silence for some time before Quentin caught movement out of the corner of his eye. He turned to see Izzy watching him closely.

"What is it?" he asked, folding his arms across his chest.

"Something is different about you," she said, her eyes studying his face.

"I've been through some pretty awful battles. I went to the dark realm and back." Izzy's eyebrows rose in alarm. He sighed and pushed away from the wall. "I'd be surprised if I hadn't changed."

"No." She shook her head, brow furrowed.

Quentin scoffed and shook his head.

"You can deny it, Que, but I can see it all over your face." She moved to stand in his way, blocking his path. "I'm guessing someone's caught your interest."

"Izzy—"

"No, don't 'Izzy' me." She smiled and leaned toward him. "You've found your mate." Quentin's heart accelerated, denial on the tip of his tongue. "I'm guessing it's the half-mage you rescued?"

"Did Griffin tell you?" Quentin narrowed his eyes. "No." She shook her head. Quentin opened his mouth, but she pressed on. "I'm not saying this because it's a problem. Though I suppose it might be—given the Council's hatred of mixed heritage. I bring it up because I'm not sure how much you know about the ancient Fae predictions."

Quentin's interest was piqued, despite himself. He'd heard fragments of the old prophecies before but had never paid them much mind—just fairytales and cautionary tales, as far as he was concerned. Still, he waited for her to continue, noting how she turned to watch the sun's slow ascent, clearly choosing her words with care. The morning light bathed her in a warm glow as she spoke, her tone thoughtful.

"You see," she said, "there's an old prophecy—of a half-being fated to bring great change."

Quentin's heart skipped a beat. Prophecies were nonsense... weren't they? He'd never been one to put much stock in Fae predictions. He'd heard of only a handful that had ever come true. But if this one was legit...

"And where did you happen to hear about this prophecy?"

"I read," she said with a small smile. "Since I'm not typically included in adviser meetings like you and Iain, I go to the archives."

Quentin smirked. "That sounds dreadfully boring. How many prophecies involving the end of times are down there?"

"Not as many as you'd think. Now shush, so I can finish."

Quentin laughed and gestured for her to continue.

"She could be the key to taking down the Council," Izzy said quietly. "Mother won't turn against them. I sense there's something... off." She frowned and looked down at her feet, swallowing before continuing. "She's not the mother you knew when you left." Her gaze lifted to meet Quentin's. "She's been touched by a darkness. Iain and I... we overheard a conversation." She glanced around—subtle but deliberate—making sure they were alone. "It appears the Council knows about the uprising. They know your friends Hera and Blythe were involved, and that Blythe's uncle—the one who should be dead—is leading it." She took a breath. "Mother didn't even flinch, as if she already knew all of it. They told her the Fae needed to be prepared to show their allegiance to the Council."

"So you're saying she knows what I've come for—and she's going to turn us away?"

"I'm not sure," she sighed. "I don't know if she really believes the Council will keep playing nicely with the Fae, or if they'll turn against us like they have everyone else. They've already pushed her completely out of the Council. It's nothing but Mages now—though I'm sure you already knew that."

The Council had already silenced the Fae, so any alliance his mother clung to was a leash, not a partnership.

"It's been that way for a long time, Izzy." Quentin watched her as she paced.

"I know, but they were still allowing her and other leaders to be present for hearings with them. That's over." She frowned. "We've seen smoke from the valleys below..."

"The Fairies?" Quentin moved toward her, alarm tightening his voice.

"We sent messengers to check on them, but there's been no response. The messengers didn't come back."

Quentin's stomach dropped. The Faeries and the Fae had always lived closely together. There was no way the Fairies would have harmed a Fae messenger—unless something else had attacked them. Which meant the Fairies could have been harmed too. His thoughts turned to Aenwyn and Nreman. Hopefully, they hadn't tried to go home.

"Mother didn't want to send anyone to look..." Izzy said.

"So she left them to die?" Quentin felt his cheeks flush with anger.

"She didn't seem to think they'd come to harm. She... I don't know. It's like she doesn't care that the messengers didn't come back. She's started preaching about looking out for our own. Trade has decreased, and we've been relying more on what little we can grow and raise here." She wrung her hands together. "Quentin, we can't grow a wide variety of crops here, and it's hard to raise livestock in the mountains... I don't know what she's thinking..."

"Maybe it isn't her making that call." Quentin rested his hand on Izzy's shoulder. "I'll figure this out."

"Quentin, we need you to do more than figure it out." Her gaze lifted to meet his. "We need you to take your place and lead us. Fix what the Council has ruined."

Quentin sighed and lowered his hand.

She raised an eyebrow.

"No, Izzy, I will. I promise. But first, I need to help our world."

"And your mate?" Izzy chewed on her lower lip.

Quentin felt the heat rise to his cheeks. "Yes. Her too."

CHAPTER SEVENTEEN

Blythe

Fasbridge Manor, Upstate, NY (Human realm) / Auroraheim (Magic realm)

Blythe and Hera sat with their legs crossed on the library floor, the dust floating slowly through the slanted late-day glow. Each worked through a stack of House-selected tomes, their pages dense with symbols and fragments of old knowledge. They were searching for clues—anything that might expose what Demetrius was seeking in the north.

Blythe wasn't sure how long they'd been at it, but her eyes were dry and grainy, as if sand scraped beneath her lids. If there was such a thing as a reading hangover, she was certain she had it. It was worse than finals week in college.

She leaned back and pressed her palms to her eyes. She cast a quick look over to see Hera stretching, joints popping after hours of motionlessness.

Blythe was about to suggest they call it a night when a sharp knock from downstairs shattered through the library's stillness. Hera sprang to her feet, her hand already on the hilt of her sword. Blythe followed suit, grabbing her blade from the side table. The two moved swiftly down the hallway, tension spiking between them as the knocking came again, stronger this time.

As they reached the top of the stairs, Blythe's heart seized in her chest. The sound was unmistakable, carrying clearly from the front door—the one that led directly to the Human realm.

She met Hera's eyes; Hera gave a curt nod, silently alerting her to take the lead. Blythe firmed her grasp on the sword's hilt and moved ahead, knowing the front door would open only with her permission.

Whoever was knocking knew exactly where to find them.

She advanced toward the door, boots whispering over the hardwood floor, and drew the rune to see what waited on the other side. The symbol flashed momentarily, then faded, exposing a window through which she saw a person standing on the porch. Dark rumpled hair. His face was shadowed, so she couldn't make out his features. His silhouette was unmistakably tall.

"Who is it?" she called through the door.

"I believe you summoned me, Keeper Fas?" His voice was mellow and warm, almost coaxing.

"My last name isn't Fas." Blythe wasn't sure why she felt the need to correct him. Perhaps she needed to distance herself from her late father and her uncle.

"My apologies." The man shifted. "I received a letter—it bore the Fas sigil." He paused. "I'm Tavian Locke."

Blythe looked at Hera, who only shrugged.

"What does he look like?" Hera whispered. Blythe had forgotten she couldn't see him.

"Dark hair, tall... I can't quite make out his features."

"Let him in." Hera stepped back, balancing her sword in her right hand.

"But Hera—"

"If he's an enemy, I'll kill him. Many things can make themselves appear to be who you think they are. The House said it would send a message to Tavian Locke and bring him here. If this is him, we'll be able to figure that out."

"How are you going to figure out if it's him?" Blythe worried at her lip again, tongue grazing the familiar split—an old wound born of nerves and silence.

Hera shrugged. "I'll wing it."

Blythe slowly shook her head but reached for the door

handle. "I hope you know what you're doing." She took a breath, pulled, and opened the door.

A gust of cold air cut in as the door opened. Illumination from the entryway washed over the man on the porch. He was at least six feet tall, with a defined jawline, his light scruff framing him in a rugged yet welcoming way. His jade-green eyes caught the light, and when he smiled, dimples creased his cheeks. A black leather jacket, worn jeans, and scuffed Timberland boots completed the picture.

He held out his hand in greeting. When Hera and Blythe didn't move to take it, he reached up to brush his hair back from his face in what she assumed was meant to seem unconcerned.

"Hello," he said, his hands in his pockets. Blythe could feel Hera just to her left, staring him down. "Hera, long time no see." He grinned in a way Blythe was sure he thought would win the heart of any damsel in distress. "May I come in?"

"That depends," Hera said, taking a step forward.

"On what?" He looked between Blythe and Hera. Blythe smirked and left it to Hera to engage him.

"That depends on whether you are who you claim to be." Blythe glanced at Hera.

"I wouldn't lie to a Valkyrie—least of all you." He pulled his hands from his pockets. "You were always the scariest of the lot. But truly, I received a summons, and if you don't need me, I'll just be going..."

"What's something you know about Quentin Hendrix that no one but the real Tavian Locke would know?" Blythe reached out to touch Hera on the shoulder. Hera lowered her sword slightly and stepped back.

"Something I know about Quentin..." He paused, thinking. "Well, he and I grew up together. How personal do you want me to get?" He smiled. "I know a lot of his dirty little secrets—like how he has absolutely no interest in being King of the Fae, or that he's fascinated by humans. He wanted to be a Sleeper Agent, too, but, you know, the pointy ears kind of give-away that he's not human."

His grin faded as his eyes flickered to Hera; whatever look she gave him was enough to shut him up.

He looked back at Blythe. Blythe glanced at Hera, unsure what to say. King of the Fae? What was he even talking about? Was his fascination with humans the reason he'd wanted to help her in the first place? She forced the thought away. Neither of those things mattered right now. She didn't want to trust this man. But she needed to know what he knew.

"Let him in," Hera instructed. Blythe stepped back further, watching as Hera did the same, allowing the man to enter.

He walked in, shifting the bag strapped across his back. He looked around as he entered, taking in the fussy, old-fashioned décor with quiet interest. Perhaps he had never been in this portal House. There were six others he could have traveled through, and she wasn't sure if they all shared the same old-lady vibes. The way he studied the portraits and the chandelier made her think he certainly had not been here before.

"So, how else would you like me to prove that I am indeed the true Tavian Locke?" He looked over at Hera, studying her posture. "If you'd like me to share something about our past, I can do that." Hera's eyes narrowed. "Or not," he added quickly.

"I think," Blythe said slowly, "we can see what the House has to say."

Hera glanced at Blythe, who gave a slight smile in return.

"The Keeper isn't the only one who decides who's welcome. It's a pretty good judge of character." Blythe stepped back and placed a hand on the stair banister. "What do you say?"

The lights fluttered, and a faint draft manifested from nowhere. The door behind Tavian banged closed with a resounding thud and locked. Hera looked at Blythe, raising one slender eyebrow.

Blythe moved toward Tavian and extended her hand. "Blythe Evans."

Tavian's face broke into a wide smile as he took her hand, his touch staying just a bit longer than necessary. "Tavian Locke. It's nice to meet you."

"Is it?" Hera slowly sheathed her sword.

"It's good to see you again, Hera." Tavian extended his hand toward her.

Hera looked at it, her glance sharp and determined. Tavian let his hand fall back into his pocket, his smile steady as their eyes met. She retreated slightly, still watching him carefully.

Blythe observed the standoff between them. Tavian was slightly taller, but Hera looked far more intimidating—it must be a Valkyrie thing. She chewed her lip, sensing a charged energy in the air between them, a twinkle that made her smile in spite of the tension. They must have really had something in the past, and judging by Hera's demeanor, it hadn't ended well.

"Since you're here, tell us what you know about the Council and the escaping demons that I'm assuming are flooding the human world?" Blythe's tone was calm, though her question hovered in the air with the poised weight of a falling blade.

"Sure, but any chance we could talk over food? Bad news always seems to go over better with a meal," Tavian said with a raised brow. "At least with those who aren't the Council."

Blythe sighed and turned on her heel, leading the way into the kitchen. The scent of freshly made coffee and baked pastries greeted them as they entered. The House had provided an ample assortment: cheeses and meats, fresh fruit, and an array of pastries with perfectly flaked crusts. The kitchen blended an old-world charm with modern convenience—wooden beams overhead, polished stone counters, and a candelabra fitted with electric bulbs. Sconces along the walls resonated with the same fusion of eras.

Blythe moved farther into the room, sat at the breakfast nook by the window, and picked up the cup of tea the House had left for her. She watched the steam spiral upward and wrapped her hands around the cup, soaking in the warmth that sank into her fingers and steadied her. Hera stood in the doorway, her stare focused on Tavian. One hand rested on her sword hilt, ready if he gave her even a hint of trouble. Blythe couldn't help noticing how calm Tavian seemed; the lack of reaction to Hera's scrutiny only unsettled her more.

Blythe gestured for Tavian to sit.

"You know, it's been a while since I've had a proper meal," he admitted with a grin. "Some sleeper agents are given positions in various governments so we can watch over events." He paused, "Or, like me, we have to play the role of an 'average Joe,' which sometimes means surviving on fast food and junk in what they call 'food deserts.'"

"Help yourself." Blythe motioned toward the spread. The House had arranged everything with its usual astonishing meticulousness.

Tavian dove in, piling his plate with bread, eggs, fruit — a bit of everything. As he finally took a bite, his expression softened, and he exhaled a quiet, satisfied breath. Hera stayed by the island, arms crossed, eyes never leaving him.

"Hera, sit. He's not going to stab us mid-croissant," Blythe said. Hera hesitated, then moved to take the spot at her side — still watching Tavian.

Blythe waited until he finished chewing. "So, the Council and the demons?"

Tavian leaned back, the easy humor draining from his face. "Right. Where do you want me to start?"

CHAPTER EIGHTEEN

Blythe

Fasbridge Manor, Upstate, NY (Human realm) / Auroraheim (Magic realm)

Steam drifted lazily from the mugs set before them. At the center of the table, a three-tiered tray was laden with delicate finger sandwiches, colorful petit fours, and biscotti that were arranged with almost theatrical care. The petit fours stood out like tiny, edible jewels—vibrant, intricate, and almost too beautiful to eat. They had agreed to speak once Tavian had his fill. However, judging by the way she was glaring at him, Blythe guessed her patience was wearing thin.

Tavian reached out, the tips of his fingers caressing the smooth marzipan bow atop one of the petit fours. He paused briefly, then popped it into his mouth. His eyes closed briefly in satisfaction. Reclining in his seat, he patted his stomach.

"Mmm," he said. "I could get used to eating like this."

Hera leaned forward, her voice shattering the silence in the cozy atmosphere. "Now that you've kept us waiting, could you tell us what you know? You've wasted enough time."

Tavian lifted his mug and paused, peering at Hera over the rising steam. "You're aware that the portal between the Dark Realm and the human realm in North America isn't being guarded, right?"

Blythe nodded, but Hera's brow tightened.

"Er—this continent we're on. In the human realm, it's called North America."

He drank, then continued. "They sent a strike team to push the demons back, but it's… not working."

Blythe's stomach tightened. Of course it wasn't. Nothing the Council touched seemed to go as planned anymore.

"They considered deploying Valkyries," he went on, "but there are too many humans around. Harder to stay hidden. Spellcasters can blend in more easily."

Hera scoffed under her breath. Blythe didn't blame her.

"Sleeper agents like me have been put on high alert," Tavian continued. "We're supposed to watch for you two—and for Demetrius."

Blythe's fingers clenched around her cup. Hearing her uncle's name still seemed like a bruise being pressed.

"No one's sure how he slipped out of the Dark Realm," Tavian said. "Some think the Warlocks helped him, but if that's true… why didn't they leave with him the first time?"

He paused, as if gathering his thoughts.

"They've known he escaped for a while. And now that they're certain he's leading a rebellion, they're scrambling to rally the factions against him. But it's not going well. Most of the Magic Realm blames the Council for letting demons through and failing to protect the portals. Some are pointing fingers at you two as well.

"Mind you, this is all coming from my keepers in the Magic Realm. I used to check in once a week, but lately, they've been contacting me daily."

Tavian set his mug down and lowered his voice. "What if I told you some of us suspect the Council has been infiltrated? Possibly by the same force driving Demetrius."

"I'd think you'd be the first to recognize that," Hera muttered. Blythe turned to her, confused. "His grandfather is on the Council," Hera said, her inflection unreadable.

A sharp beat jolted through Blythe's chest. "And you trust him to help us?"

"My grandfather isn't what you'd call... grandfatherly," Tavian said quickly. "When I turned down the Keepership in favor of a sleeper-agent role, he was livid. He said field work was beneath our family's status. My brother was finishing up his training to be the Keeper of our family House, last I heard. My father didn't care—but my grandfather, he's old-school."

He stirred his tea, the spoon tapping on the porcelain. "About thirty years ago, he changed. I was five. I remember him being kind and warm—then he became cold, obsessed with family status and appearances. He'd only been on the Council for five years at that point. My father assumed the job changed him."

He set the spoon down, his tone turning somber. "Eyra, the Valkyrie leader, told me she noticed a dark shift in the Council around the same time. She's been monitoring them, and their decisions have only grown darker, especially since the demons escaped. I haven't seen my grandfather in a while, but my brother sent a message recently that suggests he's worsened."

Blythe met Hera's eyes.

Hera hesitated, but Blythe spoke. "Demetrius is searching for something. Do you know what it is? He seemed determined to find it."

She moved to take a biscotti, its chocolate-striped exterior catching her eye.

"Well," he said, folding his hands on the table, "are you familiar with how the portals were formed?"

Blythe and Hera shook their heads.

"Didn't think so. The Council doesn't want that knowledge out there." Blythe clenched her teeth. He raised a hand to stop their objections. "And before you ask how I know—sleeper agents are trained to find what others hide. I've traveled through most of the Houses and got permission to access their libraries. My father gave me free rein of his as well. Most Keepers are just as concerned as you are—they're no longer included in major decisions, either."

He leaned back. "The Council's Great Sweep, over seven hundred years ago, was supposed to erase dangerous knowledge. You know about that?"

Blythe shook her head, but Hera gave a slow nod. Embarrassment prickled down her neck. Hera knew the story; she didn't. Again.

"When the Council changed, they destroyed stored ancient magical knowledge to keep any race from gaining too much power."

"Any race but themselves, you mean?" The words slipped out sharper than Blythe intended.

"Except they didn't," Tavian said, a wry edge to the sound of his voice. "Several of the Keepers faked the destruction. They hid the tomes inside the Houses. The Council believed the knowledge was lost, but the Keepers hoped it would protect them in the future."

Blythe blinked. The Keepers defied the Council? That... she hadn't seen coming.

"Long before the Sweep, a coalition of Mages, Warlocks, and other supernatural beings decided the open portals between realms were too dangerous. Without the Houses, creatures—good and evil—passed freely between the Dark, Magic, and Human Realms. That's where human myths came from—gods, demons, trickster fairies. All real.

"So this coalition pooled their power and created the Houses using the Rune Stones they built. These stones could both create and destroy. They hid them afterward."

Blythe pursed her lips as she thought. If the stones could destroy... what exactly was her uncle planning?

Tavian continued, "The Dark Realm was too chaotic for a House, so they sealed it with wards, needing only a handful of Mages to maintain it."

Blythe gulped. She remembered that pandemonium all too well.

Blythe raised her cup, buying herself a moment. "You think Demetrius is after one of those stones?"

Tavian nodded. "One for now. But if I were a betting man —and I'm not—I'd say he wants them all."

"How would he even know they exist? You said the Council hid the truth." Hera spoke up.

"The Warlocks helped forge the stones. Their knowledge was probably passed down. They may have told him."

"He also grew up in this House... so if there's any knowledge here, he'd probably know about it," Blythe said.

"I don't know," Tavian said. "But they can destroy. He could be planning to take down the wards—or the Houses."

"And the Council," Blythe whispered.

Tavian nodded. "And the Council."

Hera pushed her tea away. "This is all still speculation. Maybe he's after something else entirely."

"Sometimes 'probably' is all you get until you dig deeper. How far have you gotten in the House's library?"

"Not far enough," Blythe admitted.

"Then ask the House if it has anything on this." He stood and stretched. "I'd bet it does."

Blythe opened her mouth to ask when something tapped her foot. She looked down and saw a worn, leather-bound tome lying next to her. She bent to pick it up. A chill of magic ran along her back, like her own spellbook.

A pair of white gloves appeared near her foot. She smiled, pulling them on before carefully opening the book.

She gasped. The page emitted a soft glow, ink morphing like a living thing in curling inscriptions she didn't recognize. Awe prickled down her spine, chased by a flicker of fear—what kind of power was this? Acting on instinct, she closed her right eye, and the script shifted to English.

Relief washed through her, and a small smile surfaced on her lips. "Yes."

"And...?" Hera prompted.

"We need to get those stones before my uncle does."

The three exchanged looks.

"Let's get going," Hera said.

"Count me in," Tavian added, stepping away from the island.

Blythe caught the wary look Hera sent him.

"We work better alone," Hera said flatly. "This isn't a

game. We don't need interruptions or liabilities."

"We wouldn't have gotten this far without him," Blythe replied.

"We would have. The book was here the whole time."

Tavian opened his mouth, but Blythe lifted a hand to stop him. She turned to Hera, her tone hushed and firm. "We can't do this alone. If we're caught, Tavian posing as our captor might be the only way we survive."

Hera looked skeptical. "He's a sleeper agent. We don't know who's really pulling his strings."

Blythe pulled Hera aside. "I get it. I've been lied to and betrayed, too. But I must hope he's different. Besides, now that he knows what we're after, wouldn't you rather keep an eye on him?"

She wavered before adding, "Tavian has given us real information. He knows more about the Council and the realms than we do."

Hera studied Blythe for a long moment, and her shoulders slowly relaxed.

"Alright," she said. "But if he so much as looks suspicious, I take him out. No second chances."

Blythe cringed at the idea and gave a slight nod. "Deal. We'll watch each other's backs."

From the kitchen, Tavian called, "Did that book happen to say where we're headed? There's a lot of ground to cover—and three realms to search."

Blythe and Hera returned to the kitchen. "I saw some maps; I'd wager that's what we need."

"Perfect," Tavian said. "There are two stones in each realm. I don't have a clue where they are, but I'd be a monkey's uncle if they're conveniently grouped."

"A monkey's what?" Hera blinked.

"It's a human saying. Their idioms amuse me."

"Right." Hera straightened. "Let's get moving. We've got a long road ahead of us."

CHAPTER NINETEEN

Quentin

Aeloria, Fae mountain region

The room felt suffocatingly quiet as Quentin faced the Fae elders. His heartbeat hammered in his ears as he looked up at them. Enchanted light gleamed through the hall, casting subtle shadows upon the detailed tapestries lining the walls.

He never understood why they hadn't put any windows in here. It was bright and sunny outside; he'd caught a glimpse on the walk-in.

His mother sat at the center dais, gracefully smoothing the skirts of her white gown, its hem embroidered with finely crafted flora and fauna. He couldn't remember the first time he'd seen his mother on that dais—he'd been too young—but she always came across as both grounding and unreal, a symbol of their people.

Elders in their clan colors sat on either side of her, their silent expectations pressing down on him. Quentin drew a steady breath of ancient wood and lavender incense as he steadied himself and focused on the floor beneath his shoes. This was the smell of home, yet he felt no comfort. He was here to make a desperate request.

This was more than a plea; it was a struggle for the future, and he needed them to understand—and agree—to help.

He steadied himself and began.

"Honored elders, Thank you for granting me this audience. I'll speak plainly." Quentin's voice projected farther than he expected through the calm of the hall.

He cast a quick look at Griffin, Iain, and Izzy. Izzy's small, encouraging smile steadied the quiver in his chest.

"One of the portals to the Dark Realm has been left unguarded," he said, his tone confident. "And the corruption leaking through it is extending across our lands. The Council blames a handful of mixed-breed outcasts. That is a lie. The real danger lies within the Council itself—something festering in its ranks."

A ripple of unease moved through the elders. Quentin began to pace, boots whispering over polished stone. He clasped his hands behind his back, hoping no one caught the subtle tremble in his fingers.

"We've all felt the shift," he continued. "Our representatives have been pushed out of decisions that once required each and every voice. Our concerns dismissed. Our warnings were ignored. They call it order." He shook his head. "It feels like something else entirely."

One elder grumbled under his breath.

Quentin's steps accelerated as heat rose in his chest—fear for what would happen if he failed here.

"The Council looks away while darkness spreads," he said, no longer raising questions but stating the truth as he saw it. "They silence us. They uplift only the Mages."

He slowed, letting his next words settle.

"Civilizations don't fall in a moment—they rot when good people stop fighting." His tone mellowed. "The Great Houses have always chosen Keepers by worthiness, not blood. That is their ancient wisdom. Yet the Council seeks to interfere with that as well. To control the Houses themselves."

A stillness took over the chamber. Quentin felt every stare on him—some wary, some curious, some quietly afraid. His mother watched him with an expression he couldn't read, and the uncertainty twisted in his gut.

Before he could continue, an elder rose—gray-skinned, ash-haired, his purple robes whispering as he stood.

"Pardon the interruption, Your Highness," the elder said, voice coarse as grinding stone. "You speak with conviction.

But where is your proof? How do we know this is more than speculation? We have no evidence that they're trying to control anything."

Quentin held the elder's gaze, hoping his eyes didn't betray his racing heart.

"Proof," Quentin said, his voice controlled, "is in the actions of the Council itself. Their secrecy, their exclusion from the other races, their obsession with control, all point to something they're trying to hide. And if we don't act now, we may not have a chance to stop them when they get what they want."

The elder's eyes narrowed, but Quentin caught a trace of doubt within them. He continued, his volume increasing.

"I'm not asking you to believe me blindly. I'm asking you to question, to investigate. The future of the Fae—of all the realms—depends on it." The elder slowly sat down. A silence followed, laden with suspense, as every eye turned to the dais where his mother sat.

"The people they blame for releasing the demons are innocent. I know, because I was with them."

A sharp murmur rippled through the chamber, elders shifting in their seats as the force of his admission spread across them. A whisper spread through the Fae elders.

"I joined the rebellion because I believed it was the only way to stop the Council," Quentin said, tone resolute. "But I've since learned their leaders aren't being honest either. They were meant to guard the portals—and they didn't. And the Council refuses to send what's needed to push the demons back. Both sides are allowing the Dark Realm to bleed into ours while claiming to protect innocent lives. That should concern all of us."

The room stirred; the tension grew. Yet no one spoke. "I fear it's because they want the evil to spread. They don't care about anyone but themselves—or whatever end goal they're pursuing." He nodded, indicating he was done, and waited. His eyes turned to his mother.

Her glance softened.

"Quentin, as I'm sure you know, I've been attempting to reclaim my place in the Council." She rose, tidying her gown with a delicate motion, yet Quentin saw her fingers trembled, betraying the tension she refused to show. Quentin searched her face, but couldn't tell if the tremor was sympathy or doubt. The ambiguity twisted tighter than any rebuke.

The sound of her voice was calm, though imbued with concern. "I am thankful for your warning. My question is, what else is it that you seek? Surely, you didn't come here only to give us vague warnings about matters we were already concerned about."

Quentin dipped his head in a brief, respectful nod.

"Yes, please forgive me if I caused any confusion. The rebels' leader plans to send someone to seek aid in mounting a rebellion against the Council. What I'm asking for is your help in restoring balance—by confronting the Council's corruption along with handling the rebellion's failures before either can do more harm."

The room immediately buzzed faintly with low murmurs, council members leaning toward one another in low conversation. Even the audience, who had been silently observing until now, exchanged inquiring looks, their quiet conversations scarcely held back.

From his mother's left, an elder bearing pale blue skin rose to his feet, his gestures unhurried but deliberate. He swept a hand through his hair—a shock of electric-blue spikes—and fixed Quentin with eyes as keen as ice.

"You speak against the Council with such conviction," the elder began, his deep voice growling through the chamber and quieting the room. "And yet you stand here advising us against aiding those who seek to dismantle it. Explain yourself, Quentin. Which side do you stand on? Do you stand with those who would burn centuries of tradition and start anew? Or do you stand with those who would keep us beneath the power of mages?"

Quentin held the elder's penetrating look, the air around

him charged with tension. It seemed as if the room was paused, every eye fixed on him.

"My friends and I have reason to believe that while the Council is undoubtedly corrupt, the rebels are not entirely motivated by justice," Quentin began, his voice controlled while carrying pressing concern. "It was their actions—or rather, their inaction—that left the portals unguarded. They appear indifferent to the lives lost through their negligence. Instead, their leader seems obsessed with finding something he claims is needed to turn the tide of war." As he spoke, Quentin drew his hands from behind his back and directed attention to the elders.

"What I'm asking for is your aid in dealing with both threats—the Council and the rebellion. Neither can defend our people. Ideally, we would restore the old Council structure, with equal voice for everyone's races."

He paused to take a breath before continuing.

"It is my hope that this new Council will have safeguards in place to prevent the failures of the past."

"You really think true equality is possible? After everything the mages have put us through?" one of the Fae elders demanded, indicating the room. "Why should we extend such mercy if we regain a place on the Council? We Fae deserve more."

The hall erupted, subdued murmurs swelling into a clamor of heated arguments.

Council members turned to one another, voices lifted in passionate debate, while those witnessing the proceedings joined in, their shouts and exclamations filling the chamber. Quentin stood in the thick of the turmoil. He knew he had just lit a fuse—and there was no turning back. Still, he wasn't entirely sure why they were so against the idea.

He stepped back to where Griffin, Izzy, and Iain stood, their mouths agape. Izzy released a quivering laugh, the kind she only used when nerves and wistfulness tangled together.

Quentin shot her a confused look.

"I forgot how good you were at riling up the Fae elders," she said, covering her mouth as if she could trap the giggles before they escaped.

"And I knew there was a reason I missed having you around," Iain grinned, slapping Quentin on the back.

"Do you think they'll go for it?" Griffin asked, shifting his weight to one foot as he watched the turmoil before them.

"I honestly have no idea. But I sincerely hope they give us some kind of help to stop Demetrius—and that it doesn't involve the Council. I can almost guarantee that if we join forces with them, they'll turn on us as soon as the rebels are dealt with. There will never be another chance to reunite our people."

The thought twisted in his gut, a numbing memory of how quickly everything was unraveling.

Quentin sighed and leaned back against the wall, watching as his people debated among themselves. Their arguments pounded against his skull. Each shouted word reminded him how hard it was to get anyone to be united. Many of the Fae wanted a greater voice in whatever new Council might be formed; others wished to sever ties entirely and remain apart. He could feel the moment slipping toward him, the inevitable point where neutrality would no longer be an option. He had lit the fuse, and now the fire spread without him. For now, he stayed out of the fray, though he knew neutrality would soon demand its price.

CHAPTER TWENTY

Quentin

Aeloria, Fae mountain region

"Quentin."

The sharpness in her voice made his shoulders tense.

He turned to see his mother striding towards him, her voice slicing the peacefulness of the now-empty room. He sat with Izzy, Iain, and Griffin on a bench pressed against the back wall, trying to stay out of sight.

"In the future, I would be grateful if you could give me a bit of warning before you stir up such a ruckus among the elders. They won't be the same for weeks. Had I known, I could have been more selective about who attended the hearing—and spared myself the trouble of using a charm of secrecy stone."

Quentin winced. He hadn't meant to make her clean up after him. But he'd gone to her first, and he wasn't about to let himself spiral over it.

Izzy let out a nervous little giggle. "You should always assume Quentin is going to stir up a ruckus."

Iain laughed and, seeing Griffin's confused face, added, "I'm assuming Izzy also remembers the last three times Que spoke with the elder council. He has a way of poking the dragon."

"I wouldn't compare the elders to a dragon." Izzy shook her head. "They're more like snotlings."

Quentin chuckled. The laugh slipped out before he could stop it; tension always made him punchier.

"Snotlings?" Griffin tilted his head slightly. "You mean

the dumb little grubby creatures that goblins and orcs use to do their dirty work?"

Izzy nodded emphatically, and she and Iain doubled over laughing.

"That's enough," chided their mother, though the quiver in her lips told Quentin she wasn't entirely upset about the comparison. But the amusement didn't reflect in her eyes.

"To be honest," Quentin replied, rising slowly to his feet, "I did tell you what I'd seen, and I've made no secret of my feelings when it comes to how governments should run. Though I wasn't entirely sure what I was going to say until I said it." He flashed a sheepish grin and ducked his head as she narrowed her eyes at him. "But I do appreciate you making sure no one can spread the word of what was discussed." His boots scraped the dirt, restless. He hated how young he felt under her scrutiny.

Griffin cleared his throat, clearly bracing himself.

"Your Majesty, Queen Lyriana," Griffin spoke up, bowing deeply beside Quentin. "May I have a moment of your time?"

Lyriana turned her attention to Griffin, lifting an eyebrow. "Proceed."

"Quentin and I go to the dwarves next wi' the same request," Griffin explained. "We're hopin' to get their help in appealin' to their allies as well. We plan ta stop this rebellion, replace the leaders wi' ones we trust, and then take down the Council to create unity."

Lyriana studied Griffin's face. The longer the quiet stretched on, the more worried the glances Quentin and Griffin exchanged became. Quentin's pulse beat in his throat.

The anxiety in the room intensified.

"This is a bold endeavor," Lyriana said, pausing. "Raising an army against the Council is difficult enough, but to also subtly dismantle a rebellion that keeps trying, and failing, to stay below the Council's radar is another matter. How will you take them down without bringing unwanted attention from the Council?" She fixed Quentin with a penetrating stare that made him shift uncomfortably. "I propose an alternative."

Quentin stiffened. His mother's "alternatives" rarely favored him.

Quentin and Griffin shared looks before turning back to Lyriana, waiting for her suggestion.

"We assist the current rebellion in taking down the Council first," she began slowly. "Once that's accomplished, we deal with the rebel leaders. It's easier to mobilize our people against those who failed to protect us from the dark realm if we act discreetly."

Lyriana held up a hand to silence Quentin's interruption.

"In return, Quentin will agree to assume his rightful place as King of the Fae, starting now. No more wandering as a 'lawyer of the people.' You'll remain here and send envoys to seek aid from other realms, as is the proper means of requesting assistance. A king doesn't wander."

The words came like a stone on his chest.

Quentin considered his mother's proposal. He had expected nothing less than a plan meant to keep him within the Fae lands and to secure his birthright. After a few moments of thought, he spoke.

"I understand I should have taken Father's throne by now," Quentin said, his voice composed despite the magnitude of his words. "And I know I promised I'd return and assume my role once I finished helping Miles. I failed to do that. I broke our agreement."

Admitting it out loud hurt more than he expected.

His mother nodded, encouraging him to continue.

"I can't trust this to anyone else," Quentin continued. "Too many betrayals, too many untrustworthy people. I have to take care of this myself—for our people. If someone else fails, or if the Council or the rebels learn of our plans, all our efforts will be in vain, and our people will pay the price."

His mother's hand rested on Quentin's cheek. "My child, do you understand why I want you to stay?" She advanced a step and embraced him.

He froze for an instant—her affection always caught him off guard.

"Beyond the optics of having a king who does not wish to remain with his people, I've missed you and worry for your safety." She pulled back, holding him at arm's length. "There are forces moving in the hidden places that even I cannot predict, and if the Council falls, I fear it is the Fae that will be the first they blame."

Her embrace warmed him, but the weight of her conditions chilled him just as quickly.

The look in her eyes shifted to Griffin, then back to Quentin. "I will allow you to leave, but you must take Griffin and a small, trustworthy guard and return in two weeks' time. I will not permit you to join the battle against the Council. The guard I send will be adept at moving quickly and quietly."

"Mother, we're planning to fly on Ellira. It's faster and more discreet—"

"Absolutely not," she interrupted, shaking her head. "My scouts have reported seeing strange dragons in the skies. I won't risk it. I absolutely forbid it."

Heat burst in his chest, but he held back the retort.

Quentin's thoughts went to the mage who had pursued them on a dragon as they neared the Fae capital. He knew his mother was right, but still hated to concede. "Then what do you suggest? Ellira is faster than traveling on foot, and unicorns are impractical—"

"I'm not proposing either," Lyriana sighed. "To be honest, I don't know the safest route. But I do know it's too dangerous for you and Griffin to travel alone. Use dragons, carpets, or walk—but take extra guards for your protection."

Quentin folded his arms, considering her terms. "Fine, but I get to choose who accompanies us. And we postpone the coronation until this is resolved."

Lyriana's lips tightened as she deliberated. "I'll agree—on one condition."

Quentin's stomach dropped. Conditions from her were

never simple.

"That Blythe Evans girl," Lyriana said, her inflection probing. "She's the one you've recognized as your mate?"

The question punched the air from his lungs. Heat surged in his chest, humiliation and longing colliding before he forced the words out.

Quentin shot a glance at Izzy, who winced and looked to the floor.

"Don't look at her," Lyriana said. "She didn't tell me. I saw you before you left, and you hadn't found your Lunastra. Now you are back, and I can practically smell it on you. Yet you haven't completed the Æthralis—"

"And I won't," Quentin cut in firmly. "She has no interest in being with me, and I'd prefer not to go over this again."

Iain shifted uncomfortably, shaking his head slightly. Even Iain's disapproval scraped at Quentin's nerves.

"You can't simply walk away from your Lunastra—"

Quentin clenched his shaking fists and turned, his voice intensifying with frustration as he began to walk away. "I'm not walking away; I refuse to engage in a barbaric ritual." His voice faltered on the last word, humiliation burning his throat. He paused and looked back at her. "Send me the list of guards you'd like me to take. I'll choose from it, and we'll leave at mid-day tomorrow."

He hurried out of the room before she could answer, his heart throbbing in his chest.

"Oy!" Griffin called, jogging to catch up. "What was all that about, eh-tha... whatcha-ma-call it?" He sounded more worried than curious.

"It's pronounced Aa-eth-rah-lees," Quentin said curtly. "And it's best you forget about it." He looked back to make sure his mother and siblings weren't following. "I haven't been completely honest with Blythe." The admission felt harsh.

He paused.

"There are cases where one recognizes their mate and the other does not. The Æthralis would either force the nonrecognizing one to accept or break the bond at the whim of the person who imprinted. It was only used to sever bonds when a female Fae recognized her mate, and he refused her."

He moved outdoors, the fresh air welcoming. "She wasn't asking to break it. I'm sure she thinks that if Blythe and I mate, it would give the Fae some advantage over the other races."

Griffin kept pace as they walked into the open air. "What do ya mean by that?"

"I mean," Quentin said, his subdued voice, "she's only ever concerned about the Fae coming out on top. I suspect she's hoping to leverage Blythe and me to get herself on the Council. She'll put on a show for outsiders, but I know her well." Too well. Enough to fear what she'd do with power. He cast a quick look at his friend. "We'll accept her help, but we must proceed carefully. Once we've dealt with the Council and the Rebels, we can't let her manipulate the situation."

Griffin nodded. "How do ya plan ta keep her out?"

Quentin exhaled slowly. "I'll have to accept my role as King and trust that my people are more loyal to me than to her." The title still felt like an ill-fitting garment, two sizes too big. He started across the courtyard toward their rooms. "They loved my father. They fear my mother."

"How're they feelin' 'bout you, eh? Trustin' you, or just smilin' through their teeth?" Griffin asked, holding the door open for Quentin when they reached it. Quentin let out a sigh as he glanced up at the clear blue sky, watching birds soar as he considered the question.

"I'm not entirely sure," Quentin admitted. "I've been away for so long. We might need to consult Izzy and Iain to gauge the sentiment." He looked back toward the courtyard, noting that the meeting hall doors were still closed. A familiar guilt twisted in his chest. "I should never have left them with her. She's a wolf in sheep's clothing. While Izzy has a keen sense of people, I'm not certain Iain is paying enough attention. I could ask Izzy to work on the elders while we're away. If she can sway even a few elders, it might be enough to shift the balance against my mother."

"It'll help that you'll be King, aye?" Griffin's expression eased, following Quentin inside. "So, the army'll be marchin' under yer banner?"

"True," Quentin agreed, "but I'd hate for it to come down to using brute force to stop my mother. It's not a good look for the history books." And the thought of raising a hand against his own mother made his gut wrench.

"Sometimes," Griffin said solemnly, letting the door close with a firm thud, "ya have ta do what ya have ta do."

Quentin nodded in agreement, following Griffin toward their quarters. Rest now, he told himself. The way forward would demand everything.

But even as he thought it, he knew sleep would be a long time coming.

CHAPTER TWENTY-ONE

Blythe

Fasbridge Manor, Upstate, NY (Human realm) / Auroraheim (Magic realm)

Blythe turned another page of the ancient volume, her gloved fingertip following the delicate, curling script inscribed on the timeworn parchment. Her forehead creased, one eye closed, and the other narrowed as she worked to decipher the ancient language. The stale aroma of old paper drifted in the air, her scone long forgotten next to her.

"There are two stones in each of the three realms," she murmured in a hushed tone, like the room itself demanded reverence for the tome's secrets.

Hera leaned in, her breath soft against Blythe's shoulder as she peered intently at the densely packed lines. The text sparkled weakly, almost aware of their attention.

"I'd bet the Warlocks already snatched the ones from the Dark Realm," she said, frustration running through the inflection in her voice. With a sigh, she sat back. Hera had tried to read this tome before, but the letters always shifted and swirled until they dissolved into nonsense. Tavian had tried as well, only to watch the words twist into indecipherable runes.

It wasn't just the language that hid its mysteries; the tome was designed for the Keeper's eyes alone, demanding Blythe close one eye to read it, as if it required singular focus—a sacrifice of depth.

Tavian finally broke the dense silence.

"Are we screwed, then?" Tavian asked. Blythe winced. The metal tines scraped along the porcelain plate.

Hera's brow knitted. "Screwed?"

Blythe's lips twitched into a half-smile while she looked at Tavian, who fixed his eyes on her with a playful sparkle. "It's a human term," Blythe said. "It means we're in a tight spot—or out of luck. Not the politest expression."

Tavian leaned back, cradling his coffee mug in both hands, his smirk growing. "What can I say? I've got a soft spot for human profanity. Theirs are much more fun than ours." He grinned. "There's another use of that word, too. It can mean—"

Blythe shot him a look, silencing him. This was not the moment for Tavian's brand of chaos.

Hera rolled her eyes, her mouth turning up into a half-hearted smile. Tavian closed the distance with Hera, his tone lowering in a teasing whisper.

"I've always preferred things a little naughty," he teased, waggling his eyebrows.

Hera shot him a side glance, her lips twitching as if fighting back a smile. "I'll bet you do. You were the kid in school who got tied to the training dummy and used for target practice, weren't you?"

Blythe's mouth fell open as she looked at Hera. Tavian's expression likely paralleled her shock. Hera looked between them, her brows knitting in confusion. "What? That's standard discipline."

Her sincerity made it somehow worse.

"Maybe for a Valkyrie," Tavian said when he finally found his voice. "The one that sticks out to me is the time I had to write a thousand lines on why we don't summon minor demons during Runes 300."

Hera and Blythe stared at him.

"What?" His eyes scanned between the two of them. "It was one time. Technically speaking, it was an imp. But I didn't correct the professor; that would've just made me use the blood pen."

Hera shrugged and looked back down at the pages in front of her.

"Blood pen?"

"Yeah. As you write, it cuts into you and uses your own blood as the ink." Tavian shuddered.

Blythe's stomach twisted, memories of her father's punishments abruptly seeming gentle by comparison.

Her mind drifted back to her homeschooling with her father and half-brother. At the time, she hadn't known how closely she was related to them. Hera cleared her throat, pulling Blythe's attention back to the task at hand. She forced her mind back to the page, to the mission that couldn't afford distraction.

"We need to focus on getting to the stones in the Magic Realm before my uncle does. And we can't forget the two in the Human Realm."

Tavian set his coffee down, the look on his face sharpening. "Does the book give us any clues?"

Blythe flipped back a few pages, her finger following the lines of text. "There are some cryptic rhymes—like riddles. If I understand them correctly, the stones are hidden in the same places across all realms, but getting to a portal to cross over would mean backtracking. It'll take time, but humans have altered their world enough to throw everything off."

"Let's hear one of the rhymes," Tavian urged, leaning forward, his hands clasped around the mug as if anchoring himself to the moment.

Hera stood, irritation rising as she slammed her hands on the table. The crash resounded throughout the room.

"How do we even know these stones are what your uncle is after? What if they're just a wild goose chase? Are they even real?" Her voice faltered slightly on the last word, fear leaking through the frustration.

Silence was the only answer she could give, clearer than any argument.

The question remained in the air, heavy and unanswered, as they all realized how thin their leads were. How they were grasping at straws.

Tavian stretched, his arms lifting above his head as he worked out the stiffness that had built up while they sat. "Can we reach Quentin? Maybe he and Griffin can go after the second stone in the Magic Realm."

Blythe hesitated, her eyes wandering to Hera.

"He and Griffin should be at the Fae capital by now," Hera replied. Her anger cooled quickly, replaced by the practiced efficiency of clearing the table. "You could send him a message with the House's help."

Blythe looked up, addressing the unnoticed presence. "House, is that something you can help with?"

The kitchen door moaned open, but no one stood in the doorway. The door wiggled slightly—an invitation. Blythe stood, interest sparked, and followed the subtle pushes of the House. Lights wavered on, brightening the trail up the stairs, and she trailed the gentle hints ushering her to the library. A cool thread of air brushed past her ankle, nudging her in the direction of the stairs.

Entering the room, she heard the clatter of typewriter keys from the balcony above. Her heart sped up as she rushed up the spiral staircase, the metal steps squeaking beneath her bare feet. Reaching the top, she saw the old typewriter—its keys proceeding with intent, as if driven by an unseen hand—sending her a message from the House itself. She'd never get used to the House speaking like this.

A slip of paper emerged from the typewriter, the words freshly inked: You can 'call' someone through the portal door. Your Keeper book has the correct rune. Clearly say the name, and it will open a communication portal.

Blythe's lips curved into a smile. "Well, that's handy."

With fresh energy, she raced down the spiral staircase and hurried out of the library. She hurriedly moved into her bedroom, snatched up her Keeper's book from where it lay on the bed, and sped back down the stairs. As she passed the kitchen, she noticed Hera and Tavian sitting in silence—both pointedly ignoring each other, yet watching while she hurried past the door. She didn't pause, her focus sharp as she continued down to the portal door, the Keeper's book held securely in her hand.

She quickly found the rune and traced it onto the wall where the portal door would form. For a moment, nothing happened. Then, just as Blythe began to wonder if she had done it wrong, the door shimmered, quivering like disturbed water before collapsing into a whirling spiral of brightness and gloom.

At the center of the vortex, an image began to take shape —misty and wavering, yet distinctly a view of a distant place she did not recognize. Gradually, the scene sharpened, revealing the interior of a grand bedroom, its walls decorated with elaborate wall hangings and lit by the soft radiance of enchanted lanterns. Standing in the center, looking surprised but alert, was Quentin. His shimmering silver locks gleamed in the light as he turned toward her, his eyes focusing intently as he recognized the connection.

"Blythe?" Quentin's voice was clear, though tinged by the barest trace, as if traveling a great distance. Her chest loosened, the ache of separation easing for a heartbeat as his face came into focus. His expression changed from astonishment to concern. "What's wrong?"

Blythe exhaled, relieved to see him. "Sorry, I didn't mean to worry you," she began, her voice controlled despite the trace of unease at the center of her chest. "We've been going through one of the books from the library here at the House, and it seems there are six stones," she said. "Two in each realm. We're almost certain the warlocks already have the ones from the Dark Realm, but there's another one in the Magic Realm aside from what I think my uncle is after. We need to get to it before he does."

Quentin's eyes darkened as he absorbed the information, his posture straightening. "Griffin and I are already in Aeloria. We'll start the search immediately if you can give us some information on where to look and what we're looking for."

Blythe nodded, a sense of urgency tightening her chest. "Thank you. The book said the stones are hidden in similar places across all realms. It uses riddles to describe where each one is. It won't be easy," she said. "We'll read through them and be in touch once we have more information about the one in the Magic Realm."

There was an unvoiced truth in his eyes—fear, maybe, or something closer to longing. "We'll find it. Just be careful, Kitsune."

The nickname sent warmth and longing through her body. She forced the feeling down and met his eyes. "I'll try to get a message to Octo to see if he can confirm that's what they're actually after. If we know for sure, it won't feel like a stab in the dark."

Quentin nodded. "Sounds good. If it isn't what they're after, they still came across as something we could use. I'd hate to have to go to the Dark Realm to fetch those two, though. But please, as I said, stay sharp."

"You too. I'll stay in touch through the portal if we find anything else." She paused, a dozen unspoken worries pressing at her tongue, and finally settled on, "How are things going for you?"

Quentin shifted before answering. "I'm not sure if we're getting anywhere here, but I'll let you know when I know for sure." Something in his tone suggested he wasn't telling her everything. The omission stung, a reminder of how far apart they truly were. The image of Quentin began to waver, the connection straining under the burden of the distance. "Take care. We'll see this through."

With a last nod, Blythe watched as the portal gleamed and faded, the door returning to its solid form. The hush that followed seemed more oppressive than before. She stood there for a moment, her thoughts whirling. She needed to call Octo before she did anything else.

She drew a steady breath and drew the rune again, hoping he was somewhere private. They couldn't risk her uncle overhearing their plans. The glyph glowed lightly beneath her touch, responding to her magic. A mild thrum vibrated through the doorframe as if the House approved.

"Octo, please." The rune's surface sparkled, and a twisting vapor began to form, gradually forming into the image of Octo. She scanned the shadows behind him and exhaled in relief—no sign of her uncle's camp.

"Blythe." Octo's voice resonated through the mist, composed but carrying the same ethereal echo as Quentin's. "What's going on?"

Blythe spoke quickly. "We need your help. We've discovered that some magic stones were used to create the portals between realms—but they can also tear them down—and unleash far worse.

"They hold an incredible amount of power. We're worried that Demetrius is after them." Blythe ran through the information they already knew regarding the stones and what they suspected. "We're going to find the stones in the Human Realm, and Quentin will go after the other one in the Magic Realm. If he's after them, we need to know what he's planning to do—and if necessary, find a way to stop him or get them away from him."

A shadow of worry played across his features before he masked it. "I see. So you want me to spy on him and intercept if necessary?"

Blythe nodded, throat tight. She hated asking this of him.

"Perfect. I'd recommend trying to get into his tent. Check his journals if you can. If the warlocks have the stones, we need proof. Spying on the warlocks might also confirm whether they have the stones from the Dark Realm," Blythe suggested.

"I'll get on it," Octo said, his face as unreadable as ever. But the slight tightening of his jaw betrayed his concern. "I'll report back as soon as I can."

"Thanks, Octo," Blythe said. "Stay safe. We're counting on you." Her voice wavered despite her best effort to sound steady.

The image of Octo fluttered faintly as the communication rune's light gradually waned.

"I'll be in touch," he said before the portal's light faded, leaving her alone with the echo of her own fear, heavier now that she'd asked Octo to risk himself.

CHAPTER TWENTY-TWO

Blythe

Fasbridge Manor, Upstate, NY (Human realm) / Auroraheim (Magic realm)

Blythe's mind hummed with urgency as she returned to the kitchen. That recognizable shiver threaded through her back, her body's warning system sparking to life. Her conversations with Quentin and Octo ran in a loop in her head. Quentin's voice stayed the longest, sharper in her memory than she wanted to admit. The scones lay forgotten on the table, their buttery aroma wafting into the air as Blythe stepped in. Even the House became unusually still, as if listening. Both Hera and Tavian looked up at her, their eyes expectant but their lips tight with unvoiced questions.

"They're on it," Blythe said, injecting as much confidence into her speech as she could muster. The confidence sounded fragile, stretched over too many unknowns. The words carried more weight than she intended as she crossed the room and sat down, her fingers beating a restless rhythm on the edge of the table. Her fingertips chilled, colder than they should have. "Quentin and Griffin will go after the stone in the Magic Realm once we know where it is. That leaves us with the two in the Human Realm. Octo's going to try to confirm that this is what my uncle is after." And if Benjamin was involved, they needed to know that too.

Hera's nod was slow, her glance shifting to Tavian, searching for affirmation. Tavian leaned back with a soft sigh that carried the burden of the room—his laid-back demeanor scarcely disguising the tension.

"Then we've got work to do." He clapped his hands together and pushed away from the table. His chair rasped as it slid back beneath him. "We can't afford to waste any more time."

Blythe nodded. Every hour, Demetrius had a head start, tightening the noose.

"Agreed. We need to decipher the riddles and find the stones before it's too late."

Hera stood and began pacing, her footsteps silent on the aged wooden floor. "Alright. Give me the first one." She closed her eyes as if it would help her focus.

Blythe inhaled, letting it out slowly as she perused the verses from the tome.

The letters twinkled subtly, arranging themselves as if anxious to be spoken.

The words resounded in her thoughts and off the walls of the quiet room while she recited them aloud:

"One guards the dawn with riddled face,

A lion carved in timeless grace.

Its silence holds the burden of kings,

Where desert breathes and memory clings.

The other weeps from mountain's brow,

A silver braid unbound till now.

She fell for love, betrayed by lies,

Her tears cascade where mist still cries.

Find the gaze that never blinks,

Seek the braid where sorrow sinks.

Two truths await where legends sleep—

One carved in stone, one carved in grief."

Hera stopped in her tracks, her eyes snapping open as she repeated the riddle. "Weeps from mountain's brow..." she thought aloud, furrowing her eyebrows. "That could be literally anywhere."

"Probably a waterfall," Tavian added.

"It's the same location in all three realms. We need to think of a northern location with a waterfall... Demetrius said they'd be going overseas, so if they were traveling north—probably to the area in the Magic Realm that coincides with Maine—and then going overseas, we're looking at Greenland, Iceland, Ireland, Scotland, the UK, or Europe..." She frowned.

"Well, that certainly narrows it down," Hera muttered.

Sarcasm was her coping mechanism, apparently.

"The other weeps from mountain's brow, A silver braid unbound till now. She fell for love, betrayed by lies, her tears cascade where mist still cries." Tavian mused, leaning forward. "There's a spot like that near some old ruins in the Magic Realm. I visited it as a kid. Back before things with my brother and family went sideways. Demetrius was going north and east?" Blythe nodded. "It was to the north of where I lived. I'd bet there's something similar in the Human Realm—maybe in an old park or a nature reserve."

Blythe's fingers followed the worn edges of the aged volume. "Then that's where we start." Resolve enveloped her like a suit of armor.

"Hold on." Hera flipped a chair around and straddled it. She always got sharper when Blythe needed her. "What if whatever natural markers were destroyed when humans put up buildings or something? How would we know?"

"I suspect there's some sort of magic preventing that kind of thing. Old magic—the kind tied to the Houses, not the Council," Tavian said with a shrug. "But you make a good point."

"All we can do is try to find it," Blythe conceded.

Hera fixed Tavian with a look. "Can you pinpoint that location on a map? If we match it with a map from the Human Realm, we'll know exactly where the stone is hidden."

Blythe scanned the kitchen, her thoughts swirling. "House... could we get some maps?" she asked, her speech a subtle plea to the House. A soft tap on her foot drew her attention downward, where, to her surprise, three rolled parchments had appeared at her feet. She picked them up quickly and unrolled each one on the table.

The maps unfurled, revealing identical topographies—mountains, rivers, and valleys mirroring each other—but the names and cities varied. One was clearly of the Human Realm, another of the Magic Realm, and the last, with its darker hues and ominous landmarks, must have belonged to the Dark Realm.

"These are perfect," Blythe murmured, spreading the maps side by side. If they were wrong, they'd lose days they didn't have. "Now we just need to match the location across the realms."

Hera approached, her look hardening while she looked over Blythe's shoulder. Tavian did the same from the other side, his finger gliding over the map of the Magic Realm. "I grew up in Veloria—right there in Vyrendale. It's one of the old border cities—half magic, half ruin," he said, his finger settling on a spot that would match with France in the Human Realm. "I remember we traveled north, to here." He pointed to a land mass north of the country he had first indicated. "We flew over the strait there, up to here." He moved his finger toward the northwest coast of Scotland. "It was called Eas a' Chual Aluinn."

"That would be Scotland—Scotland, here," Blythe murmured, reading the maps for any signs or symbols. "That name sounds like Scottish Gaelic... Would they really use the same name in the Magic Realm?"

"Well, you know, our worlds used to be joined. Your oldest languages would likely match up with our oldest ones," Tavian explained, studying the map.

"Where's the closest portal to that location?" Blythe's mind was spinning with this information. It was fitting too neatly. It couldn't be this easy.

"Here." Tavian pointed to a location on the Human Realm map near Inverness, Scotland.

Blythe leaned down, looking over the map.

"That's Loch Ness..." Blythe's face tensed while she traced the path with her finger. "How was Demetrius planning to get there from here?" She pointed to the continent that corresponded to North America on the Magic Realm map.

"I'm not sure," Hera admitted, her frown deepening. "Are you certain that place fits the riddle?"

"No," Tavian stroked his chin. "But I remember being told the location was used for powerful magic centuries ago. I'm sure there are waterfalls in other places, but none were particularly symbolic, as far as I know." He paused. "As for getting there... could he have been planning to take an airship?"

"Not a chance. They're rebels, remember?" Hera countered, shaking her head.

"Unless he intended to commandeer one," Blythe suggested, lifting her shoulders in a half-shrug. Blythe had a feeling her uncle had never shied away from taking what wasn't his.

"That's possible," Hera conceded after a moment.

"Alright," Blythe said, standing and stretching, her muscles objecting after so much time hunched over maps and books. "If we're sure that's our target, how do we get there quickly?"

Tavian's mouth curved into a grin. "I can take care of that. I got my pilot's license a while ago. I'm fascinated by planes. The Council was generous enough to procure one for me, which I now use to ferry sleeper agents. We use magic to keep our movements hidden from Humans." He winked. "How about a flight across the great ocean to Inverness?"

"Inverness?" Hera echoed, scowling.

"That's what it's called in the Human Realm," Blythe explained, pointing to the corresponding spot on the map.

Hera shrugged, a small smile blossoming. "Alright, let's go."

Blythe caught Hera's smile lingering too long on Tavian, a thread she wasn't sure she wanted to tug.

Tavian was already rolling up the maps—brisk, efficient. "Let's pack some supplies," he said, the parchment snapping into tight rolls under his hands. "We can take my car to where I stash the plane."

Somewhere in the walls, the House moaned. Whether it was in approval or warning, she couldn't tell.

Hera looked at Blythe—one brow lifted, sharp and skeptical—as if she'd spoken another language.

"It's how we travel instead of by dragons or carpets or whatever you all use. Humans don't have access to magic travel." Blythe paused, the faintest smile emerging at her lips. The House had the habit of anticipating their needs, and she suspected this time would be no different.

"I'm betting the House has us covered for supplies," she said, glancing up as the lights above flickered in response.

Following her hunch, Blythe moved up the stairs, her fingers drifting lightly along the banister as she ascended. The polished wood warmed under her touch, as if greeting her. She held her breath as she came near the closet door, her footsteps creaking quietly on the worn floorboards. If the House didn't provide, they'd lose precious time.

When she opened the door, the perfume of cedar and aged paper greeted her. Inside, three backpacks sat, perfectly aligned, as if they'd been placed there moments before, waiting for them. She reached out, brushing her hand over the cloth of one. The House's signature, neat and precise supplies.

She pulled the backpack toward her and unzipped it. The contents were organized, each item fitting together like pieces of a puzzle: a sleeping bag, ready-to-eat meals, water bottles, a change of clothes, and a compass. Her fingers caressed the soft leather cover of her magic book, tucked securely into a side pocket, ready to be called upon when needed. She pulled it out, running her hand over the aged leather.

The book's mass centered her in the reality of the challenges to come. Cold pooled low in her chest, whether in anticipation or warning. She inhaled the whiff of leather and parchment mingling with the lingering aromas from the kitchen below. Blythe slid the book back into place and slung the pack over her shoulder. The strap dug into her shoulder, a reminder of the burden they carried—more than the physical load, but the responsibility of their mission.

When she returned to the kitchen, Hera was already standing, her eyes narrowed in focus as she studied one of the maps. Hera always anchored herself in strategy when fear filtered in. Tavian was by the door, holding the other maps, his glance drifting from Blythe to the backpacks she carried.

"That was fast."

"Thanks to the House," Blythe said with a small smile, handing one to him before giving the other to Hera.

Hera accepted hers with a nod. Blythe set her own bag down on the floor. Tavian's grin returned as he slung his pack over one shoulder and handed his maps to Hera.

"The House never disappoints," he said. A cupboard door clicked into place somewhere in the hall, as if in agreement. "Let's hope the plane's as ready as we are."

Hera rolled up the maps and tucked them into her pack. They moved quickly, checking to make sure the bags held everything they might need. Tavian added a few more snacks before Blythe led the way outside. The air outside was in sharp contrast with the warmth of the House. The sky deepened to blue above them, the sun just starting to sink toward the horizon, throwing long shadows across the ground.

Tavian's car was parked just beyond the porch. Blythe eyed the sleek, dark vehicle, out in place of the old-world Victorian charm of the House. Quentin would've teased her for judging a car by its aesthetics. Hera loosened the strap of her pack, mouth clenched. He opened the trunk, and they loaded their packs inside.

As they climbed into the car, Tavian took the driver's seat, and the engine growled to life. He clutched the steering wheel and guided the vehicle deftly down the driveway toward the road.

Blythe tried not to think about the last time she'd been in a car—leading rebels toward the Dark Realm.

Cold stung her fingertips in her body's warning to stop spiraling. She couldn't let the thoughts in. Inevitably, they led to maybes and regret, and she didn't have the mental spoons for that.

The car sped down the road, the landscape blurring past the tinted windows. Tavian tapped the steering wheel with experienced familiarity. Blythe stared out at the shifting scenery, her thoughts whirling alongside. Every bump in the road echoed the uncertainty running through her mind. If they failed, the realms wouldn't survive the fallout.

Maybe someday she'd ride in a car for something ordinary—grocery shopping, going to work. Maybe Quentin would be there for that version of her life, if they lived long enough to reach it. A life not spent attempting the impossible and trying to save the realms.

"Can I ask you something?" Tavian said, eyes still on the road.

She blinked, pulled from her spiraling thoughts. "What?"

"Is it true you can cast magic without a Talisman?"

Her pulse stumbled. "How would you even know that?"

Tavian shrugged one shoulder, but there was nothing casual in the glance he flicked her way.

"I read once that half human–half mages could use wild magic. Raw magic. The kind that doesn't need a Talisman to channel it."

He glanced at her, just long enough for her to see the worry there. "I didn't know if it was real. Not until now."

Blythe looked away, pulse thudding in her ears. Wild magic. Every possibility twisted together in her mind, tightening like a snare. She didn't know what she was—or what they wanted her to be—and the not-knowing was its own kind of terror.

But the realms were hanging by threads she didn't have the luxury to ignore.

She forced a steady breath. "Whatever I am… it doesn't matter. We just have to get through this."

Tavian nodded, jaw set. "Then we will."

Blythe pressed her palm to the cool glass, watching the world blur into shadow. Exhaustion tugged at her bones, but beneath it, something else stirred—fear, yes, but also resolve.

Ahead of them, the road stretched into the dark, and somewhere beyond that, an airfield waited. A plane. A waterfall. A stone that could change everything.

Blythe straightened in her seat as the headlights cut through the dusk.

They were committed now. There was no turning back.

CHAPTER TWENTY-THREE

Octo

Northeastern Auroraheim

Octo stepped out of his tent, joints cracking as he stretched his arms above his head. The camp lay still, shrouded inside the hush of the night. Most of the rebels were either on patrol, their footsteps softened by the forest floor, or deep in slumber. They trusted Demetrius far more than Octo did, and that blind trust irritated him.

The air was thick with the earthy smell of moist leaves and pine. A faint mist hovered on the ground, swirling gently around the tents in a white shroud. Only a distant owl and the rustle of broken leaves broke the quiet. Octo moved with deliberate care.

The night air pricked at his exposed arms. It was nothing compared to the deep cold of the Arctic waters, breaking through ice into a snow-choked world. He shoved down the memories he rarely let surface. As he walked, he cast a careful glance around the clearing that served as the camp's heart, his eyes roaming the shadows for any trace of activity. The campfire had burned down to embers, throwing out a dim orange light that barely penetrated the darkness around it.

A faint light wavered in Demetrius's tent. Light at this hour was unusual. Octo moved quickly toward it. Through the tent's fabric, he saw the outlines of three figures, their shadows painted along the canvas, turning and merging like apparitions as they moved within. Something was wrong. He felt it before he heard the voices. He peeked around to confirm no one was watching before creeping across the clearing to hide behind a nearby tree. The ground was soft beneath his feet as he moved.

As he drew closer, the voices reached him—low and subdued. Octo stayed concealed in the darkness, inching nearer until he stood just outside the tent. His breath thinned as he strained to listen. If Demetrius caught him, the questions wouldn't just be uncomfortable—they'd be dangerous.

"...Complaints have reached me, Demetrius," a rough, disdainful voice said. Octo ground his teeth. Zelos Dredmore. That man was a sea urchin's spine buried under his skin, sharp and impossible to ignore. He clenched his jaw and listened.

"Your followers are growing restless," Zelos continued. "They believe you haven't done enough to protect the portals."

"They're impatient," Demetrius replied. "They don't see the full picture, but they will soon enough. The Council has been kept busy, scrambling to secure the portals we've left open. By the time they realize what's happening, it'll be too late. It's a means to an end."

He edged closer, piecing together the fragments of their conversation.

"And what of the stones?" Zelos asked, his voice fading to a barely audible whisper. The stones—Blythe was right. "You've promised that once they're all in our possession, we'll have the power to crush the Council. But can you really reach the human realm to gather the remaining ones?"

Demetrius snickered lowly, fingers rapping on the table in a slow, intentional cadence. "The Council is spread thin. They're fighting a losing battle. By the time they realize what we are up to, we'll have everything we need. When we strike, the Council will be caught completely unawares, their defenses shattered." Octo heard papers shuffling. "I had hoped to use my niece to get the stones from the Human Realm, but she's taken off with Hera." Octo's mouth set in a hard line. Blythe was just a tool for this rebellion. "I'm not sure what they're up to, but it's not a problem. She served her purpose for now and got you and the Warlocks out of the Dark Realm. You have the ones from the Dark Realm, and we will get the stones from this realm. I have friends in the Human Realm that I believe can be relied on to get the stones there."

"We will need her later, Demetrius," Zelos said.

"I realize that." Demetrius snapped.

Octo felt the strain from where he crept. His nerves tightened. Hopefully, Blythe and Hera could get to those stones before whoever Demetrius had there could reach them, and he'd have to make sure Demetrius wouldn't use her in whatever way they were planning. If Blythe was right, and Demetrius and his followers managed to gather all six, they'd all be doomed. The cold finally permeated him—fear, not weather.

"We have to have all six and the Unbound," Zelos growled. "We can't destroy the Council and the portals without them."

Octo searched his memory for the term Unbound, but it meant nothing to him.

"We will get them," Demetrius said dismissively. "We can go through The House of Fas to get to the Human Realm. If Blythe went there, she'll let us through to meet with my ally."

Octo's nerves jolted. The House of Fas. Fasbridge Manor. Blythe.

He could not let Demetrius go there. Inevitably, Blythe wouldn't be there. She'd be out looking for the stones.

A tense silence followed, shattered merely by the crackling of the lantern inside the tent. Octo caught a cold sweat from on his brow.

Zelos's voice cut through the quiet, his tone cautious. "You speak with confidence, Demetrius. But are you sure she will help? I suspect she knows you didn't protect the portals, and she's still upset about the Dixon boy. I'm sure she blames you for that. We cannot do it without the Unbound."

Miles's death still haunted them all.

Demetrius slammed his fist on the table.

"I know this, Zelos!" he snarled, the anger in his voice faintly contained. Octo felt the tension radiating from inside.

An uneasy hum ran through the canvas, as if the night wind listened for trouble.

The third voice, Melya, another Warlock, spoke up, her inflection measured but no less severe.

"Are you certain the stones and the Unbound girl will be enough? The Council holds resources, and if they catch wind of our plans—"

"They won't," Demetrius interrupted, his voice firm. "They believe the knowledge of the stones was destroyed when they did their first sweep of the Houses. The Houses had guarded that knowledge for centuries. They overlooked that the Warlocks kept their records even after their banishment. The stones will grant us the power we need. With them, we can control the portals, manipulate the realms, and strike at the heart of the Council when they least expect it."

"Fine. We focus on getting the two here, and then we meet up with whoever you have in the Human Realm to get those..." Zelos's shadow paced back and forth in the tent.

"My ally will get those stones to us. They won't fail me. Not again," Demetrius purred.

Octo's breath faltered.

Octo listened as a chair protested beneath the weight of someone sitting.

"Who is this ally?" Melya asked, attention captured.

Octo strained to hear Demetrius's response, his heart fluttering in his chest as he waited for the name that could change everything.

"Don't worry about that now. We get the two stones here, then my contact will get me the other two from the Human Realm," Demetrius said dismissively.

Octo's brain whirred, dread coiling tight in his gut. Blythe and Hera had met an ally of Quentin's who was supposed to be helping them. What if that ally wasn't theirs, but Demetrius's? He trusted Quentin, but Quentin's trust could easily be betrayed. Octo had warned against letting too many in on what they were doing. He hoped Quentin's trust in his friend was well-placed—for all their sakes.

The night felt colder than ever.

CHAPTER TWENTY-FOUR

Quentin

Aeloria, Fae mountain region

Quentin's breath steamed in the brisk air as he stared into the darkened sky from the edge of a clearing. The aroma of pine and moist soil rose from the undergrowth. He tightened the sword strap. It was an awkward weight for a man trained to fight with quill and argument. He missed the serene surety of ink more than he wanted to admit.

Griffin paced nearby, his boots grinding on the gravel path step by step. Griffin's jaw worked; impatience was his armor.

"I've seen moss grow faster than this," he muttered, eyes surveying the dense forest.

Quentin's stare was unwavering on the shade growing between the trees, unease stinging at the back of his neck. "My mother's instructions were clear. The team is coming with us. It's more than just adding numbers. It's about showing unity."

He hated that "unity" often meant being paraded as a symbol rather than trusted as a leader.

Griffin only murmured something skeptical, but didn't argue. Dwarves prized deeds over ceremony; a show of numbers could backfire. Quentin understood his friend's apprehension: the Dwarves were notoriously reclusive and difficult to impress. The prospect of a small entourage might seem like overkill, but Quentin knew his mother's insistence was strategic. Going with just Griffin wouldn't suffice, regardless of Griffin's standing with them.

A rustle snapped the quiet; both men stopped cold,

hands drifting to weapons. But it was not an ambush. Iain emerged from the dense shrubbery, broad-shouldered and welcome against the gloom.

"Apologies for the delay," Iain rumbled. "I had to argue with Mother for her to agree to my coming—Izzy didn't win that one."

A group of individuals came into view behind him. Quentin's eyes roamed over them, and he released a relieved breath. His mother had listened to his request for team members: Freya, the diplomat; Cael, the scout; and Rhys, the battle-hardened fighter.

Griffin's eyes narrowed, measuring the newcomers. He nodded in acceptance. Quentin knew that, despite his friend's reservations, Griffin would grow to value the added strength.

"Ready to move?" Quentin asked.

"Always," Iain replied. "Mother briefed us. Unless there's more we need to know?"

"No." Quentin shifted the bag on his back. "Let's go."

They moved under a tightening canopy; the atmosphere grew thinner, and the smells of wildlife sharpened. They moved up the slope, the forest's natural musk giving way to the sharper, mineral fragrance of the mountains.

Hours slipped by in a tense silence, broken only by the crunch of leaves and the whisper of branches overhead.

"Everything okay?" Griffin fell in beside him.

Quentin pursed his lips. "Just a feeling."

Something shifted in the underbrush, gone before Quentin could pinpoint it.

Griffin held out an arm. "Fan out. Meet back here."

The group dispersed, moving as quickly and quietly as they could, hoping that if someone were following them, they'd catch them by surprise.

Quentin scanned the shifting shadows as he walked. The only sounds were his own breathing and the stirring of birds and other creatures in the forest. Quentin knew the others had trained for this kind of terrain. They moved as one, silent and practiced.

A yelp sounded from behind Quentin. He turned and ran toward the sound. He burst through the bushes into an open space where Iain had pinned an individual in a long cloak to the ground.

"Don't move!" Iain ordered, a knife pressed to the stranger's ribs—close enough to draw blood if needed.

"Get off of me!" A muffled female voice snapped.

Quentin jogged over as the others emerged from the surrounding forest. He sank down beside Iain and the figure, reaching down to pull back the hood.

A sinking sensation hit him.

"Izzy?" Iain leaped back.

Quentin felt a complicated tug of relief braided with exasperation.

"Are you insane? I could have killed you!" Iain snapped.

She slowly rolled over and sat up. "That wouldn't be a problem if your first move wasn't to attack."

"We're on a dangerous mission; of course, we're going to attack first," Iain growled.

"Enough." Quentin's voice sliced through the argument. "Izzy, Mother told you not to come. I can only assume she hasn't changed her mind just because you were skulking behind us?"

He hated being the one to carry his mother's orders—hated that he had to be stern with her.

"I wasn't skulking," she grumbled, standing and wiping the dirt off her brown pants. "I was coming to join you..."

"By following us at a distance and not making yourself known?" Griffin grunted.

"Mother doesn't know you're here, does she?" Quentin studied her face. Her cheeks were red, her blue eyes cast downward. That was enough of an admission for him.

"You're going back," Iain said, grabbing Izzy by the elbow. She yanked it free.

"No," she glared at him. If looks could kill, Iain would be

a goner.

"We can't risk sending her alone. Council allies would use her to get to you," Freya said.

Rhys nodded. "She comes with us. We can't afford to waste time going back, and we need everyone who's here."

"My mother will kill us if we don't take her back," Iain argued.

"Mother will kill me if you bring me back," Izzy snapped.

"Your mother won't actually kill you. But the Council will," Freya said flatly.

"Stop," Quentin's voice rang out through the argument. All eyes turned to him. "We keep moving forward. I'll deal with my mother and take full responsibility for keeping Izzy safe."

"She got herself here; she could get herself back," Cael offered.

"She got lucky," Iain shot back, narrowing his eyes.

"I can take care of myself, thank you," Izzy said, pulling her cloak back to reveal the sword fastened to her belt. Her cloak had hidden the weapon well. "I've had training."

"Yeah, in court etiquette," Iain mumbled.

"Och, Iain, just leave it be," Griffin muttered, hitching the bag higher on his back. "Ye came yerself?"

Izzy gave a nod.

"Right. We've dawdled long enough. Time tae get movin'."

Iain grumbled but fell in line. They didn't have time for more discussion, and naturally, the group followed Quentin's orders.

They walked in silence, everyone absorbed in their thoughts, yet staying alert for anyone sneaking up on them. Izzy fell in step beside Quentin. Quentin felt time passing, though in the forest, the only signs were the shifting light and his growing weariness. They ate jerky and drank from their canteens as they walked, not risking a pause for a meal break.

Time dragged, each hour a slow bruise; Izzy's presence at his side helped, yet he wished Blythe could see this—see him leading. He hoped she was safe and that he was making the right choices. Leadership, he was learning, was mostly a matter of guessing in the dark. But the thought only sharpened the ache of her absence.

"We've entered the Dwarven lands," Griffin said as the terrain beneath their steps grew rockier and the trees sparser. The Dwarves hid their cities well—entrances were carved to confuse and to test those who sought them.

The cliff face towered ahead of them, an imposing wall of rock. Quentin's eyes scanned the surface, searching for the hidden entrance he knew existed inside.

Griffin pointed. "Here." They had reached a section of the cliff where the stone rippled and shimmered faintly in the moonlight. A gentle drone thrummed underfoot as if a chord struck in the earth in response to their presence.

Quentin raised a hand. "Hold."

His fingers skimmed the cool stone; a faint vibration answered beneath his palm. Griffin swapped places with him and drew out the patterns and mouthed the invocation; the rock groaned and slid aside, revealing a narrow passage.

"Griffin, you're in charge now," Quentin instructed, gesturing for Griffin to lead the way into the faintly lit tunnel. Quentin's eyes met Griffin's—trust and warning braided together.

"Stay close," Griffin grunted. "Ye'll be lost if ye wander off."

Deeper in, the tunnel opened up; the walls smoothed to polished stone, and the fragrance of melted metal rose, joined by the steady hammering of forges.

Emerging from the tunnel, they entered a cavern so expansive it seemed to spread without end into the darkness above. A furnace's glow painted the ceiling in molten orange. Massive furnaces lined the cavern walls, their fiery glow projecting lengthy shadows. Quentin looked closer and noticed Dwarves moving with skilled precision, their hammers ringing out in a regular cadence as they worked.

This was a living forge where the quintessence of the earth was transformed into works of art and power.

Out of the darkness, a figure materialized, his authoritative presence eliciting immediate respect. He noticed Griffin at the front and greeted him with the dwarven salute, a hand to his heart and a bow of his head.

"M'liege," Thrain rumbled, stepping forward. He was broad and compact, with a beard plaited in silver and gold. "Name's Thrain, Master o' the Forge. What business drags outsiders tae our gates?"

"We've come tae speak wi' me uncle," Griffin said gruffly, hands resting atop his battle axe as he propped himself on it. A flicker of recognition passed through Thrain's eyes—family, but not warmth. Griffin's grip held tightly on the haft—a tacit warning.

Quentin moved ahead, his hand resting lightly on the hilt of his sword. "Thank you for receiving us, Master Thrain. We seek your aid in a matter of great importance. The dwarves are unmatched in strength, and their metalcraft can counter magic."

Thrain's gaze was piercing, eyes flicking over each member of the team before settling back on Quentin. "Aye, I ken why ye've come. Word o' yer quest's reached my folk already. But mark me well—our steel's not handed out for naught. The Dwarves dinnae fight for causes that serve no gain. If ye want our axes, ye'll earn them."

A trace of frustration tightened Quentin's jaw as he met Thrain's gaze. "The threat we face is not ours alone. It endangers all realms. We need to remain united, or we will all fall."

Thrain examined him for a long moment, the quiet broken by the clanging of the hammers. "Words dinnae win wars. We're folk o' deed. Prove yer cause, and ye'll have our steel."

"Freedom's no' enough for ye?" Griffin said, low and sharp.

Thrain narrowed his eyes at Griffin. "Mind yer tongue,

Griffin—son o' Dragoon, chief o' the Silverback clan. We dinnae bend the knee tae the council, and we sure as stone don't take orders from you."

Griffin straightened, lifting his chin as he leveled a hard stare at Thrain.

Quentin's breath hitched. This wasn't going as he had hoped. "You said that we could prove our cause is worthy. What must we do?"

"There is a task," Thrain said, slow and deliberate, a glint of iron in his smile. "Beyond these walls lies the Dark Passage—stone that fights back, tunnels that twist and swallow. Deep within is a gem our forgers have sought for generations. Bring it back, and ye'll have our aid."

Even Griffin, who feared little, had gone pale at the name. Griffin stiffened beside Quentin, fingers clenching round the hilt at his side. "Ye want us tae march into that gods-forsaken hole and fetch a gem? That's not a task—it's a death sentence."

Quentin felt a shift in the air; this was worse than he'd feared.

Thrain didn't flinch. "If ye mean tae earn our steel, ye'll prove yerselves. The Passage is cruel, aye—but if yer cause is true, and the Gods favor ye, ye'll find what waits in the dark."

Quentin glanced at his team, the resolve in their looks echoing his own. "Then we accept the challenge. We will return with the gem."

The words tasted like iron. Commitment, cost, and the weight of every life depend on them.

"Quentin—" Iain began. "We can't take Izzy into that."

Izzy's expression flickered, then smoothed into neutrality.

Quentin met Iain's eyes. He thought of his mother—of duty and cost.

"You'll stay here with her," he said. "If we do not return, take Izzy to Aeloria and send word to The House of Fas."

Iain sputtered, but the order stood. He stepped back, jaw

locked.

Quentin stepped toward Griffin and Thrain.

Thrain's gaze eased, just a shade, beard twitching as he spoke. "Ye've leave tae rest in our halls. The road will test yer mettle. Take the trials or be stripped to bone."

They followed Thrain through winding tunnels, the hammering fading behind them. When they emerged, a city opened before them—streets carved from the mountain, forges burning like suns, and passages that led deeper into the mountain. Thrain spread his arms.

"Welcome ta Umbrahold, m'liege," Thrain announced, motioning toward the city before them.

Thrain led them to a building that shone softly from its windows. Quentin wondered how the Dwarves maintained an appearance of day and night, for no light came in from the outside. Griffin seemed more at ease in this place than he had been in Aeloria. They were led inside, and Thrain promised them food and shelter. They entered a tavern whose chatter died at their arrival.

Rhys let out a humorless huff. "Well, this will be fun," he mused.

CHAPTER TWENTY-FIVE

Quentin

Umbrahold, Dwarven stronghold

Quentin's gaze swept the room, taking in the patrons' open stares. The tavern was low-ceilinged and stone-walled, with thick beams running overhead. He ducked beneath one of the low-hanging wrought-iron chandeliers. Weapons and banners lined the walls; the oak tables bore grooves and scars from years of rowdy use. A roaring fire filled the hearth, pushing back the cavern's chill.

The dwarf patrons, broad-shouldered and bearded, watched them with narrowed eyes.

Mugs sat untouched. The usual banter had died; an uneasy silence settled between the tables, taut as a drawn bowstring.

"What does one need ta do ta get a good ale 'round here?" Griffin bellowed, breaking the silence and grinning as he strode to the bar. His voice echoed off the stone, and the spell broke.

A few patrons grunted; the tension eased as Griffin's energy spread. Not all the dwarves relaxed; a few still watched them with flinty suspicion. The barkeep, a gruff-looking dwarf with a thick red beard, eyed Griffin for a moment.

"Ha! At last, a soul who can light a room wi' more than just a torch!" the barkeep roared, filling a mug and sliding it to Griffin.

The team followed Griffin's lead, moving toward the bar as murmurs of conversation gradually returned, though wary eyes stayed fixed on them. Quentin sat at the bar, nervous despite the hearth's warmth. Every hour spent here was an hour Demetrius gained, and Quentin couldn't shake the fear that Blythe and Hera were facing those dangers alone. He wished he could reach Blythe through a comm-portal again, even for a heartbeat—just to hear her voice steady him.

Iain announced he was heading up to bed, took his key from the barkeep with a curt nod, and headed for the stairs. Quentin didn't need magic to read the frustration in Iain's heavy steps.

"What's his trouble?" Griffin asked, dropping onto the stool beside Quentin.

"He's upset because I asked him to stay behind with Izzy," Quentin replied, glancing at the stairs.

"I'm not staying behind while you all go into danger." She slid onto the stool on his other side, clearly having lingered within earshot.

Quentin tensed. "This isn't up for debate. Mother would never forgive me if all her heirs walked into near-certain death. I need you here—safe."

Izzy's defiance didn't waver, but her gaze softened a touch. "I get why you're doing this, but that doesn't mean I have to like it."

"I don't like it either," Quentin admitted. "But you need to be strong here—for all of us. Promise me you'll look after Iain. He's stubborn, but he'll listen to you. If anything happens to me, you must keep the kingdom steady."

"I'll stay with him. You'd better promise me you'll come back."

Quentin met her gaze. "That's the plan." At least he hoped he would. But fate had a habit of rewriting plans.

Quentin glanced around the tavern. Cael and Rhys were deep in discussion by the fire; Freya spoke quietly with the barkeep.

"I'm heading to bed," Izzy announced, pushing her stool back and rising.

"Sleep well," Griffin called as he leapt up and bowed with

exaggerated flair.

"You too," Izzy responded with a faint smile. She gave Quentin a nod, which he returned, and retrieved her room key from the bartender. As she ascended the stairs, her footsteps were silenced by the roar of the tavern's evening revelry.

Griffin took another swig. "So, what's yer plan, boss?"

"We leave early, and hopefully, when we succeed, you can get some of your brethren to take my brother and sister back to Aeloria," Quentin replied.

"They won't like that," Griffin said gruffly.

"Too bad. I won't let them risk their lives and the future of the Fae." Quentin's voice trailed as he stared into his tankard.

Griffin raised an eyebrow.

Griffin leaned in. "There's more to it, innit?"

Quentin nodded slowly. "Iain's hiding something—and whatever it is, he's willing to stay behind for it. He'd have argued to come."

"Aye," Griffin mused, his eyes narrowing thoughtfully. "What's he up to?"

"That's the question," Quentin said, swirling his drink.

Griffin took another sip of his ale, his gaze steady on Quentin. "Might be worth keepin' an eye on him. If he's up to somethin', it could be important."

Quentin nodded in agreement. "I plan to. He never keeps things from me for long. Maybe Izzy knows more than she's saying."

Griffin's expression grew serious as he contemplated the gravity of Quentin's words. "Aye, boss. Might be best we sort it out on our own. We'll keep a sharp eye on him—can't be lettin' any surprises slip through."

They sat, thoughts heavy despite the tavern's rising noise. They drained their mugs. Quentin excused himself and headed up to his room for bed.

Quentin slept fitfully, his mind circling Iain and the mission. At the morning chime, he gathered his gear. The group moved quickly, the previous night's talk lingering between them.

He cast one last look at Umbrahold, quiet in the dawn, and led the team toward the Dark Passage.

CHAPTER TWENTY-SIX

Blythe

Travel to the air strip in Upstate, NY

The steady sound of tires on pavement gave way to the crunch of gravel as the car shifted beneath them. Blythe and Hera sat in the back, separated from the outside by tinted glass. Anticipation tightened the air in the car. Every mile they traveled was another mile Demetrius gained—and Blythe couldn't shake the fear that the Council or the Warlocks might reach the stones first.

Blythe leaned forward while Tavian steered onto a narrow dirt road and stopped at an empty security gate. Trees crowded in, almost hiding them from view.

Tavian rolled down the window, tapped his security pass on the panel, and the gate opened with a groan. Beyond, Blythe saw that the airfield and airplane hangars stretched out, with long shadows in the cool evening. The setting sun lit the horizon in orange and pink, casting the scene in an eerie, dreamlike light.

The car eased to a stop outside a hangar, and Tavian turned off the engine. He stepped out, a dark silhouette in the fading light, and crossed to enter a side door.

The large hangar door rumbled open, its echo rolling across the empty field. Tavian reappeared, climbing back into the car. He steered the car inside and parked it where shadows hid it from prying eyes. Hera leaned in, breath catching at the sight of the small plane waiting in the building's center. Under the hangar lights, the aircraft gleamed like a silver bird.

"What is that?" Hera whispered.

Tavian, quick with a smile, replied, "That's a private airplane. This will be unlike any ride you've had—might even beat a dragon or a magic carpet. It's nice to be in a climate-controlled space while soaring."

"Less risk of falling, I'd imagine?" Hera said, a quiver of unease threaded her humor.

Blythe caught the tremor in Hera's voice.

Tavian shrugged. "If you mean falling out, yes. Our magical flying is more reliable."

"Is this really a good idea?" Hera asked, her eyes darting nervously to the plane as if seeking assurance from the machine itself. Blythe moved to the back of the car to retrieve their luggage.

"It's all we've got," Blythe said. "We can't take a commercial flight, and a boat would take too long—honestly, it'd probably be just as risky."

"Planes aren't that bad. You'll see." Tavian hefted a bag onto his shoulder, his nonchalant attitude seemingly unshaken. He set off toward the plane. Blythe hung back, helping Hera unload the rest of their gear.

Equipment rustled, and zippers rasped as they readied for takeoff.

Blythe cast a glance toward the cockpit, where Tavian was already immersed in his pre-flight checks. He glanced up occasionally, checking the horizon.

Tavian finished with a nod, his gaze returning to them as they completed their own preparations.

"Everything's set," he said. "Let's get seated."

Blythe glanced around the plane's interior. It was surprisingly spacious, with enough room for their equipment and for them to settle comfortably for the flight.

As Blythe and Hera strapped themselves into their seats, Blythe took a deep breath. Jet fuel and sterile cabin air filled her lungs. The plane slowly pulled out of the hangar and began taxiing down the runway, the rumble of its wheels on the tarmac resonating through the cabin. Her heart raced with pre-flight anxiety. She watched the hangars shrink behind them, the world blurring into twilight.

They gained speed, lifted, and the ground fell away—stars pricking the dark as the world shrank below. Blythe glanced at Hera, whose knuckles were turning white as she gripped the armrests of her seat. The ordinarily unflappable woman was visibly tense, her calm fraying at the edges. Blythe met Hera's eyes and offered a reassuring smile. Hera grimaced; Blythe kept her sympathy to herself—better not to try to comfort a Valkyrie.

Minutes passed before Hera's fingers unclenched and relaxed. She kept watching the dark below until her shoulders finally lowered and her breath slowed. Blythe closed her eyes and let sleep edge toward her.

They flew through the night; city lights twinkled below as Blythe's thoughts turned to strategy and a cautious hope.

She pictured Quentin's silhouette against a firelight she'd seen once. For a moment, the ache of missing him and the fear of losing him braided together. She wished she could talk to him, even for a moment.

Benjamin's shadow loomed at the edge of her thoughts—the threat he posed, the choices he'd made, the danger he still represented.

The tightness in her shoulders loosened as if someone had eased a hand from her back. A faint chill threaded through her, the same cold that always came when fear and longing tangled together. One step closer now. With Hera and Tavian at her side, she felt steadier, and she let herself hope that Quentin had someone watching his flank as well.

The plane hit the runway, and the cabin shuddered

through her. Across from her, Hera's fingers dug into the armrests. Her face had drained of color; her mouth was a thin line. Blythe kept her mouth shut. There would be time for jokes later.

As the plane stopped, Hera sagged with relief. Blythe unbuckled her seatbelt and rose, making her way to the cockpit. Tavian was finishing up his post-flight notes, his expression focused yet relaxed. He turned before she spoke, offering a knowing smile.

"So, how'd Hera handle the landing?" he teased, glancing past her to where Hera was hastily gathering their supplies.

"She was fine," Blythe lied smoothly, a hint of amusement in her tone. "I'm hoping you have a vehicle to get us to both the stone and a portal to get back to the magic realm."

"Of course," Tavian replied, his eyes flicking back to his clipboard as he finished jotting down notes. "And as for the portal manor, I should hope the keeper will let us through."

Blythe arched an eyebrow. "Why is that?"

Tavian set his clipboard down on the instrument panel and met her gaze with a small, almost mischievous smile. "He's my brother."

A jolt of surprise shot through her at the reminder. She'd known he'd turned down a keepership, but she hadn't realized it was one House they might need access to.

He still didn't look like someone who would have been a Keeper. Keepers were akin to lords, their positions appointed by the magic that governed the realms.

"I suppose I should have told you sooner," Tavian continued, his voice light, though an undercurrent of something more ran beneath it. He stepped closer, and the cockpit seemed to shrink around them.

"There's more to my past than I've said," he added. There was something unspoken in his tone—was it about his brother? Or about the House he'd walked away from?

Blythe's breath hitched. She stepped back before she

realized she'd moved.

"Is that so?" she asked, her voice steady, though she couldn't quite mask the edge in it.

Tavian's smile remained, though his eyes took on a more serious glint.

"It is. We both have ties to the Keepers, and we both made our choices for a reason. You accepted your Keepership—maybe because you didn't know you could refuse it, maybe because you knew someone else wouldn't have been the right fit.

"I realized I could do more outside a House. Being the brother of a Keeper doesn't make me any less committed to what we're fighting for."

Blythe nodded slowly, trying to process this new information while keeping her emotions in check.

Something in his tone hovered between challenge and invitation. Blythe couldn't quite tell. What she did know was that she wasn't ready to delve into whatever strange feeling she was getting from him.

"I actually knew that about you already," she said, a bit more briskly than she intended. "Anyway, we have stones to find."

Tavian's expression remained unreadable, but he nodded in agreement.

"Of course. But, Blythe," he added, his voice softening again, "You don't have to shoulder all of this alone."

"I appreciate that," she said, keeping her tone neutral. "But right now, we have a mission."

Tavian gave a small nod of understanding, though there was a hint of something like disappointment in his eyes.

"Let's get to it."

CHAPTER TWENTY-SEVEN

Blythe

Inverness, Scotland

They stepped out of the plane into fresh air, permeated with earth and the far-off promise of rain. Another hangar waited ahead, its wide bay door open. Beyond it, she could see the trees in the distance, past the airstrip and the metal fence.

Their destination waited several miles beyond the tree line.

Hera slung her pack over her shoulder and joined Blythe and Tavian as they moved toward a waiting vehicle, a rugged all-terrain vehicle, built for this kind of trip.

Tavian climbed into the driver's seat, his usual air of confidence seeming to return as he took control of the vehicle. Hera settled into the back, while Blythe took the passenger seat beside him. The engine rumbled to life, and they set off—the tires kicking up dirt as they sped away from the small airstrip toward their destination.

They drove in silence at first. Blythe couldn't shake the feeling that Demetrius was just one step behind them. She kept her eyes on the horizon, where the forest came further into view with every passing minute. She wondered where Quentin was now—whether he was safe, whether he was thinking of her too.

"So, what do you know about this place we're going to?" Hera asked from the back seat.

Tavian handed Blythe his phone. She skimmed the first result. "Okay, listen to this—'Eas a' Chual Aluinn is the tallest waterfall in Britain, dropping a massive 200 meters—almost four times the height of Niagara Falls.'"

She peered at the screen. "It's in the Highlands, near Loch Glencoul. Says here the hike's about 6 miles round-trip, but it's boggy and unmarked. You can also see it from a boat if you're not up for slogging through the mud."

Blythe flicked through again. "Oh, and the name means 'waterfall of the beautiful tresses.' That's kind of poetic."

She peeked up. "So... majestic death trap or scenic detour?"

"Either sounds fun to me," Hera said with a laugh.

Tavian's grip shifted on the wheel while maneuvering a rough patch of road. "Death trap is what I'm worried about. If the stone has been there for centuries, who knows what kind of defenses it might have built up?" He smiled. "At least we won't have to worry about getting through the Portal Manor."

Blythe's mind drifted back to Tavian's brother. She had so many questions—about Tavian, his past, and how much she could fully trust him. Benjamin's choices still haunted her—a reminder that even family could turn dangerous when power was involved. But now wasn't the time to investigate those uncertainties; they needed to focus on the task at hand.

"How much do you trust your brother?" she asked, keeping her voice neutral.

Tavian didn't answer right away. His gaze stayed fixed on the road ahead, but Blythe could see the strain in his jaw. "My brother... he's a complicated man. We've always been close, but our paths diverged a long time ago. He stayed in the family business. I didn't. But I do believe he'll help us. He may be tied to the Keepers, but he's no friend of the Council." Something in the way he said it made her wonder what he'd given up, and why he avoided talking about it.

"Even if your grandfather is?" Hera spoke up.

"He's not fond of our grandfather, either," Tavian said with a frown.

Hera leaned forward, interest sparked. "So, if he's not with the Council, what's his angle?"

Tavian sighed, his face troubled. "He's a pragmatist. He'll do what benefits him most, and right now, helping us is the best way to secure his own interests. But don't mistake that for loyalty. If things start to look bad, he won't hesitate to protect himself, even if it means leaving us to fend for ourselves."

Blythe absorbed the details, filing them away as the scenery started to shift. Scraggly birch and rowan trees dotted the hills like abandoned sentinels, their branches contorted by years of Highland weather. Mist wrapped low to the ground, looping around rocks and pooling in hollows.

The trail emerged ahead, little more than a suggestion —muddy, uneven, and carved through bog and scree. Tavian slowed the vehicle, steering carefully around waterlogged dips and jagged outcroppings. The silence stretched, expansive and eerie, broken only by the far-off cry of a gull or the quiet rustle of the grass. It felt less like a forest and more like a place the earth had never fully welcomed.

As they continued forward, the tension among them grew palpable. Blythe could feel it in the way Tavian's gaze kept sweeping between the road and the terrain.

"We're close," Tavian murmured, his voice hushed. "The path to the waterfall should be straight ahead."

The terrain changed as they neared the falls. The moorland unfolded ahead, bleak and sodden, with heather clinging to the earth.

Something brushed past the edge of Blythe's awareness —silent, patient, cold.

For a heartbeat, she wondered if Benjamin had found a way into the Human Realm. If he did, would he know what they were after and where to find them?

They stepped out of the car into a calm of wind and mist, the air damp and tinged by peat. Packs thrown over their shoulders, they began the hike—footwear sinking into the soft earth with every step. The trail was barely marked, winding through heather-strewn moorland and past jagged outcrops jutting from the earth like old bones.

As they climbed a soft incline, Blythe paused. A low, far-off roar could be heard like rolling thunder. The further they walked, the sound grew louder, becoming more forceful until it saturated the air with a measured rhythm. The waterfall was near.

The wind carried hints of wet rock and mildew. They crested the rise, and before them lay a winding river, a silver thread snaking through the moorland toward the base of Eas a' Chual Aluinn. The waterfall thundered down the cliff face in a glistening torrent, mist rising in ghostly plumes. Blythe quickened her pace, pulled toward it. Behind her, Hera's sword rasped free, but Blythe scarcely noticed the sound. She knew only one thing: the stone was behind the falls.

They dropped their packs at the foot of the cliff, the ground coated in spray and moss. The climb was steep and treacherous, the rock face slick and unforgiving. Blythe led the way, fingers finding holds in the timeworn stone, boots sliding but never failing. The waterfall's roar filled their ears and rattled their bones.

After what felt like an eternity, they reached a narrow ledge halfway up the cliff. Mist drifted around them, and the falls crashed beside them, so close that the spray soaked their clothes and blurred their vision. Blythe pressed forward and ducked behind the curtain of water.

The world shifted.

Behind the falls, the noise lowered to a muffled roar. A narrow cleft in the rock opened into a small cave, hidden from view and preserved through the centuries. The space within was cool and still, saturated with dampness and something ageless—something watching.

At the cave's center rested the stone.

It was half-buried in the earth, its surface coated with moisture and engraved with ancient runes that glowed dimly in the faint light beating like a heart. Blythe approached, the vibration of magic rising in her ears, quivering through her chest. It felt familiar. The stone in the desert. The one at her dig site. Similar, but not the same.

She crouched next to the stone, her breath quick.

"This is it," Tavian said. "The first stone in the Human Realm."

Blythe drew a steady inhale, carrying the load of their mission on her shoulders. They had found one stone. It felt... wrong. Too easy. She studied the runes.

"We need to move quickly," Hera said, her voice tense. "We don't know how long before someone else shows up."

Blythe nodded, putting out her hand to trace the runes with her fingers. The instant her fingers touched the runes, cold flared up her arm, sharp as ice beneath her skin. She gasped and jerked her hand back. The stone's magic was powerful—wild and unbridled, like a storm trapped beneath her skin.

"We'll need to disable whatever defenses it has," Tavian said, his voice composed but focused. "Then we can extract it."

Blythe stood, her thoughts swirling as she weighed their options. They had reached this far, but she knew this wasn't the real challenge.

CHAPTER TWENTY-EIGHT

Octo

Land of Valoria

He waited for the camp to quiet, for the fires to dim and the warlocks to sleep, before he moved. The climb was slick and treacherous, but he proceeded with caution. He scaled the cliff, the spray soaking him through.

At the ledge, he took cover behind the curtain of water before entering the cave.

The air inside hummed with enchantment, and the walls resonated as if they were breathing. At the middle rested the stone—half-buried, inscribed with runes. Magic pulsated in his chest, echoing the relentless rhythm of the sea.

He moved nearer, heart beating fast. This was the proof Blythe had dreaded. If Demetrius and Zelos controlled the stones, they controlled the portals—and the realms themselves.

Then—movement in the dark.

Octo froze, ducking behind a pointed stone as two figures entered. Their eyes shone red, and as they came deeper into the cave, he began to recognize their voices.

"There it is," Zelos said, stepping forward.

"Care to do the honors?" Melya asked, the sound of her voice silk over steel.

"Don't mind if I do." Zelos reached for the stone. It flamed in his hand, radiating with power, then diminished as he slid it into a pouch at his hip. "Three down. Three more to go."

"Do you think Demetrius's friends in the human realm

will really get those stones for us?" Melya asked, following him as he headed for the exit.

"They'd better. And Demetrius had better get the Evans girl on board. Our plans depend on it."

Their voices dissolved beneath the waterfall's roar. Octo remained motionless, every muscle locked until the last echo of footsteps dissolved into the spray.

Octo slipped from the cave—swift and silent, nerves firing.

He had to reach Eyra and the Council. The balance between realms was tipping fast, and Zelos's scheme was darker, deeper, and more insidious than anyone had feared. He could only hope Blythe and Hera were faring better in the human realm.

There was no time to wait for Demetrius's group to descend. Octo launched himself down the mountain, intent on reaching the coast before they did. They couldn't know he'd left the main group to follow them. He needed a cover: an errand, a meeting, anything plausible. Anything to mask the truth of his espionage.

The path back was a slog through wet brush and sucking mud. Octo pushed through, his boots settling into the wet ground, drawing in short, measured breaths.

He reached the shoreline and dove in, parting the water with desperate speed. The swim was faster than before, but it drained him—limbs burning, lungs aching, thoughts blurring at the edges.

As the rebel camp came into view, Octo's awareness sharpened. The camp buzzed and thrummed with activity—scouts returning, fires crackling, voices growing louder—but he avoided the main paths, slipping into a shadowed alcove near the outer perimeter.

There, below a canopy of twisted branches, he knelt and drew out his bewitched mirror. The surface glistened, waiting. He had to report what he'd seen before Zelos's plan advanced another step.

When Eyra's image appeared, her authoritative presence carried a comforting antithesis to the disorder in Octo's anxious mind. Her piercing eyes met his, full of concern and expectation.

"Eyra," Octo's voice had a low, urgent murmur. "I've found something critical. Blythe reached out to me several days ago, suspecting that Demetrius was after the magical stones used to create the portals. I followed Demetrius and a few warlocks when they left camp, and Zelos confirmed her suspicions. They already possess three of the stones—and three remain. Whatever they intend, it cannot be good. If Demetrius controlled all six, the portals—and the realms—would be his to command."

He hesitated, jaw tightening. "And Benjamin's involvement only makes it worse. He's bitter and angry, making him unpredictable—and dangerous. They also said something about needing someone or something they called the Unbound. I think that might be Blythe."

Eyra's expression stiffened as she absorbed the news. "Are you certain? What do the stones do, and what is an Unbound?"

"Yes, I'm certain," Octo replied, his voice composed in spite of the seriousness of the situation. "But I don't know exactly what the stones do, or what that term means. Blythe said they were used to form the portals and could also destroy them. To what end, I'm not sure. Maybe to let the dark realm spill into ours unchecked, or to let magic-born cross freely into the human realm. Either way, the why matters less than stopping them."

Eyra's expression stiffened as she absorbed the news. "If they succeed, the fallout will be devastating. We must act quickly to secure the portals and counter Demetrius's scheme."

"Indeed," Octo said, his eyes narrowing. "I'll collect additional information about their goals for using the stones. Blythe must retrieve the ones from the human realm, and we need to make sure Quentin and Griffin secure the others here."

"Agreed," Eyra said, her tone authoritative. "I'll coordinate with the Council and prepare a strategy to counter this threat. Keep me abreast of any news."

"I'll send updates the moment I have more information," Octo replied.

The mirror's surface darkened as the communication ended, leaving Octo in the soft radiance of the moon. He slipped the mirror back into his pouch; the impact of what he'd learned settled hard across his shoulders. Pale daybreak light edged over the horizon. He wondered how many understood the truth and how many were helping hide it.

Octo's thoughts sped as he made his way back to the heart of the camp. The rebels' routine continued, the sounds of their preparations blending with the morning birdsong. He observed the busy scene with a sense of detached urgency, aware that every single moment mattered.

Octo was deep in thought when one of the rebel commanders approached—a tall, weathered man with a gruff demeanor. "You look like you've stared down a sea wraith, Octo," the commander remarked, his tone edged with concern.

"Not quite," Octo replied. "All's well."

The commander nodded and moved on.

Time was running out. Everything they'd fought for rested on a knife's edge, and Octo knew that swift action was required. He needed to alert Blythe and Quentin, prepare them for the confrontation ahead, and ensure the dark forces were contained before they could wreak havoc.

CHAPTER TWENTY-NINE

Quentin

Umbrahold, Dwarven stronghold

Quentin and Griffin stood near the entrance to the Dark Passage. The wind blew through the narrow canyon—a warning of what lay ahead. Just as he advanced, a familiar mental tug pulled at him. He froze, tilting his head slightly, listening.

"What is it, Que?" Griffin asked.

Before he could respond, the air around them shimmered faintly. A soft light emerged from the small communication stone hidden in his pocket. He pulled it out, noticing the distinct light pattern that signaled a direct connection from Octo.

The group tensed, watching as Quentin activated the stone. A faint image of Octo appeared in view, projected by the stone's magic. His expression was pale and solemn.

"Octo," Quentin greeted, keeping his voice even despite the tension winding inside him. "What's going on?"

"Quentin," Octo began, his voice pressing, "I've got bad news. Blythe was right—Demetrius is after the magic stones. The Warlocks have obtained the two from the Dark Realm, and they just secured one from the Magic Realm. I don't know yet what Blythe's status is. Have you heard from her?"

"No, not yet. I know they were heading out to get one of them, though." A sharp worry cut through him.

"I also overheard Demetrius about someone—he's got an ally who's going to help him get the stones from the Human Realm."

Quentin felt the bottom drop out of his chest. If Demetrius got the rest, the realms wouldn't stand a chance.

"Did you hear where the other stone in the Magic Realm is?" Quentin asked, his thoughts scrambling.

Octo shook his head. "Not yet. But I'll let you know as soon as I do."

"We're in a tight spot," Octo continued, sensing the tension. "But if you can get the Dwarves on board quickly, maybe we can still beat Demetrius to the stone in Sylvannor."

Quentin nodded, his decision made. "We'll finish here as fast as we can. Once the Dwarves are with us, I'll connect with Blythe, and hopefully, by then, you'll know where the second Magic Realm stone is. But we'll need to move quickly. Demetrius won't wait."

Octo's image wavered. "I'll remain alert here and delay them as much as possible while I try to gather more information. But you'll need to hurry."

"We will," Quentin promised. "Stay safe, Octo. We'll meet up with you as soon as we can."

The connection faded, and the stone went dark. Quentin slipped it into his pocket and turned to face Griffin and the others. He'd never been prone to anxiety—not until this mission.

"Let's get this done," he said, his tone strong. "We need the Dwarves, and we need them now."

Griffin nodded, the conviction in his eyes matching Quentin's. "Then we'd better not waste any more time."

With that, Quentin led the way into the Dark Passage. Even under pressure, a thin thread of hope held. They might still have a chance to shift the balance in this war.

The group shared looks as they began their descent into the darkened pass. The night before, over drinks at the pub, they'd carefully avoided discussing what might await them. Quentin half-wished he'd asked, but he had to trust they were ready. They were the best of the Fae. And they had a fearless Dwarven warrior. They could handle this.

They had to. He had to believe they would succeed, that

he would be reunited with Blythe—and find a way to mend the relationship he'd broken. The longer he was away from her, the sharper the pang became. For someone unaccustomed to feeling needy, the sensation was strange—and painful.

Quentin forced himself to refocus on the mission. The canyon walls pressed in, rough stones looming on either side, casting elongated shadows that shifted with every footstep. The breeze became colder. The only sounds were their boots grinding over loose stone and the far-off, eerie howl of wind floating through the narrow passage.

Ahead, Griffin led the way. His presence comforted Quentin, reminding him that Griffin knew this terrain far better than he did. The rest of the team, each thoughtfully selected for their skill and courage, followed in tense silence.

Quentin could feel the shadows closing in on them. The pressure of the mountain above and the uncertainty of what was in store below. He wondered what test of strength or cunning they'd have to overcome to get the gem and earn their alliance. The doubt persisted, but he knew better than to ask. The Dwarves were proud and secretive. They had offered their help, but it would not come easily.

"Stay close," Quentin murmured.

As if in response, the ground began to tremble. A distant grumble rose from the depths of the earth. The group halted, hands snapping to their weapons. Quentin's heart beat rapidly as he scanned the shadows, looking for the origin of the disturbance.

The path before them split open with a deafening crack, exposing a yawning gorge that vanished into darkness. Its jagged walls plunged into a current of molten lava that bubbled and churned far below, throwing a ghostly red glow up through the passage.

"Och aye, this is the mighty trial, is it?" Griffin snorted, eyeing the chasm like it'd offended his ancestors. "Standin' here starin' at a glorified hole, tryin' not tae nod off. I've seen fiercer fissures in me uncle's beard, and he's been dead twenty years!"

Quentin nodded, his thoughts already racing as he considered their options.

"We'll need to cross carefully," Quentin said, calm in the face of the rising unease. "Griffin, you're the expert on Dwarven trials. Any advice?"

Griffin's sharp eyes swept along the uneven edges. At last, he let out a satisfied grunt. "Dwarves dinnae make things easy, right enough," he muttered, squinting at the rock face. "But we don't deal in daft impossibles, neither. There's always a way if ye've got the spine for it."

He jabbed a thick finger toward a line of near-invisible steps inscribed on the chasm wall. "There. See them wee bastards? That's our path. We'll need tae tread light, though—one slip, and it's a long, screamin' drop tae regret."

"Oh, good. I was worried today might lack mortal peril," Freya muttered.

Quentin signaled for the team to follow Griffin's lead. One by one, they edged along the narrow steps, their movements cautious.

As they made their way across, Quentin couldn't get rid of the feeling that this was wasting time. The mission pressed on him, heavy and relentless.

Finally, they reached the other side. Solid ground met their feet, and Quentin let out a slow breath of relief, though he knew this marked just the start. The real test awaited deep within the heart of the Dwarven tunnels.

"Keep moving," he urged. "We're not out of this yet."

Griffin nodded, the look on his face hardening while they advanced into the darkness. As they moved further into the Dark Passage, a small trace of hope steadied him, stoking his determination. They would find the stone, secure the Dwarves' alliance, and turn the tide in the battle for the realms.

CHAPTER THIRTY

Octo

Land of Valoria

The camp lay silent, save for the pop of a dying fire and the soft rustling of leaves. Octo waited in the shadows, focused on Demetrius's tent. What he'd overheard still churned in his mind. He couldn't afford to leave anything to chance—not with the stones, and not with Demetrius's plans.

Demetrius and the Warlocks had returned the day after him. From what he could gather, no one had mentioned his disappearance—thankfully. He'd been listening closely to the low talks around camp. Word of entire villages being wiped out by creatures from the dark realm was spreading, and unease simmered through the camp. The rebels who had joined the cause before "rescuing" the Warlocks were becoming restless. Their anger toward the Council remained, but now it was beginning to shift toward Demetrius and his allies.

Octo crossed paths with Bertolf, freshly returned from warning the other Werewolf nations. He wasn't his usual peppy self. He looked ten years older—not physically, but in his demeanor. Lean and weary from countless strains, his angular features had lost their youthful softness. His brooding gray-blue eyes studied Octo as he approached.

"Where did you run off to, Octo?" he asked as they walked the perimeter of the camp, careful to avoid the prying eyes and ears of their fellow rebels. He slid his hands inside the pockets of his fitted green jacket, its seams reinforced for travel. His weathered boots moved softly over the leaf-strewn ground.

"You know what—no. Better not to tell me." He smiled, momentarily, and the age vanished from his face. "I'm just glad you're here. And okay."

"Thank you."

Bertolf hesitated, then lowered his voice. "The were-worlf clans listened. Most of them, anyway. They won't trust Demetrius. Or the Council. Not after what I told them." His jaw tightened. "They'll fight—but only for the right side."

Octo's chest eased with a breath he hadn't realized he'd been holding. "Good. That's exactly what we needed."

"I'm guessing whatever you were up to has something to do with Blythe, Hera, Quentin, and Griffin," Bertolf said with an impish grin. "I'd be happy to help, if you want backup."

"I appreciate it," Octo replied, clapping him on the back. "But for now, it's better if you keep your head down. Go grab some dinner. I'll check in with you later."

Bertolf nodded and loped off, leaving Octo alone with his thoughts. He could have asked him to keep watch—but he knew better. In their wolf forms, Werewolves shared thoughts with their pack. Even if Bertolf wanted to keep a secret, he wouldn't be able to. His suspicions would pass through the bond, unspoken but known.

Still, Octo hoped Bertolf's youth might work in their favor. Maybe the others would chalk it up to juvenile nerves.

As the last of the rebels on night watch passed by, Octo moved, his steps light and soundless as he slipped toward Zelos's tent. Zelos had gone to meet with Demetrius, so Octo didn't have much time. He'd trained for moments like this, when stealth was his only ally. He steadied his pulse with slow breaths as he approached. The subdued brightness inside flickered. He paused, listening to any sound within. Hearing nothing but the soft hum of voices far off, he lifted the flap just enough to slip inside.

The interior of Zelos's tent was crowded with maps, scrolls, and unusual relics that radiated a faint, uncanny illumination. Octo didn't understand magic, but he hoped he wouldn't need much knowledge of it to find what he was looking for. A large table dominated the center of the room. Fortunately, he didn't need light to see—merpeople had long adapted to the pitch-black depths of the ocean floor. Octo's gaze shifted to the corner of the tent, where a small chest sat half-hidden underneath a heap of robes. His gut told him this was what he needed to investigate.

Moving quickly, he crossed the tent. The chest itself was simple, but the lock was anything but. He knelt beside it, tracing the elaborate patterns carved into the metal. Pulling a small pick from his belt, he began working on the mechanism, every sense sharpened. He knew he didn't have much time. When the lock opened, Octo hesitated, looking around once more. Shadows played across the tent walls, but nothing stirred outside. Drawing a steady inhale, he lifted the lid.

Inside, nestled among folds of black velvet, were two stones, each no larger than a fist. The energy they radiated was so dark it appeared to engulf the light. Octo's breath caught for a beat. These had to be the stones from the Dark Realm. He couldn't take them now; that would raise suspicion. And though he didn't know much about magic, he knew most enchanted objects emitted a distinct magical signature. If he took them and stayed in the camp, he'd be discovered for sure. He'd have to retrieve them another time.

But how did Demetrius even know about them? Octo hadn't heard their legend until Blythe. Maybe the stones were secrets kept by the highest Warlocks. Demetrius wasn't one of them; he must've learned in the Dark Realm. His escape was still a mystery. Some said he'd never gone at all, but then how did he know about the stones? Questions piled up that he didn't have time to unravel.

He searched for anything that might expose more about their plans. He found maps—some of the Dark Realm, others of the human world—with locations circled and signified by enigmatic runes. Then the sound of voices outside grew louder.

Octo paused.

The tent flap rustled, and shapes passed across the entrance, sending a flood of panic through him. Quickly, he rolled the map back up, replaced it in the chest, and closed the lid just as the flap lifted slightly.

Octo dropped to the floor, slipped beneath the tent wall, and rolled out, flattening himself against the earth. He lowered the tent fabric as Zelos and another person entered. It was Melya.

"We must move faster," Zelos said, soft-spoken and urgent. "The Council is closing in on our movements, and they're making progress with guarding the portals again."

The lantern flared, their shadows thrown across the tent walls like a twisted puppet show.

Melya nodded as she moved toward the chest. Octo's breath caught when she reached down, brushing her hand over the lid. Tension hung in the air, and a drop of sweat slid down his neck. If Melya opened the chest and found anything out of place...

"So, tomorrow we set off for the second stone in the magic realm?" Melya said at last, turning away from the chest. Octo exhaled silently in relief. "I suspect the stone there will be more heavily guarded."

Zelos sat back as he spoke. "What are your thoughts on this ally of Demetrius's? Do you think they'll be trustworthy? If they're caught, it could ruin everything."

Melya sat across from him. "Demetrius and the others have been very clear about how much they hate the Council. They'll do whatever it takes to see it fall. But as long as this ally knows nothing of our true intentions with the stones, we should be fine. They think they're helping us gain power to take down the Council and the barriers between all the realms." She reclined in her seat. "Things were better when we could pass freely between them. The humans worshipped us."

"Better than that—they feared us," Zelos chuckled. "The Council is doing exactly what we need them to. Everything is going according to plan. Soon, we will have the stones, the Unbound, and Demetrius positioned where we need him to carry out the final steps of our plans."

Octo's mind raced as he absorbed the information. This was far worse than he'd feared. Did Demetrius know all of this? Could he really be okay with it? Was he a pawn in Zelos's strategy?

The conversation between Melya and Zelos continued, but Octo knew he couldn't stay hidden much longer without risking discovery. He inched away from the tent, moving with the silence of a spirit. He sprang to his feet and tore into the forest, skirting the edge before angling back toward his tent on the far side of camp.

He moved swiftly as he went over what he'd overheard. The risks had multiplied. He had to warn the others. But first, he needed to figure out who Demetrius's ally in the human realm was, and how to reach Blythe and Hera before it was too late.

He could reach Quentin through his communication stone, but Blythe had none. There was still a chance the second stone could be taken before he found it. They'd have to determine where it was. He thought of the maps in Zelos's tent. He should've studied them harder. He'd have to get back inside to look again.

Octo moved quickly towards his tent. There had to be some way to contact Blythe. Maybe Eyra would know—no. The siblings, Nreman and Aenwyn, would know. He changed direction and moved quickly toward their small tent.

"Pssst!" He made the sound soft, trying to wake them without alerting anyone else.

Octo crouched by the entrance of their tent. If anyone could help him reach Blythe, it was them.

The flap of the tent rustled, and Aenwyn's head peeked out, eyes narrowing as they adjusted to the darkness.

"Octo?" she said, her voice colored with both surprise and irritation. "What in the name of the gods are you doing?"

"I need your help," he whispered. "It's important—Zelos

is planning something big, and I need you to contact Blythe right away. I can reach Quentin on my own."

"What's going on?" Nreman asked, voice groggy but shaded with concern.

"It's better if I don't say," Octo replied quietly. "But I need to reach Blythe right now. I have no way to contact her. Do you?"

The siblings shared a look. Nreman nodded. "We can help. There's a spell we've used before. Risky, but it should get a message through."

Aenwyn pulled a small, distressed leather pouch from inside her cloak. "It'll drain some of our energy, but it's the fastest way. We'll need something personal—something Blythe would recognize as yours. Come inside."

Octo ducked through the tent's narrow opening and crouched to avoid the low ceiling. From beneath his tunic, he drew a silver pendant on a thin chain—an old keepsake from childhood, trident-shaped talisman.

"This should work."

Aenwyn took it gently, her fingers lightly brushing his as she did.

"Here," Nreman said, handing over a quill, ink, and a piece of parchment. "Write what you want her to know."

Octo accepted the items and placed them on the small stool Nreman offered. He quickly scrawled out the warning, folded the note, and passed it to Aenwyn.

"Let's do this."

Nreman had already drawn a casting circle in the dirt, the pendant placed at its center. Aenwyn added the note. The siblings moved with fluid skill. Nreman began to chant, his voice muted and lilting, while Aenwyn cradled the pendant, focusing her energy.

Power hummed through the air, raising goosebumps along Octo's arms.

Aenwyn's eyelids quivered shut as the pendant began to emit a soft light. Nreman's chant deepened, the ancient words thrumming with power. Then, with a final utterance, the parchment burst into flame and vanished.

"It's done," Aenwyn's voice wavered. With trembling hands, she passed the pendant back to Octo, who slipped the now-warm pendant over his neck once more.

"The message will reach Blythe soon," she continued. "She'll see an image of the talisman. If she accepts it, the note will appear—and she'll be able to respond."

"Thank you. I need to get back to my tent."

Nreman placed a steadying hand on his shoulder. "Be careful. If they suspect you're onto them..."

"I know," Octo said grimly. "I will."

He turned to leave, but Aenwyn stopped him.

"Octo, if you ever need help, anything at all, don't hesitate. We're in this together."

He met her gaze. He nodded, then slipped out into the shadows as the tent flap closed behind him.

He scanned the darkness out of habit. Every rustle of dried leaves felt like a watcher, as if the night itself knew what he was doing. The weight of it pressed harder with each step. One truth cut through the noise: Demetrius had to be stopped.

CHAPTER THIRTY-ONE

Quentin

Dark Passage, Umbrahold, Dwarven stronghold

The tunnel walls closed in around them as Quentin led the way through the Dark Passage. The air was oppressive and damp, wafting the smell of earth—and a trace of something wrong deeper in the mountain. The soft gleam of the few lanterns they carried barely pierced the dark, casting long, flickering shadows that crawled across the rocky walls. Every step reverberated sharply, as if the stones themselves were hissing warnings of the dangers ahead.

The team moved in silence. Quentin kept his hand close to the hilt of his sword, his senses on full alert. He couldn't shake the feeling that they were being watched—that something old and hungry waited just beyond the glow of the lanterns.

After what felt like an eternity, the passage widened into an underground chamber. The ground underfoot was uneven, strewn with jagged rocks and the remains of ancient battles. Scattered were rusted weapons, shattered armor, and bones partly sunk into the dirt. A faint glow shone forth from the far end of the cavern, where a rocky plinth stood, holding the object of their quest: the gem the Dwarves had sent them to retrieve.

"There it is," Griffin whispered, his voice barely audible in the deep silence. His eyes fixed on the glowing ruby, his expression tight with focus.

But Quentin wasn't looking at the stone.

Before anyone could speak, the darkness burst to life.

Dark, twisted creatures pulled themselves from the walls, eyes gleaming with red light. Lanky and skeletal, all claws and elongated limbs, they separated naturally from the darkness.

"Form up!" Quentin shouted, his voice shattering the silence in shock. The team snapped into formation, weapons flashing free.

Rhys's arrow whistled past Quentin's ear, burying itself in a creature's skull.

The creatures attacked with unnatural speed, their claws slashing through the air with deadly finesse. Quentin parried a blow aimed at his head, the impact shuddering up his arm. He struck back with a quick blow, but the creature dodged easily, its movements seamless and unnerving.

Griffin was fending off two of the creatures at once, his axe swinging in wide arcs that kept them at bay. The Dwarven warrior fought with savage skill, his strikes precise and deadly. Yet even he struggled to hold his ground against the ceaseless onslaught.

One of the creatures lunged at Quentin, its claws aimed for his chest. He barely managed to block the attack, but the force sent him lurching back. Another creature grabbed the opportunity, slashing at his leg. He cried out as the claws tore through his armor, leaving deep gashes in his thigh.

He staggered, barely able to keep his footing. The creature moved in for the kill, its eyes gleaming with intent. Quentin swung his sword in desperation, but his strength was ebbing, and his sight was blurring.

Just as the creature's claws were about to tear into him, a flash of steel cut through the air, severing its arm in one clean stroke. Griffin appeared at Quentin's side, axe raised and expression grim.

"Get up!" Griffin barked, pulling Quentin to his feet. "We're not done yet!"

Quentin gritted his teeth, pushing the pain to the back of his mind. He couldn't afford to be weak—not now. He raised his sword again, this time with fresh resolve. Together, he and

Griffin fell into a brutal rhythm, covering each other without a word.

But the monsters continued coming. For everyone they struck down, two more took their place. Quentin's muscles trembled with exhaustion, and he knew they couldn't keep this up for much longer.

"We need to get to the ruby!" Griffin shouted, his voice strained with effort.

Quentin nodded in understanding. The stone was their only hope. If they could retrieve it, maybe this would all end. Maybe it held some kind of power—or the creatures would vanish once it was claimed.

Adrenaline surged through Quentin as he cut a path toward the pedestal. The closer he got, the more they focused on him, as if they recognized what he meant to do. He was almost there—just a few more steps—when, out of the corner of his eye, he saw one of the creatures leap toward Griffin, its claws aimed directly at his heart.

"Griffin!" Quentin shouted, his voice cracking with fear. Without thinking, he threw himself in front of the Dwarven warrior, taking the full brunt of the attack. The creature's claws tore into his back, and he cried out in agony—the pain so fierce it punched the air from his lungs. He fell to the ground, the scent of iron filling his nose. The last thing he saw before everything went black was Griffin's horrified face.

When Quentin awoke, he tried to move, but pain locked his limbs in place. His body felt impossibly heavy. He lay on the cold, unforgiving stone, the sound of battle still raging around him.

But above the noise, he heard Griffin's voice, shouting something in a language he didn't understand. A dazzling burst of light filled the cavern, and a powerful force surged through, shaking the air.

The pain in Quentin's back began to lessen, replaced by a spreading warmth. He forced his eyes open and saw Griffin standing over him, the gem glowing in his hands. The creatures recoiled from the light it emitted, their forms unraveling into darkness as the stone's power overwhelmed them. A sharp, crackling hiss surged through the cavern, rattling his bones.

"Quentin!" Griffin shouted, his voice laden with relief. "We did it! We've got the gem!"

Quentin forced a faint smile, the relief in Griffin's voice lifting his spirits. They'd done it. The gem was theirs, and the creatures were gone.

Griffin lowered himself beside Quentin. "Hold on, my friend," he said, the timbre of his voice gentler now. "We'll get ye out of 'ere."

Quentin nodded, though even that small movement emitted surges of pain through his body.

"Remind me to have words with those Dwarven leaders," he muttered. "Their trials are absurd."

Griffin chuckled. "Aye, I will."

With Rhys's help, Griffin lifted Quentin to his feet, and together they began the long walk back to Umbrahold to see Thrain.

CHAPTER THIRTY-TWO

Quentin

Umbrahold, Dwarven stronghold

By the time Quentin and his team made it back to Umbrahold, his legs shook with every step he took. Even with Griffin and Rhys supporting him, each muscle in his body screamed in protest. The throb of his wounds—blunted by adrenaline—was beginning to return with renewed intensity.

When they eventually came out from the dark pass, Izzy rushed over, anxiety carved across her face. She skidded to a halt, her eyes homing in on Quentin, who, he assumed, must have looked worse for wear.

"What happened?!" she cried out, immediately stepping in to take Rhys's place. Her smaller frame was surprisingly strong as she helped Quentin hobble along.

"Some fool went an' played the hero, takin' the blow meant for me," Griffin said, his tone casual but edged with concern. He cast a sidelong glance at Quentin, his eyebrows knitted together despite his attempt at levity.

"Sounds about right," Iain chimed in, his expression dry as ever. Sarcasm colored his tone, but Quentin caught the respect beneath it.

Quentin tried for a shrug and immediately regretted it. "You'd have done the same."

"Still nae smart," Griffin chuckled, though his eyes remained locked on the trail before them.

"How bad is it?" Izzy asked, pausing just outside the tavern where they had been staying. She gave Quentin a quick, assessing look before glancing back toward the door. She was already moving, always quick to act. "I'll see if they have a healer." Handing Quentin off to Iain, she hurried inside to find help.

"Quit fussing," he muttered, his voice husky but tinged by exhaustion. His body ached, and his head pounded with the thought of their journey. "I'm fine."

Ignoring his protests, they half-carried him up the groaning stairs to his room, each of them well aware that it had been far more than a close call. Quentin's thoughts drifted back to the battle—the moment when time felt like it would slow as the enemy's blade came crashing down toward Griffin. If he hadn't jumped in...

Once inside the room, Quentin collapsed onto the bed with a groan. The mattress felt heavenly, though his body still ached. He let out a breath, closing his eyes for a moment, hoping for some peace from the constant whirl of worry about Blythe in his mind.

"I'll have a word with Thrain, see if he'll talk to me uncle 'bout lendin' their axes to our cause against Demetrius and that blasted Council," Griffin said, not wasting any time as he made for the door. He looked back at Quentin before leaving, a wordless understanding exchanged silently. He knew Griffin understood that they'd need to leave for the second stone as soon as possible.

Not long after, the Dwarven healer arrived—her expression calm as she began tending to Quentin's wounds. She moved with the seasoned skill of someone who had seen far worse injuries in her time. Her hands were firm as she applied a salve to the cuts and bruises marring his body. Then she handed him a vial of some strong-smelling draught; just the fragrance of it made his stomach revolt.

"Drink up," she said, her voice brisk but gentle. "It'll put fire back in yer bones." Quentin grimaced at the taste but downed it, knowing they had no time to waste. He needed to be back on his feet as soon as possible.

"Thank you," he muttered, leaning back against the bed's

headboard. The scratches on his back had stopped hurting, much to his relief. The healer gave a curt nod before gathering her things and leaving the room. Iain, Freya, Cael, and Rhys departed shortly after to fetch food and restock their supplies so they could leave as soon as possible.

As the room emptied, Izzy remained in the doorway. Her arms were folded firmly over her chest. Her thoughtful expression didn't match the tension in her posture. She lingered in place for a while, biting her lip as if deliberating whether to speak.

Quentin watched her. "Izzy," he whispered, wincing as he repositioned himself in the bed. "What's on your mind?"

She wavered, glancing at the floor before locking eyes with him.

"It's probably nothing, but..." She trailed off, clearly hesitant to say her thoughts out loud. Her eyes flitted toward the door, as though checking to make sure they were still alone.

"Izzy, you're not the type to worry over 'nothing.' What is it?" Quentin pressed, his voice gentle.

She let out a small breath, rubbing the back of her neck. "It's Iain. I don't know what it is, but something's wrong. I can feel it. I can't place it, but I just—" She stopped, grasping for the right words. "It's like he's hiding something. I don't know, but it's bothering me."

Quentin frowned. He had noticed, too. Iain had consistently been somewhat goofy, but never secretive. Sneaky wasn't a word he'd ever associated with him. However, Izzy's instincts were rarely wrong. If something was off with Iain, it wasn't something they could afford to ignore, especially not now.

"We'll watch him closely," Quentin said, trying to reassure her. "If something is going on, we'll figure it out."

Izzy nodded, though the worry in her eyes didn't fade entirely. "I just hope we're not too late." She sighed again, her shoulders drooping slightly. "I don't want to jump to conclusions. I could be wrong. But first Mother, and now him?" She shook her head. "Something is going on that I just don't understand."

Quentin studied her for a moment. Izzy didn't like doubting people, especially not her twin. But if Iain was hiding something, they couldn't overlook it when so much was at stake.

"Follow your intuition," Quentin said after a beat. He winced as he shifted his position.

Izzy relaxed a little, despite the doubt that remained in her eyes. "I just... I don't want to believe he'd turn on us."

"I don't want to either," Quentin admitted. "But with Demetrius out there, working behind the scenes, we can't rule anything out." And the Council was still hunting them, with Benjamin leading the charge. He had no illusions about how far Benjamin would go to kill Blythe.

She glanced toward the door as if looking for Iain to walk in at any moment. "You get some rest."

Quentin gave her a smile. "Thanks, Izzy. We will leave for that second stone tomorrow." If they didn't reach the second stone before Demetrius, everything they were fighting for would unravel.

Izzy stepped back, pausing in the doorway. "Try not to play the hero again," she said with a strained smile. "We need you in one piece."

Quentin laughed quietly, though the pain in his side turned it into more of a grimace. "No promises."

As she left, the room fell into silence. His thoughts spun, refusing to settle for sleep. He lay back, staring at the ceiling, the dancing lantern light throwing unsettling, shifting shapes over the walls.

His mind turned over everything—the mission, the gem, and the growing suspicion about Iain. Could it be possible that Iain was working against them? The idea seemed unthinkable, but with Demetrius pulling strings in the shadows, anything felt possible, and trust was growing scarce.

His last thought before exhaustion at last took hold of him was of her. Blythe. He needed to survive. Not just for the mission, but for her. If he failed, she'd pay the price too.

CHAPTER THIRTY-THREE

Quentin

Umbrahold, Dwarven stronghold

Quentin's eyes flew open, heart hammering. For a moment, he lay perfectly still, gaze darting around the dark room. What had snatched him out of sleep? He scrubbed a hand over his face, forcing himself upright.

He slid out of bed, muscles tense, ears listening intently for any sound. The silence bore down around him, and still there was a slight change in the air, the faintest trace of movement just beyond the door.

He froze, waiting. The stillness felt wrong—until he remembered where they were: an inn deep underground, within the mountain. He swung his legs out of bed and crossed to the window. It must have been night; he couldn't hear the furnaces running. Their steady roar had sounded outside when they'd walked through Umbrahold.

He moved back to the bed, leaving the window open. A slight current of air flowed in through the opening, though it couldn't quite be called a breeze—not like the ones aboveground. He wondered if Griffin felt the same strangeness above ground that he felt down here, missing it.

Quentin's eyes narrowed as he stared into the dark beyond the window, mind sifting through the fragments of his dream. His breath hitched as flashes returned.

Demetrius stood by the verge of the void; his face distorted—not in pain—but in something far worse: a twisted mix of mockery and victory. Shadows spiraled around him, alive and shifting.

"Blythe..." Demetrius's voice possessed a throaty growl, warped as if a dozen voices spoke in unison. "You can't run. You can't hide."

The council had risen behind his uncle, their forms distorted, spreading into giant silhouettes of shadow. The arcane darkness pulsing from them was stifling, pressing on Quentin's chest. He saw Blythe move—to reach Demetrius and pull him back from whatever madness had claimed him—but her hands slipped straight through the figure. No warmth. No resistance. Just a bleak emptiness.

Demetrius's laughter resounded in the air, a spine-tingling, hollow echo inside Quentin's mind. Then the shadows reached out—not just for Demetrius, but for everyone. He watched in horror as, one by one, his friends were dragged into the darkness. Nreman was first, pallid face, arms outstretched in a frantic appeal. Aenwyn followed, her wordless wail frozen in her eyes. Octo, Bertolf, Griffin, and Hera—all yanked into the endless void without a sound.

Quentin had fought, struggling to keep his footing on the thinning soil below him, yet the grip was unstoppable. The darkness wrapped around his legs, climbing higher—cold and immovable. He strained, but it was no use. He was next.

As the shadows snaked tighter around him, one last individual stood in the dream's dimming glow: Blythe. Just as he reached for her, his fingers barely grazing the edge of her sleeve, the darkness descended over him.

And then... his voice. His own voice. "It's okay. You'll be okay."

Quentin blinked, shaking his head as the memory faded away. A cold sweat dampened his skin. He pressed his palms into his eyes, attempting to banish the lingering dread. What in the Dark Realm was that? It wasn't like any dream he'd ever had before. It had felt too real. A premonition? But he didn't have those. He didn't have magic.

Were Blythe and the others in danger? Was his subconscious trying to warn him, or was it just his fears taking shape in a nightmare?

If he could see her, he'd know she was safe. But he couldn't get in touch with her. She was in the human realm, and he couldn't risk a human seeing something if he tried a magical means of contact. The distance between them felt like a wound he couldn't heal.

He knew sleep wouldn't come easily again—not after something like that. With a deep sigh, he moved away from the window.

He dressed as quickly as his body would allow, then stepped into the hall. If he couldn't sleep, he might as well make himself useful. He needed to find out if Griffin had spoken with Thrain and arranged the meeting with the Dwarven leaders. They needed to secure their support before they could go after the stone.

His limbs felt stiff and unnatural as he descended the stairs, the familiar scents of woodsmoke, stale ale, and something frying in the kitchen drifting up to meet him.

He found Griffin and Rhys already in the tavern, talking quietly by the hearth. The flames threw shifting light across their faces, and both men looked just as restless as Quentin felt.

"Couldn't sleep?" Griffin asked, glancing up as Quentin approached.

"No," Quentin muttered.

"Same here," Rhys added, raking a hand through his hair.

Quentin nodded grimly. "We need to secure the Dwarves' help, and fast. Demetrius and the Council aren't going to wait for us to gather our strength."

If either side reached the next stone first, they'd gain the advantage, and the remaining stones would become far harder for the others to claim.

"Had a word with Thrain," Griffin said. "Told the others already—figured I'd let ye rest. They'll meet us come first light."

Quentin nodded again.

The three of them sat in silence, the tavern still dim and half-asleep around them. Griffin leaned back in his chair, boots planted wide, arms crossed over his chest as he watched the door with the patience of someone who'd spent too many mornings like this.

Quentin let his gaze drift between them. No one spoke; there was nothing left to say that hadn't already been said. The quiet wasn't uncomfortable—just heavy, the kind that settled over people who'd survived the same night and were bracing for the same dawn.

A floorboard creaked upstairs. Someone was finally stirring.

Quentin looked up as Izzy entered the room, her complexion wan.

"You ready?" She glanced between the three of them. She looked ethereal in a pale blue floor-length gown. Leave it to his sister to pack a dress for a mission. She looked calm, but her eyes revealed everything she wasn't saying.

"Any word from Blythe or Hera?" Quentin asked, turning to Griffin, who was stretching.

"Not yet, far as I ken," Griffin grumbled, scratching his beard and eyeing the door. "She ought tae be at the first stone by now."

She should have.

And with the Council hunting her, with Benjamin leading the charge, silence was normal, but terrifying.

A hollow ache settled in his chest, the kind that only absence from someone you love could carve. He tried to focus on the task ahead, but the worry lingered anyway, a quiet pressure he couldn't shut out.

"They'll check in soon," Rhys said. "I'm sure of it."

"If something happened…" Quentin started.

Izzy shook her head gently. "We'll deal with it. But first, we get the Dwarven elders on our side."

"Ready for me to gather everyone?" Rhys asked, rising from his seat.

"As ready as we'll ever be," Quentin replied, straightening his shoulders. He scanned his team—Griffin, Rhys, and Izzy—worn, bruised, but unbroken. Rhys went upstairs to fetch Iain, Freya, and Cael.

Once they regrouped, they made their way through the serpentine routes of the Dwarven city. The walls around them emitted a soft glow infused with supernatural stones embedded in the rock. One by one, the forge fires began to burst into flame. It gave the place a sense of life with stone and flame waking together.

At a fork in the path, Thrain joined them from the left.

"This way," he said, leading them toward an opening in the cavern wall.

Two armored Dwarven guards stood watch at the entrance, their axes crossed in a ceremonial stance. They moved aside as Quentin and his companions approached.

At the end of the tunnel stood the large carved wooden doors of the Dwarven elders' chamber. Detailed symbols shone dimly along the frame.

"Looks like the elders are ready," Griffin explained, pointing to the symbols. Quentin paused at the doors, shooting a sidelong look at Izzy and the rest of his companions.

Griffin gave him an encouraging nod.

Quentin drew a breath, squared his shoulders, and pushed the doors open.

His boots rang out on the smooth stone floor as he stepped into the Dwarven Council Chamber, Freya close behind, ready to assist in the diplomacy that would be needed to convince the elders to help. The moment pressed in about him like the low ceiling overhead, and though he stood tall, he felt familiar tension tighten across his shoulders.

Seven Dwarven elders, each covered in heavy robes decorated with clan sigils and ancient metals, sat in a semicircle behind a raised stone dais, their eyes watchful.

It was time to make their case, but Quentin's thoughts kept slipping back to the girl who still hadn't called. Sometimes he wondered how anyone who imprinted managed to survive the constant distraction.

At the far end of the broad stone table sat a muscled dwarf, his stance stiff and imposing. His frame was wrapped in intricately etched armor, each plate engraved with runes and battle marks that spoke of centuries of tradition and war. Deep-set, sharp, unyielding eyes tracked the group as they entered. A long, snow-white beard spilled over his chest in braided strands, matching the coarse, frizzy tufts of hair crowning his head like frost on granite.

"Ye're early," the dwarf remarked, his rough voice filling the room. "I take it ye've come with news, or more trouble."

"Bit o' both," Griffin said with a crooked grin. "Well met, Uncle Garruk."

"State yer purpose," rumbled the figure to Garruk's right, his beard braided with silver and stone.

"Elder Falbrook," Freya whispered. As a diplomat, she prided herself on knowing the names of every elder from every nation, a skill honed through extensive travel and dedication.

Quentin stepped forward. "Thank you for granting me an audience, Elders. I come not just on behalf of my people, but on behalf of all who reside within the Magic and Human realms. I wish I were being dramatic, but in truth, the time for unity is now, or everything we know will fall."

He paused, then continued. "We need your help. The Council grows bolder by the day, and the rebellion I once supported is beginning to mirror them. They no longer fight for equality—only power."

Garruk leaned back in his chair, eyes narrowing as he studied them. "Ye've done what few outsiders ever manage and retrieved the ruby. That's no small feat. Only those the mountain deems worthy can claim it. It's our measure, our test o' true allegiance. And ye passed."

He paused, voice dropping to a gravelly rumble. "But takin' on the Council? Standin' against Demetrius himself? That's a different beast entirely. Ye're askin' for more than aid—

you're askin' us to stake everything we have."

A low murmur passed through the elders, but Falbrook raised a hand, silencing them. "Go on."

Quentin steadied his nerves with a breath before he began.

After laying out the full truth, he let the silence settle. "That's why we're here."

Several of the elders stiffened at the mention of the stones.

"The Stones of Binding are legend," the lone female elder snapped, her eyes narrowing.

Quentin met her stare. "They're real. Two have already been taken from the Dark Realm, and one from this realm is likely in Demetrius's hands. If he gathers all six, he'll tear the realms open. None of us will survive what comes through. We have friends pursuing the ones in the human realm right now."

Garruk leaned forward, his expression hard to read. "And what, exactly, does Demetrius plan to do with them?"

"He means to reunite all six. If he does, he can collapse the magic of the Houses, eliminating the barriers in the portals between the human and magical realms, as well as the portals between both realms and the dark realm. With all six, he could tear down the boundaries. The dark realm's creatures—banished there for a reason—would flood back into the human and magical worlds. More than they already are from the two portals left unguarded. And Demetrius would rule over the chaos."

Silence swept through the chamber.

Garruk let out another grunt. "And what of the Council? You expect us to align with them against this traitor?"

Quentin shook his head. "The Council is nearly as corrupt. They've allowed their fear of half-bloods, hybrids, and dissenters to turn into policy. The darkness didn't just reach Demetrius—we suspect that it's corrupted much of the Council from within as well."

The female dwarf looked to Griffin, whose expression

was grim.

"He speaks true," Garruk rumbled. "The Council's cursed mandates started long before they tossed us outta their gilded halls—laws tae keep us in the dark while they sit pretty, hoardin' magic and favor."

Falbrook swept his gaze around the room, voice low and sharp. "And the Fae? Bah. They're no better. Perched on their mountain, drippin' with power, lookin' down their noses at the rest of us. I've yet tae see how throwin' in with you lot changes anythin'. When we crush Demetrius and his Council, what do we get, eh? Another boot on our necks?"

Quentin let out a breath. "I understand where you are coming from. Historically, the Fae and Mages were unkind towards others, believing themselves to be above them." He shook his head. "I don't agree with it. I never have. However, Demetrius is using the deep-seated anger of all the races who feel mistreated to rally support. But he doesn't want justice for anyone. He wants control. We're not asking you to choose between Demetrius and the Council. We're asking you to help us build something better — to fight both of them. Together."

"Quentin 'ere is the 'eir to the Fae throne," Griffin stepped up beside him. "I trust 'im. He is as honest as any dwarf I've ever met. I trust 'im wit' the lives of me and mine."

A tense silence settled over the room, the kind that felt as though one stood on the edge of a bridge or chasm, waiting to see if the rope would hold.

Finally, the female dwarf spoke. "You come spoutin' tales of war, rot, and betrayal. And now ye ask us tae gamble our kin, our homes, our way o' life."

She continued, voice like gravel. "Tell me this—what proof have ye that you're different? That you won't turn out like the rest o' them, sittin' high while we're left in the dirt?"

Quentin met her gaze without flinching. "You don't. All you have is hope that we can make a better world. You've seen what happens when we let fear and tradition decide the future. If we do nothing, Demetrius will break the realms open.

The corruption will spill into each realm. And there won't be a home left for any of us to defend."

The elders studied him for a long time. Then Falbrook turned to the other elders and began speaking. Whispers passed back and forth, some in the old tongue, others in terse grunts.

At last, Garruk raised his hand again. "Ye'll have our answer by nightfall. 'Til then, our halls are yours—eat, rest, and treat 'em as your own, but don' go far."

Quentin bowed his head in thanks, then turned and followed Izzy and Griffin out of the chamber. The doors closed behind them with a deep, echoing thud.

"How do you think it went?" Izzy asked.

"As well as it could've," Quentin murmured.

Griffin grunted. "They'll come around. They're stubborn, not stupid. They know what the alternative is. They know what the Council has done to them, and they don't trust a Mage to make things better."

Still, the stone was in Demetrius's hands. Blythe was silent. And the clock was ticking faster every day. This wait would cost them.

He could only hope the Dwarves made the right choice—and that Blythe would still be safe to fight beside him when the time came.

They made their way back through the winding tunnels toward the inn, the weight of the elders' silence pressing on all of them. By the time they reached the tavern's hearth, the adrenaline had faded, leaving only exhaustion and the dull ache of waiting. Hours blurred into restless pacing, half-finished meals, and glances toward the door each time footsteps echoed in the hall.

At last, a dwarf messenger appeared in the doorway, helm tucked under one arm. "The elders request yer presence," he announced, voice clipped with urgency.

Quentin rose at once. Izzy and Griffin followed, tension coiling through the air as they retraced their steps through Umbrahold's winding tunnels. The forge fires burned brighter now, casting long shadows that fluttered across the stone.

When they reached the chamber, the guards stepped aside without a word. Quentin exchanged a final look with Izzy and Griffin before pushing the doors open once more. Inside, the Dwarven elders sat assembled again, their stern gazes fixed on the group as they entered.

Garruk stroked his thick beard thoughtfully, his eyes narrowing as he studied Quentin and his team. He then leaned forward, his voice low and firm. "I'll rally me kin," he said. "We'll stand with ye—against the Council, against the rebels, all of 'em."

His gaze hardened. "But mark me words—once we step into this, there's no turnin' back. So ye'd best be right."

Quentin exchanged a glance with his companions.

"We are, and we're ready," he said, his voice unwavering. "And we'll do whatever it takes to stop them."

Garruk gave a slow nod. "Right then, it's settled," he said, his voice like gravel. "We'll be ready tae move when the time comes."

He leaned forward, eyes glinting with fire. "In the meantime, we'll dig intae the Council's affairs. If there's cracks in their ranks—any weakness at all—we'll sniff it oot. Dwarves ken how tae find fault in stone."

Quentin felt a wave of relief wash over him. It was a small victory, but it was one step closer to stopping Demetrius and safeguarding those they cared about. They weren't alone in this fight, and that made all the difference.

As they left the hall, Quentin's thoughts drifted back to Blythe. Wherever she was, whatever danger she faced, they were one step closer to protecting her. They still had a long road ahead, but at least now, they had more allies in the fight to come.

Izzy's voice cut through the heavy silence—a quick, clean flick of a knife. "Now we go for the stone?" Her tone was steady.

He didn't answer right away, his thoughts still far from where they were. Finally, he nodded.

"Yes. Let's pack and leave as soon as possible."

CHAPTER THIRTY-FOUR

Blythe

Eas a'Chual Aluinn, Scotland

Blythe leaned in over the glowing runes, thoughts snapping into place as she studied them. The energy from the stone was palpable, pressing into her skin. The beat of her heart fell into step with the pulsing symbols.

"We should first identify the protective wards," Tavian said, keeping his tone even. "The runes might be tied to traps or defensive spells. We should tread lightly."

Hera stepped next to her, glance sweeping the shadows. "I'll keep an eye out. If anyone's coming, I want to know before they're on top of us."

Tavian crouched and pulled a small pouch from his bag. He emptied its contents—a collection of fine powders and magical reagents—letting the powders spill into a thin, shimmering ring.

"This should help us detect any active magic," Tavian explained. "If there are any traps or wards, this circle will reveal them."

Blythe steadied herself and leaned closer to the runes. The symbols were ancient and intricate, their designs twisting into complex patterns that shifted and changed as she looked. She could almost feel the magic flowing through them, alive and aware. Not for the first time, she felt as though she'd come late to the party, completely unprepared.

"This cluster here...," Tavian said, pointing to a cluster of symbols, "they're channeling the primary energy. If we can neutralize them, we might be able to access the stone."

He got to work, sprinkling a fine dust over the runes. The powder gleamed and flared, disclosing faint, nearly invisible barriers around the stone. Each barrier trembled with a pale sapphire radiance as it came into view.

"Any mistake could trigger a defensive reaction," Tavian said quietly, focusing.

Blythe nodded. The cave seemed unnervingly quiet as Tavian worked, while Hera remained a steady presence.

Something tapped her boot, catching her off guard. She looked down to see the glowing image of a trident at her feet. When she extended her hand to touch it, she jolted as a piece of paper appeared in its place.

"Octo," she whispered.

She spread out the paper. The trident symbol flared for a heartbeat and then faded. Ink gathered on the surface, rising into words as if pulled from the air itself.

"Blythe, Zelos is moving. Demetrius has a contact in the human realm. I don't know who yet. Zelos wants the portals open for some reason. He wants the humans to worship them. They're also after something, or someone, called an Unbound. You and Hera need to be careful. I'll try to find out more. Stay on guard. Something's coming. — Signed, Octo."

Unbound. The word struck her like an echo. Zelos had said it before. She remembered now the whisper she wasn't meant to hear. She hadn't known what it meant then, but now the dread settled deeper.

The pendant image could only mean Octo, and the message confirmed it. She touched the edge of the paper, half expecting it to vanish. It didn't.

Her pulse stuttered. Something's coming. The cave suddenly felt too small, the air too thin.

She pivoted away from Tavian's work and hurried to Hera. "Hera, I got a message from Octo."

She handed the paper to Hera, who read it, her frown deepening. She looked past Blythe toward Tavian, then back at

Blythe.

"I don't know… it might not be him," Blythe murmured.

Hera scowled, folding the paper and handing it back. "We'll just have to stay on our guard."

Blythe nodded in agreement.

She slipped back to Tavian's side, careful not to break his concentration.

After several tense minutes, Tavian let out a relieved sigh. "That's it. The primary wards are neutralized."

Blythe reached for the stone carefully, her hand poised above it. The runes had calmed, their gleam less intense but still present. She calmed the energy, guiding it into a more stable form. The symbols dimmed to a soft, steady light.

"Got it," Blythe said, her voice a mix of exhaustion and triumph. "The stone's magic is under control. We can extract it."

She reached into her pack and pulled out a specially prepared pouch for mystical objects. As she picked up the stone and placed it inside, a sense of accomplishment flooded her. She tightened her grip on the pouch. She wasn't letting this out of her sight. She wished she could tell Quentin they'd succeeded, even just to hear his voice for a moment.

"Let's move," Hera said firmly. "We need to get out before anyone notices."

The three packed up quickly, leaving the cave as quietly as they'd entered. They carefully descended the cliff face, the spray from the waterfall moistening the stone under their boots. Once on solid, marshy ground, they began the hike back toward the car, the mist hanging onto their clothes.

Blythe felt the stone humming faintly in her bag, a low vibration that matched her steps. She followed Tavian through the trees with Hera bringing up the rear, her gaze flicking across the woods. The walk back to the car felt longer than the trek in. Once they were inside, Blythe shot Tavian a quick glance. Without him, they would never have figured out how to disable the defenses around the stone.

As the marshy landscape slipped away behind them, she let out a slow breath. They had secured the first stone. Her thoughts shifted to the next one. Would it be this straightforward? It hadn't been easy, but she had expected monsters or traps or something more violent.

Tavian broke the silence. "We need to hurry. There's no telling where Demetrius is with the ones from the magic realm."

"Quentin and his crew should be getting the second one," Hera added. "But out here, it's just the three of us. If the Council or the Rebels have armies, we're on our own."

"Where to next?" Tavian asked, glancing back.

Blythe pulled out the maps from her bag and used a light spell to illuminate them. As the car bounced along the road, she studied the locations while Hera leaned over her shoulder.

"Looks like the second one is in Africa," Blythe murmured, looking over the map. "Egypt, specifically."

Hera frowned. "Why the hesitation?"

"If I'm right, it's in the Valley of the Kings," Blythe said.

"And that's bad?" Hera glanced at Tavian, searching for an answer.

"It's a heavily protected site with limited access."

"You're an archaeologist, right?" Tavian asked. "You could claim you're there for a dig."

Blythe's eyes narrowed. "When did I tell you that?"

From the edge of her vision, she saw Hera go still, her hand settling near her sword.

"You didn't," Tavian replied casually. "The Council included it in the brief. They thought you might try to return to your old life."

A thin chill slid down her spine—the same cold that always came when danger brushed close.

"It's a possibility," she admitted, her head already spinning through the logistics. "But I doubt we can trick the Egyptian government that easily."

"We also can't just stroll in there," Hera pointed out.

"We're both wanted by the human realm."

Tavian drove in silence, each of them contemplating their next move. Finally, Blythe spoke up, her eyes casting a quick look to Tavian. "You're a sleeper agent, right?"

Tavian shifted uneasily. "Yes, but what are you getting at?"

"Maybe you can infiltrate the site. Use some magic to help us get in," Blythe suggested.

Tavian smiled. "You're overestimating my abilities. Sneaking three adults into a dig site unnoticed is… tricky."

"Maybe you're overestimating it," Hera countered. "It's remote enough."

"Not that remote," Blythe said dryly. "They have a Pizza Hut with a view of the Valley of the Kings."

Hera shot her a look. "You're not helping."

"I'm just being realistic," Blythe said. "If it's hidden at a dig site, how do we know it hasn't already been uncovered?"

"Our ancestors wouldn't have left something that powerful for a human to stumble upon," Tavian said, matter-of-fact. "It's still there."

Blythe exhaled, her mind tugged back to the dream she'd had days—maybe weeks—ago: the sun-scorched dig site, her knees sinking into hot sand, the shimmer of a magical stone half buried beneath centuries of silence. She'd uncovered so many enchanted artifacts over the years. Apparently, the ancestors had never been great at hiding their secrets.

Tavian paused, weighing something. "We scope it out first. Plan from there. Head coverings are common. You'll blend in."

"I guess we don't have a choice," Blythe said, resignation settling in. "This map isn't precise enough. We'll have to follow the coordinates."

"Or…" Tavian pulled out his phone and handed it to her. "Google Earth?"

"What?" Hera looked confused as Blythe opened the app and began typing in coordinates.

"Brilliant! I can't believe I hadn't thought of it myself," Blythe said under her breath, quickly entering the coordinates from the map into the phone. The satellite images loaded, providing a detailed view of the Valley of the Kings. She zoomed in, studying the valley from above.

"Here," Blythe said, pointing at a section of the valley that wasn't part of the typical tourist routes. "This is our spot —isolated, with an old excavation site nearby where I had been working before my father's passing. If the stone is anywhere, it's likely hidden somewhere within that area."

Hera bent forward, peering at the screen. "Looks like a lot of rocky terrain. Could be tough to reach without raising suspicion."

Tavian looked back from the driver's seat. "We'll need to approach at night. Fewer people around, and we can use a cloaking spell to mask our presence from anyone watching."

Blythe's mind was already mapping the route. "We'll need gear—ropes, climbing equipment."

"I can handle the climbing," Hera said confidently. "If we have a plan, we can make it work."

Tavian smiled slightly. "And if we run into any obstacles, that's where I come in. A little magic can go a long way in places similar to this."

Blythe appreciated their confidence, even as pressure tightened in her chest. "The Council and the Rebellion may have people in Egypt as well. We're not the only ones looking for these stones, and the Council is still looking for us."

"And if Benjamin's anywhere near Egypt..." She swallowed hard, forcing the words out. "He won't hesitate to kill me."

"True," Tavian agreed, glancing at the GPS as they drew near the airport. "But I think we have a head start. The Council underestimates you—that's their mistake—and the Rebellion likely doesn't know what you're doing."

As they pulled into the airport, their plane waited exactly where they'd left it. Once inside, Tavian began moving about, performing his pre-flight checks.

"We'll call Quentin from the air," Blythe said, her tone clipped with firmness. "He needs to know where the second stone is in the magic realm."

She spread out the map, eyes flickering across the parchment as her finger glided over the marked locations. "Kemetra… Aferra. Does that sound right to you?"

Tavian nodded. "Yeah. I've never been, but I've heard there are pyramids—massive ones—that mirror the human realm's. It makes one question whether humans would think aliens built ours, too." He grinned at the thought.

Blythe rolled her eyes, then rolled the map, tucking it away with care. A tight coil formed low in the pit of her stomach, a mix of anticipation and worry she couldn't untangle.

Once ready, the plane took off smoothly, the drone of the engine forming a calming rhythm. As they gained altitude, Blythe reclined in her seat, her thoughts tumbling. Securing the first stone had been a major victory, but the risks were only growing.

"If we act fast, we'll get it before anyone else does. We just need to trust the plan." Tavian said, calm and certain.

Blythe wasn't convinced. She'd seen how fast things could spiral, and the thought of both the Council and the Rebellion converging on the same location made her skin crawl.

She shifted in her seat and scanned the cabin, then focused on the window, its polished pane ideal for channeling magic. She inscribed the communication rune across the glass. The lines twinkled lightly, then burst to life, radiating in the dim light of the plane's interior.

The window undulated like disturbed water, and Quentin's face emerged from the distortion, eyes wide with alarm. He clearly hadn't expected the call, especially not mid-flight.

"Where are you?" he asked, his gaze scanning the cabin behind her.

"We're on a plane, heading toward the next stone," Blythe replied. "I needed to confirm its location. Are you familiar with Kemetra? Aferra?"

She shot a look over her shoulder just as Hera approached, map in hand.

"Here," Hera said, offering it without hesitation. She couldn't see Quentin, but she clearly understood Blythe wasn't talking to herself.

Blythe unrolled the map and pointed to the marked region.

"Yes, I know it," Quentin said. "We've just finished getting the Dwarves on board. We'll head there next. Stay safe, Kits."

His image began to fade as the ripples swallowed his face.

"You too," she said under her breath, exhaling as the window stilled once more. The moment his face vanished, the ache returned—sharp, familiar, impossible to ignore. And for the first time, she didn't ignore it. She didn't try to explain away her feelings for him.

Maybe she was finally letting herself want him.

She leaned back, her thoughts drifting. A thin chill slid down her spine—Quentin and Griffin heading into Kemetra, trying to breach the Valley of the Kings. What was it called there, and did it look the same?

Her thoughts drifted to the dream she couldn't shake: the darkness that had infiltrated both Demetrius and the Council. Maybe it was symbolic. A warning of corruption on both sides. But her gut whispered otherwise. It seemed genuine. Tangible. If they were cut from the same cloth, wouldn't they share secrets too?

And if they did… then the Council might already be waiting.

Maybe it was paranoia. But in a universe where magic twisted truth, and loyalty blurred, paranoia felt like survival.

◆ ◆ ◆

After flying through the night, they touched down in Egypt, with darkness still enveloping the desert. The team moved quickly, collecting their bags and making their way through the private terminal. Tavian had already arranged a vehicle while they'd been in flight, and they loaded it with their gear before setting off.

The drive was quiet as they approached their destination. The night bit at their skin, colder than expected, and the vast dunes lay out in front of them, illuminated only by the soft gleam of the moon.

"When we get there, we can't afford to linger in one spot, or we'll risk getting caught."

Hera, sitting next to her, checked her weapons and gear one last time.

The car bumped along the rocky terrain as they neared the Valley of the Kings, and the ancient landscape came into view. The cliffs and valleys rose like silent sentries carved by centuries, stirring a soft amazement in Blythe.

"This place," she murmured, "always amazes me. It was my favorite dig site."

Tavian glanced at her from the driver's seat. "Let's hope we find the right place."

They parked at a distant ridge, far from the patrol routes. The team unloaded their equipment and began the trek on foot, staying in the shadows as they approached the isolated section of the valley Blythe had identified earlier.

Blythe's gut feeling was sharp, and every scrape of sand felt too loud amid the calm.

Hera crouched down, signaling for them to stop. "There's movement ahead," she whispered.

Hera peered through the darkness, her vision focusing. "Could be a patrol. Or… someone else."

Tavian moved forward, speaking quietly. "I'll handle it. A simple illusion spell should keep them from noticing us."

He raised his hand, murmuring a few words under his

breath. A shimmer spread through the air, bending light and shadow until the terrain around them transformed. Blythe watched as the figures in the distance moved past without glancing in their direction.

"Nicely done," Hera whispered.

Tavian's jaw stiffened. "Let's keep moving."

They continued onward, reaching the dig site hidden in a shallow valley. Blythe knelt, map unfolded across her knee as she confirmed their position.

"This is it," she said quietly, apprehension twisting through her. "The stone should be nearby."

Hera and Tavian shared a brief, tense look.

"We find it," Hera said. "And we get out."

Tavian's grin didn't touch his eyes. "Right. Simple as that."

His grin was thin. Nothing about this would be simple.

CHAPTER THIRTY-FIVE

Quentin

Traveling Valoria to Aferra (Magic Realm)

After days of travel across Valoria and the sea, Griffin called in a favor in Raferi and secured passage on a dune glider. It waited for them at the desert's edge. Quentin knew of dune gliders but had never seen one. He imagined them as a cross between a manta ray and a desert dragon.

Hours later, the plains gave way to the hot, steamy dunes.

Quentin stepped over the last dune, boots sinking into the scorching sand, and froze.

There it was.

The dune glider loomed ahead, half-buried in the golden drift like a creature resting between worlds. Its body stretched wide and low, leathery wings folded tightly against its sides. Its hide shimmered iridescent scales that caught the sunlight, refracting it into dancing patterns across the sand.

Its head lifted as he approached, eyes like warm amber watching him with eerie intelligence. A row of ridged fins ran down its spine, pulsing with magic. The air around it felt charged, like the moment before a storm breaks.

Quentin swallowed hard.

The creature didn't move, but the sand beneath it rippled as if responding to its breath. He could feel it—a deep, elemental rhythm syncing with his own heartbeat. This wasn't just a mount. It was a force of nature.

And it was waiting.

Griffin groaned, and Quentin couldn't help but chuckle.

"This won't be as bad as flying on Ellira, Griffin," Quentin said, smiling amiably at his friend.

"You don't like flying?" Izzy asked, standing next to Griffin and gazing up at the dune glider in amazement. "I personally love it."

"We dwarves be meant fer land, nae air," Griffin grumbled.

She smiled and threw her arms around him in a friendly hug. "Don't worry, Griffin. I'll sit in front of you so you can hold on to me."

"No," Iain cut in, moving Izzy away from Griffin. "You will ride between Freya and me. Griffin can ride between Rhys and Que."

Izzy pouted, but didn't argue. One by one, they climbed onto the large back of the dune glider, settling between its fins. Once they were all secure and braced themselves, the creature lifted its head and let out a low, resonant hum that vibrated through the sand.

The air around them shimmered, heat and magic intertwining as the dune glider unfurled its wings—wide, leathery sails that caught the wind like ancient banners. With a sudden surge, it launched forward, skimming just above the desert surface, its body undulating in rhythm with the dunes below.

Sand kicked up in a golden spray behind them, and the wind roared past their ears. Quentin squinted against the rush, his fingers tightening around the fin as the creature accelerated. It didn't gallop or flap—it glided, as if the desert itself parted to let it pass.

The horizon stretched endlessly, but the dune glider moved with purpose, drawn by instinct—or magic—toward the distant pyramids of Kemetra. Their jagged silhouettes rose from the haze, towering and ancient, casting long shadows across the scorched land of Aferra.

Above them, the sky burned blue and cloudless. Below, the dunes whispered in every shifting ripple. And between them, the dune glider soared—silent, swift, and unstoppable.

Quentin could hear Griffin's groans over the rush of wind as the dune glider skimmed the crests of the dunes and dipped into their valleys. Each descent sent a ripple through the creature's body, and Quentin silently prayed that Griffin's stomach would survive the ride.

They traveled for hours, the sun sinking behind them until the desert was cloaked in shadow. At last, the glider slowed, wings folding as it came to a halt at the edge of a narrow trail carved into the sand.

Quentin swung down first, the others following in silence.

The trail wound into rising foothills, jagged silhouettes etched against the fading light. Shadows stretched long and warped across the path, twisting into shapes that didn't feel entirely natural.

Quentin pressed forward. But with each step, the silence grew thicker, more oppressive. His boots crunched against gravel, and still—no wildlife, no wind, no sound.

Only the sense of unseen eyes. Watching. Waiting.

A flicker of movement caught his attention. He raised his hand, signaling the others to stop.

"What is it?" Izzy asked, stepping up beside him.

Quentin's gaze narrowed. "I don't know..."

Griffin glanced around, gripping the haft of his axe tightly. "Smells like a bloody trap," he muttered, eyes darting through the shade. "Place's too quiet by half—like it's holding its breath."

A harsh, guttural voice called out from behind a ridge. "You there! Halt!"

Cloaked figures emerged from the rocks, each bearing the crest of the Council: a silver chain against a black field, and intricately designed cloaks billowing around their forms. There were seven in total, and as they moved closer, Quentin took a step back, feeling their gaze settle on him.

Beside him, Iain drew in a sharp breath, the sound quick and tight. Quentin glanced over, but Iain's face was unreadable.

A tall, imposing figure stepped forward, his eyes narrowed under the hood of his cloak. "State your names and your purpose here."

Quentin clenched his jaw. "We're passing through. On official business." He held up a medallion marked with the House's emblem, but the man only sneered.

"Official business?" the man scoffed. "You must be aware that Fae are prohibited from entering lands outside their own territories. And as for dwarves..." He glanced at Griffin with a look of contempt. "They are not permitted above ground at all."

Izzy stiffened. "Since when are there restrictions on where we can go? The realms are open to all."

"Not anymore," the man replied, his tone cold and dismissive. "By order of the Council, all beings are to remain within their ancestral lands. For the safety of all, each person must keep to their own territories."

Quentin's stomach dropped. He'd heard whispers of such policies, but hadn't believed the Council would go this far. "And what of those who travel for duty or alliance?" he demanded. "You can't just—"

"Silence!" the man barked, his voice echoing across the rocks. "You are in violation of the mandate. For this, you will be detained until your fate is decided by the Council."

Griffin bristled, stepping forward despite Quentin's warning glance. "Detained? Just for bein' here? Since when did walkin' through the wrong patch o' dirt become a bloody crime?"

One of the soldiers—a wiry woman with dark, intense eyes—smirked and raised her weapon. "Since your kind stopped respecting boundaries. You may think yourselves above the laws, but the Council will see that justice is served."

A flash of Benjamin's face cut through Quentin's mind. Cold, loyal, unyielding. If he were here, he'd be thrilled to see this in person.

Quentin's hand dropped to the hilt of his sword, his jaw

tightening. "We won't be detained," he said, tone flat and dangerous. "We're not enemies of the Council."

"Not enemies?" The leader laughed, a mirthless sound. "You're Fae, traveling with a dwarf. To us, you're nothing but rebels, stirring trouble. Surrender now, or face the consequences."

The group tightened formation, weapons rising. Quentin knew they had no choice. With a slow nod to his friends, he whispered, "Stand your ground."

The soldiers closed in, brandishing their weapons. Quentin's sword flashed, blocking a strike aimed at his side. Griffin swung his axe, meeting one of the soldiers' blades with a bone-rattling clang. Izzy darted between the attackers, her movements fluid and precise as she dodged a barrage of spells.

"Stay close!" Quentin shouted over the din, his eyes scanning for a path of escape.

But their enemies were relentless, pressing in from all sides. The Council's soldiers moved with a rigid, almost mechanical precision, their strikes calculated and unforgiving. Quentin felt his strength waning under the onslaught, his arms burning with strain as he blocked blow after blow.

Just as the fight began to slip away, Iain's voice rang out, cutting through the chaos. "Quentin! The ridge!"

Quentin looked up sharply, spotting a narrow pass that led higher into the rocks. If they could reach it, they might lose their pursuers in the winding trails.

"Go!" he shouted, breaking away and sprinting for the ridge, the others close behind. Griffin brought up the rear, swinging his axe in a wide arc to fend off the soldiers. They scrambled up the rocky slope, stones skittering beneath their feet as they climbed.

The soldiers followed, but the narrow path slowed them down, giving Quentin and his friends precious moments to gain ground. At last, they reached a small plateau, overlooking a sheer drop on one side and a steep climb on the other.

Breathless, Quentin turned to face their pursuers. "This

ends here," he said, raising his sword, the words echoing off the rocks.

The soldiers' leader sneered, his eyes filled with contempt. "You think you can defy the Council and escape?" He raised his hand, and dark tendrils of magic coiled around his fingers, crackling with energy.

Before he could move, a low, rumbling growl echoed from the shadows. The soldiers froze, their eyes darting toward the source of the sound. From the depths of the rocks, a creature emerged—a massive, stone-skinned beast with eyes like molten lava. The sand vibrated beneath its steps as it approached.

The leader's face paled.

"A sentinel..." he whispered, his confidence faltering.

The sentinel's growl reverberated through the rocks—deep and menacing—its red eyes fixed on both Quentin's group and the Council soldiers. The air around it shimmered with an unnatural charge.

"That's from the dark realm..." Iain whispered, fear threading through his words.

Quentin didn't need to be told twice. He turned to his companions, his voice low and urgent. "We need to move. Now. Stay low and don't look back!"

As they edged back, the sentinel's gaze snapped to them, and it snarled, taking a lumbering step forward. Its taloned feet scraped against the stone, sending sparks flying as it approached—each step landing with slow, deliberate menace.

The Council soldiers were the first to scatter, scrambling back down the slope. "Forget them!" the lead soldier shouted to his companions. "Let's get out of here!"

Quentin's muscles coiled tight as he glanced at his friends. "We go right, down the cliffside—carefully but fast. That thing's not here for us alone."

The creature let out a roar—an ancient, guttural sound that seemed to echo from the depths of time itself. It lifted one massive, clawed hand, and a wave of power blasted outward, shattering stone and sending chunks of rock flying in all directions. A wave of scorching heat rolled off its body, baking the air around them.

"Now!" Quentin hissed, grabbing Izzy's arm and pulling her toward the cliff's edge. Griffin didn't hesitate despite the drop; he leaped down first, finding handholds with practiced ease.

Iain was next, scrambling over the edge, his fingers slipping but catching onto a rocky outcrop just below. Rhys, Freya, and Cael hurried after him. Quentin and Izzy followed, moving as quickly as they could. Claws raked across the cliff above them.

"Don't look back!" Griffin shouted from below. "Just keep moving!"

Rocks crumbled underfoot as they descended. The sentinel, undeterred by the cliff's edge, stretched an arm down, swiping mere inches from Izzy's head. She yelped, pressing herself flat against the rock face.

"Quentin!" she gasped, her face pale.

Quentin scanned the cliffside until he spotted a small crevice—an opening, a dark, narrow opening—just big enough to hide in. "There," he said, pointing. "One at a time—get in."

They quickly slipped into the crevice, pressing themselves into the darkness. The sentinel's hulking form loomed above, its heated gaze scanning the cliffside. For a tense moment, it hesitated, sniffing the air.

The creature's eyes burned brighter as it let out a frustrated snarl. It lingered a moment longer, then finally turned and retreated up the cliff with thunderous, resounding steps. Quentin and the others held still until the sounds of the sentinel faded.

When he was sure the creature was gone, Quentin let out a slow, shaky exhale. He turned to the others, relief mingling with a sharp edge of anger. "That... was closer than I'd like."

Izzy nodded, still catching her breath. "Why was it here

at all? Those creatures are bound to the dark realm—it should never have made it this far into ours."

Griffin shook his head, his expression grim. "Council's sittin' on their hands while these things slip through like smoke."

Quentin stared toward the trail below, the path they'd abandoned to escape. "The Council soldiers weren't patrolling. They don't patrol in that large of numbers," he said. "They must have been waiting."

Iain shifted his weight, gaze fixed on the ground. "Coincidence," he muttered.

Quentin shot his brother a look. Iain didn't meet it. He exchanged a glance with Izzy; her lips were pressed tight. "One thing is clear: the Council's mandate grows more dangerous by the day."

Iain leaned against the rock, wiping sweat from his brow. "Whatever they're planning won't end well—not for them, and definitely not for us."

Quentin nodded. "Which means we need to find the stone. It's the only chance we have of standing against whatever the Council and the rebels are unleashing."

"We go where you go," Freya said, almost anticipating him suggesting they stay behind.

"Time to start walking," Rhys muttered, already turning toward the trail. Quentin looked around at their group.

A grim silence fell across the group as the reality of their situation set in. They were alone, caught in the middle of a storm driven by the Council and the Rebellion. With every step, they felt the balance tipping ever more precariously. The wind didn't return. Even the desert seemed to be holding its breath.

CHAPTER THIRTY-SIX

Quentin

Kemetra, Aferra

Quentin pushed through the golden sands, his eyes scanning the rock walls around them. The cavernous landscape shimmered under the punishing heat. Sandstone cliffs and dunes stretched beneath the burning sun; their edges blurred in a haze against the light. There was an eerie quiet—thick and unmoving—that clung to the air in this part of the Magic Realm. No winds stirred the dunes, and no birds flew overhead. It felt untouched, suspended.

"Hmph. Wonder how close this is tae the human realm," Griffin muttered, squinting at the horizon. "If it's the same, here's hopin' Blythe and Hera've got it easier than we do. This place's got all the charm o' a sunburned grave."

Quentin nodded, his eyes narrowing at the distant shapes on the horizon. Dark, angular structures jutted from the sand, their outlines sharp against the cloudless sky. At first glance, they looked like plain pyramids, but on closer inspection, etched with runes that pulsed faintly with light. These pyramids seemed far more ancient—older than any human-built monuments Quentin had seen in books. It was as though humanity had once mimicked something glimpsed in a forgotten age. "The realms were connected once," Quentin murmured, eyes fixed on the distant pyramids. "Maybe the humans modeled theirs after the ones here—or maybe the Magic Realm lent them a hand."

Freya stepped up beside him, shielding her eyes from the relentless sun. "Right now, the only thing that matters is finding the stone before Demetrius or his minions do."

"Alright then, killjoy," Rhys muttered, rolling his eyes.

The group drifted into quiet conversation—some trying to distract themselves from what lay ahead, others already calculating their next moves.

Quentin tuned them out. He drew in a slow breath, the dry air scraping his throat, and focused on the subtle thrum beneath his feet—magic, faint but steady. The stone was close, its energy pulsing through the sand, whispering from the ruins ahead. Whether buried deep or hidden within one of the ancient structures, it was calling.

And he was listening.

"Let's keep moving," Quentin ordered, urgency tightening his voice. "We're close. I can feel it."

They trudged across the dunes, their footsteps sinking deeper into the soft sand. Magic thickened around them—suffocating and relentless.

In the distance, rising from the desert floor, stood a massive stone structure: angular, towering, and ancient. It lacked the distinct triangular form of a pyramid.

Quentin adjusted the strap of his satchel. The second stone was somewhere inside that ruin. They had to reach it before Demetrius's forces did.

Unease crawled beneath his skin, growing sharper with every step.

As they neared the structure, the air began to vibrate with magic. The walls shimmered faintly. The entrance was a gaping archway, flanked by towering statues of robed figures. Their faces were worn smooth by time, but their watchful stance remained ominous.

"I'll take a look," Iain said, stepping cautiously toward the archway. Before he could get far, a sharp, commanding voice echoed from above.

"I wouldn't do that if I were you." A jolt shot through Quentin. He looked up just in time to see a figure descending from the sky, cloaked in dark robes, a staff glowing with energy that seemed to absorb the light. Cold dread slid through him.

It wasn't Demetrius, but he knew who it was.

"Melya," he hissed under his breath.

Zelos's right hand—and one of the last people he wanted to see here.

The warlock landed lightly before them, her dark eyes scanning the group, a slow, predatory smile curling across her lips.

"I wondered when you'd show up, Quentin," she said smoothly. "I was hoping you'd be a little slower. I have strict orders to retrieve the stone, but..." Her gaze flicked over his companions. "This could be fun."

Quentin's jaw clenched. "We're tracking someone. That's all."

A simple lie. Broad enough to be believable. Vague enough to hide the truth.

Melya's smile sharpened.

"Tracking someone," she echoed. "How convenient. Especially since Zelos was so certain you four didn't vanish for nothing." She glanced around. "Where are the Unbound and the Valkyrie, anyway?"

Quentin's pulse kicked up. Unbound? She couldn't mean Blythe.

"He said you'd go after the stones," she continued, her tone almost playful. "He said you'd try to beat him to them. Do you even know what they're for?"

Quentin kept his expression still. He had a suspicion, but he didn't know. Not fully. He suspected she did, though.

Melya smirked, her eyes glinting with amusement. "You don't have the power to use them. So why bother?"

She tilted her head slightly, "Or do you know who does have that power?"

"We don't have time for this," Quentin said tightly.

Iain took a step forward, but Quentin raised a hand to stop him. He knew better than to underestimate a warlock—especially one as powerful as Melya.

"No," Melya agreed, "you don't. And Zelos will be thrilled to know he was right about you."

Quentin narrowed his eyes. "Zelos sent you to slow us down?"

Melya laughed. "No. As I said, I came for the last stone in this realm. But stopping you—or even slowing you down —would be my pleasure." Her fingers twitched, and a swirl of dark energy coiled around her hand, ready to strike.

Quentin's mind raced. They couldn't afford a battle here, not with the stone so close. "We don't need to fight. The stone isn't yours."

"No, it isn't yours," she snapped, her tone growing more dangerous. "You think you can waltz in here, take the stone, and defeat the Council and Demetrius? You're fools if you think you can win this game."

"This isn't a game. We're not trying to defeat Demetrius," Quentin lied coolly. "We're with the rebellion."

"Oh, everything in life is a game. It keeps things fun! If you're really with us, then why did you and Griffin left under the guise of getting the Fae and Dwarves on our side—only to create your own little group to come after what we've been seeking?" She lifted one slender eyebrow, a slow smile crossing her face. She laughed. "It's good you don't think this is a game since you're already losing."

Of course, she knew. Someone must have told her.

Warlocks didn't just sense things. If they could, they would have stopped them before they ever left camp.

Unless... they wanted them to get this far. Let them get the stones for Zelos.

Iain reached for his weapon, but Quentin remained still, thinking fast. "It's not about winning," he said. "It's about balance. The rebellion's no better than the Council, and you know it. You're a piece on someone else's board."

Melya's eyes flashed with anger, and for a moment, Quentin thought she might unleash her magic. But instead, she lowered her hand, the energy dissipating into the air.

"Maybe you're right," she said coldly. "But it doesn't matter. We now know where you stand, and we will have all the stones soon enough. You'll help us, whether you mean to or not. The prophecy will come to pass. It's already in motion."

A ripple of dark energy coiled around her feet like a creeping shadow.

"Try not to die before you're useful."

Before either of them could react, Melya vanished in a swirl of shadows, leaving the air unnervingly still.

Quentin exhaled slowly, tension bleeding from his muscles.

"What in blazes d'ye think she meant by that?" Griffin muttered, staring like he'd seen a ghost. "I suspect she's gone tae tell Demetrius and Zelos..."

"Why wouldn't she just attack us here?" Izzy whispered.

"She was outnumbered, and she knows the Council has people nearby," Freya offered.

"She could've wounded some of us, but it would've brought the mages down on her, too," Cael added.

"We don't have time for this. Let's move," Quentin said.

They turned back toward the ruin. It loomed darker, as if waiting for them. The stone was waiting inside and time was running out. He wondered if Blythe felt the same pressure tightening around her, wherever she was. The thought sharpened his urgency.

CHAPTER THIRTY-SEVEN

Quentin

Kemetra, Affera

"How are we even going to find our way to this stone?" Izzy whispered, the cavern's shadows swallowing her voice.

"Very carefully," Griffin said, his lips twitching with faint amusement.

"Har har har," Iain said flatly, fingers tightening on his staff. "Your humor isn't helping here."

"Neither are you at the moment," Izzy snapped, her eyes narrowing.

"Stop it. Both of you." Quentin's tone sliced through the rising tension, firm and steady. He stopped walking and turned to face them, the weight of leadership in his gaze. "We must push forward. The stone is close, and every second we waste gives Demetrius or the Council Mages time to get here. Let's move."

And if Benjamin was among them, he wouldn't hesitate to use Quentin as bait to get to Blythe. Demetrius may even do the same thing to get her. The Unbound.

Without waiting for further argument, Quentin led the way into the narrow crevice; the sound of their footsteps was muffled by the sandy floor. The tunnel stretched ahead—an oppressive corridor of cool stone etched with the marks of forgotten ages. Ancient glyphs lined the walls, faintly glowing with the soft hum of dormant magic. Their torches flickered, casting eerie, shifting patterns on their tense expressions.

Izzy trailed her fingers along the carvings, her brow furrowed. "These wards aren't just to keep people out. They're designed to keep… something in."

Griffin snorted, his grip tightening on his pickaxe. "Brilliant. Somethin' lurkin', waitin' tae chew us to bits. Just give me a shout when it's time tae smash its face in."

The air thickened with each step, as if the magic embedded in the walls pressed against them, testing their resolve. Iain's sharp intake of breath made them all stop short; he raised a hand and pointed toward the ground ahead. A faint line of glowing runes crossed the path, their pulsing in a slow, steady rhythm.

"Warding trap," Izzy muttered. "Step past that, and it'll trigger something nasty." She crouched to study it.

"How do we disengage it? Can any of you work magic?" Iain asked, looking around; everyone shook their heads.

"I have something that might work." Cael stepped forward, producing a pouch. "I have a powder that supposedly disengages wards. I'm not sure it'll work, but I can try."

Quentin exchanged a look with Griffin. "How long?"

"If you want me to do this right, it'll take a few minutes," Cael replied, sweat gathering at his brow as he knelt and began to sprinkle the powder over the runes. The wall's glyphs flickered in response. "Unless you're ready to deal with whatever curse this thing throws at us."

Iain muttered, "Just don't take all day."

The minutes dragged as Cael worked, spreading the powder slowly and in specific patterns over the glyphs. Finally, the glowing line faded into the stone, and he exhaled shakily, standing. "Done. But there will be more."

"How much of that powder do you have left?" Freya asked, anxiety leaking into her words.

"Hopefully enough," Cael said with a frown.

They pressed on, the tunnel winding deeper beneath the sands. The traps grew harder to spot. Griffin's keen eye for weak points in the stone saved them from collapsing walls, while Cael's magic powder unraveled the traps as they found them.

At last, the tunnel opened into a massive chamber. The air was colder here, carrying a faint smell of decay that prickled at their noses. Above, crystals embedded in the ceiling cast an eerie light across the room, bathing the space in a ghostly glow. At the center, a pedestal rose from the ground, and atop it sat the stone. It pulsed faintly, its glow rising and falling with the chamber's hum.

"There it is," Quentin said, his voice almost reverent.

"Don't touch it yet," Rhys warned before anyone could step farther into the space. "Go ahead, Cael."

Cael moved closer to the pedestal and pointed to the glowing runes encircling its base. "Those wards are deadly. Give me time to disable them."

Griffin's expression darkened as his gaze shifted to the far end of the chamber.

"Time's runnin' short," he said sharply, gesturing ahead. "Look."

Out of the shadows emerged a towering figure, its form carved from black stone. It moved with an unnatural grace, the jackal-shaped head swiveling toward them. Its eyes glowed with an eerie green light, and the sound of grinding stone accompanied each predatory step.

"Focus on the wards, Cael," Quentin ordered, drawing his blade. "Griffin, Iain, and I will handle this." He glanced toward Freya and Izzy. "Stay back."

The construct roared, the sound vibrating through the chamber and making their bones hum. Griffin charged first, dodging a massive swing that sent shards of stone flying. His pickaxe struck with a loud crack, chipping away at glowing runes etched into the creature's body. The construct faltered, its movements stuttering for a moment before resuming.

Rhys had positioned himself beside Freya and Izzy, firing arrows in rapid succession. Each one carried a small explosive that detonated harmlessly against the beast's stony exterior.

"Izzy!" Quentin shouted, ducking a vicious strike as his blade flashed. "Where's its weak spot? Can you see it?"

"Anything glowing!" Izzy yelled back. "Chest or back—anything exposed! That's how magical beasts work!"

"I can't see it!" Quentin dropped flat, narrowly avoiding a swipe, then sprang up.

"Anytime now!" Iain growled, slashing at the creature's leg. His blade clanged off harmlessly.

"There!" Freya cried, pointing. "Its back—just below the spine!"

Griffin ducked under another swing, landing a powerful strike on its knee joint that made it stagger. Quentin seized the opening, leaping onto its back as his blade plunged into a faintly glowing core at the base of its spine. The construct froze, its limbs jerking spasmodically as light spilled from the wound.

"Now, Griffin!" Quentin yelled, his voice urgent.

Griffin threw his axe, striking the construct squarely in the chest. With a deafening crash, it collapsed, its lifeless body scattering into rubble.

"Let me make sure nothing else comes after us," Cael called, continuing to spread the powder to disarm the protective symbols. "I'm almost out of this stuff, but hopefully it's enough to get past these wards." Once the runes faded and disappeared, he nodded.

Quentin stepped to the pedestal, his hand hesitating over the stone before grasping it. Power surged through him, visions crashing through him in a torrent of destruction, betrayal, and secrets. He gasped, snatching his hand back.

Iain stepped forward with a small pouch and scooped up the stone. "We have it," he said, his voice steady despite the turmoil in his eyes. "But we need to move."

As if on cue, the sound of pursuit echoed from the tunnel behind them.

"Move!" Quentin commanded.

The group sprinted, their boots pounding against the stone floor as they raced through the dimly lit chamber.

The ground beneath them trembled as the ancient

chamber reacted to their frantic escape. Stones rained from the ceiling, and the glyphs lining the walls pulsed erratically, as if sensing the chaos.

Griffin skidded to a halt at a sudden drop ahead. "Gap!" he shouted. Without hesitation, he leaped across, landing hard and reaching back to help Izzy follow. Cael, Freya, and Rhys jumped in rapid succession across the chasm.

Quentin was next, blade still drawn, landing hard. "Iain, hurry up!" he barked, extending a hand to steady his brother as he stumbled, nearly toppling over the edge.

Behind them, the pursuit grew louder. Their enemies poured into the chamber, torches throwing frantic shadows against the walls. The glow of weapons and spells lit the tunnel in flashes of fire and frost.

"We're not going to make it!" Izzy said, breath hitching as she clutched a stitch in her side.

"Yes, we will!" Quentin shot back.

Iain stopped short in the middle of a narrow passage, the others halting behind him. "Cael, do you have any other magic tricks in that bag of yours?!"

"I have a portal stone, but it will only work once," Cael said, digging into his pack and pulling it out. "It'll take a minute to activate."

"Then do it!" Quentin ordered, planting himself in front of Cael and raising his blade. "Griffin, Iain, Rhys—cover him! Izzy, Freya, behind me."

The group formed a protective circle around Cael, Freya, and Izzy as he knelt, the stone glowing with a brilliant, shifting light. His voice rose above the din, weaving the words needed to activate the stone.

A burst of energy tore down the passageway as their pursuers unleashed a volley of magic. Fireballs and shards of ice streaked toward them.

"Move!" Quentin shouted as the group parted, narrowly dodging the attack.

Griffin grunted as he swung his pickaxe, shattering a

jagged spear of ice that nearly struck Izzy. "This is bloody madness!" he barked. "How much longer, Cael? I'm roastin' like a turnip in a forge!"

"One more minute!" Cael shouted.

The air around them shimmered as the teleportation spell took form, the faint outline of a shimmering portal swirling into existence.

"We don't have a minute!" Quentin grunted, slashing his sword to deflect a bolt of energy.

"Just hold them off!" Cael barked.

Steel rang, and spells cracked through the tunnel, mingling with the snarls and shouts of their enemies. Izzy hurled a dagger, her aim true, striking one of their pursuers and slowing the advance.

The portal solidified, its swirling energy casting an eerie blue light across the tunnel.

A thunderous roar erupted behind the council mages, shaking the ground. A massive figure emerged from the shadows. A towering construct with sigils etched into its stone body, each one glowing with a heat that rolled off it in waves. It lunged forward, driving the group apart as its clenched hand crashed down, leaving a crater in the floor.

"Those idiots must have triggered something!" Izzy shouted.

"Go! Now!" Iain cried as the portal fully opened.

Quentin didn't hesitate. "Through the portal!" he shouted, shoving Izzy forward. Freya followed.

One by one, they leaped into the glowing vortex. Griffin went next, narrowly dodging another swing from the construct. Iain stumbled as he followed. Cael steadied him and went through. Rhys went next.

Quentin dove through the portal as the construct's fist came crashing down behind him. For a heartbeat, his stomach lurched as the world twisted sideways.

The portal closed with a flash of light.

They hit the ground in a tangled heap on a scorching

desert plain, sand scraping their skin as the setting sun bled across the dunes. Quentin pushed to his feet.

"Everyone... alive?" he panted, scanning the group.

"Barely," Griffin muttered, dusting himself off.

Quentin allowed himself a moment to breathe. A flicker of Blythe's face cut through the haze. Hopefully she was having a safer time getting the stones in the human realm.

"At least we got the stone," Freya said, trying for optimism, though her voice trembled with exhaustion.

CHAPTER THIRTY-EIGHT

Blythe

Valley of the Kings, Egypt

As Blythe, Hera, and Tavian edged through the excavation site under the dark desert sky, an unnerving quiet hung over it. Every shadow felt poised to move.

"Tavian," she murmured, "be ready."

He nodded, magic gathering at his fingertips, as if prepared to release it at any second.

Hera turned, scanning the distance. "We have company," she warned, barely audible, but Blythe felt the tension rising in her friend's stance.

A spell arced through the air, sizzling with crackling energy. Tavian reacted first, snapping a barrier into place that deflected it with a searing flash. Shadows emerged from the darkness—a team of Council agents, hidden until now. Their eyes shone, and without hesitation, they struck again, unleashing a barrage of spells.

Blythe launched into action, calling a protective incantation that wrapped around them in a shimmering shield.

"Move!" she shouted, dodging another spell and firing a blast of energy that hit one of the agents squarely, hurling him backward.

Tavian countered with a gust of wind that swept a pair of agents off their feet, flinging them into the rocks behind them.

"There's more coming!" he shouted, gritting his teeth as he deflected another volley.

The agents regrouped. "Surrender now!" one shouted.

"Wait!"

Blythe froze. She knew that voice.

A figure pushed through the line of agents. He wore the dark cloak of a Council Mage. The hood shadowed his face, runes and symbols were stitched in glowing silver thread along the edges.

"Well, well, well."

The figure raised a gloved hand and pulled back his hood, revealing a sharply cut crown of black hair and the beginnings of a dark beard shadowing his jaw. His eyes gleamed—cold, calculating, and far too amused.

He stepped forward, boots sinking into the sand with each deliberate stride.

"Benjamin," Blythe said quietly.

A breath of cold brushed her spine, quiet but unmistakable.

Beside her, Tavian stiffened. Hera snarled, low and feral.

"Oh dear," Benjamin said, his voice dripping with mock concern. "You're in quite the mess now, aren't you?" He laughed—a sharp, grating sound. "No House to shield you. I wonder... will the House finally recognize its true keeper once you're dead?"

His laugh twisted into a maniacal cackle as he raised his hand. "Kill them all. And bring me the stone."

His smile didn't reach his eyes—it never had.

Benjamin's team began to move forward as he backed away, magic crackling around them.

"Oh yeah, big brave Benjamin—always leaving others to clean up his mess!" Blythe spat. "I'm done with you." Her magic flared through her, sharp and hot.

The advancing mages' steps were steady as they moved toward them. Blythe didn't hesitate; she channeled her energy. Explosions of light and heat lit the night as they struck her targets, who staggered back in pain and confusion.

Just as an agent lunged at her with a magical lance, Blythe twisted, unleashing a razor-bright burst of power that sent him sprawling. She met Hera's gaze, and they nodded—a silent agreement to go all out. Hera leapt forward, grabbing a pair of daggers and slashing at the nearest agent, a ferocious display of skill as she weaved between Blythe's and Tavian's spells.

The ground trembled as Tavian invoked a powerful incantation, and jagged spikes of earth erupted from the sand, blocking the agents from closing in. Blythe seized the chance to unleash a burst of white-hot brilliance, stunning the enemies just long enough to drive a final, potent shockwave through the air, scattering the remaining Council agents.

Breath ragged, they stood back-to-back, surveying the aftermath. The desert was eerily quiet once more, the Council agents lying still among the sand and stone.

Hera wiped a trickle of sweat from her brow. "Well, so much for sneaking in."

Blythe smirked. "I think we made our point." She gestured toward the darkened ruins ahead. "Let's go. We're not leaving here without that stone."

"That felt too easy," Hera muttered, glancing at the agents in various stages of consciousness and recovery. Benjamin was nowhere to be seen.

"I'm not questioning it," Tavian said, starting toward the path.

"We need to move," Blythe noted, spotting one agent rising to his feet, holding his head as blood oozed between his fingers.

"Okay, let's go," Hera said. Blythe sprinted down the path they had been taking before the ambush. As they advanced deeper into the ruins, strange, rhythmic energy thickened the air, growing stronger with each step. The walls were etched with ancient symbols that shimmered faintly, as if alive. Blythe felt a subtle resistance in the air—a warning, or perhaps a final test. The stone had to be close.

"Do you feel that?" Tavian asked, his voice tense as he glanced around. "It's almost like... the air is pressing back."

Blythe nodded, her senses attuned to the peculiar aura. "Yes. The magic here is ancient—it feels like the other one."

Ahead of them, at the end of the narrow passage, a soft glow emanated from a cavernous chamber. The three of them entered cautiously, eyes scanning every corner. In the center of the chamber, a pedestal held the stone, radiating a faint, ethereal light. It was roughly the size of a fist, black with dark blue veins glowing in slow waves.

Hera stopped abruptly. "Wait. Look." She pointed to an intricate network of symbols carved into the floor, spiraling outward from the pedestal like a trap ready to spring.

"Enchanted runes," Tavian muttered, inspecting them closely. "They're rigged to react to movement." His gaze locked on Blythe. "One wrong step, and this place will come down on us."

Blythe surveyed the chamber, calculating. Her spells had always been a blend of instinct and training, but these runes would require precision. "I think I can disrupt them, but it'll take a moment." She reached into her pack for her Keeper's book.

"We've got your back," Hera assured her, weapons at the ready. "If anyone else is lurking, we'll handle them."

"But please, hurry," Tavian whispered anxiously.

Blythe found the page with the disabling spells and quickly studied it before beginning.

Blythe stepped forward, murmuring an incantation as she channeled her magic into the floor. Her energy flowed into the runes, trying to unweave them without triggering the trap. She felt the resistance in the enchantments—like fighting against knotted threads that twisted tighter the harder she pulled.

Tavian's hand shot up. "Blythe, we've got company!"

From the shadows, more agents emerged.

"They must have called reinforcements," Hera muttered.

They didn't hesitate, hurling spells with ruthless efficiency.

Hera leapt forward, deflecting one spell with her dagger and throwing a second enchanted blade that caught an agent in the shoulder, sending him staggering back. "Blythe, keep going! We'll hold them off!"

She closed her eyes, isolating herself from the chaos around her as her magic wrapped around the runes.

Beside her, Tavian laughed.

"Come on! Is that all you've got?" he taunted. "I know you trained to be better than this! Or is the Council sending disposable agents?"

Blythe tuned out the words around her, bringing her focus inward and allowing herself to be consumed by her magic. She felt more alive than she had in weeks. She began to feel as if she wasn't herself anymore. As if something—or someone—else had taken control.

Her eyes opened just as an agent slipped through Tavian and Hera's defenses, boots skidding across the sand as he lunged—dagger raised, eyes locked on Blythe.

She didn't think. She didn't have to.

Her magic snapped awake, faster than lightning. A shockwave burst from her chest—raw and instinctive—slamming into the attacker mid-stride. He flew backward, hit the wall with a crack that echoed through the chamber, and didn't get up.

Blythe didn't watch him fall. Her focus tunneled in. One last thread of the runes remained—tight, stubborn, resisting her grip.

She pushed harder.

The floor lit up in a wave of blue, the enchantment unraveling all at once, like breath released after a long-held scream.

Then it was gone.

Magic drained from her in a rush, leaving her hollow, brittle at the edges. She staggered, caught herself, and turned toward the fight—Tavian and Hera locked in combat, spells flying, blades flashing.

No time to rest. Not yet.

"It's done!" she shouted, grabbing the stone from the pedestal.

A boom sounded from somewhere deep within the hallways.

Instantly, the room shook. The ground split and cracked, and rocks began to fall from above.

Another boom like the steps of a giant followed, shaking the ground beneath them.

"Time to go!" Tavian yelled, pulling Blythe along as Hera covered their retreat, throwing a last flurry of dagger strikes at the remaining agents.

They dashed back through the passages, narrowly dodging debris as the temple began to collapse. Shouts sounded behind them. Some agents gave chase, but were slowed by the chaos around them; some were caught beneath falling stones or blocked by walls that collapsed.

Finally, the three of them burst into the open desert air just as the ruin crumbled behind them silencing the shouts and roars. They moved quickly away from the cloud and stopped to catch their breath, bruised and exhausted but victorious.

Hera looked at the stone in Blythe's hand, her eyes gleaming with relief. "Well, we did it. That's one more that the Council and the Rebellion can't control."

Blythe nodded, the stone's power vibrating faintly against her palm.

"Now we just need to make sure it stays that way."

A flicker of Quentin's face flashed through her mind—steady, grounding. She hoped he was still alive. She longed to see him again, to breathe in the worn leather and cold mountain air that always clung to him, sharp enough to clear her thoughts.

Hera nodded in agreement. The three of them made their way across the desert, their minds still buzzing from the adrenaline of their escape. They moved quickly, keeping an eye on the dark horizon for any other agents who might be lurking, but it was clear for miles in every direction. The silence pressed in around them—too still after the chaos inside the ruins.

After they reached a small outcrop, Hera paused and stretched, looking up at the stars. "We've had worse nights," she said with a tired smile.

Tavian let out a chuckle, his gaze flicking between the two of them. "You know, I've got to hand it to you both," he said, almost conversationally. "Pulling off something like this with only three of us? Impressive."

Blythe exhaled, relaxing a little.

Tavian's voice softened with an unusual calm. "Which is why I hate that it has to end this way."

Before either Blythe or Hera could react, Tavian's hand shot forward, and a ripple of magic snapped from his palm. A blast of force slammed into Blythe, hurling her against a rock.

"Tavian!" she shouted, struggling against the spell that held her. His magic was ironclad. She panicked, reaching for her magic, a guttering candle always just out of reach.

Hera, too, was pinned, her body held rigid by an invisible force as Tavian stepped closer. His face, usually open and good-humored, was cold, almost indifferent.

"Tavian," Hera hissed through clenched teeth, her expression twisted with anger and disbelief. "What in the dark realm are you doing?"

Blythe glanced down and noticed the stone sparkling on the ground. She'd dropped it.

Cold dread pooled in her gut.

He lifted the stone and turned it over in his hands, inspecting it with detached curiosity. "I'm doing what needs to be done, Hera. You didn't really think I'd let the two of you keep these, did you?"

Blythe's heart sank as she realized the depth of his betrayal. "So, this was all a setup? You never planned to help us. You're working for the Rebellion?"

Tavian tilted his head, a slight smirk on his face. "Working with the Rebellion, Blythe." His eyes hardened in a look she'd never seen on him before. "Not for them. Unlike you two, I know the stakes. The Council and the Rebellion, they're not so different. But the Rebellion… well, they have something worth fighting for. A chance at something better."

He raised his hand, and, in an instant, the second stone—the one Blythe had hidden was yanked free along with the pouch it resided in, flying into Tavian's palm. He poured the first stone out of the pouch into his other hand. His eyes bright with triumph as he held both stones, faint energy sparked between them. Blythe's stomach twisted. She'd handed him everything he needed.

"Enjoy your stay out here," he sneered, backing away. "I doubt you'll last long once the desert creatures catch your scent. But maybe you'll get lucky. Or maybe not. Maybe the Council will find you. Who knows?"

"Tavian, don't do this!" Blythe cried. "The rebels don't want peace. They're letting the dark creatures escape!"

Tavian ignored her and retreated, step by step. "Don't worry, Blythe. Everything will work out in the end."

With a last, mocking bow, he turned and began to walk away. Blythe and Hera struggled against the magical bindings, but Tavian's spell held fast, growing even tighter as he put more distance between them.

Desperation ate away at Blythe. She couldn't let him get away with the stones, not after everything they'd risked.

She forced herself to focus, pulling at every thread of energy she could reach. But it held firm—unyielding, built to trap and never release. Her wild magic wouldn't come—it felt burned out, like a flame that had guttered too long and needed time to recover. The hollow helplessness made her want to scream. Beside her, Hera's expression hardened into something lethal. "When we get out of this, I swear I'm going to tear him apart."

Blythe forced a small nod, her gaze locked on Tavian's retreating form.

CHAPTER THIRTY-NINE

Quentin

Kemetra, Affera

They moved quickly, urgency snapping at their heels as they returned to the dune glider. The beast would need to carry them one last time—far enough to find passage across the sea to Valoria, and from there, on to Aeloria. The glider waited exactly where they'd left it, resting in the sand.

They had not been gone from the coastal city for more than a few days, but upon their return, they found it burning, smoke clawing at the sky.

"What… what happened?" Izzy asked, her voice soft with horror.

A screech tore through the sky, and they all craned their necks to see a large, dark shape descending toward them, its mouth and claws open, ready to grab them.

"Roc!" Quentin shouted, recognizing the beast from their books of lore he had read as a child.

The dune glider howled and whipped around with surprising speed, lifting its massive mouth to bite the creature.

"Everyone off!" he shouted. They all leapt off the beast, rolling across the sand as the Roc dove. They quickly moved into defensive positions, weapons drawn. Rhys didn't wait; he immediately began firing arrows at the creature.

"Incoming!" Griffin shouted. Quentin turned to see what he hoped was just a mirage but feared was not. Dozens of people were walking toward them. As they drew closer, he saw their heads tilted at unnatural angles, with overly large eyes and mouths that gaped with huge fangs.

"What the dark realm are those?!" Iain shouted, clutching his sword.

"Mirrorfiends," Izzy said, terror etched into her words. "They take on the shape of those they kill… but it's not quite right…"

"Well, we'll kill 'em again all the same!" Griffin snarled, standing with his axe at the ready.

A sharp whistle cut through the air—then the clash of steel followed.

Quentin moved instantly. His sword was already drawn, intercepting the first blow with a hard exhale. Rhys barreled into an attacker, shield up, driving them back with sheer force. Iain ducked low, sweeping a leg and sending another crashing to the ground. Griffin let out a roar, axe swinging wide, catching the glint of torchlight as it met flesh.

There was no time to speak. The fight had found them.

Quentin glanced over his shoulder just long enough to see Freya dragging Izzy behind a toppled pillar, shielding her with one arm while drawing her sword with the other. Izzy's eyes were wide, breath sharp and uneven, but Freya stood between danger and his sister.

Quentin dipped his head—a silent thank-you, before turning back to the fray.

Steel met steel.

He dodged a wild swing, countered with a sharp jab to the ribs, then pivoted to block another strike from the left.

Time blurred.

The battle became rhythm: parry, slash, dodge, strike. A dance of survival. Dust billowed around their feet, kicked up by boots and bodies. Grunts, shouts, the clang of weapons—each sound sharper than the last.

A blade scraped his shoulder. He inhaled, twisted, and drove his sword into the attacker's thigh. They fell with a cry, and Quentin didn't wait to see if they would rise again.

Another came at him—taller, heavier. Quentin feinted left, then slammed his elbow into the man's jaw, following with a brutal slash across the chest. The man staggered, blood blooming as he collapsed.

Quentin's breathing turned harsh and uneven. His shirt clung to him, soaked in sweat and grit. He scanned the battlefield and now saw Freya and Izzy back-to-back, swords drawn and fighting.

They were barely holding.

"We need to get out of here!" Iain shouted.

Quentin nodded. He battled his way to each of his allies, shouting at them to make for the sea. As he went, he glimpsed the dune glider locked in a fierce struggle with the Roc. They couldn't help it—they had to go. Now.

The group ran, blades flashing as they fought their way down the winding path toward the shore. The terrain was unforgiving: loose stone and jagged roots. Quentin led the way, blood streaked across his cheek, eyes locked on the horizon.

"There has to be a boat somewhere," he muttered, more to himself than anyone else. "There has to be."

Behind him, Griffin grunted as he shoved an attacker off the trail, sending the creature tumbling to the ground. Freya stayed close to Izzy, her sword in one hand and dagger in the other, slick with effort, her chest heaving. Her sword arm trembled, but she didn't falter.

The path opened suddenly, revealing the sea—dark, churning, and vast. And there, half-submerged in the shallows, was something impossible: A vessel.

Not made of wood or metal, but of woven kelp and glowing crystal. Runes pulsed along its sides, and a faint hum vibrated in the air around it.

They didn't have time to question it.

A shout rang out behind them—more enemies, closing fast.

"Go!" Quentin barked.

They splashed into the surf, climbing aboard the strange craft as arrows hissed past. Freya hauled Cael up just as he slipped. Rhys shielded Izzy with his body, dragging her into the vessel's heart. Iain stumbled in right behind them with Griffin bringing up the rear.

Quentin reached the helm. There was no wheel, no sail, just a glowing orb set into the center.

He touched it.

The vessel lurched, then shot forward, skimming across the water with unnatural speed. Behind them, the attackers reached the edge too late.

Quentin didn't let go of the orb. He could feel it: ancient magic, volatile and alive. It was taking them somewhere. Somewhere safe. For now.

They had escaped.

But only just.

"Will this take us to Valoria?" Izzy asked, her voice barely rising above the hum of the waves.

The orb in Quentin's hand glowed steady and warm.

"It would seem so," he murmured, a faint smile tugging at his lips. He eased down onto the deck, muscles aching, head tipping back against the side of the vessel. The gentle rocking of the boat lulled him in a rare moment of peace after the chaos. Blythe's face shimmered through his mind, calming him. He prayed to whatever Gods existed that she was still safe.

Griffin dropped beside him with a grunt. "Well, that was fun."

Quentin chuckled, eyes still closed. Leave it to Griffin to find joy in a death-defying battle.

The sea stretched around them—vast, quiet, and endless. Valoria awaited.

CHAPTER FORTY

Blythe

Valley of the Kings, Egypt

With the stones gone and Tavian's betrayal still burning in their thoughts, Blythe and Hera found themselves stranded in the Egyptian desert, with no magical artifacts to aid their journey home. His spell had worn off, leaving them alone in the cooling sand, the silence absolute and unnerving. Night draped the dunes in an eerie quiet, broken only by their footsteps. Their immediate goal was to reach civilization—perhaps find a port where they could blend in and eventually return to the United States.

Several days later, disheveled and exhausted, they finally arrived in Cairo. Small spells kept them hydrated and alive as they crossed the brutal desert. In Cairo, Blythe used a soft glamour spell to nudge a dock worker's perception, guiding his eyes away from her and Hera as they slipped aboard a cargo ship bound for New York City. Hidden among crates and barrels, they survived on stale crew rations pilfered from storage when no one was looking.

When they finally disembarked in the U.S., they were met with a tension she didn't recognize—sharp, electric, distrustful. The harbor bustled with people hurrying about, eyes flicking over strangers with thinly veiled distrust. Police sirens echoed from blocks away. Blythe and Hera slipped through the streets, observing the shift.

Broken windows, abandoned shops, and the uneasy murmur of crowds painted a picture of recent chaos. Hera motioned Blythe to stop, her face tight with unease. Across the street, a news broadcast flickered on a television inside a bar, casting a ghostly glow on the few patrons huddled around it.

"...an increasing number of mysterious attacks," the reporter's voice was strained. "Officials still have no explanation for the surge of violent incidents occurring across the country. Tensions have risen, with many blaming neighboring communities and accusing outsiders of being involved in these violent outbursts."

"Mimics," Hera whispered.

As Blythe and Hera lingered outside the bar, the news broadcast took a chilling turn. The reporter's tone shifted from urgent to grim, her expression tense.

"In a recent statement from the new administration, drastic measures are being put in place to combat what officials are calling 'a foreign threat.' Effective immediately, borders will be closed to all but essential personnel, and emergency powers have been granted to expel foreign nationals from the country. The administration has declared its intent to 'take care of our own' and handle this without outside interference."

Gasps and murmurs of disbelief rippled through the patrons watching the TV. A weary bartender muttered under his breath, "So they're really doing it... closing up and leaving everyone else to fend for themselves."

Hera gripped Blythe's arm, her whole frame drawn taut. "They're sealing themselves off from the rest of the world. They don't even realize what's really happening, and they're abandoning everyone else to face it alone."

A man nearby scoffed bitterly. "Can you blame them? With all these attacks and those... things crawling out of nowhere? I'd say it's about time we stopped letting strangers in, stopped trusting anyone we don't know."

A sick twist coiled in Blythe's gut. She'd seen enough of the Council's divisive methods in the Magic Realm, and now the same fear, paranoia, and isolationism were gripping the human world. With this new administration feeding it, the situation was unraveling fast. Borders would close, people would turn on each other, and the dark creatures would continue their onslaught unchecked.

They turned away from the bar's doorway and slipped back into the street, blending into the shadows as they continued toward The House. Her House. A chill threaded through the air, sharp enough to raise gooseflesh. A colder thread slid beneath her skin—her magic's warning, subtle but unmistakable. As they walked, Blythe clenched her fists, her mind racing through the facts. Not only were they racing to stop the Council and the Rebellion, but they now had to contend with a human world fracturing along the same dangerous path.

And Quentin was somewhere out there in the chaos of the magic realm—too far to reach, too far to help. The distance ached.

Blythe caught the lingering looks Hera drew. The headscarf she'd kept on to hide her ears wasn't what people reacted to—plenty of humans wore them—but Hera's movements had a wrongness that pricked at attention.

"We need to get back to the Magic Realm before someone notices," she said.

"Agreed," Hera murmured.

CHAPTER FORTY-ONE

Blythe

United States, New York City - travel to Upstate, NY

The trip back to the House of Fas passed without incident, which felt wrong in itself. Blythe had expected either the police or Council agents to pop out, cartoon-villain style, and apprehend them. Hera displayed some incredible pickpocketing skills, acquiring enough money for bus fares. They arrived in the town near Fasbridge Manor and hiked the remaining seven miles.

Blythe wasn't sure what she had expected when they approached the House, but seeing it unchanged, untouched, sent a ripple of unease through her. The air hummed faintly, the way it always did when the House was paying attention.

Once they set down their stuff, Blythe quickly called Quentin. They needed to meet at once.

"Tavian double-crossed us," Hera snarled, voice rough with fury.

"That's nae surprising. I've seen rocks do more unexpected things," Griffin grumbled. Blythe saw the group gathered behind Quentin, the portal carved into the wall before her.

"It's impossible to know where anyone's alliances lie in times like these," a young woman to Quentin's right said. Blythe wasn't sure who she was.

"I knew we shouldn't have trusted that bastard," Hera bit out. Blythe decided against reminding her that she had recommended giving him a chance—she wasn't sure what the Valkyrie would do if reminded of that poor choice.

"It seems to happen a lot these days," Quentin's expression tightened. "We got ours. If we can at least keep this out of their hands, we have a bit of an advantage."

"There's strength in numbers, though, Quentin," Hera countered. "He has the numbers."

"Not much we can do about that," Quentin countered.

"Since we are all in relatively safe locations for now, when and where do we want to meet? We could come to you, but I think it's best we reunite in Aeloria," Quentin asked.

"I agree," Hera nodded. She glanced at Blythe, who looked confused. "That's the capital of the Fae."

"I'll go to the Dwarves to help coordinate their joining us," a woman said from behind the others. She stepped forward, long red hair catching the light. "Hi, I'm Freya."

Quentin gestured to the group behind him. "Blythe, Hera—this is Rhys, Cael, Freya, Iain, and Izzy."

"I'll go with you," Rhys offered.

Quentin nodded. "Yes. Okay, Freya and Rhys, go to Umbrahold and check in on where they're at. As soon as we land, we will separate."

"Okay. How do we get to Aeloria?" Blythe pronounced the unfamiliar name slowly.

"We will start making our way there by land. You can call Ellira. She knows the way."

"Will do," Hera nodded, glancing at Blythe again. "You have thoughts?"

"When don't I?" Blythe's thoughts tangled as she leaned against the cool stone wall, eyes scanning the room as if seeking answers in the familiar surroundings. She'd hoped the House would steady her. It didn't.

"Two enemies," she murmured, her voice barely above a whisper, though the words settled heavily between them. A thin chill threaded beneath her skin. Her magic's warning, quiet but insistent. "Demetrius and the Council." She shook her head slowly. "And honestly, I'm not sure which is worse. We have only one stone out of six."

Hera was quick to respond, her usual fire dimmed by the truth they both knew.

"But we've seen what the Council is capable of. We've lived it. And Demetrius—he's... ruthless. But he's also driven by a personal vendetta. His agenda, twisted as it is, is rooted in something... personal. We'll get the stones."

Quentin's voice cut through the thick quiet that had taken root in the room, calm and steady.

"The Fae are reaching out to their allies," he said, his gaze meeting Blythe's, as if trying to pull her back from the edge of her racing thoughts. "If we can keep the nations from isolating themselves like the Council wants and remind them of what the world once was, we might just have a chance."

Quentin paused before continuing. "Also, we ran into Melya, who seemed to call you Unbound? Does that mean anything to you? Earlier, Demetrius seemed to imply he needed you for something involving the stones."

A sacrificial lamb. Was that what she was meant to be? Did the stones kill their wielder... or do something worse? And Unbound. Were they calling her that because she had no Talisman at all? Was that why they needed her?

"We also need to convince them that Demetrius's way is not the only one," Hera added.

Blythe lifted her gaze to Quentin's, feeling the weight of Hera's words.

They were right, of course. The Fae had allies, and Blythe understood the importance of unity, of collective strength. But how could they ever hope to unite the nations when the forces against them were so intent on dividing everything?

Blythe closed her eyes for a moment, steadying her breath. The pull of her emotions was overwhelming. She opened her eyes again and met his gaze. "I want to believe we can do it. But sometimes it feels like we're losing ground with every step we take."

"We won't lose," Quentin said, determination unmistakable in his voice. "We'll fight for both worlds. Together."

Blythe inclined her head, resolve settling in. If she had to trust in anything anymore, it would be the strength of the people fighting beside her.

"Okay," she said quietly, a new sense of purpose settling over her. "We'll fight."

"Fetch Ellira. We will see you soon, Kits," Quentin said.

Blythe's heart skipped a beat. Something in his voice tugged at her. Steady, familiar, and too close to hope.

She pushed the thought aside, focusing on the task at hand. She couldn't afford distractions. Not now. There was too much at stake. The weight of Quentin's words echoed in her mind: We'll fight for this world, Blythe. Together. It was a promise. Or was it a plea?

"Right," she muttered, pulling herself together. "I'll call Ellira."

Their call ended, and Blythe moved toward the stairs to reach her study and use the House to contact Ellira.

She hurried up the stairs and moved down the hallway. The door to the study opened, and she stepped inside, heading toward the spiral staircase. At the top, she heard the clicking of the typewriter as the House wrote out a message for her. She moved around the desk to read the paper protruding from the old metal typewriter:

Ellira has been called. Rest. She will be here soon.

"Thank you," she whispered, fingertips grazing the cool metal.

She forced herself back into the hallway, each step weighted with exhaustion and the knowledge that everything was shifting again. Ellira was coming. Hera was waiting. And the world wasn't going to pause for her to catch her breath.

CHAPTER FORTY-TWO

Blythe

Aeloria, Fae Mountains

Blythe clung to Ellira's back as they soared through the sky, the wind tearing through her hair and drowning out all sound but its own deafening roar. Hera, infuriatingly, seemed entirely at ease with this mode of transportation. Blythe didn't understand it. Surely clinging to the back of a massive, winged creature with nothing between her and a thousand-foot plummet was far worse than the illusion of safety an airplane offered—with its walls, floor, and roof pretending you were in the safety of a vehicle on the ground. So long as you didn't look out the window and ignored the turbulence.

She had no idea how long they had been in the air. Time lost its meaning in the clouds. But when Ellira finally touched down on a patch of grass nestled among jagged mountains, their peaks swallowed by mist, Blythe could have dropped to her knees and kissed the ground pope style.

"Blythe and Hera! A relief ya survived yer trip!" came Griffin's unmistakable voice. "I'll ne'er get used to ridin' one of them!"

She turned to see his stocky form lumbering toward them, his grin stretching wide.

"Hello, Griffin," Blythe said with a smile, hugging him tightly. Hera offered him a respectful nod, which he returned with a grunt and a wink.

Then she heard it—his voice.

"It's good to see you."

Blythe turned, and there he was. Quentin.

Something inside her eased at the sight of him, like a knot she hadn't noticed finally untied. A faint warmth pushed back the ever-present chill within her. She wasn't sure what she'd expected—awkwardness, distance, maybe the hollow echo of everything left unsaid. A tether she hadn't wanted to need.

And damn it, he still looked good.

"It's good to see you, too," she said, forcing her tone to stay even as she met his eyes—steady, unreadable, the way they always had been.

The smile that crossed his face sent a flutter through her belly. He looked away, as if he, too, felt the awkwardness.

Griffin cleared his throat, and Hera muttered, "Get a room..." before another voice joined them.

"You must be Blythe!" Blythe recognized one of the women she had seen in the communication portal. "We weren't really officially introduced. I'm Izzy, Quentin's sister." She elbowed the boy who could have been her twin in facial structure and body shape. "And this is Iain, our brother." He grunted and shifted away from her. "He's my twin." Well, that explained the similarities.

Izzy swept up to Blythe and hooked her arm through her own, gently leading her across the field in the direction from which they had come.

"Come! We have so much to talk about. I'm dying to learn about the human realm and your side of all the adventures you and Quentin were on."

"Izzy, give her a break." Iain pulled his sister away. "She's not here to be your new best friend."

"No, but if Quentin has imprinted—"

Did everyone know about that? Heat rushed up her neck. Was it just that obvious to those who came from this world? The thought made her feel icky, as if a deep, dark secret had been plastered across a billboard for everyone to see.

"Enough," Quentin's voice sounded strained and uncomfortable. He ran a hand through his hair in his patented nervous habit.

"No, it's fine," Blythe said, unable to bear the pressure any longer. "I'd love to chat with you, Izzy, but I think Quentin, Griffin, Hera, and I should speak first. We have some important things to discuss."

"I'll just take this one away…" Iain grabbed Izzy by the arm and dragged her off as she loudly protested. "Let us know when you need us!" he called back over his shoulder.

"Sorry about that." Quentin had moved over to stroke Ellira's nose as she nuzzled into him.

"It's fine…" Blythe noticed Hera and Griffin moving away, talking quietly with each other. Griffin gave a brief wave as they disappeared into the hedges. She exhaled, steadying herself. "This imprinting thing…"

"It's not important," Quentin began, but she needed to get this out of the way.

"It is. There's been so much else going on—but clearly it's not a secret, and everyone knows about it." Blythe looked down at the grass, the cool evening breeze brushing past her. A faint breath of him reached her—worn leather, sweat, and the cold bite of mountain air. The scent hit her with a rush of memory and longing she wasn't prepared for.

The distant chatter of the others faded as Quentin stepped closer, his shadow stretching across the field.

"I didn't tell them," Quentin said. "Izzy and my mother guessed—they're perceptive like that…"

Blythe shook her head. "I didn't think you did. I've been thinking," she began, her voice low and hesitant. She met his eyes—steady but guarded. "Neither of us asked for it. And we can't pretend it's not there, or that it doesn't mean something. To you, at least. I mean, I guess it means something to me too, but…"

Quentin's expression sharpened, and he nodded slowly. "It's not just a bond. It's a need. I don't want it to be a weakness, but sometimes it feels like it already is."

She swallowed and rolled her shoulders back, forcing

the tightness to ease. "I need you to understand—we can't let it control what happens between us, or what we do. The rebellion, the Council—those things must come first. We can't afford distractions."

He stepped closer still, the heat of him brushing against her skin. Her breath hitched a tight pull blooming low in her stomach before she could stop it.

"I can't help but be distracted by it. I need you to know... I can't control what this imprinting does to me. I will do anything to protect you—anything. It's what the imprinting has made me."

His words landed between them. Blythe focused on her breathing. In, and out. Trying to ignore the desire blooming within her.

"Maybe we stop fighting it," she whispered. "Maybe we should stop pretending we can just set it aside. I must. Because it's real. But we promise we'll keep it in check, together."

Quentin's eyes softened, a fragile hope breaking through as he breathed out. "Together."

Blythe felt something inside her give way. A soft, aching surrender she couldn't fight anymore.

She moved first, just a breath closer, and he met her halfway.

The kiss wasn't tentative. It was deep and trembling, born of fear and relief and the impossible pull between them. The warmth and pressure of his lips against hers consumed her.

For a moment, the world froze around them.

Then Quentin drew back with a small, almost reluctant smile. Blythe's body leaned after him before she caught herself, stopping the instinct to chase the kiss, to pull him back. Not now. Not yet.

"We should join the others," his voice came out in a husky breath. "They're waiting—and time isn't on our side."

Blythe nodded, brushing a loose strand of hair behind her ear.

"Right."

Quentin reached for her hand lacing his fingers through hers as if it were the most natural thing in the world.

The contact jolted through her. Her pulse stumbled, then quickened, warmth blooming up her arm and settling low in her chest. She tightened her grip before she could think better of it.

As they walked toward the city, the stress between them hadn't fully eased, but it had shifted—into a quiet understanding.

Hera and Griffin were waiting near the gate, their expressions a mix of impatience and guarded hope.

"Ach, finally," Griffin grumbled, scratching his beard. "Thought ye'd wandered off into yer own skulls and forgot the way out!"

Blythe glanced at Quentin, who offered a brief nod. The group moved on, walking towards the sparkling city as the sun began its slow descent beyond the horizon.

"Freya and Rhys sent word," Iain ran over to join them. "The Dwarves will help us, and they've sent word to their allies—the Gnomes and Stone Elves. If they can get the Stone Elves on their side, the Woodland and Mountain Elves may follow suit."

"I spoke with Octo earlier, and he said he was on his way to get the Merfolk and their allies," Quentin added.

The Council and Demetrius know the stones are in play, and Demetrius has all but one. And Benjamin? He's just waiting for his chance to take the last stone, and Blythe with it."

Blythe's gaze moved over her friends, taking in the weight of their mission and the fragile threads holding them together. The fight was only beginning, and her thoughts churned so heavily that the city blurred around her as they walked.

Quentin brushed his shoulder against hers, pulling her back to the moment. When she looked over, he gave her that familiar grin. The flutter in her stomach nearly unraveled her composure, but she managed a smile in return.

CHAPTER FORTY-THREE

Blythe

Aeloria, Fae Mountains

Nerves fluttered under her skin as she stood outside the Throne Room. Quentin stood nearby, silent, arms crossed, watching her pace across the polished stone floor. A cool breeze swept down from the peaks, brushing across her face. She brushed them away with a frustrated huff.

"I hate waiting," she muttered.

"Better to wait and be prepared," Quentin said. "We only get one shot to convince them."

Hera lay sprawled on a bench, her braid trailing to the floor. She squinted up at the ceiling, then muttered, "Fae, Dwarves, Gnomes, Elves, Merfolk... getting that lot to agree on anything? Might as well ask a thunderstorm to hold still."

Blythe opened her mouth to reply, but the double doors groaned open behind them.

A Fae guard stepped through, his armor a shimmer of silver and green, ceremonial and spotless. He bowed low, eyes never quite meeting theirs.

"They're ready for you."

The chamber beyond was a mosaic of light and unease. Sunlight poured through arched windows, catching on crystal inlays that webbed across the domed ceiling like veins of frozen lightning. The air smelled faintly of salt, stone, and old magic.

At the center, a circular table dominated the space—seven chairs spaced evenly around it, each carved in the style of its occupant's homeland.

Lyriana sat tall at the far end, her robes flowing like water. Garruk was beside her, arms crossed and jaw set. Next to him, a stone elf perched stiffly. A mountain elf leaned back, eyes scanning the room like a hawk. The woodland elf beside her tapped a finger against the table, rhythm sharp and impatient.

The mer-woman's hair shimmered like kelp, her gaze unreadable. The gnome adjusted his spectacles, feet dangling above the floor, his expression somewhere between curiosity and dread.

Around the edges of the room, their entourages waited —silent, watchful, and visibly uncomfortable. Cloaks rustled. Fingers twitched. No one leaned too close to a neighbor.

Blythe stepped forward, the moment settling on her shoulders like a mantle.

Each bore the sigils of a realm on their garments: the swirling waters of the Mer, the mountain runes of the Dwarves, and the golden tree of the Fae. She couldn't quite make out the ones on the various elves and the gnomes.

Quentin stepped forward and bowed. "Thank you for agreeing to this meeting."

"Let us hope it's worth the risk," the mer-woman said, her voice like rushing water. "We do not gather lightly."

"We know," Blythe said, steadying her voice. "The Council is corrupt. Demetrius's revolution is not what we were led to believe."

Garruk grunted. "And ye've brought a stone with ye?"

Blythe stepped forward and unwrapped the blue stone in her hand. Its glow shimmered in slow waves across the floor. Murmurs spread through the chamber. Even Queen Lyriana's serene mask cracked.

"We believe Demetrius is trying to unite the stones to tear down the barriers between realms," Quentin said. "He wants chaos. Power. Rule without restraint."

"Worship from humankind," Hera added.

"And you want to stop him?" the woodland elf asked.

"Yes. But we need your support. Real support."

"What you're proposing would drag all of us into war," the gnome leader said, voice low and grave.

"So be it, then," Griffin growled, his voice like gravel. "Waitin' won't save a soul. By the time we blink, there'll be no bloody kingdoms left to defend!"

Before anyone could reply, the chamber doors slammed open behind them.

Gasps rippled across the room.

Tavian stood in the doorway. His hair was matted with dirt, his shirt stained with dried blood, one hand pressed to his side.

"Wait," he rasped. "Don't act yet. You don't know everything."

Hera drew her sword and started forward, stopping only when Griffin threw a burly arm in front of her.

"Wait," he muttered. She swore under her breath but obeyed.

Blythe fixed Tavian with a hard stare. "You've got some nerve showing your face here."

"I had to make it look real," Tavian said, stumbling forward. "Demetrius doesn't trust easily. If I'd taken only one stone, he'd have known I was lying—and I wouldn't be standing here."

"Where are the stones?" Hera growled. Blythe might have been terrified to face Hera, but Tavian stood his ground.

"I told Demetrius I was angry with my grandfather—that I believed the Council was under dark influence."

Lyriana chuckled. "A double-double agent. How convenient."

Hera scoffed. "At least that part wasn't a lie..."

Tavian's face tightened. "I said I wanted to help him and needed to see what Blythe and Hera were really up to. When I found out they were trying to stop Demetrius, I realized I could gain his trust by taking one stone. He demanded I get both. I couldn't say no. I'm not suicidal."

Hera's grip tightened on her sword. "You expect us to believe you?"

He winced. "Demetrius has the same dark aura my grandfather has. Both the Council and Demetrius wanted you to get the stones for them—I'm sure of it."

"So you just handed the stones over to him?" Tavian flinched at Blythe's tone.

"I did think it was too easy to beat the Council agents…" Hera muttered.

The mer-woman raised an eyebrow at Tavian before turning to Quentin. "Tavian contacted Octo, and Octo contacted me after Tavian handed over the stone."

Tavian attempted a bow, but pain cut the motion short. "I stopped at Locke Manor on my way. Dug through records, anything I could find on the stones and the Council's corruption. My theory? Demetrius made a pact—something ancient and twisted—while trapped in the Dark Realm. Maybe the Realm itself demanded it. I don't think he escaped alone."

"Bah, this muddies the brew," Griffin muttered, brow furrowed. "Like tossin' a goat into a gearworks—nothin's runnin' smooth now."

"No," Quentin said. "This clarifies things. We no longer have the luxury of mistrust."

"Speak plainly," Lyriana said coldly. "If we are to stand together, we must unify our strategy. Tavian Locke—what's your plan?"

"I continue as I am," Tavian said. "Demetrius thinks I'm loyal. The Council believes I'm spying on him. Neither side knows I've been here."

"Are you lying to them both?" Hera asked.

Tavian had the decency to look ashamed. "Yes—and no. I haven't told the Council about the stones, and I haven't told Demetrius that you suspect he's up to something nefarious. But I have warned the Council that he's preparing a rebellion, and I've told Demetrius things that could help him defeat the Council."

"And what do you hope to accomplish by lying to everyone?" Blythe snapped. "How can anyone trust you?"

"They can't," Tavian said. "That's the point. No one does. But I'm still here—still fighting for the people I care about. My family lives in a Portal House. If Demetrius tampers with the stones' magic, what happens to them? What happens to the barriers keeping the realms balanced? And the Council… they already see non-Mages as lesser. If they win, the rest of you don't stand a chance."

"That would work in your favor," Hera muttered.

Tavian shot her a sharp look. "Except it wouldn't. Not when the people I love aren't Mages." His eyes flicked between Hera and Quentin before rising to the platforms. "I grew up between here and Locke House. You've been my family as much as they have. I don't want to see any of you harmed."

Queen Lyriana rose and stepped forward. "I have watched you grow, Tavian Locke. I want to believe you, but belief must be balanced with caution. Tell us everything you know about the Stones, and then I will have you escorted out so that we may continue our discussion."

"And tell us why you look like you've been to the Dark Realm and back," Izzy chimed in. "You really look terrible."

"I had a run-in with some dark creatures on the way here." His voice hitched, as if the memory was raw. "The Stones were integral in creating the portals. What I found at Locke House—and from speaking with Demetrius—is that the Old Ones had a reason for not sealing the Dark Realm completely." He paused, gathering himself. "We parasitically draw life-force from the dark creatures feeding on those banished there. If the Dark Realm closed, our power would collapse. We'd be back to fire and coal."

He hesitated, jaw working.

"I think it would be better if we did. It's wrong to banish people to the Dark Realm, and it's wrong to drain the life-force from anyone—evil or not. There were more portals before. But, I believe Demetrius intends to continue using the dark realm, but also to cause more chaos by eliminating the barriers between the realms entirely. He loves chaos. Probably why he doesn't care what Blythe is up to. He figures if she's causing distrust, it'll create more chaos."

His expression tightened, shoulders lifting in a helpless gesture. "But that's all I have to share for now." Turning to Hera, he pleaded, "Please believe me—I want the same as you. I want this evil and destruction eliminated once and for all. If sealing the portals is what it takes to protect humans and keep the dark creatures contained, then we should do it. We survived before without draining life from others."

"Where are the Stones, then?" Blythe repeated.

He frowned and had the good sense to look ashamed. "Demetrius has them." He looked back up at her. "But they're useless without the one you have—and you."

"Me? Why me?" She tried to ignore the chill creeping up her back.

"I'm not sure," he admitted. "He has called you 'Unbound' and apparently needs you for the stones."

Queen Lyriana nodded. "Thank you, Tavian. We will fetch you when we are done talking. Guard, escort him to another chamber while we continue our discussions and see that our healer takes a look at him."

Tavian bowed and followed the guard out. Blythe glanced at Hera, who watched him go with an expression she couldn't read.

Iain's gaze stayed fixed on the door, shoulders drawn tight. A hush settled over the chamber.

Lyriana turned to Quentin. "Now. What do you propose?"

Quentin stepped forward, voice firm. "We help the rebels take out the Council first."

A sharp, instinctive panic flared in her chest. The Council was corrupt, yes, but helping Demetrius felt like stepping into a trap she'd spent weeks trying to escape. And Quentin... why was he the one suggesting it?

Blythe's pulse spiked, her magic flickering uneasily beneath her skin, cold as ice in her veins. "What?"

He turned, facing her. "Demetrius doesn't want you dead—at least not yet. He thinks you're misled. If we eliminate the Council, we can turn our full efforts to stopping him."

"So we help him topple the Council, then hope we can outmaneuver him afterward?" Hera asked.

Lyriana's voice was quiet, but resolute. "We give Demetrius the stone—conditionally. He dissolves the current Council and reinstates the old structure with representation from all races."

"No," Blythe said flatly. "Absolutely not. We can't trust him."

"He already has more stones than we do," Lyriana replied.

"We're not givin' up our only bloody edge!" Griffin barked, fists clenched. "Might as well toss our beards in the fire and call it a day!"

A murmur rippled through the chamber.

Lyriana met each gaze, calm but implacable. "If we don't take the Council down first, it won't matter. They'll wipe us out before we ever reach Demetrius."

"And you think Demetrius will just step aside afterward?" Hera asked.

"No," the stone elf said, her cool grey eyes studying them. "Right now, we're scattered, defensive, and vulnerable."

"This is madness," Quentin's voice dropped, rough. But he could already see the tide turning. The leaders were nodding.

Lyriana's eyes moved from face to face, noting the quiet nods spreading through the room.

"You're being overruled," Lyriana said gently. "I'm sorry. But the decision is made."

Blythe felt the decision closing around her like a door, leaving her with no room to push back. She clenched her fists at her sides. Every instinct in her recoiled. This was wrong.

Giving Demetrius the stone was handing him the keys to their destruction. But she looked at her allies. Izzy stared at the ground, and Iain's face was harder for her to read. He looked almost… pleased, though she couldn't imagine why.

A knot tightened in her chest, the taste of surrender bitter on her tongue.

"Fine," she said. "But when this all blows up in our faces… just remember we tried to stop it."

Queen Lyriana nodded. "We will have Tavian arrange a meeting. I think it's best to hold it in neutral territory. Octo told us that Demetrius is moving on toward Brilane. I'm sure he's making himself ready for an attack on the Council. We can arrange a meeting at the abandoned stronghold of Virethorn Keep. Quentin, Blythe, Hera, and Griffin, we will send you with a small entourage. I am hoping that, in his desire to have our support, he will not try anything…"

"And if he does try something?" Blythe braced herself, chin lifting.

"Then he will learn exactly what an army of Fae, Dwarves, Elves, Gnomes, and Mer-People can do to him and his followers," Queen Lyriana said darkly.

"He needs our armies too much to risk it," Quentin said, sounding more convinced than she felt.

Quentin cleared his throat and looked toward Blythe.

"And me," Blythe said, because she knew she was part of the bargain whether she liked it or not.

"I guess we will see," Hera muttered.

Somewhere above them, a draft stirred the banners, a faint rustle that felt like a warning.

CHAPTER FORTY-FOUR

Blythe

Aeloria, Fae Mountains

The sun had long since dipped behind the mountain ridge, casting the palace courtyard in gold and shadow. Blythe wandered along the outer edge of the Fae castle, her boots crunching softly on a moss-strewn path behind the main hall.

The air carried a faint charge of magic, like ozone after a storm, along with the sweet, syrupy scent of duskberries and the light brine from the Merfolk's nearby campsite.

She didn't know what had drawn her this way until she heard voices—two familiar ones—low, tense, and unmistakably private.

"I'm not here to apologize," Tavian said quietly. "You wouldn't believe me if I did."

Hera replied, edged and weary. "Smart of you. Saves us both the lie."

Moonlight filtered through the high canopy of whispering silver leaves, their branches swaying gently overhead in the mountain breeze. Her fingers grazed the curve of a marble column as she turned the corner, the stone cool and smooth beneath her touch.

She stopped just behind a tall hedge of flowering duskberries.

There was a long pause. Blythe's hand brushed a branch. Thorns pricked her palm, and she drew it back, stifling the yelp in her throat.

"I never meant to hurt you," Tavian continued. He dragged in a shaky breath. "The hardest part wasn't pretending to betray you. It was knowing you'd believe I meant it."

The silence stretched, sharp enough that Blythe worried they'd hear her heart beating.

"You did mean it," Hera finally said. "You were angry. You were reckless. You played both sides and nearly lost everything. We could still lose everything. If you had just told us—"

"I couldn't tell you," Tavian said. "If I had, and Demetrius had gotten to you first, if you'd cracked, if you'd slipped, it would've unraveled everything."

"You think so little of me?" Hera's voice was sharper now, brittle with something close to pain. "We are tortured from childhood and beyond as part of our training. A Valkyrie never gives in."

Once again, Blythe was grateful she had not been raised as a Valkyrie.

"No," Tavian said. "I think so much of you. Too much. That's why I couldn't risk it."

Blythe watched through the gaps in the hedge as they stood beneath an old willow, its hanging tendrils swaying like silk in the breeze. The tree's roots curled around the base of the stone fountain, where water murmured quietly.

Hera's stance stayed guarded, though her shoulders had dropped.

"You hurt us," Hera said, her voice low. "We were just another step in your mission. Like we didn't matter."

Tavian stepped closer, slow and careful. "You mattered. Always."

"Then why didn't you let me in?" Hera's words were sharp. "I would've helped you. You didn't fight for me back then, either."

Blythe felt the shift. Whatever this was, it ran deeper than the recent betrayal. It reached back farther than anything Hera had ever shared with her.

Tavian faltered.

More silence. Blythe pressed her lips together. Something in the pain of their voices rooted her in place like the stone beneath her boots.

"I trusted you when I told myself I never would again," Hera said, her voice hoarse. "I let you in. You know I don't do that. Not easily. Not ever."

"I didn't take that for granted."

"You threw it away."

Tavian closed his eyes. "It wasn't that simple."

"No," Hera said, eyes glinting. "It never is."

Another step closer. She didn't back away.

"I thought if I could just… fix things," Tavian said, "bring down the Council, prove I was more than my name—maybe then I'd be worthy of the person I wanted to be with."

Hera's laugh was short and bitter. "So you lied to that person instead?"

For a heartbeat, the air between them pulsed with something unspoken. Blythe watched as Hera's hands twitched at her sides, as if she didn't know whether to strike him or reach for him.

Finally, Hera looked away. "You're a coward."

"Yeah," Tavian said. "Probably."

"But that doesn't mean I stopped—" She caught herself, teeth clamping down on the word that nearly escaped. Frustration tightened her features. "Just… go. Before I forget all the reasons I should never trust you again."

Tavian nodded slowly, though his eyes lingered on her longer than they should have.

He turned and walked away, disappearing down the garden path.

Blythe waited until she was sure he was gone. Then she stepped out from the hedge, brushing a few duskberry petals from her sleeve.

Hera didn't flinch, but her expression shuttered instantly. "Eavesdropping now, are we?"

Heat prickled at her cheeks. She should have walked away, but the words had rooted her in place.

"I didn't mean to," Blythe whispered. "I was just walking.

I heard voices. I didn't want to interrupt."

Hera exhaled, but didn't respond.

"You don't have to trust him," Blythe said after a moment.

Hera's eyes flicked to her, tired and shadowed. "Good. Because I don't."

"But" Blythe continued, stepping closer, "if you do... You should do it with your eyes open. Know what he's capable of. Know what you're risking. But also... know what you're choosing."

Hera turned away, arms wrapping tightly around her middle. "I don't want to choose. I want things to be simple again."

"I know. But nothing about this is simple anymore."

A breeze drifted through the garden, stirring Blythe's hair against her cheek and lifting the scent of lavender from the nearby planters. The wind carried the hum of distant conversation from the elven camp—muffled, indistinct. Everything here felt peaceful, but it was the kind of quiet that comes before a storm.

For a long moment, neither of them spoke. Hera looked over her shoulder, her gaze sharper now. "You're one to talk about trust."

Blythe blinked. "What?"

"You've been keeping Quentin at arm's length since the Dark Realm," Hera said. "You flinch when he gets too close. But you know he'd die for you—you know he would."

Blythe looked away, jaw tightening. The accusation scraped against old wounds, stirring guilt she didn't want to face. Hera was right.

"He's not perfect," Hera said, "but he's not a liar. He's not Tavian. And still, you're pushing him away like he's the one who broke your heart."

A thin chill slid beneath Blythe's skin, her magic's warning, or maybe just fear.

"I'm not—"

"Yes, you are." Hera frowned. "He did what he did because he needed to keep you close— to make sure you were safe."

Blythe narrowed her eyes. "Because dragging me into the Dark Realm was keeping me safe? Miles—"

"Don't bring him into this," Hera snapped. "You can't keep blaming Quentin for Miles choosing to follow us into the Dark Realm." Hera stepped toward Blythe. "Quentin has imprinted on you—that means he would literally lay down his life for you."

Hera exhaled, frustration flickering across her face. "He believed we had the strength and numbers to handle the Dark Realm. Rather naïvely, if you ask me. I even warned him. But sometimes he thinks he knows better and doesn't listen. He's young."

Hera waved a hand. "Yes, I'm young too, but I've seen things in my years he can only imagine." She shook her head. "I would trust Quentin with my life, and I don't say that about many people. He didn't tell you because he was protecting you. Sometimes following orders means keeping secrets from those we love."

Blythe looked down at her boots. The hem of her cloak brushed their tips, heavy with dew. "People who said they cared about me left or turned on me. I thought I knew Dorian... and then found out he was my father." Her voice dropped. "I was wrong about everything."

"So now you're scared of being wrong about Quentin."

Blythe swallowed hard. "We... kissed."

Hera's expression didn't change, but her eyes sharpened. "Ah. That would complicate things."

"I don't know what it meant," Blythe whispered.

"You do," Hera said. "You're just afraid to say it."

Blythe didn't answer.

Hera stepped forward, gentler now. "He's not going to betray you."

"You can't promise that."

"Yes, actually, I can," Hera rubbed a hand over her face, exasperated. "His imprinting on you literally means he cannot betray you. He doesn't want to. It would hurt him too much. I can promise you'll regret it if you keep running. We all need someone, Blythe. Even you. Especially you."

Blythe blinked hard, forcing the burn behind her eyes to stay where it was by changing directions. "You still love Tavian, don't you?"

Hera didn't answer right away. When she did, her voice was almost too soft to hear.

"I never stopped."

Blythe nodded. "Then maybe that's worth trusting even if it's only once more."

Hera gave a humorless smile. "What about you?"

"We're going to try. But we can't let it get in the way of what we need to do."

Hera shook her head. "I will never understand how complicated emotions can be. War is easy. Feelings are hard."

Blythe laughed. "Truer words were never spoken."

They stood together under the falling night. The silence felt fragile.

Above them, the stars began to pierce the dusk, scattered like forgotten promises across the deepening sky. A moment of peace amidst her tumultuous thoughts.

CHAPTER FORTY-FIVE

Blythe

Aeloria, Fae Mountains

The morning air in the landing field just outside the Fae capital bit with a chill that sank through Blythe's cloak, nipping at her fingers as she clenched them into fists for warmth. Frost coated the moss-laced stones beneath her boots, crunching faintly with each impatient step she took. Thin rays of sunlight filtered through the tall silver-leaf trees that lined the perimeter, glinting off carved archways where couriers and emissaries murmured in hushed voices.

Fae, Dwarf, Gnome, Elf, and Merfolk brokers gathered in careful lines, bundled in cloaks dyed in the colors of their nations. Blythe could smell the earthy tang of cold stone and pine sap, and the sharper scent of burning sage—protective magic—wafting from a nearby fire basin.

"It's a risk," Hera said, as though picking up a conversation only she remembered. "Meeting with Demetrius and Zelos? We're outnumbered. There are too many warlocks loyal to him and too many disillusioned people from all the races. They hold the edge."

"What's another risk?" Blythe lifted her shoulder. "At this point, just getting up and continuing in the morning feels dangerous."

Quentin's hand found hers—warm, steady—a grounding touch that steadied Blythe more than she cared to admit. For the first time in a long time, she let herself lean into it. The way her heart lifted scared her almost as much as it soothed her.

"We drew the line. We've got the last stone, and you, Kits. We have to try. We can't win by fighting them and the Council at the same time," he said.

"Let's just hope Tavian didn't sell us out," Griffin muttered, his breath rising in front of him as he scanned the horizon near the gates.

"Let's hope Demetrius bought the story," Iain said from Quentin's other side.

"Let's go," Quentin said, pressing the teleportation stone into Blythe's hand. "It's keyed to our destination. The Council's too distracted to track these right now."

Blythe's smile was thin and humorless. "Well, that's a relief. I wasn't looking forward to hiking and swimming from the Sierra Nevada to Europe or Great Britain."

Hera, Griffin, and Quentin exchanged glances, then stared at her.

Realization hit a beat late. She exhaled. "Right. Sorry. Fae Mountains to Auroraheim."

Tavian joined them, flanked by two guards in ash-gray armor. His robe was streaked with dust, one sleeve darkened by a smear of dried blood. He didn't limp, didn't wince—just walked forward and handed her a folded parchment.

To Blythe, Hera, Quentin, Griffin, and entourage—
You are to present at Virethorn Keep.
Arrive by sundown. Stone in hand. No tricks.
— Demetrius

Blythe's breath faltered for a moment.

"Here we go," Hera said, a wry, almost grim smile flickering across her face.

CHAPTER FORTY-SIX

Blythe

Virethorn Keep

Evening sunlight bled through thinning clouds, the last golden rays catching on the tips of wild heather clinging stubbornly to the rocky hillside. Blythe stopped short at the crest, breath catching.

Virethorn Keep rose ahead like a half-forgotten memory. The ruin stretched along a narrow promontory jutting into the dark waters of Veilmere Sound, a mirror of Loch Ness in the human realm. Wind coiled off the water in sharp gusts, carrying the briny tang of the lake and the faint metallic sting of old magic. A thin chill slid beneath her skin, quiet but insistent.

The castle, though crumbling, was vast. Its curtain walls traced the natural rise of the hill, partially collapsed in places, leaving jagged teeth of ancient stone jutting toward the sky. A single weather-worn tower loomed in the distance, its battlements broken, ivy spilling down its sides. The gatehouse had long since fallen, but the remains of its arch still stood, massive and proud, scarred by time and battles lost to memory.

"Legend has it that before the Portals were guarded, there were more of them," Iain said from behind Blythe. "Each place that mirrors another in the Human realm is said to have been a Portal House. This is one of them."

"Legends are convenient," Hera said. "Do you have any proof?"

Quentin shook his head. "Just what was passed down from generation to generation. So while some of it might be true, there's no way of knowing how much."

Torches had been lit along the perimeter, the flickering flames throwing elongated shadows across the ancient stone. The ground was uneven, covered in patches of frost-glazed grass and black moss, and Blythe could feel the faint pulse of old magic vibrating beneath her boots, residual enchantments that must once have protected the stronghold, now fractured and gone.

She stepped forward slowly, boots crunching over loose gravel and frost-kissed grass. The lake below lapped against the rocky shore in a deep, slow rhythm that echoed in her bones. Mist swirled just above the water, giving the entire scene the feel of a haunted battleground, held together by willpower alone. She had visited Urquhart Castle in the human realm during a study-abroad semester, drawn to its myths and tragic grandeur, but even that place hadn't carried the magical weight Virethorn Keep did.

Shadows danced across the inner courtyard. The keep's high inner walls enclosed the area like the ribs of a long-dead beast.

In the center stood a single basalt plinth, flanked by twin thrones carved from obsidian—ornate, terrible, and waiting.

Demetrius sat in one.

Next to him, on the matching throne, sat Zelos. The Warlock leader's white hair gleamed like bone, and his violet robes shimmered with runes that pulsed dimly with power. He exuded the stillness of someone accustomed to being obeyed.

Blythe spotted Octo off to the side. He inclined his head so slightly she wasn't sure she'd imagined it.

Demetrius's voice came first, smooth and cold. "Tavian tells me you want to talk. We'll speak plainly."

Zelos rose and stepped forward, long fingers spread as he gestured with the ease of a diplomat. "We propose an alliance. The stones should be reunited—not to shatter the barriers, but to control them."

Hera's hand dropped to her sword hilt, but Blythe stopped her with a silent touch on her forearm. The air crackled like the charge before a lightning strike.

Glancing around, she saw Iain hovering near the back of their group, shoulders drawn tight as if he wished he were anywhere else. Her attention shifted as Quentin stepped forward and spoke.

"Control is a beautiful word. But we've seen what it becomes in the wrong hands."

Zelos's expression hardened. "Your answer?"

"I say no," Blythe added, her voice ringing against the stone. "Not if it's built on threats."

Demetrius's eyes met hers. "You don't see the bigger picture yet. Once the Council is dismantled, I will usher in a world of safety—guarded portals, balanced powers. Think of it."

"You're also ignoring the fact that the portals we went through aren't guarded. It's your fault, not the Council's." Blythe folded her arms over her chest.

"Odd you would feel the need to defend the Council," Demetrius tilted his head. "Had it not been for me and my rebels, you'd be dead right now because of them."

A flicker of doubt twisted in her gut. She hated that he wasn't entirely wrong.

"We don't need another overlord," Quentin said. "We need shared responsibility. If you are truly proposing unity, prove it. What will your new council look like? How will the stones stop the escaping evil from the dark realm?"

Zelos's hand rose. A low hum vibrated through the air as violet flame curled around his fingers, carrying the faint scent of ozone. "Then let this be a show of faith. Give us the stones, and we will seal off the dark realm once and for all—after we take down the Council."

Griffin muttered incoherently behind Blythe. It sounded vaguely like, I'll be an Ogre's uncle, but she wasn't sure if that was what she'd heard.

"We will no longer let dark creatures feed on our people just to keep our buildings lit," Demetrius said, his voice steady. "There are other ways. The Council has imprisoned innocents, and worse—allowed them to suffer so we could have lights and enchanted homes. Tell me that isn't wrong."

A hard knot formed in her throat. No answer felt right. Not one she could speak aloud and still live with.

Blythe's pulse stumbled, just once.

"What did you need me for?" She asked, her gaze fixed on Demetrius. She searched his face for the shadow she was certain lived there. But it wasn't visible. Not now.

"You have no idea how powerful you are, do you?" Zelos asked with a wry smile.

Blythe lifted her shoulders in a shrug, aiming for nonchalance. "Does it really matter? Obsessing over your own power feels a little narcissistic."

Demetrius shook his head, as if disappointed in her answer. "Your power isn't tethered to an anchor or shared source. Your mixed blood gives you an almost unending fount to draw from."

Her magic stirred beneath her skin in icy shards, restless and uneasy, as if it sensed what was coming.

Zelos's voice followed like a confirmation of that dread. "Mixed beings, the Unbound, those without anchors or limits, created the stones—and the barriers. You're the only one of your kind we know of. You're the only one who can wield them."

"Then if that's the case, why don't you just give Blythe the stones?" Hera's annoyance seeped into every word.

"Because she doesn't know how to use them," Zelos snapped. "She could just as easily destroy herself—and all of us—as succeed. We can help her."

Blythe's eyes flicked between Zelos and Demetrius. For a moment, just a breath, she thought she saw it: a faint shadow clinging to their outlines, like smoke trying to take shape. But when she blinked, it was gone.

Her magic shrank inward, a cold sweep pulling back from her limbs until it knotted tight at her center.

Her thoughts scattered, refusing to settle.

"We could help her," Quentin argued.

"Do you have magic?" Melya's irritated voice cut in from Blythe's right.

Quentin didn't answer. Instead, he drew the glowing stone from his satchel, holding it for all to see. The stone's runes flared as he held it—once, twice—before a low hum echoed through the ruins, as if it could sense its brethren near.

Demetrius straightened. "You give it willingly?"

"We want peace," Blythe said. "Not subjugation. You will get it when we are certain you're true to your word. I agree that no one should be used or tortured to improve others' lives. We will use the stones to stop the Council close off the dark realm, and that's it."

A long moment passed. The stone flared brighter, then dimmed.

Demetrius reclined slightly, fingers steepled. "You drive a hard bargain, Niece. But you don't seem to understand. You don't hold the cards here."

"I wasn't aware we were playing a game, Uncle," Blythe gritted her teeth. "You're gambling with people's lives. People are dying because you left the portals unguarded."

Murmurs rose among Demetrius's rebels gathered around them.

"Interesting that you would accuse us of gambling with people's lives when your lover's brother has been feeding the Council all of the information you've been learning." Zelos grinned in what could only be described as a victory smile.

Blythe glanced at Quentin, whose eyes widened, the only sign of the blow he'd just taken. Behind him, Iain had gone utterly still, as if Zelos's words had frozen him in place. A spark of anger flared—not at Quentin, but at Zelos for aiming the blow so precisely. She wanted to reach for him, but the moment was too public.

"It's so hard to trust people these days, isn't it?" Zelos drawled.

Demetrius sighed. "I understand where you're coming

from, Blythe. I really do. However, we needed to show the people how ineffective the Council is. Their power is waning." He shifted in his throne, and Blythe caught a glimpse of something dark against the skin of his neck. When she looked again, it was gone.

"You agree the Council has done bad things, yes?" Zelos asked, interrupting her thoughts.

"Yes, of course," Blythe said, resisting the urge to roll her eyes.

"And you agree all people deserve representation." Demetrius tilted his head, watching her. There was something in his eyes darker than she remembered.

"Yes, of course, we agree to that," Quentin said, his impatience seeping out of every word.

"Then why are you pushing back against helping us accomplish this?" Demetrius asked, looking between Blythe and Quentin. "Under the new Council, I want to establish that you and Quentin would be free to have whatever life you choose. Quentin would be able to rule the Fae as he is destined to do. The current Council would strip him of that power and dictate what he and his people can do, which makes it particularly odd that his brother would help them."

Blythe clenched her fists. He was making a persuasive argument, and the elders of their allies would want to work with him if this were true. She felt the walls closing in. Quentin spared her the decision.

"We'll work with you," Quentin said quietly, as if each word cost him something. "The elders—Fae, Dwarf, Elf, Gnome, and Mer—have agreed, but only on two conditions: a new, inclusive council must be formed, and the portals must be guarded. They want the escaped evil returned to where it came from."

Blythe's stomach dropped. He'd said it—the words she couldn't.

Quentin met their eyes. "Can you agree to that?"

Zelos inclined his head. "We accept. As a show of good

faith, you keep that stone, and we will gather our troops to march on the Council. Go and rally your forces. We will assemble outside Brilane to take the Council down. Give us that stone, and we will show you how to use it. But know this—betrayal will be repaid in kind."

"Agreed," Hera said in a low, dangerous voice. "If you betray this agreement, you will regret it."

A brittle silence followed, sharp as the winter air. Then Quentin turned, and the others fell in behind him. Blythe didn't look back at the obsidian thrones or the shadows clinging to the ruined walls. She didn't trust what she might see.

The group slipped beneath the broken archway, boots crunching over frost and gravel. Iain trailed near the rear, quiet and unreadable, and Blythe felt the weight of that silence settle between them like another threat.

CHAPTER FORTY-SEVEN

Quentin

Just Outside of Virethorn Keep

The walk back felt slower—each step dragging under the weight of what Zelos had revealed. Quentin kept his eyes on the broken path ahead, though he could feel Iain's presence behind him like a stone lodged beneath his ribs. Blythe brushed her fingers along a collapsed wall as they passed; the air was icy, but Quentin barely felt the cold. They stopped on the hill overlooking the keep, the ruin shrinking behind them while the truth about his brother pressed closer.

Hera leaned against a large oak tree, its leaves gone with winter's approach. "That was a trap," she muttered. "Militant diplomacy."

Tavian stepped out from the shadows. "And not exactly the best outcome. Once we take out the Council, we can figure out what to do about Demetrius and the Warlocks."

Hera didn't even look at him. Her gaze had locked onto Iain.

"What about you?" she said, voice low and sharp. "Zelos claims we have a leak. Care to explain that, Iain?"

The group stilled.

Iain froze where he stood, half a step behind the others, as if hoping the shadows would swallow him.

Quentin turned slowly. "Iain?"

Iain's throat bobbed. "Quentin, I—"

"Answer her," Quentin said, the words tight.

Iain's shoulders sagged. "The Council approached me weeks ago. They said they needed updates. That it was... important."

Hera stepped closer. "And you believed them?"

"I believed someone finally thought I mattered," Iain snapped, the words bursting out before he could stop them.

Silence hit the group like a blow.

Quentin stared at him. "You told me you didn't want responsibility. That you were happy being left alone."

"I lied," Iain said, voice cracking. "I was tired of being the useless brother. The one no one listened to. The one who didn't matter to the Fae, or the Council, or even to you."

Quentin flinched.

Iain pressed on, voice shaking. "They told me I could help. That I could be part of something important. That I could prove myself. And I wanted that. I wanted it so badly I didn't think about what it would cost."

Octo's voice rumbled from the right. "Whether you meant to or not, you compromised us."

Iain's eyes dropped. "I know."

Blythe stepped closer to Quentin, her presence steady but quiet.

Quentin swallowed hard. "You should have come to me."

"I didn't think you'd listen," Iain whispered. "You're the golden one. The future ruler. The one everyone looks to. I'm just... me."

"That's not an excuse," Hera said. "It's a confession."

Iain didn't argue.

Quentin's voice was barely audible. "I trusted you."

"I'm sorry," Iain said, and for once, he sounded like he meant it.

"You're going home," Quentin said, turning away before the words could break him. "And you're staying there."

He didn't wait to see Iain's reaction before turning his attention to the others. He couldn't.

"Did you notice the shadow?" Octo asked, his deep voice cutting through the cold air. "On Demetrius?"

Quentin shifted his gaze. Octo stood like a carved monolith against the dying light. Bare-chested despite the cold, massive enough that Quentin felt small beside him.

Blythe spoke before he could. "I thought I imagined it."

"You did not," Octo said. "There was a mark on the back of his neck. A symbol I didn't recognize. It vanished as soon as I saw it." His arms folded across his chest, muscles tightening. "The Demetrius I knew is gone. The man who returned from the Dark Realm is not the one who left."

Quentin's stomach twisted.

"I wondered if he was a changeling," Octo continued. "Or a shape-shifter. But no. It's him. Just… altered."

"I think he brought something back with him," Tavian said quietly.

Quentin's voice came out lower than he intended. "I wonder if the Warlocks did something to him…"

"Like a control spell?" Tavian's expression sharpened. "Possibly. Their magic draws from darker places and tends to be… more nefarious."

"Is that the truth?" Blythe asked, eyes narrowing. "Or just propaganda? Like what they spread about half-lings?"

Tavian winced. "Yes and no. The propaganda exaggerates. But it's not entirely false."

He glanced around, as if the trees themselves might be listening. "If I understand correctly, Warlocks draw their power directly from the Dark Realm."

He'd suspected as much, but hearing it aloud made the air feel thinner.

Tavian continued, unbothered by the weight of what he was saying. "The reason no one has tried to close off the Dark Realm portals isn't just politics. It's because they can't. If those portals were sealed, the entire energy grid of the Magic Realm would collapse. Houses would lose function. Spells relying on ambient magic would die. And the Warlocks, who originate from the Dark Realm, would be powerless."

"So they're not actually planning on closing it off," Hera said, her voice quieter than usual.

"No, they want the portals wide open so they can play gods in the human realm," Octo snarled.

"They don't just draw passive power," Tavian added. "They reach into it. Shape it. Channel it into weapons, rituals, whatever they need. It's corrupted energy. Fundamentally corrupt."

Blythe huffed. "Has no one thought to build an alternative? Transition away from an evil-dimension dependency? Water power works great."

Tavian let out a humorless laugh. "Plenty have thought about it. But breaking that tie would destabilize every magical system we've built. It's not as simple as flipping a switch. Even the Houses would be affected, they'd either collapse… or worse, overload."

Quentin frowned. "Overload?"

"The Houses aren't just homes," Tavian said. "They're living circuits. They regulate how much dark energy gets filtered into this realm. If you block the flow without cutting the source, the pressure builds. Like stuffing magic into a bottle and shaking it. Eventually, it bursts."

"But the Houses aren't on all of the portals," Blythe said, brows furrowing.

"No," Tavian agreed. "They're built on some that connect the ley-line currents that run from them. The Dark Realm is the source. Magic bleeds through the portals and runs underground in ley-line currents. The Houses sit at the intersections, where those currents converge."

Blythe frowned deeper. "Then why not build the Houses directly at the portals?"

"Because Dark Realm energy is volatile," Tavian said quickly. "It needs to be diluted first. Strongholds were once built at the all of the portals. Most fell. Some became cursed. Others were swallowed whole."

"So the Houses regulate the flow?" Hera asked.

Tavian nodded. "Exactly. Without them, the ley lines would overload. Magic would leak. Destabilize. That's why closing the portals isn't as simple as slamming a door. The entire realm is wired into them. There are far more ley-line intersections than portals."

Quentin looked back toward Virethorn Keep, its silhouette jagged against the horizon. "So, Virethorn Keep could be on one."

"Exactly," Tavian said. "That's why no one's tried to truly seal off the Dark Realm. And why the Warlocks feel so powerful, they're tapping the same energy we rely on, but without filters. It's like comparing a windmill to a lightning strike."

"Then how were they trapped so long?" Griffin muttered.

"That's a good question," Tavian said darkly. "I suspect they weren't as trapped as they want us to believe."

A cold tremor rippled through Quentin. Blythe's voice broke the silence. "So if we shut the portals, if we win, what happens to everything?"

Tavian met her eyes. "That's the question, isn't it?"

Silence settled over them, heavy as the winter air.

"Well," Hera muttered, "guess it's time to round up those armies we promised."

Quentin exhaled slowly, the weight of what they were walking into pressing heavier with every step.

CHAPTER FORTY-EIGHT

Blythe

Brilane, Auroraheim

A thin mist curled around their ankles as the allied armies gathered on the emerald slopes outside Brilane. Dawn broke in soft hues across the sky, banners lifting as the rhythmic clink of armor rippled through the ranks.

Fae warriors stood tall in silverleaf plating that glinted like sunlight on water. Dwarves hefted runed axes and staves, their faces set in grim determination. Merfolk, armored in glistening scale plates that shimmered with each step, moved in tight formation beside rebel mages cloaked in deep midnight blue.

A line of werewolves stood along the ridge to the east —tall, broad-shouldered figures in leather and steel, their eyes sharp in the morning light. Some remained in human form, weapons strapped across their backs; others waited half-shifted, claws glinting, fur bristling in the dawn breeze. At their center stood Bertolf.

He looked different. Somehow he was older, steadier, the weight of his journey carved into the set of his jaw. When his gaze swept the field and briefly met hers, he dipped his head in a small, solemn nod. The werewolf clans had come. And they had chosen *her* side.

A tightness eased in her chest; relief and gratitude tangled together.

Blythe stood behind the front rows of troops with Quentin and Tavian, her heart thudding hard beneath her ribs. The last time she'd been in this city, she had faced the Council, arguing her innocence against their charges. The memory of riding behind Quentin on Ellira as they soared toward his apartment came rushing back.

Behind her, an army stretched that shouldn't have existed. Justice, at long last, might be reclaimed.

Across the valley, Brilane rose into view. The great city shimmered like a dream—perched atop a broad hill that overlooked the world like a crown set in stone. Its spires were delicate yet unyielding, reaching upward like fingers of carved ivory, and the walls wrapped around the city in protective arms. Light spilled from enchanted lanterns along the parapets. It was beautiful. And it stood in their way.

Blythe spotted Demetrius and Zelos near the edge of the group of Warlocks and angled toward them, Quentin and Tavian close behind.

Demetrius turned as they approached, hands folded neatly behind his back. His cloak rippled in the wind, shadows flickering at his heels like loyal hounds. Zelos stood beside him, rigid and regal in violet robes, fingers curled around a silver-topped staff that shone faintly with magic.

"I'm glad to see you've joined us," Demetrius said, his voice smooth.

Zelos lifted a brow. "Did you bring the stone?"

Blythe nodded, her throat too tight to speak.

"Good." Demetrius smiled—an expression meant to be warm, paternal. But it crawled across her skin like frost. She hated how familiar it felt.

"I've thought this through," Blythe said, her voice low and deliberate. Resolve settled in her bones like a weight she could no longer set down. She knew Quentin wouldn't like what was coming.

Demetrius and Zelos watched her silently and expectantly.

"I'm going to use the stones," she continued. "First to dismantle the Council. Then to seal the portals to the dark realms."

Beside her, Quentin went still—the kind of still that spoke louder than shouting. His jaw tightened, a single muscle ticking once before he forced his breath out.

Zelos's gaze sharpened, but he said nothing.

"Quentin, I sense you have some reservations about this," Demetrius said, looking between the two of them.

"I have to," Blythe said, cutting off Quentin before he could speak. "He knows I do. If we're serious about stopping the Council and protecting the realms, this is the only way. I'll strike the Council first—then seal the portals. No more leaks from the Dark Realm. Ever."

Demetrius didn't blink. "And if it destroys you?" he asked, still watching her as if she were a puzzle he hadn't finished solving. "What then?"

A cold line traced down her spine.

Quentin's breath hitched.

"Yes," Zelos said, his voice low. "That kind of power could consume you."

She glanced at him. His tone was grave, but something in his eyes gleamed—too bright, too pleased. It didn't match the warning.

"I'm the only Unbound here, so I have to. At least I'll have made everyone safer." The words tasted like stepping toward her own execution.

Quentin's jaw clenched, and he looked away, swallowing hard. His hand brushed hers once before falling back to his side. She knew he didn't agree—not entirely—but he understood they needed to stop the evil from destroying everything.

She waited for Zelos to speak. If the Warlocks drew their power from the Dark Realm, surely they wouldn't want the portals closed off.

Demetrius studied her for a long moment. Blythe felt his gaze, heavy and appraising, like a general sizing up a weapon rather than a person. And then she saw a smear of darkness creeping just beneath his skin before vanishing once more.

He folded his arms slowly.

"You're certain?"

"I am."

Zelos arched a pale brow but said nothing.

Demetrius turned slightly, glancing toward the armies behind them. When he looked back, his expression was unreadable—thoughtful, distant.

"You'll get your chance," he said finally. "When the time is right, I'll give you the remaining five stones I carry."

Only then did Blythe notice the ache in her lungs.

Demetrius continued, "And as a show of good faith, you'll keep the one you currently possess. Guard it. And don't lose your nerve, girl. There may not be a second opportunity."

The word 'girl' scraped across her nerves.

"I won't," she said.

Zelos inclined his head with something like respect—or amusement. "Then may the magic favor the bold."

They were standing on the edge of something vast. Something final.

A chill settled beneath her skin. She would see this through. Even if it killed her.

Blythe, Quentin, and Tavian turned to return to their friends. She glanced up toward Brilane and spotted movement above the walls—winged figures descending from high ledges with impeccable grace. Valkyrie. Dozens of them. Clad in gleaming armor, their wings trailing iridescent threads of light, they landed in perfect formation outside the gates. Behind them, mages assembled on the battlements, long robes catching the wind, staffs glowing with stored magic. Gone were the people flying along on dragons or magic carpets, heading to and from their business.

"'Ere we go!" Griffin's voice rang out from her left.

Blythe turned, catching sight of the dwarf with his axe raised high, eyes gleaming.

"Let's do this!" Tavian shouted, bolting toward Hera.

"We'll get through this, Kits," Quentin whispered to her. She wasn't sure if he was reassuring her—or himself.

He was so close she could breathe in his scent of worn leather and cold mountain air, threaded with the faint warmth of his skin. The mix steadied her, settling something restless inside her chest. She slipped her hand into his and gave it a gentle squeeze, their fingers fitting together with an ease that made her pulse jump. When she looked up, he was already smiling, and she couldn't help but return it.

A horn sounded—low, resonant—and the allied forces surged forward. The ground shuddered beneath Blythe's boots. Chanting rose from the spellcasters at the front, ancient words carried on the wind. Runes lit the air like flickering embers, forming protective wards around the vanguard.

Above, dragons wheeled and dove, their riders locked in aerial combat. Flames streaked the sky; some came so close that Blythe instinctively dropped, the heat brushing her scalp.

As they descended the hill, the sun crested behind them, casting long shadows across the battlefield. Ahead, a line of Valkyrie stood like a wall of light and power, their mounts' wings outstretched. A quiet awe swept through her.

The creatures were stunning. Horns curved from their foreheads, their brilliant white bodies clad in golden armor that shimmered like sunlight on water.

The mages on the wall raised their staffs. Bolts of radiant magic lanced upward, crackling across the sky like lightning made of glass. Mist above the city twisted into a vortex, the air humming with raw arcane energy.

Blythe paused for half a heartbeat, the charged air prickling across her skin, the taste of metal sharp on her tongue. Then the world erupted.

The Valkyrie cried out and launched into the fray—some soaring to meet dragons midair, others diving toward the ground troops.

Blythe broke from the ranks with Quentin and Tavian, pushing toward the wall.

They weren't alone. Demetrius, Hera, Eyra, Griffin, Octo, Zelos, and a cadre of shadow-cloaked Warlocks joined them, cutting a deliberate path through Brilane's twisting streets. The city shook with chaos—buildings ablaze with magical fire.

The Council Spire loomed ahead, tall and gleaming like a blade stabbed into the heart of the capital. Every street leading to it was barricaded—steel and sorcery woven together.

Demetrius moved with grim purpose. Blythe saw the sweat streaking his brow, the sword in his hand replacing the magic he had once wielded. He fought with precision, not brute force—commanding, calculating.

Zelos was another story. His Warlock magic lashed out in violent bursts—shadows binding sentries to walls, dragging Valkyrie from the sky. Blythe caught glimpses of him muttering incantations, his eyes glowing violet. The stones Demetrius carried glimmered faintly from his pocket with each surge of Zelos's power. Did the stones pull from the Dark Realm, too?

Griffin tore through enemies with brutal efficiency. His double-headed axe shattered shields and split enchanted armor. Blythe had no idea how he managed to stay upright through the shockwaves. But he did.

Octo moved like water unleashed. His trident spun in wide arcs, disarming and disrupting. His armor gleamed like obsidian coral, and the tendrils of water he conjured cracked against Valkyrie shields.

"On your left!" he shouted.

Blythe turned just in time. She raised her hand, and raw magic burst from her fingertips. The Valkyrie flew backward, the blast cracking the flagstones.

The stone in her pocket burned hot, as if it could feel her power. Heat bloomed through her body, her ears ringing from the force of it.

The mother and daughter duo fought like mirror images, their mounts' wings tucked close and golden armor flashing as they carved through enemy lines. Blythe couldn't look away. Their strikes were lightning fast, their cries rolling through the battlefield like distant thunder. They took to the air only when space opened around them, preferring the brutal grace of close combat.

Quentin stayed close. Blythe watched him move through the chaos with a precision that felt almost choreographed, always circling back to her.

She reached out, instinctively siphoning the leftover energy from her spell. Her fingers glowed with pale blue fire, the heat prickling across her skin. She'd never done that before and wasn't sure why she had now.

"You alright?" Quentin asked, breathless.

"I am now," she said, voice taught as she pushed forward as Brilane burned.

CHAPTER FORTY-NINE

Quentin

Brilane, Auroraheim

Smoke drifted between shattered spires and marble facades. Magic clashed with steel in every alley, every courtyard, every skyway. Heat rolled off the fires in waves, carrying the acrid odor of scorched stones. Blythe kept moving, pulse throbbing, stone burning, gaze locked on the Spire.

Her boots slammed over cracked stone as she led the assault team through the heart of the city. Behind her, the others advanced like a living storm: Demetrius, Quentin, Hera, Eyra, Octo, Griffin, Zelos, and a cadre of Warlocks—forged for one purpose: reach the Hall of Elders and end the Council's rule.

The Council's tower rose at the far end of the city like a temple of judgment. Grand and imposing, it stood with the self-righteous serenity of something that believed it could not be brought down. Its clock tower rose above everything, a watchman of old power, its pristine white walls now haloed in smoke.

"That's where we're going," Blythe said, out of breath. "Straight through them."

"Here." Demetrius appeared at her side, pressing the pouch of stones into her hand. "If you break your word—"

"I won't." She met his gaze with a hard, unflinching look as she added her stone to the five in the pouch.

"Take cover!" Quentin shouted as a massive dragon dove from the clouds, its jaws widening, fire gathering like burning gold between its teeth.

They scattered, each running and ducking to escape the

inevitable torrent of flame the beast carried in its maw.

Blythe bolted into an alley, boots sliding on loose stone as heat blazed past the entrance. The blast lit the walls in violent orange, the air shuddering with the dragon's fury. She pressed herself against the shaded brick, chest heaving, the pouch of stones in her hand pulsed hot against her flesh.

For a second, she thought she was alone.

A figure came out from the smoke at the far end of the alley. Broad-shouldered, dark-haired, and familiar in a way that made her stomach lurch before her mind caught up.

Ben.

His silhouette wavered in the haze, half-lit by the burning city behind him. He wasn't armed, not visibly, but tension radiated from him like warmth from a forge. He was covered in dust, blood, and grime. Proof that he'd fought his way here just as she had.

His eyes locked with hers. They were determined and carrying a thousand things he'd like to throw at her.

"Blythe," he breathed, as if he'd been searching for her.

Her heartbeat raced. "Not now."

"You don't get to decide that anymore."

She straightened, magic tingling along her fingertips. "I really do."

Ben moved a step closer, boots trampling over broken stone. "You're walking into the Council's jaws with six stones burning a hole in your hand. You think I'm going to let you do that?"

"You don't get to 'let' me do anything," she snapped.

Another explosion shook the street behind them. Screams echoed. The dragon roared again, but the alley felt secluded, like the world had reduced to the two of them.

His lips curved into a predatory smile.

"I didn't come here to talk to you, half-breed."

She licked her parched lips. "Then what did you come for?"

"To end you."

Her jaw tightened. "I don't know what I ever did to you that has made you hate me so much—"

"You didn't have to do anything but exist." His voice rose, sharp and vicious. "Every time you walked into a room, he looked at you like you were special. Chosen. And I was nothing. You stole everything I was supposed to be."

She didn't have to ask who he meant. Dorian. Their father.

He'd loved her Mother even though it was illegal. Had he favored her for that reason?

Something in her chest twisted, old fear, old shame, and the memory of every time he'd made her feel small. She shoved it down, hard. She didn't have room for that anymore.

"I didn't ask to be the Keeper!" She shook her head. "I would have handed it over to you if I could."

"You could have refused! You were just too selfish and stupid to do so! You're disgusting. An abomination. And it will be my pleasure to kill you!"

A cold prickle slid down her arm, settling in her fingers. Her magic stirred, ready.

"I look forward to seeing you try," Blythe whispered. "But I don't have time for this right now."

She backed up toward the alley entrance.

Ben's hand snapped up. A blast of magic rushed through the air toward her.

She dropped and rolled, heat brushing her cheek as it scorched the wall behind her. She came up on her feet without thinking, breath sharp in her throat.

A second blast followed immediately, getting closer and hotter. She leapt out of the way. It grazed her shoulder, ripping through her sleeve and singeing her skin. Pain flared white. If she'd moved a heartbeat slower, it would have taken her head off.

Instinct took charge. She flung her hand forward, a wild flood of power. She felt it flow from the stones, through her core, and rip from her palm. The magic snarled, twisting midair like something alive. For a split second, she wasn't sure she'd aimed it at him at all.

Ben threw up a shield too late. The blast struck him full force, slamming him backwards into the wall. Stone cracked. Dust fell. He hit the ground hard, coughing, fury twisting his features.

He pushed himself up, staggering. "You think that's enough to stop me?"

He charged.

Blythe reacted before she could think—another burst of magic, fiercer this time, powered by fear and the stones' hungry pulse. The ground beneath Ben shuddered. The wall behind him groaned.

Then everything gave way.

The upper half of the building collapsed in a roar of stone and splintered beams. Ben's eyes widened as the rubble collapsed, consuming him in a cloud of dust and debris.

The impact shook the alley. A final chunk of masonry thudded into place, sealing him beneath a sharp mound of stone.

Silence followed—heavy, awful.

Blythe stared at the pile, chest tight. A faint groan, or maybe just shifting rubble, resounded from somewhere inside it.

Alive. Or not. She couldn't tell.

A memory glimmered. Ben sneering at her in lessons, Ben shoving her in the sitting room, Ben whispering poison in her ears when he believed no one was listening. And under it all, the smaller, quieter truth that she hated: the child in her had hoped that maybe, just maybe, he could grow up and she could have a friend.

Her stomach knotted.

"I didn't want this," she whispered, voice scarcely heard over the distant screams and crackling fires. "I didn't..."

Another explosion rocked the street. Quentin shouted her name somewhere far off.

Blythe tore her stare from the rubble. The guilt stuck to her like soot, but she forced her legs to move.

She turned and ran, leaving Ben buried in the ruins as the city burned around them.

CHAPTER FIFTY

Blythe

Brilane, Auroraheim

Smoke swallowed her as she sprinted back into the street, the roar of the battle slamming into her like a wall. The world hadn't paused for her fight with Ben; it had only grown louder, hotter, more desperate. Dragons wheeled overhead, their shadows cutting across the burning rooftops. Spells cracked like thunder. Steel rang against steel.

Quentin spotted her first, relief flashing across his face before he masked it with focus. "There you are—move!"

She fell into step beside him, breath sharp, shoulder throbbing where Ben's blast had grazed her. The guilt clung to her like soot, but there was no room to feel it, not with the Hall looming ahead, not with the stones pulsing in her hand like a second heartbeat urging her forward.

"I think Ben's dead," she said, the words rough, barely audible over the chaos.

Quentin's head snapped toward her. "What happened?"

"Later," she said, forcing her gaze forward. "We have to keep going."

Demetrius, Hera, Eyra, Octo, Griffin, and the Warlocks regrouped around them as they pushed deeper into the city. The streets narrowed, funneling them toward the Spire. Magic flared in the distance. It was bright, violent and unmistakably defensive.

The Council was bracing for them.

Blythe tightened her grip on the stones. What—who—she'd left behind would have to wait.

They had reached the final stretch.

Ahead, Council loyalists blocked the road: Valkyries in gold-and-silver armor, their mythical mounts pawing the stone with horned hooves; mages stationed on rooftops and balconies, casting bolts of sun fire and force downward. Between them and the Hall, magic lit the air like a lightning storm trapped in a cage.

Griffin barreled into the front ranks with a war cry, his axe cleaving through a line of armored sentries. "Clear the damned road!"

Quentin was already beside him, darting into the opening Griffin had made. The Fae rolled low beneath a swing, elbowed a mage in the ribs, and kicked another into a shop window with shattering glass. He fought without spells—just instinct, muscle, steel, and grit. One after another, his enemies fell unconscious in his wake.

Hera and Eyra flew overhead in unison, their mounts' wings slicing through the smoke. Eyra hurled her spear into a Valkyrie mid-flight, sending her tumbling, while Hera flipped off her mount, drew twin blades, and carved a path through the chaos with elegance and rage before landing back on her mount's back.

Below, Octo wielded his trident with brutal efficiency, twisting to knock back a wave of foot soldiers before conjuring a wall of water from the steam rising off the fires. He flung it forward in a crashing arc, drenching enemy spellcasters and shorting out their enchantments.

Zelos stayed near Demetrius, calling shadows to their defense. The warlock's hands moved quickly, lips curled in concentration as black magic spiraled around him in ribbons. "Valkyrie incoming!" he shouted.

Blythe snapped a shield into place, blocking the hail of knives, spears, and arrows that rained down upon them. She blocked most, but some broke through, and her companions dodged out of the way.

Blythe saw an opening and shouted, "Stay close! If I fall,

grab the stones from me."

Flame flared near her, forcing her to drop low. She lifted a hand and sent a surge of raw magic straight through the open window of a tower, blowing apart a battalion of archers. It poured from her like a river breaking its banks, unrelenting.

She felt it again—that strange separation. Like the magic was moving through her, not with her. Like it had its own will.

A faint dizziness tugged at the edges of her vision.

She just hoped it wouldn't break her while it did whatever it was doing.

The closer they drew to the Hall of Elders, the more resistance they met. Barricades lined the avenues, Valkyrie forming phalanxes with their winged mounts, while mages behind them chanted in unison, their hands raised. But nothing could stop the team's momentum. Not now.

"We're nearin' the bloody gates!" Griffin bellowed, voice rough as gravel. "Left flank, move yer arses and follow Octo!"

The Hall emerged at the end of the square. Its white façade glowed with magical reinforcement. The green trim and gray roof gleamed like freshly polished armor. The central clock tower loomed above them, its face unmoving.

Standing at its front steps were two dozen Valkyrie, arrayed like statues. Their spears glowed with spell-enhanced light. Their expressions were grim.

Blythe stepped forward, and the others formed up around her. "Ready?"

"Get the stones ready!" Demetrus shouted.

She poured the stones into the palm of her hand. The moment her fingers closed around them, they hummed in unison. Power lanced through her veins, sharp and blinding.

Fear and awe collided in her chest—too much, too fast—her vision bending at the edges as if the world were tilting.

Her vision blurred for a second as colors bent, and magic sang inside her bones.

She felt a hand on her back.

"I've got you," Quentin said, steadying her.

Blythe steadied her focus, the world snapping back into clarity.

The Valkyrie captain raised her spear.

"Advance," Blythe said.

And they did, one final charge, straight up the steps of the Hall of the Council.

CHAPTER FIFTY-ONE

Blythe

Brilane, Auroraheim

The Council Chamber loomed ahead. Blythe could see the golden runes etched into the doors, shining faintly. Magic clung to them—old, layered, and dense. She didn't recognize half the symbols, but she felt their presence deep in her bones.

She didn't wait.

The stones in her hand flared, heat rushing up her arm as she thrust her palm toward the doors. The magic hit hard —white,-blue, and blinding. The runes sparked, resisted, then cracked one by one.

The doors groaned, shuddered, and blew open; the blast shoved her back a step.

Inside, the atrium stretched upward. Goldleaf ceilings, floating lights that looked like stars, and marble floors that glowed faintly underfoot. It was beautiful in a way that made her stomach turn. Statues lined the walls. She didn't recognize them, but she didn't trust them either.

"Go!" she shouted, and they rushed in.

The guards were waiting. Blythe barely registered their robes before the spells started flying—lightning, frost, fire. The air filled with the metallic tang of ozone.

Griffin charged first, axe raised. He struck an ice wall, shattering it like glass.

"Path's open!" he barked.

Zelos swept in behind him, shadows pooling around his feet. Blythe saw him drag a mage backward with a tendril of black energy.

"Keep moving! Don't give them room to regroup!" he snapped.

Octo moved like water, his trident spinning. Blythe caught glimpses of him between pillars, binding mages in conjured kelp. Demetrius hung back, loosing arrows with sharp precision. His face was pale. He looked tired.

Blythe didn't stop. A sigil drawn in midair turned into a hammer of wind. Sunfire scorched the floor ahead. Her hair lifted, caught in a storm she couldn't see.

The floor vibrated beneath her boots, urging her onward.

"Second wing incoming!" Hera shouted from above.

Blythe looked up. Hera and Eyra were vaulting across the balconies above, spears flashing in the dim light. Their mounts had been left outside, but they clearly didn't need them. The speed and height they cleared on their own were breathtaking—muscles coiling, boots striking stone with barely a sound, hair whipping behind them like banners in the wind. In that moment, Blythe finally understood why the old Vikings claimed their kind could fly without wings. They moved as if gravity were only a suggestion.

Quentin stayed close. Blythe felt him more than saw him, fists flying, body moving like liquid.

"Left hallway!" he called.

An explosion rocked the eastern wing. Blythe jerked back.

"They're trying to collapse the corridor!" Demetrius warned. His voice was strained.

Tavian stepped up and cast something; she didn't know what, but the ceiling held just long enough for Griffin and Octo to pass.

"We ain't stoppin' now," Griffin snarled, voice thick with grit. "Not 'til every last one o' those bastards is bleedin' in the dirt."

They kept moving.

The corridor narrowed. Murals stretched across the

walls—Council propaganda, Blythe guessed. She didn't look too closely. At the end stood another set of doors, carved with snarling griffins.

"Let me try," Zelos said. He laid his hands on the wood. Shadows curled around the lock. The hair on Blythe's arms rose as a soft whispering, too shaped to be wind and too wrong to be language. It stirred from within the shadows. "It's keyed to blood and oath. Council magic. Won't open unless you're one of them."

"I've got this," Eyra's voice came from behind them.

Of course. She was a Valkyrie. Not just any Valkyrie, but one of the top. She moved forward and placed her hand on the door.

The enchantments flared, then folded.

The doors parted.

And the Council's sanctum waited.

They could hear more troops coming from behind.

"Go—we'll hold them off!" Eyra shouted, half pushing Blythe forward.

The air inside the circular inner chamber was heavy, soaked in the scent of incense. At the center of the room, a raised dais stood like a throne of judgment. Seven chairs sat around it, each carved from a different magical material: crystal, obsidian, redwood, bone, sapphire, ironwood, and ivory. Six of them were occupied.

The Council.

Blythe stared at them as recognition hit low and hard. She knew their faces, had memorized them in the time she'd spent defending herself in a sham trial, each of them watching her as if she were something they'd stepped in. Ruthless in their serenity.

Now it was her turn.

One of them, an elder mage with golden eyes that twinkled like a dying sun, rose slowly from his seat. His robes shimmered with woven enchantments, his voice echoing unnaturally through the chamber, amplified by the stones and spells embedded in the walls.

"So you've come," he said. "The traitors. The rebels. The criminals."

"Don't waste your breath," Blythe said, stepping forward, voice steady. "There's something rotten in this realm, and it's clinging to you. We're here to tear it out—before it spreads any further."

A ripple of offense spread through the circle of mages. Another, seated to the right of the golden-eyed speaker, leaned forward with a sneer.

"You are a naive fool," he spat. "You stand beside a man who carries the stain of the dark realm inside him. That evil has slept beneath our world since time began. Perhaps it would have been more worth it to seal off that place forever."

Demetrius's gaze hardened, but he didn't speak. His silence spoke volumes.

From the far end of the circle, another mage rose, his posture poised and grandfatherly—but his eyes were sharp, predatory.

"Do the right thing, Blythe," he said, voice smooth, coaxing. "Use the stones to seal the portals. Destroy Demetrius and his followers, and you will be free. This war will end. We will owe you a great debt."

Blythe's breath caught. The resemblance was undeniable. His features were a weathered mirror of Tavian.

Beside her, Tavian's expression tightened.

"Grandfather," he said coldly.

The older man smiled thinly. "I did what I could for you, Tavian. You were headstrong. Idealistic. Too reckless. I see now... I should have cut you off completely. Allowing you even to become an agent was giving you too much."

"You raised me to believe in justice and merit. But when it came time to act, you chose power over truth," Tavian snapped.

"You have no idea the burden of ruling," the elder mage said sharply. "And she—" He pointed at Blythe. "She carries the key to the realm's destruction. The stones don't belong to you, girl. They were never meant for mortal hands."

Blythe felt the stones stir in her grasp, as if they too were aware of the moment. For a heartbeat, she feared they'd been right about her all along. The air wrapped around her fingertips. Power so vast it defied comprehension hummed through her bones.

"No. People like me made them." Blythe snapped. "I will do what they should have done."

"Their theatrics are over. End this." Demetrius barked. He stepped forward, shoulders squared despite the wear of battle and the ache in his magic-starved body. "Do it, Blythe! You know the truth about them. You've seen their corruption. You've seen the cost."

Her mind reeled. The chamber spun.

She looked from one face to the next: Demetrius, who had lied and manipulated, but fought for freedom; Tavian, shaken; Quentin, steady beside her; the Council, polished, serene, unmoved by the thousands dead outside these walls.

And the offer. Peace. Safety. An end.

All she had to do was sacrifice Demetrius.

"Blythe?" Quentin's voice reached her, quiet but anchoring. "Follow your heart."

His nearness grounded her, a tether in the storm. Her fingers clenched around the stones.

And her heart felt as if it would leap out of her chest.

"I came into this realm as a stranger," she said slowly, lifting her head. "And you tried to make me a scapegoat. You told me I was dangerous. A mistake. A threat."

The Council sat frozen, watching.

"But here's the truth," Blythe continued, stepping forward. "You are the mistake. You're the danger. And you're terrified someone finally has the power to challenge you."

The golden-eyed mage's lip curled. "Don't be foolish, girl."

"Too late," Blythe said.

With a scream, she hurled the full power of the stones into the center of the chamber.

Magic detonated in a blinding torrent of light that was raw, chaotic, and cleansing.

Council members staggered. Spells shattered. One fell from his seat, screaming as the power uncoiled around him like divine fire.

The walls cracked. The runes scribed into the ceiling exploded like dying stars.

Zelos let loose a howl of triumph and launched a spear of shadow into the heart of the circle. Octo swept his trident wide, deflecting a retaliatory blast. Griffin leapt over the railing, his axe raised, bellowing a war cry.

Her hair whipped around her face, but it wasn't her face anymore. Not really. Her body felt suddenly weightless, as if her bones had turned to smoke. Each stone tugged at her core, as if invisible threads were pulling her upward. Her feet lifted from the ground, and the six stones rose with her, circling her body, moons caught in orbit.

She saw it all from somewhere else: above, behind, nowhere. The girl in the air wasn't her, not anymore. She watched herself hover, watched the magic burn through her like a storm with no center.

And emotion slipped away, leaving only distance. Just awe. Just the quiet, terrifying certainty that she wasn't the one in control anymore.

The Council had no time to regroup.

Glass shattered above. Blythe saw Hera and Eyra crash through the high windows, spears already mid-flight. Two guards dropped before they hit the ground. The sisters' armor caught the light, blazing gold in the storm of magic.

And then—her. Or her body without her in it.

Was this what they'd warned her about? Was this what she was becoming?

The woman—her shape, her face, her voice—raised her hands.

"This is your judgment," she said.

Blythe didn't remember speaking. Didn't feel her lips move. But the words echoed through the chamber, an already--sealed verdict rolling back to them.

Power surged. The air tasted like metal and smoke. Her vision blurred at the edges, but she could still see it, still see them. The Council, unraveling. A shadow peeled away from their bodies. It twisted and coiled, a mass of writhing void, serpents made of nothing, and then it moved.

It didn't flee. It chose.

The cloud shot toward Demetrius, slamming into his chest with an impact that jolted Blythe backward. She saw his body seize, his eyes go wide with recognition or horror, maybe?

A scream clawed up her throat but never made it out.

Then the shadow disappeared into him, swallowed whole.

Like it had always belonged there.

Like vermin fleeing fire.

Her heart lurched. She'd been right. It hadn't just been the Council. That same rot—whatever ancient thing had corrupted them—had touched him too. Maybe long ago. Maybe just now.

The world cracked.

Fire. Stone. Light. Pain.

A shock wave tore through the chamber, lifting her off her feet. She felt herself fly—untethered, unmoored—before the ground slammed into her and everything went white.

She watched herself fall as if the body hitting the floor wasn't hers at all.

CHAPTER FIFTY-TWO

Blythe

Brilane, Auroraheim

The sulfur hit her nose first.

Her vision dragged its way back into focus, her skull throbbing. The ceiling spun above her. No, not a ceiling anymore. Just sky. Gray, endless, smeared with smoke. Somewhere nearby, metal clashed, magic cracked, and someone screamed.

Blythe groaned and rolled onto her side. The floor, what was left of it, was split and blackened. Marble reduced to ruin beneath her palms. She forced herself up, one hand flat against the scorched stone.

Above, smoke curled through the jagged beams, broken ribs clawing at the sky. Fire danced along the balconies, hungry for whatever hadn't been reduced to ash. The tapestries still hung. Somehow.

Her lungs stung. She coughed and pushed to her feet.

Splinters of the dais lay in fractured heaps. The center of the floor had collapsed entirely, a charred crater smoldering like the earth had decided to swallow the Council whole—and be done with it.

Maybe it had.

She looked down. The stones were still in her hand—warm, dim, stirring with a sluggish glow of something half-asleep. Six of them. A cold thread of fear slid through her.

They were warm, alive, responding to her—because of her.

The Council had called her dangerous, unstable, a threat.

Clearly they were right. The thought hit harder than the

blast that had thrown her.

She slipped the stones into the magical pouch and then into her pocket before taking a slow, calming breath.

The battle hadn't stopped. Mages and Valkyrie clashed with her friends near the archways. They didn't know. Didn't feel it the way she did. The weight that had settled over the Hall the second they walked in… gone.

Like waking from a nightmare.

"Blythe!"

Quentin's voice punched through the haze. She turned.

He jumped the wreck of a column, landing beside her with a grimace and blood on his sleeve. "You're hurt."

She swayed. He caught her elbow.

"This whole place is about to come down." He wrapped his arm around her waist to help her stay upright. "Let's get you out of here, Kitsune."

Behind him, chaos unfolded. Eyra spun her spear into a blur, shielding Demetrius with barely a breath between attacks. Zelos flung shadows like waves.

Griffin was yelling again, something loud and unintelligible, and probably gleeful. He enjoyed battle far too much.

The west wall buckled under another explosion. A spray of stone and smoke rained down, a glass shard whizzing past Blythe's ear, the unmistakable sting of a warning shot.

"I saw them die," she whispered, the images seared in her brain. "The Council. Gone. I felt it. It was like the stones and I were… in sync." Her brain, unhelpful as ever, supplied: not the band.

Quentin's grip tightened around her hand. "Then you did it."

"But something escaped," she said. "It went into Demetrius."

He didn't answer. There wasn't time.

Her legs buckled as she stepped forward, but they held. Quentin wrapped an arm around her, steadying her as they limped out of the chamber and into the wrecked hall. The battle was winding down. Word of the Council's fall was spreading fast.

When they stepped outside the building, a quiet wall of stillness hit her.

No shouting. No clashing steel. Just silence—sharp, strange, and weighted. As if every soldier on both sides had paused, unsure what the end of the Council actually meant.

Then movement.

Eyra landed beside Hera, her mount's wings folding in tight. Demetrius stood nearby, barely upright. Zelos let the shadows bleed out around him, his expression unreadable. Slowly, heads turned toward the crater where the Council had once sat.

Griffin whooped. "Ha! Told you she'd do it!"

But no one cheered. Blythe could feel it, no one trusted it. Not fully.

Movement flickered at the edge of her vision. A cluster of werewolves emerged from the smoke, some limping, some supporting others. And there—Bertolf.

He was streaked with soot, hair wild, shirt torn down one side, but unmistakably alive. When he spotted her, his eyes widened.

"Oh, good," he called hoarsely, "you're not dead. I was really hoping I didn't run all that way just to avenge you."

Despite everything, a laugh scraped out of her. "You look terrible."

He grinned, teeth sharp and bright against the grime. "You should see the other guy."

A nearby werewolf groaned. "We *did* see the other guy, Bertolf. He's fine. You tripped over a body."

Bertolf shot him a betrayed look. "It was a very dangerous body."

Blythe shook her head, warmth blooming in her chest. He was alive. They all were, for now.

She looked back. The Hall that had held executions, laws, and decisions carved in stone lay in ruins.

But they were still here.

Zelos was already issuing orders, sending Warlocks to tend the wounded and scout the upper levels of nearby buildings. The shadows coiled at his boots like something hungry learning patience.

Octo dipped his head toward Blythe. "You did it."

"No," she said quietly, eyes flicking again to Demetrius. "Not yet."

Griffin was helping to free a trapped rebel from beneath a slab of marble when he looked over.

"What's the plan then, General?" Griffin rumbled, voice thick with grit.

She nearly laughed at the title—nearly.

General. Right. Because nothing said "qualified" like almost dying twice in one afternoon.

"We need to make sure Ben is either dead or otherwise taken care of. We find the others. We regroup. And then we deal with the portals and Demetrius. Winning this battle hasn't end the war. We need to move."

"We will." Quentin brushed her cheek, brief and grounding. "But first… let's make sure you stay upright."

"I'm fine."

"You always say that right before you pass out."

She smirked. "Then help me."

"I was already planning to, Kit." She put her arm around his shoulders, leaning heavily against him.

"Ye said somethin' 'bout Ben?" Griffin called over the noise.

Blythe pointed toward the alley where she'd left him buried under rubble.

"He was under a fallen wall."

"I'll check." Griffin signaled another rebel to help the fallen and took off toward the alley.

She looked back as they limped away.

One last glance at the burning ruin behind them, the sky opening wide above the wreckage. Stars were visible through the smoke. Somehow.

"You have them?" Quentin asked quietly.

She nodded.

"Good. We need to move before Demetrius comes for them."

She rested her head against his shoulder. "Right."

There was no time for rest. The world hadn't righted itself just because the Council had fallen. The stones still needed to be used on the portals. Whatever Demetrius had become, he had to be stopped later.

She thought back to what she'd seen. That thing. Whatever it was. That darkness, shapeless and hungry, sliding into him—

No. She hadn't imagined it.

She twisted to look through the smoke.

Demetrius still stood, hunched and leaning hard on a broken wall. Exhausted. Or…No. Not just exhaustion.

Her stomach lurched, a wave of nausea rising as the truth clicked into place.

"It infected him," she said quietly.

Quentin's brow furrowed. "What did?"

"The darkness. From the Council."

"You sure it wasn't—"

"I know what I saw." Her voice dropped low. Firm. "I saw something clinging to them before. And now it's all in one place—inside him."

Quentin's mouth pressed into a thin line and he sped up, hurrying her out.

They reached the hills outside of Brilane just as the last light bled from the edges of the city. Ellira was waiting, tail twitching. She let out a pleased huff and nudged Blythe, the gentle touch of a concerned friend.

"I'm okay, girl," she whispered.

"A miracle, that," Tavian said, appearing from the trees. "Freaking miracle," he added.

"Really?" Hera deadpanned beside him.

"Would you prefer I say—"

"Tavian," Blythe and Quentin snapped in unison.

"It's a human word," Blythe offered, waving it off.

Hera rolled her eyes. "I'll never get used to them..."

"No time," Quentin said.

A shadow passed overhead. Eyra's mount dipped low, wings kicking up dust as she shouted down to them. "Griffin checked the alley—Ben's gone. The rubble was moved."

She didn't wait. She wheeled back toward the city before anyone could answer.

Blythe's stomach dropped, a cold jolt shooting through her. Gone. Not there. Did that mean he wasn't dead?

Quentin moved on before she could let the fear settle.

"Griffin, Octo, and Eyra are staying behind for clean-up. And if what you said about Demetrius is true, the rest of us need to get to a portal—fast. We need to seal off the Dark Realm. Locke House should still be clear, right, Tavian?"

"How many can Ellira carry?" Blythe asked, scanning the group.

Hera whistled. From the trees, her mount stepped through, hooves heavy, armor gleaming under the blood and dirt that had spattered on it during the battle. The unicorn's horn was crusted with drying crimson, a stark reminder of what it had carved through. Blythe was sure its fur used to be white, but now it looked like a Pollock painting of red and brown. Blythe watched as the beast strode up to Hera, nudging her gently.

"This is Saphira," Hera said affectionately. "It's been far too long since I've ridden her in battle. It was good to have her again."

"I'm riding with Hera," Tavian said with a grin that made Blythe snort despite everything. Hera shot her a look.

"You look like the cat that swallowed the canary," Blythe shot at Tavian, who smiled.

"I haven't heard that one yet. I like it."

"Humans have such strange sayings," Hera mumbled,

mounting Saphira. "What is a cat anyway?" She shook her head. "You coming?" she called to Tavian, who rushed over and jumped onto Saphira behind Hera, moving closer to her. Blythe thought she saw a bit of a blush on Hera, but just as quickly as she saw it, it faded.

Quentin helped her onto Ellira's back and mounted behind her. He sat so closely that she feared she might be blushing too.

The mounts took off—Hera and Tavian ahead, while Quentin and Blythe followed.

Blythe wouldn't say she was getting used to flying this way. Maybe it'd be more accurate to say that she had slightly less terror as the ground fell away with every beat of Ellira's massive wings.

The wind picked up as they rose, the burning city shrinking beneath them. Blythe looked back.

A cold current sliced past her cheeks, sharp enough to clear the smoke from her lungs.

She didn't know if she'd ever see that place again.

But if she did… she hoped it would be under a fairer administration.

CHAPTER FIFTY-THREE

Blythe

Brilane, Auroraheim to Locke House, Auroraheim

The frigid wind tore through Blythe's hair as they soared above the countryside, the sharp edge of evening air stinging her cheeks. Below, mist rolled over dark hills and dense forested ridges, drifting across the land like silver smoke. The rising sun cast soft silver-gold light, stretching long shadows across fields tinted pale lavender and smoky blue as daylight slowly returned.

And then she saw it.

The dragon dipped lower, its wings slicing through the night like blades. Below, a fortress stretched across the river. Its pale stone, glowing silver in the moonlight, cast long shadows over the water through its arches.

The towers rose quiet and watchful, their windows flickering with candlelight—too warm, too human—against the cold hush of the sky. Beyond, the gardens lay geometric and perfect, but strange from above like runes cut into the earth. The bridge spanning the river, connecting the stronghold to the road, gleamed, a spine of light and stone.

High above, illuminated flags flapped and snapped in the breeze—dragons, phoenixes, ancient trees, symbols she didn't recognize—fluttering atop towers streaked with dew and traced with luminous spells.

As they drew closer, new details emerged: griffins perched watchfully on the parapets, feathers rustling. A few took flight, and Blythe momentarily feared they might attack, but instead they descended toward the river, soaring past the open drawbridge to land in the water.

A sharp inhale caught in her chest as they passed over a garden within the outer wall. Topiaries shaped as mythical creatures moved slightly, as if alive. Fountains spilled not water, but floating droplets of glowing liquid that shifted color with the fading sun.

A place like this shouldn't exist. It felt sacred—like flying straight into the pages of a half-remembered story she'd never expected to live inside.

"That's a castle." Her voice shook, finger raised toward the towers gleaming beneath them. It looked just like the images she'd grown up seeing—textbooks, documentaries, postcards. But this wasn't the human world anymore. That much was clear.

Quentin chuckled, eyes dancing.

"Yes," he said. "Here it's Locke Castle—or Locke House. In the human realm, they call it Prague Castle."

Blythe frowned, thinking back to her visits to Prague Castle in the Czech Republic. "That castle's a working palace. You can take tours, and the president lives there. How can it be a portal hub if humans are walking through it every day like it's nothing more than a pretty building?"

Quentin nudged Ellira into a glide toward a grassy clearing tucked near the base of the outer wall, trailing behind Hera and Tian as they descended to land.

"It's not like The House of Fas," he said, his voice softer now. "There's a whole section that's hidden—shielded by old magic in the human realm. Only the Keeper can access it. In our realm, they can move through the entire keep."

He glanced at her. "I've never quite understood how they manage it. I don't think I'd be terribly comfortable having tours of my House."

Blythe raised an eyebrow but didn't press. Quentin just gave her a lopsided smile.

Ellira touched down gently, and Quentin hopped off before helping Blythe dismount. His hand stayed briefly at her waist.

Tavian was already stretching, the slow, instinctive motions of someone shaking off sleep. Hera was speaking quietly to her mount, and then the unicorn walked off toward the water. Blythe assumed it was to drink, but once it reached the edge, it plunged in—ducking under and coming up again, shaking its head.

"Bath time," Hera said with a laugh.

Blythe looked back at the castle. The awe hit harder than she expected, scraping against the exhaustion still clinging to her bones.

"Let's go see my brother!" Tavian called cheerfully, walking toward the drawbridge entrance.

"He's the Keeper?" Blythe clarified.

"Yeah. He was happy to take it when I didn't." He glanced back at her. "Hopefully, he still feels that way."

They crossed the lawn in silence, the castle rising ahead. The drawbridge led them through the open gate and into a large courtyard. Tavian led the way across and up white marble steps toward the front entrance. The door—massive, wooden, marked by time—bore symbols carved deep into its surface. Tavian knocked three times in a rhythm that felt almost ceremonial.

The door creaked open.

And there he was.

He could've been Tavian's reflection—same features, same sharp eyes—but steadier somehow.

"Tavian," the man said in a voice with quiet authority. "And guests."

He stepped forward, giving Blythe, Hera, and Quentin a subtle nod.

"Hey, Soren—long time no see," Tavian said, hugging him. Blythe would be eternally grateful that the two of them dressed differently with different hairstyles.

"Come in. There's much to talk about."

Warm air met them as the doors opened wide, scented

with herbs and something cooking. Inside, the castle opened into a world all its own.

Tapestries blanketed the walls with scenes from both magical and mundane history—wars, rituals, the earliest Keepers. Chandeliers hung overhead, glowing with enchantment instead of flame.

They moved through carpeted corridors and down stone hallways inlaid with symbols that shone faintly beneath their feet. Light from the stained-glass windows spilled across the floor in rich, shifting colors.

Soren walked with purpose through each turn until they reached a heavy door bound in iron. Its emblem—the twin trees, one inverted—felt somehow familiar.

It opened as he approached. Beyond lay a room unlike anything Blythe had ever seen—a chamber that was part war room, part sanctuary. The kind of space where plans were made and secrets kept.

"Please tell me you had nothing to do with the attack on the capital." His voice was calm, but edged with steel.

Blythe looked to see Soren staring at his brother, who had the good sense to look sheepishly away.

"Okay, so you did. Tell me your side, and then I'll allow you to do whatever it is you've come here for, if I determine your reasoning makes sense."

Where Tavian was charming and flirty, Soren was serious. Straightforward.

He led them into a sitting room where the House—or perhaps the Castle—had laid out tea, biscuits, and small finger sandwiches. As they settled in, Blythe weighed her options, trying to decide how best to begin.

The warmth of the tea felt impossibly gentle after the chaos she'd just survived.

Quentin didn't waste any time before diving in.

He told Soren everything, from Blythe's issues with the Council to her rescue from prison and then her kidnapping after she'd helped them. He held nothing back. Which was probably for the best, because their next task was to address the portals. Shock flashed across Soren's face before he masked it.

Since Soren was a Keeper and they'd come to his House, it only made sense that he should know what they were after.

Blythe only hoped he'd agree to what they decided needed to be done. They were running out of time.

CHAPTER FIFTY-FOUR

Blythe

Locke House, Auroraheim

Soren listened, hands folded, as Quentin told the story. Blythe tried to tune him out. She didn't need to be reminded of the nightmare she'd lived through over the last—however many weeks it had been. She'd lost track of time. Had it been months? She wasn't sure.

She looked toward the window. Through the window, snow drifted past. It had been early autumn when all of this began. Now winter was arriving. The whole season had passed. A whole season.

When Quentin finished, their plates were empty, and exhaustion pulled at them. The House had cleared away the empty tea cups, and they sat in an uncomfortable silence with nothing but the sound of the cuckoo clock ticking slowly on the wall. Tavian, Blythe, Quentin, and Hera watched Soren, who had risen from his seat and stood by the window, staring out at the darkness.

Blythe shot Tavian a look, who shrugged. Clearly, their twin bond didn't include knowing what his brother was thinking.

"And Grandfather is dead," Soren said after a long, dragging silence.

"I'm fairly certain," Tavian said. "Yes."

Soren stood still, staring out the window. That yes fell flat between them.

"If there'd been another way—" Blythe started.

"There wasn't one," Soren cut in. "The council has been

doing terrible things for a long time. Things were getting worse. Demetrius left the portals unguarded. Untold horrors are spreading through the magic and human realms."

He turned to face them again. Soren's face was a stone mask—Tavian's emotions turned outward, his face turned to granite.

"So you came here to decide what to do about the portals —how best to use the stones."

"Yes," Hera said. She was watching Soren, her face just as unreadable. She'd be great at poker, too.

Blythe's thoughts felt slow, muddled—like wading through fog.

"I do not know much of the stones," Soren said, "but if you wish to look in the library to determine how to instate safeguards and put the evil back where it belongs, you are most welcome."

Blythe unclenched her fists. Her nails had left crescents in her palms.

"Thank you," Tavian whispered. "About Grandfather..." His voice broke ever so slightly.

A muscle jumped in Soren's cheek.

"Now's not the time," Soren interrupted. "Follow me."

He led the group out of the room and down a hallway. A large wooden door opened for him, revealing a set of spiral stairs descending into darkness.

As Blythe followed, she couldn't help but wonder if he was taking them to a dungeon. The air grew cool and damp as they went down.

At the bottom of the stairs was another door, which opened for Soren. Inside was the grandest library Blythe had ever seen.

When she first walked in, she saw a massive stone fireplace with two chairs in front of it. Just beyond stood a large mahogany desk with a tall chair behind it. On the desk sat a typewriter that looked remarkably similar to the one in the library at Fasbridge Manor.

From the floor, she could look up and see the spiral staircase winding all the way to the top, each landing opening into a circular gallery lined with floor-to-ceiling shelves

Blythe, Hera, and Quentin stood frozen just inside, staring upward, trying to take in everything—the intricate wooden carvings on the shelves, the wrought-iron railing that didn't look sturdy enough to keep someone from toppling over one of the upper floors onto the stone below.

Blythe was pulled from her awe by the sound of a typewriter clacking away.

She watched as Soren walked to the desk and read the paper.

"The House knows what book you need."

Blythe felt something tap her foot and looked down to see a hefty brown tome so old she feared it might crumble if she touched it. She bent to pick it up, letting the book fall open naturally. The letters did the same strange trick that the Keeper's books at The House of Fas had—when she looked with both eyes open, the letters continually moved, and she couldn't read them, but if she closed one eye, the words stopped.

"I'm not sure why I bother trying to read over your shoulder," Hera grumbled. "It's gibberish."

"It's Keeper's Script," Soren corrected her. "What does it say?"

He had taken the seat behind the desk, watching her with that unreadable expression. Blythe wondered if Tavian had tried to make him smile when they were kids. Or maybe he hadn't always been this serious.

She shook her head. Focus.

The others settled in—chairs, floor, wherever they could. Blythe took a breath and turned her attention back to the script, letting the silence stretch as they waited for her to speak.

She crossed the floor and set the book on the desk, open to the page it had naturally fallen to.

Pulling the stones from her pocket, she examined them.

"They still have magic left, but if what I'm reading is correct, we can use them to fix our portal problem. I'm just not sure their magic will remain after that."

"Well, that's fine, right?" Tavian said, sitting on the rug in front of the fireplace, legs stretched out and leaning back on his palms. "We just need to restore the safeguards, and we're good to go."

"We can't just put guards up," Quentin said from a bookshelf to Blythe's right, where he'd been perusing titles. "We need to close off that dark realm and send the evil back inside."

Blythe shook her head and began to pace, turning the thoughts over in her mind.

"When the stones were made, they were created with a specific purpose—to limit the number of portals, focus the magic, and establish safeguards to prevent beings from each realm from easily passing through them. The Houses served as the borders between the Human and Magic Realms, while the dark realm's portals in the human and magic realms were more loosely guarded, as the Magic Realm and the Houses needed the energy to keep them powered."

She studied the stones in her hands, their runes glowing faintly in the light.

"If we close off the portals to the dark realm, we also cut off the magic in the Houses, leaving those portals unguarded. Of course, we'd like to think all magical beings are good and kind, but humans have a plethora of lore and stories from the time before, when magical beings came and did both great and terrible things to and for them. We can't go back to that." She continued to stare at the stones, thinking aloud. "I was able to channel their magic through me to take out the Council. That may have been a one-time deal. I don't think we could use them to cast all the evil that has escaped back unless we somehow managed to round them all up into one place, as we did with the Council."

"It'd be like herding cats," Tavian said with a chuckle.

"Herding what?" Hera stared at him.

Blythe cut in before he could answer. "We can't use the stones for that. We'll need to go and fight the evil back into the dark realm—or else eliminate them."

"Okay, so some of us go into the human realm and take down the demons and such there, then come back," Hera said, crossing her legs. "It won't be easy, but it's doable. I'm sure we could round some people up to go in and take care of that."

"You're overlooking something. The Council has been sending agents to take out the evil. But new creatures just replace them. The portals must be closed before the evil is taken out."

Silence fell as they processed Blythe's words.

"So, if I'm understanding correctly," Soren spoke up, twisting a pen between his fingers, "the only way to block the dark realm's portals is to close them entirely, which would then eliminate the Houses' magic and the power in the Magic Realm. Those who went to the human realm would be able to pass back through, but there'd be no way to limit who traveled either way."

"The book explains that the Houses channel the portal magic. Without them, other portals would pop up along the ley lines." Blythe leaned against the desk. "I don't know how many—but it would be too many to guard."

"So what's our other option, or is this the only one?" Quentin asked. "Just close the Dark Realm off and hope?"

She exhaled, the truth settling like a stone in her chest.

"We close all of the portals."

Tavian swore under his breath.

CHAPTER FIFTY-FIVE

Quentin

Locke House, Auroraheim

Quentin didn't realize he was holding his breath until Blythe said it—"We close all of the portals." His chest hollowed.

No one spoke. Even the House was still.

She meant it. Of course she did. And she would follow through, even if it meant splitting the worlds forever, and her stepping into the half he could never follow. He'd promised his mother, and he had no doubt she'd find a way to hunt him down in the Human Realm, closed off or not.

The others discussed logistics. Hera was already volunteering to gather reinforcements. Tavian, unsurprisingly, offered without hesitation.

"I'll go with you," Tavian said simply. "You shouldn't face that alone."

It wasn't what he said that made Quentin's stomach clench. It was the look in his eyes. The kind of look that could follow someone into battle or through fire without question.

Quentin turned away, jaw tight. He focused a crack in the stone floor to anchor him.

Blythe wasn't looking at him. She was staring at Hera.

"Hera," she began gently, worry threading through her voice. "You don't have to go. You're not—"

"I do." Hera cut her off—quiet but firm. She met Blythe's eyes and softened, just a bit. "This is the kind of fight I was made for, remember? If I don't go, who will? And I trust myself more than I trust half the warriors we'd drag from the barracks."

"But if people see your ears—" Blythe began.

"I'll hide them," Tavian said, stepping in before she could finish.

Quentin swallowed hard, a bitter tang rising in his throat. He didn't speak. He couldn't. If he opened his mouth, something inside him might crack wide open. Instead, he stepped back into the shadows of the tall shelves, out of their line of sight, and pressed a palm on a shelf, steadying himself.

He had imprinted. His soul had chosen her before he could stop it. A tether he hadn't asked for but couldn't sever. And now, she might walk away into the human realm, into danger, into a world where he couldn't follow without standing out like a lighthouse in a thunderstorm.

Fae weren't built for that world. Not his kind. Not with ears and eyes that marked him. He'd last a day at most.

And Tavian would go with Hera. Would fight beside her. Watch her. Protect her. Because, of course, Blythe would choose to go to the human realm. That was where she felt most at home.

He'd always known imprinting didn't guarantee being accepted. But he hadn't expected the burn of it, his heart exiled with her.

He stepped forward then, needing her to see him. He caught her eye, and for a moment, it felt like the whole room disappeared. Just her, and the truth between them. He didn't say it—he couldn't. But maybe, just maybe, she'd already sensed it.

If she had, she didn't show it.

She only gave him that small, brave smile—the one he'd memorized long ago—and turned back to the others.

Quentin barely registered Hera's voice until it cut through the room with unmistakable finality.

"Blythe, you're not going."

Every head turned.

Blythe's heart stalled. She blinked at her, stunned. "What?"

Hera met her gaze evenly, her voice calm, but edged with urgency. "You need to stay here with Quentin. Demetrius is still out there, and we both know he's not just mad. He's corrupted. Something's twisted him, and if he's left unchecked, he could tear the magic realm apart from the inside. Tavian and I can handle the human realm with help from others. But you and Quentin need to make sure there's a free realm to come back to."

Blythe opened her mouth to argue, but Hera raised her hand.

"I mean it. You're the only one who has a link to both realms. You're stronger than they are. And Quentin—" she glanced at him briefly "—is probably the only one stubborn enough to keep you alive while you do it."

That drew the smallest twitch of a smile from Tavian, but Quentin didn't move. Not even a blink. Hera's words sent lightning through his chest, staggering relief threaded with an emotion too heavy to name. Was she saying this because she believed it? Or because she knew it would tear him in two if Blythe left?

Blythe turned to him, expression unreadable. His heart thudded loud enough that he was sure she could hear it. She looked back at Hera. Her words had carved out a thin, dangerous thread of hope.

"Are you sure?" Blythe's voice softened. "You're walking into a literal war zone."

Hera shrugged with a crooked smile. "Wouldn't be the first time. Besides, I'd rather face demons than be stuck babysitting you two. Far too much unresolved tension."

Tavian made a choking sound that might've been a laugh, or a curse. Quentin watched as Blythe stared at the floor for a long second, then nodded slowly.

"All right," she whispered. "We'll stay. We'll deal with Demetrius."

Quentin let his eyes fall shut for a heartbeat.

She was staying.

For now.

And that—for the first time since she'd spoken of sealing the portals—felt like enough to breathe again.

"So… how do we actually do this?" Soren's voice came from behind the desk, low and even. Quentin had nearly forgotten he was still in the room.

"We will gather troops to bring with us to the human realm," Hera said, rising to her feet.

Blythe drew in a slow breath, too controlled to be casual, and Quentin knew she was already calculating the cost of whatever came next.

The room fell into a brittle silence until the steady clack of the typewriter sliced through the stillness. Soren's eyes tracked the machine as its keys struck, one after another, the bell chiming softly before the carriage slid back with a metallic sigh, ready for the next line.

"Soren?" Blythe's voice was barely audible.

"We don't have time," he said flatly, yanking the paper from the typewriter. Without a word, he handed it to her.

Blythe took the page, her fingers brushing the edge, eyes scanning the message:

An order has gone out from the capital. Demetrius has seized control and issued a decree for the arrest of Blythe and her companions. He accuses them of smuggling dangerous magical artifacts. He's hunting the stones.

"We need to close the portals," Soren added. "Now."

"What happens to the Houses when the portals are closed?" Blythe asked quietly.

Quentin looked at Soren, and for the first time, Soren glanced at Tavian—his fingers tightening around the paper, his façade cracking before he could hide it.

"I don't know," Soren whispered. "I'd have to see if there was information about the Houses from the time before."

He hesitated, the smallest flicker of worry crossing his face.

"But if their magic relies on Dark Realm energy flowing

through the ley lines, then once the portals are closed, the Houses will lose their power."

He watched as Blythe looked back down at the paper and then up, locking eyes with Hera. She looked at Quentin as if she wanted to scream that they couldn't do it, not yet. They needed time. Or perhaps that was Quentin projecting his own feelings. Hera had become such a close friend and ally through all of this. He couldn't imagine facing any of this without her.

Hera stood. "You and Quentin need to go back to the Fae."

"The Fae?" Blythe's mind was having a hard time catching up.

"They can protect us," Quentin agreed. "You and I will leave on Ellira as soon as you close the portals."

They all rose and moved quickly toward the door.

"I'll open the portal for you and Hera," Soren said to Tavian. A look passed over Tavian's face that was mirrored in Soren's. The brothers hugged, and Quentin saw a look cross Blythe's face before she pressed her lips together. Quentin wondered if Soren would ever see his brother again.

"Are we sure the stones won't harm you while you do that?" Quentin asked aloud. Blythe elbowed him. "What?" He looked at her, and she nodded towards the brothers. "Oh." He hadn't realized he was interrupting a moment.

"They won't," Soren said as he stepped back from Tavian, still looking at his brother. "I have to believe that everything will work out as it's supposed to," he added, glancing toward her. "We need to hold onto something."

"And hope there's enough left to open a portal again—so we can bring Hera and Tavian home," Blythe whispered.

CHAPTER FIFTY-SIX

Blythe

Locke House, Auroraheim

Blythe watched as Tavian stood facing the portal, arms folded, expression locked in place. But the tension in his shoulders betrayed him. Soren stood a few feet away, not moving either. She swallowed the lump in her throat. She would not cry. Not now. Not here.

"I'll bring her back," Tavian said finally, without turning.

"I know." Soren's voice was steady. "Just don't make me come into that awful human realm to find you."

It was barely anything—and somehow, it was everything. They stepped in close, their foreheads touching for a heartbeat, twin shadows in the flickering portal light. Then Tavian turned, jaw clenched, and walked toward Hera without another word.

Hera faced Blythe.

Silence hung between them.

It was harder than Blythe expected, standing in front of her this way. Her best friend. Her sister in everything but name. Hera, who had fought beside her when it felt like the world was burning. Who had dragged laughter out of her when she thought she'd forgotten how.

"You don't have to do this," Blythe whispered.

Hera's smile tilted, wry and weary. "You say that like it's true."

Blythe shook her head. "What if I never see you again?"

"You will." Hera stepped in, pulling her into a hug so tight it hurt. "You'd better. I am not dying in the human realm just so you can name your first unicorn after me and call it a tribute."

Blythe laughed. "You'd hate that so much."

"I would haunt you for eternity."

They pulled apart, but their hands stayed clasped for a moment longer.

"Stay alive," Blythe said, nodding toward Tavian.

"I will," he said, giving her that familiar, lopsided smile.

Blythe looked back at Hera.

"And you—don't be a hero unless you have to."

"Oh," Hera said with a wink, already turning toward the shimmering light. "I always have to."

Then she and Tavian stepped through the portal.

Blythe stared at the space they'd vanished from, the magic already thinning.

The portal didn't explode, flash, or scream when it closed.

It just blinked out.

Blythe dropped to her knees before she even realized she'd moved.

It wasn't graceful. It wasn't brave. It was just grief.

Soren didn't speak. Didn't interrupt. The House didn't hum around her, didn't wrap her in a blanket of gentle magic. Her House would have. This one stayed still. There was nothing but the sound of her breath—the sharp, broken way she tried and failed to keep it steady.

For a heartbeat, she wanted to undo everything. To tell Hera and Tavian that they would find another way. They had to.

But she knew they wouldn't.

They couldn't.

Her fingers found the pouch. The moment she touched the stones, they quivered beneath her skin. Waiting. Watching. Wanting.

Time to finish it.

She rose slowly.

Soren stood beside her. “Ready?”

“Yes,” she lied. She wasn’t ready. She doubted she ever would be.

Soren opened the book to the page that showed them how to handle the stones.

“Let’s take this outside. I don’t know what will happen to the House once the portal closes,” Soren said, his voice quiet, steady.

Maybe one day she’d learn how he stayed that calm while everything inside was coming apart.

They stepped out into the field beyond the Castle, the night closing around them. No torches. No moon.

Snow drifted down in slow, deliberate spirals, catching faint glimmers from the rising sunlight behind them. It kissed her skin, cold, fragile, and almost reverent. Each flake melted on contact, leaving behind a chill that felt deeper than the weather.

The ground was soft beneath her boots, blanketed in white. The air held that peculiar silence only snowfall brings. Thick, expectant, as if the world itself were holding its breath.

She looked up. The Castle loomed behind them. Ahead, the field stretched out, a blank canvas where a story would have to begin.

And Blythe felt it—that strange, fragile moment between endings and beginnings.

Soren assisted by drawing the necessary markings. Blythe knelt, placing the stones in their spots—each one falling into place with a finality that made her chest ache. They pulsed once, then again.

She pressed her palm to the center and closed her eyes.

It ripped through her, a burning cold that stole her breath. Power surged from the stones, from her blood, from the marrow of her bones. It wasn’t just magic. It was everything.

She felt the portals closing. One after another, each slammed shut like a door on a scream. The rhythm of the world faltered, stuttered, and then went still.

Her vision fractured. The air around her pulsed with heat and silence, and somewhere deep inside, something screamed.

And still, she held.

And then—

Silence.

She gasped, falling forward. Her hands slipped on the ground as she collapsed. The stones lay inert. She could feel it. They were dead and lifeless.

"Blythe?" Quentin's voice came from a distance. She expected him to be right there, but when she looked up, she saw Soren holding him back.

"Soren?" she whispered.

No answer.

The air had changed—flattened. The Castle had fallen silent.

She turned, heart sinking. Nothing moved. No soft pull of enchantment.

It felt like the heart of the world had stopped beating.

And Blythe was left in the dark.

CHAPTER FIFTY-SEVEN

Blythe

Locke House, Auroraheim

Time wasn't being kind. Not in a dramatic way, but in the slow, heavy way that made every breath feel too large.

Blythe sat in silence, palms pressed flat against the frozen ground. The magic was gone. And even with Quentin and Soren somewhere nearby, it felt as if she were sitting in a tomb.

"We need to go, Kits," Quentin said quietly, his words gentle, almost apologetic.

She swiped hastily at her face, pulling herself back together.

"Yes," she whispered. Then, realizing he probably didn't hear her, she added, "Let's go."

She didn't feel ready. But readiness didn't matter. The Castle couldn't protect them, and Demetrius surely knew where they'd gone. They could rest when they reached the Fae. She gathered the stones in her hands, tears pricking as she realized there was no magic left inside them.

Soren turned, starting towards the dark castle.

Blythe followed him. "I don't think we would've been able to do this without you," she said, her voice rough from grief. "Thank you—for everything."

Soren inclined his head once, the gesture small but steady. The air around them felt hollow without the magic from the stones and castle. Blythe drew in a slow breath, bracing herself for what waited beyond this place.

The ground shook as Ellira walked to join them from

where she'd been resting at the other side of the field. Her wings twitched, tail swishing with impatience. The scent of fresh snow clung to everything.

Soren turned to her then.

"Take care of each other," he said simply. "And if you fail..." He paused. "Don't fail."

It was meant to be dry—a joke—but it hit too close to the truth.

Quentin stepped in and offered his hand. Soren didn't shake it; instead, he clasped his forearm in a warrior's farewell.

"Watch her," he murmured.

"With my life," Quentin replied.

Blythe climbed onto Ellira's back in silence, Quentin behind her. She didn't look back—not at the Castle, not at Soren.

Ellira's wings beat against the ground, and the wind lifted them into the sky. Her limbs and eyelids felt heavy with exhaustion, but there was no time for sleep now.

They soared through the light snowfall into the cold morning air, the quiet broken only by the rhythmic flap of wings and the roar of wind in their ears.

Quentin nodded behind her. "Demetrius will feel the portals closed, the magic fading. Especially if what you suspect is right—that there's an ancient evil from the dark realm inside him. This will have severed that connection. The Warlocks will know. Their magic will be gone. And they'll blame you."

She didn't respond right away.

"He's got the armies now," Quentin went on. A cold prickle slid down her spine. "He's rallied most of the realm under fear and lies. But I have the Fae. And Griffin will ensure the Dwarves are with us. There's no way the Merfolk will turn against us either, so long as Octo's on our side.

"We may even be able to win the Valkyrie over. They followed the Council because that's who they are—steadfast, always. If Eyra convinces them that Demetrius was responsible for everything, and that the evil affecting him was rooted in the Council, then there's no way the Valkyrie would stay with him. We still stand. With all of them, the elves, gnomes, and fairies will go with us."

She turned slightly. "Because I'm your what? Your friend? Your ally? I'm half Mage, half of the very people who oppressed everyone else. Unbound according to the Warlocks, whatever that even means."

"But you were oppressed, too. And you risked your life to save them all. Plus..." He hesitated. "If you were mine—consort, wife—whatever you'd call it—you'd be theirs too. The Fae would see you as their queen. One of us. Joined in blood."

The words dropped like stones in her stomach.

It wasn't that she didn't trust him. After everything they'd been through, how could she not? Hera had made her promise she'd let go of what happened before they went into the Dark Realm. Miles's dying hadn't been his fault. She didn't blame him, and her feelings for him had changed. She wasn't angry at him anymore. Not after everything. But this? This was different. Binding herself to someone, not out of love, but out of strategy... or survival?

She looked out across the horizon.

"I don't know if I can do that," she said finally.

"I'm not asking you to," Quentin said. "Just think about it."

Silence stretched between them. But it wasn't heavy—not this time.

"I will." She leaned into him as Ellira moved beneath them, his chest firm and warm at her back, every shift of his breath brushing her spine.

And for the first time in a while, she meant it.

Far beyond the treetops, the final traces of night melted at the horizon, and the sky warmed into a brilliant new day.

CHARACTER LIST

MAIN CHARACTERS

Blythe Evans
Race: Half Human / Half Mage
Age: 24
Role: Keeper of Fasbridge House (The House of Fas); former archaeologist

Quentin Hendrix
Race: Fae
Age: 28
Role: Rebel strategist; former lawyer; dragon rider; Fae prince/heir

Hera Eyundal
Race: Half-Valkyrie / Unknown
Age: 22
Role: Warrior of the rebellion

Griffin
Race: Dwarf
Age: Unknown (appears mid-40s)
Role: Axe-wielding warrior; son of the chief of the Silverback Dwarf Clan

Tavian Locke
Race: Mage
Age: 30
Role: Council agent; double agent allied with the rebellion

REBELLION LEADERS & ALLIES

Demetrius Fas

Race: Mage
Age: appears late 40s
Role: Leader of the rebellion; Blythe's uncle

Zelos Dredmor

Race: Warlock
Age: Unknown
Role: Warlock advisor aligned with the rebellion—motives uncertain

Eyra Eyundal

Race: Valkyrie
Age: 40s (appears ageless)
Role: Valkyrie commander; spy

Melya

Race: Warlock
Age: 30s
Role: Guide from the Dark World; close-combat fighter

Xander

Race: Vampire
Age: Unknown (appears early 30s)
Role: Enigmatic ally who aids in Blythe's rescue

Octo

Race: Merman
Age: Unknown (appears ~30s)
Role: Rebel fighter, scout, strategist; Prince of the Mer people

Bertolf

Race: Werewolf
Age: 19
Role: Scout and messenger for the rebellion

Aenwyn

Race: Fairy
Age: Older than 200 (appears early-20s)
Role: Herbalist and healer of the rebellion

Nreman

Race: Fairy
Age: ~200 (appears mid-20s)
Role: Healer and alchemist of the rebellion

FAE ROYAL FAMILY

Queen Lyriana Sylvannis Hendrix

Race: Fae
Age: Appears early 50s
Role: Regent Queen of the Fae; Quentin's mother

Iain Hendrix

Race: Fae
Age: 24
Role: Prince of the Fae; Quentin's younger brother; Izzy's twin

Isolde "Izzy" Hendrix

Race: Fae
Age: 24
Role: Princess of the Fae; Quentin's younger sister; Iain's twin

Race: Golden Draak (Dragon)
Age: 15

Role: Quentin's mount and loyal companion

FAE DELEGATION

Freya

Race: Fae
Age: Appears mid-30s
Role: Diplomat of the Fae delegation

Cael

Race: Fae
Age: Appears early-30s
Role: Stealth scout of the Fae delegation

Rhys

Race: Fae
Age: Appears late-30s
Role: Warrior of the Fae delegation

ANTAGONISTS

Benjamin Fas

Race: Fae
Age: 23
Role: Captain of the Council Guard; Blythe's hostile half-brother

The Council

Race: Seven Mages
Age: Varied - Elders
Role: Authoritarian rulers of the Magical Realm; judges of Blythe's fate

DECEASED

Miles Dixon

Race: Mage
Age: 25
Role: Magical intelligence agent; Blythe's former boyfriend and loyal protector

Dorian Fas

Race: Mage
Age: Died around age 50
Role: Former Council magistrate; Blythe's estranged father

PORTAL HOUSES LIST

The House of Fas (Fasbridge Manor)

Location in Magic Realm: Valoria
Location in Human Realm: Northeast United States, North America

Locke House (Locke Castle)

Location in Magic Realm: Auroraheim
Location in Human Realm: The Czech Republic, Prague; Prague Castle

Tepetl Wasi (Teōcalli Tepetl)

Location in Magic Realm: West Coast of Rynoriah
Location in Human Realm: The Historic Sanctuary of Machu Picchu, Peru

The House of Nipaluna

Location in Magic Realm: Southern coast of Pyragarde
Location in Human Realm: Port Arthur, Tasmania; Port Arthur Historic Site

Shuk-Dral Khang (Shuk-Dral)

Location in Magic Realm: Central and East Thalyora
Location in Human Realm: Lhasa, Tibet: The Potala Palace in Lhasa

House of Nymtharil

Location in Magic Realm: The coast of Nymbrasil
Location in Human Realm: Unknown to humans

Marakora Kasteel

Location in Magic Realm: On the coast, South West of Kemetra
Location in Human Realm: Cape Coast, Ghana, Africa; Chateau le Marara

ACKNOWLEDGEMENT

My deepest thanks to the Under the Canopy Writer's Group, whose insight, encouragement, and sharp eyes carried this story through every stage of its evolution.

To my beta readers, thank you for your honesty, your enthusiasm, and your willingness to dive into early drafts with open hearts.

To my editor, whose guidance strengthened this books in ways I could never have achieved alone.

And to my family—thank you for your patience, your belief in me, and your unwavering support. I couldn't have written a single page without you.

PRAISE FOR AUTHOR

"Winter's writing is evocative, painting vivid images that linger in the reader's mind long after the last page is turned." - Goodreads review by Brooke

"I love a main character that's full of angst. Interesting world building. Fun fantasy world." - Goodreads review by Mrs. Winter

"The author has done a wonderful job of giving us an intriguing look into a world of lore with interesting characters. This book is compelling to read, filled with complicated relationships, characters with mysterious backgrounds, and difficult situations to navigate. For the reader of anything fantasy, this book will not disappoint." - Goodreads review by Brooke

LEGACY OF SHADOWS SERIES

In a world divided into three realms, Blythe has spent her life hiding the truth of what she is—until the ruling Council accuses her of a crime powerful enough to ignite a war. Branded a threat and hunted for her mixed heritage, she is thrust into a rebellion she never asked for and a destiny she never wanted.

As Blythe uncovers the secrets of her lineage and the lies that shaped the realms, she is drawn into a dangerous alliance with Quentin, an enigmatic Fey whose loyalties are as mysterious as his past. Together, they challenge an oppressive hierarchy determined to erase anyone who doesn't fit its rigid order.
But when the portals to the Dark Realm are left unguarded after the warlocks' release, demons begin spilling into the human and magic realms—relentless, hungry, and multiplying. The conflict deepens as Demetrius, Blythe's uncle and the rebellion's charismatic leader, insists he can end the invasion if he finds a legendary weapon capable of destroying the Council and "restoring peace."

Blythe isn't sure which is more dangerous: the Council hunting her for what she is, or the rebellion courting catastrophe under Demetrius's command. As the realms fracture and darkness spreads, she races to uncover the truth behind the weapon, the prophecy tied to her, and the forces manipulating both sides of the war.

Caught between a corrupt regime and a rebellion spiraling out of control, Blythe must decide who she can trust—and who she's willing to become—before the fate of all three realms is sealed.

Legacy of Shadows is a sweeping fantasy saga of identity, rebellion, and the cost of power, following a young woman fighting to claim her place in a world determined to define her.

Legacy Of Shadows: The Keeper's Rebellion

"Legacy of Shadows: The Keeper's Rebellion" is a captivating fantasy novel that delves into a world where magic and humanity collide. Follow Blythe, a young woman burdened by her unique heritage, as she faces accusations of a grave crime by the ruling council of witches. Forced to confront her identity and navigate treacherous alliances, Blythe joins forces with Quentin, an enigmatic Fey, to uncover the truth and challenge an oppressive hierarchy. As tensions rise and their feelings intertwine, Blythe must embrace her dual heritage to become a beacon of hope in a world on the brink of chaos. Prepare for a thrilling journey of resilience, self-discovery, and the extraordinary power within.

Legacy Of Shadows: The Unraveling

They opened the way. They didn't expect the darkness to follow.

After barely escaping the Dark Realm, Blythe hoped the worst was behind her. Instead, demons have begun spilling into the human and magic realms—relentless, hungry, and growing in number. Her uncle, Demetrius, insists he can stop the invasion… if he finds a legendary weapon powerful enough to destroy the Council and "restore peace."

Blythe isn't convinced.

Demetrius's rebellion has already left the portals unguarded and the realms exposed. The Council, meanwhile, hunts Blythe and Hera for their mixed heritage, determined to erase them before the prophecy can unfold. With danger rising on every side, Blythe and her friends race to uncover the truth behind the weapon before Demetrius does.

But the deeper they dig, the more impossible the choice becomes: Stop the rebellion that may be courting disaster, or stop the Council that wants them dead.

And as the demons and evil spread across the realms, one truth becomes terrifyingly clear— Whoever controls the weapon will decide the fate of all three worlds.

BOOKS BY THIS AUTHOR

Legacy Of Shadows: The Keeper's Rebellion

"Legacy of Shadows: The Keeper's Rebellion" is a captivating fantasy novel that delves into a world where magic and humanity collide. Follow Blythe, a young woman burdened by her unique heritage, as she faces accusations of a grave crime by the ruling council of witches. Forced to confront her identity and navigate treacherous alliances, Blythe joins forces with Quentin, an enigmatic Fey, to uncover the truth and challenge an oppressive hierarchy. As tensions rise and their feelings intertwine, Blythe must embrace her dual heritage to become a beacon of hope in a world on the brink of chaos. Prepare for a thrilling journey of resilience, self-discovery, and the extraordinary power within.

Devil's Hope

In "Devil's Hope," Cassielle finds herself ensnared in a web of secrets and unearthly powers amidst the enigmatic streets of New Orleans. When a routine investigation spirals into a perilous journey of self-discovery, Cassielle must confront dark forces that threaten to unravel the fabric of reality itself. With the guidance of enigmatic Loa spirits, Nibo and Samedi, Cassielle delves deep into the heart of the city's mysteries, uncovering long-buried truths and facing sinister adversaries at every turn. Filled with pulse-pounding suspense and mystical intrigue, "Devil's Hope" is a captivating urban fantasy that plunges readers into a world where danger lurks in the shadows and hope flickers like a flame in the night.